CROSSROADS

By Andy Duncan

Beluthahatchie and Other Stories

Edited by

F. Brett Cox

and

Andy Duncan

C R O S S **R** **O** **A** D S

Tales of the Southern

Literary Fantastic

TOR® A Tom Doherty Associates Book | *New York*

ACKNOWLEDGMENTS

We wish to thank Joel Bernstein for getting this project
started, Shawna McCarthy for keeping it going, and
Jim Frenkel for seeing it to completion.

CROSSROADS: TALES OF THE SOUTHERN LITERARY FANTASTIC

This book is printed on acid-free paper.

Edited by James Frenkel

Book design by Michael Collica

A Tor Book
Published by Tom Doherty Associates, LLC
175 Fifth Avenue
New York, NY 10010

www.tor.com

Tor® is a registered trademark of Tom Doherty Associates, LLC.

Library of Congress Cataloging-in-Publication Data

Crossroads : tales of the southern literary fantastic / edited by F. Brett Cox and Andy
Duncan.—1st ed.
      p. cm.
   "A Tom Doherty Associates book."
   ISBN 0-765-30813-4
   EAN 978-0765-30813-9
   1. Fantasy fiction, American—Southern States. 2. American fiction—Southern
States. 3. Southern States—Fiction. I. Cox, F. Brett, 1958- II. Duncan, Andy, 1964-

PS648.F3C76 2004
813'.0876608975—dc22   2004046030

First Edition: August 2004

Printed in the United States of America

0 9 8 7 6 5 4 3 2 1

For Jeanne and Sydney

CONTENTS

Introduction | *F. Brett Cox and Andy Duncan* 11

A Plate of Mojo | *Honorée Fanonne Jeffers* 17

The Wounded | *Richard Butner* 29

The Map to the Homes of the Stars | *Andy Duncan* 43

Under Construction | *James Sallis* 63

Houston, 1943 | *Gene Wolfe* 69

See My King All Dressed in Red | *James L. Cambias* 97

My Life Is Good | *Scott Edelman* 115

Rose | *Bret Lott* 143

Boar Lake | *Mark L. Van Name* 159

The Mission | *Jack McDevitt* 169

The Moon and the Stars | *Marian Carcache* 179

The Specialist's Hat | *Kelly Link* 185

Christus Destitutus | *Bud Webster* 201

Ool Athag | *Don Webb* 213

The Yukio Mishima Cultural Association
   of Kudzu Valley, Georgia | *Michael Bishop* 223

The Last Geek | *Michael Swanwick* 235

Slippered Feet | *Daniel Wallace* 241

Alabama | *Kalamu ya Salaam* 255

Madeline's Version | *F. Brett Cox* 273

Tchoupitoulas Bus Stop | *Lynn Pitts* 285

Water Dog God: A Ghost Story | *Brad Watson* 293

Mankind Journeys Through
   Forests of Symbols | *Fred Chappell* 305

The Mikado's Favorite Song | *Marian Moore* 319

The Perfecting of the Chopin
   Valse No. 14 in E Minor | *Sena Jeter Naslund* 331

Making Faces | *Ian McDowell* 343

Every Angel Is Terrifying | *John Kessel* 361

So much has been written about the literature of the fantastic, and so much more about the literature of the American South, that to attempt even a brief discussion of the crossroads where they meet seems both daunting and redundant. But perhaps a few points merit repeating.

"The fantastic," as scholar Brian Attebery has suggested, is a useful, broad, base-line term to encompass all types of nonrealist literature: science fiction, fantasy, supernatural horror, you name it. Locating stories of fantasy and the supernatural within a southern tradition is easy enough, from the trickster tales of Brer Rabbit and the singular visions of Edgar Allan Poe through a host of works by everyone from Charles Chesnutt and Mark Twain to James Branch Cabell and Robert E. Howard to Zora Neale Hurston and Truman Capote.

On the other hand, the idea of "southern science fiction" may appear more problematic. Given science fiction's ongoing concern with the effects (good or ill) of technology, its assurance that there will be a tomorrow different from today, doesn't it run counter to the accepted image of southern literature—rooted in history, schooled in defeat, bowing to tragedy and fate? Isn't science fiction about gadgets and change, while southern fiction is about people and tradition?

Like most either/or formulations, this one shortchanges both sides. Both science fiction and southern fiction are accomplished and diverse bodies of literature, much larger than their stereotypes. And especially in the past quarter century, southern fiction has steadily acknowledged a South that is increasingly urban, increasingly connected with the rest of the world, increasingly subject to change—changes that began well before the Civil War, and accelerated thereafter.

Indeed, the history of the South is on many levels a history of collision with, and absorption of, technological change, from the cotton gin and the Gatling gun to the Tennessee Valley Authority and air conditioning to the U.S. space program, headquartered in the South at Houston, Huntsville, and

Cape Canaveral. Just ask the many southerners who watched the Saturn rockets being floated downstream from Huntsville, en route to the Apollo missions. As for the southern willingness to embrace such change, author Harry Crews has observed that any southerner who grew up with a wood-burning stove, however picturesque, would cheerfully take an ax to it if presented with an electric range. No surprise, then, that William Gibson, the leading voice of the "cyberpunk" movement of the 1980s and inventor of the term "cyberspace," was born in South Carolina and grew up in Virginia.

More broadly, what southern literature and the literature of the fantastic share is a rootedness in the particularity of place—"landscape as a shaping force," as Alabama native Gregory Benford observed in his groundbreaking essay "The South and Science Fiction." The Mississippi of William Faulkner and Richard Wright and the Georgia of Flannery O'Connor and Alice Walker are akin to Bradbury's Mars, Tolkien's Middle-Earth, Baum's Oz, and the German forests of the Brothers Grimm. All are lands simultaneously real and imagined, luminously inventive yet as accessible and specific as the reader's backyard. In another recent essay, Candas Jane Dorsey—who hails from another fabulous realm, namely Canada—noted that even the most out-of-this-world narratives are dependent on readers' need to be "grounded" and "to recognize the landscape." After all, Dorsey writes, "in order to transcend, we have to come *from* somewhere."

All the stories you are about to read come from somewhere. They also realize, as Dorsey further notes, the importance of "standing on the basis of landscape and hurling the story away from us." In so doing, they may defy expectations of what it means to be southern, to be fantastic, or, in a couple of cases, to be a story. Almost all the authors included in this book are southern natives or residents or both, but not all the stories are set in the South. Some of the stories are clearly identifiable examples of the science fiction and fantasy genres; others are not. Some of the authors are best known for their work within these genres; others are not. From the outset, we decided to limit the contents of the book to living writers, but to include newer voices as well as the usual suspects. We made no effort to obtain stories of any specific geographic, thematic, or aesthetic identity. We did not, for instance, seek a clutch of stories set in New Orleans, that most fantastical of southern cities, yet found them anyway;

likewise, we did not intend a set of metafictional musings on the southern literary canon, but here they are, too. These stories enrich a Table of Contents that, while not necessarily "balanced," is varied, adventurous, and, we hope, entertaining.

It has been said that literature should provoke at least one of two responses: "That's just how I feel," or, "I never thought of that before." It is our fondest hope that you will find in the following stories both recognition and surprise, whether or not you consider yourself southern—or fantastic.

—F. Brett Cox and Andy Duncan

CROSSROADS

HONORÉE FANONNE JEFFERS

A Plate of Mojo

*Honorée Fanonne Jeffers has won awards from the Rona
Jaffe Foundation and the Bread Loaf Writers Conference.
Her first poetry collection,* The Gospel of Barbecue, *won
the 1999 Wick Poetry Prize and was a finalist for the 2001
Paterson Poetry Award. Her second book of poetry is* Out-
landish Blues *(Wesleyan, 2003). Her work has appeared in*
Callaloo, Brilliant Corners, Dark Matter: A Century of
Speculative Fiction from the African Diaspora, Indiana
Review, The Kenyon Review, Ploughshares, Prairie
Schooner, *and elsewhere. A native of Alabama, she holds
an M.F.A. from the University of Alabama and is assistant
professor of English at the University of Oklahoma. This
marks the first publication of "A Plate of Mojo."*

In the end, Pearl never tried to kill anything or anybody, but no one wanted to believe that after all these years because small things, like the way a woman's flesh slowly moves beneath her skirt or her lips curve upward over a gap-toothed smile, can mark that woman for life. The food on her plate that comes from nowhere but makes a full belly is a sign and talk that has slowed down to a bare whisper can hurry up loud again. Talk runs like water down a road leaving mud in its rutted wake.

It's simpler than that, though. No one could explain Pearl or how she and Brother got here, what cabbage leaf their mother, Rosalie, had overturned to retrieve them and no one was going to know because the mother was gone now. Rosalie was dead and had been for years so how was somebody going to find out who had been walking in and out of that back door for thirty years? Pearl wasn't talking. Rosalie dead. Brother gone up North someplace, the best thing for him really.

So Pearl starts working in the white folks' kitchen when she didn't have to. Pots and pans can stop bullets, an apron is a second, rougher shell of skin and you can say "no matter" to what happens outside or what is said. If you don't need the money, you can take it, as long as you conjure nothing with your body or hands but a meal. Because then you can prove the daughter is nothing like the mother.

She got to be working some root just like her Mama cause how her mama get her own house? How she get all that land?

And how Pearl still staying on that place? Where she get the money?

Ain't no man coming out the back door now but you can bet they's one sniffing round. The mama ain't never had no shame, you know that girl don't either.

And if they ain't sniffing, what's wrong with that girl Pearl? Why can't she find nobody? She think she too good for a colored man or she saving it for somebody else?

Umph. It's a scandal. Something in that milk ain't clean.

2

Pearl is glad she is finally five and the first day of school isn't at church either. Pearl and Mama and Brother come to Red Mound Primitive Baptist early most Sundays so they can get a good seat and there are so many colors of people, a field like flowers in it. Different colors like her and Brother and Mama. The best part is the singing when Sister Jones stands up and closes her eyes and then starts singing a song about running along and running along and the Hand of God comes out of the mountains and sweeps the sinner away like dust and sometimes Mama starts crying, "Jesus!" in the middle of the song and sways her body back and forth. The worst part is after service, Mama smiling peace at the women, never the men, and speaking, "Hey y'all." And there is smiling back with mouths and the women fan away heat with handkerchiefs but the women's eyes cut at Pearl and Mama and Brother. And the women suck their teeth when Mama walks on past them down the middle aisle. Mama holds her head straight above the buttoned-up collar and she won't look down at Pearl or Brother. Mama's fingers squeezing Pearl's small hands and making red marks on her skin.

The first day of school Mama calls softly to Pearl in bed, "Pearl. Pearl? Get up now," and walks around gathering clothes, heating water in a tin pail to wash Pearl's and Brother's face and hands. Ten more minutes and then again, still softly but a little louder. "Pearl. Come on now, baby." Grits and fried chicken and biscuits with cane syrup sweet and hot lemon tea and Mama is singing a made-up silly song and laughing and promising all the letters to Pearl. Pearl will be just like Brother, so smart and eating those books like they were cake. Yes she will. Mama lets Pearl wear her favorite dress that is too short, coming up to her calves and Brother making a hooting sound at the sight of Pearl's legs. Mama says, "Stop it now. My baby girl looks good to me!"

Pearl knows the way to school; she has walked down the road every morning with Brother and Mama before she stays all day this first time. Mama thinks two miles is too long for the both of them to walk alone and too long for Pearl anyway so Mama picks Pearl up in her arms and strides fast across the dirt road. "Mama, I can do it; put me down!" Mama not listening and kissing Pearl a hundred times on her forehead and Mama looking at Brother beside them and ruffling his loopy curls with her long fingers and then putting them back in place. The first day, Rosalie drops them off at eight and picks them up when Teacher rings the big bell at two and those hours in between Pearl longs for Rosalie. Brother sits on the other side of the room out of reach, his round glasses sitting on the tip of his nose. He reads a book because Teacher lets him do as he pleases since he has moved past the other children. Pearl tries to sound out the words like Mama taught her. Where are the letters Mama has promised Pearl will be hers?

At noon, Pearl follows the other children in looking underneath the seat for her lunch pail and then the door to the schoolhouse is opened. A white man opens the door and comes inside, points his finger at several children in the room. He does not remove his hat. "You and you and you and you." Pearl looks over at Brother shaking his head back and forth at her and his finger at his lips. "You and you and you. Come on now, y'all; I ain't got all day." He points to a child, a girl, sitting in front of Pearl and Pearl rises with her. "No, uh-uh, not you." Pearl scuffs her shoes back and forth on the floor and then sits down. The children leave with the white man on a wagon heading for Mr. Big John Pinchard's fields and they won't be back until November.

These are the lessons Pearl remembers about a father: first rule of thumb is there is nothing wrong with a rich man as long as he is sweet. As long as he walks the miles after dark to see your mother, his shiny shoes coated with red dust, the brow of his face streaming with sweat. Waits for your mother to finish feeding chickens and slopping hogs and says a grateful "Thank you, Rosalie" for the pail of hot water she brings to him to wash the dust off those shiny shoes. Wipes his mouth with a clean white handkerchief after every bite of her simple food. Smiles and watches his children eat that food as if his nourishment depended on their own. Reads to Pearl and Brother from the big book he brings with him each evening. Kisses the heads of his ivory son and yellow daughter and pull the covers up to their chins. Opens the quilt of his and Rosalie's bed when the thunder and rain starts and lets his frightened daughter climb in between them. Rises well before dawn, holds the mother's slender chocolate and cream hand over his heart and then quietly closes the door of the house. Promises the mother that she and their children will never have to work the fields, that the house and the land will always belong to her. As long as he keeps his promises.

3

When Pearl took over for Aretha as cook, the whispers got louder. Even though Pearl kept to herself and fanned away men like so many dragonflies, only worked hard and brought home honest money, they would not let her the daughter forget the mother. She is too young to have moved that quickly through the ranks in five short years. From freelance washerwoman to maid to cook, and by the time she was twenty-four, there was Pearl. And there was Aretha "retired" at the young age of sixty-three. A joke really since Aretha had at least twenty more years of work left in her.

Aretha's footprints on the floor of the Pinchard kitchen, her mother's footprints before her and if the old folks' had been there, they could have told about the women in Aretha's family back to the plank of the ship, the ones who had stirred their spoons in Pinchard stew but now Mr. Big John had taken to his sickbed and Aretha was out. The doctor telling Mr. Big John straight out for a while now that sweets were off-limits, and now that he thought of it, bread, potatoes, and too much meat might be better left off Mr. Big John's plate as well. It wasn't that Mr. Big John is too sick to move; it was that the man is too fat to get up and walk. Lazy. Even a thought of getting up off that featherbed made him sweat.

Sometime after Mr. Johnny Junior's Mama died, Mr. Big John just seemed to lose the need to move. Funny. Devotion hadn't seemed one of the couple's excesses but Mr. Big John laying his fat self up in bed all day long was proof of his oddity. Grave dirt was nurturing his love.

Miss Lucy, Mr. Johnny Pinchard Junior's wife, trying to get rid of Aretha for five years anyway, ever since Miss Sally died and here was her chance. Could Aretha read the special recipes for foods that Mr. Big John requires? No? Oh, well, then. The truth was Miss Lucy was scared of Aretha. Miss Lucy remembered—who can forget?—that one afternoon before Miss Sally's death when Aretha lost her mind and forgot where.

There wasn't any actual digging in the soil and dirtying of the fingernails that day it happened, only an admiration of the yellow blush roses and azaleas in the outside beauty. The black servants performing their magic trick, the presenting of iced tea in high balls and the clearing away with no tinkling of silver on glass. Black invisibility is so cherished. The sun hot and white female pecking orders being established and that will make anyone hungry. Miss Sally and her ladies sat down to eat dinner at two o'clock and that's when they found Aretha's strange gift. Between the slices of the thinnest light bread, coated by the most aromatic of homemade mayonnaise: dark meat chicken salad. Some of the more delicate ladies who had never tasted dark meat a moment in their lives (never mind about their husbands) took sick and it was almost a year for the post office to stop losing Miss Sally's invitations in the mail.

Make a cook happy and keep her that way; a family knew it well, and Miss Sally should have known it better. Suppose one day the lady of the house starts looking in the pots. That makes a cook get all crotchety, like a woman discovering the obscene truth that little boys follow close behind her with mirrors on the tops of their shoes. The kitchen is a cook's domain even if she does work for a family. A black woman has to have peace somewhere in this world but a white lady can forget herself and start prying open lids and sticking her actual nose two inches from bubbling food. Now you know that's plain nasty. Next thing, the cook's nerves get frayed and she might forget herself as well, leave a jar of homemade mayonnaise out the icebox all night long, then serve the whole batch in some dark meat chicken salad the following day at a garden party.

What remained in the front of folks' minds was a strange gratitude for Aretha's situation. At least seventy years after emancipation they could call it Aretha's "retirement" instead of "sold further down South" or "taken out in the woods and left to starve." Come on and thank God for little favors. In the front of their minds, though, was another thing.

Just let a body take sick with the rheumatism for a week before Thanksgiving season and some folk will have your job before you can say jack rabbit.

Aretha got her moods but what is Miss Lucy thinking bringing Pearl's mess into her house. That's like trading the devil for the witch.

Ain't nobody never been worried about Mr. Big John before. I bet you Mr. Johnny Junior the one who thought of this.

I guess Mr. Johnny the real one who need some healing.

There were accusations of left-handed activity (what mojo had Pearl done to make Aretha take sick in the first place?) but neither Aretha nor Pearl responded to that talk. Aretha always had a real even disposition; it took one to deal with Miss Lucy. Besides, Aretha was sanctified, never cheap with her church donations at Red Mound because she did believe in tithing. In the time-honored tradition of generations of house servants before her, Pearl cultivated a smirk starting in the corner of her mouth.

Aretha couldn't let it go and showed up the day of sewing circle. Maybe Pearl was getting tired of the cooking of breakfast, the boiling of water to wash the dishes, the preparation for dinner and supper, the boiling of water to wash those dishes. Maybe Pearl was tired of Miss Lucy and her airs. Miss Lucy sitting around on her sofa draining glass after glass of iced tea with the other ladies, drawing pretty pictures of dresses, then handing them to Sister Jones who kneeled for hours on the Oriental rug tracing and cutting out the elaborate patterns from tissue paper and then took the patterns home and transformed them into beauty.

May Lois saw Aretha through the window and rushed downstairs to the kitchen. Uh-oh now, here it comes but Miss Lucy rang her bell and May Lois had to hurry up and carry out a tray of sandwiches and sliced pound cake to the parlor. There was a bare-bones "How do, Miss Aretha" and then a hurrying away. When May Lois got back, running, Aretha was turning redder than usual—she was a meriney colored woman in the first place— and struggling to stand up from her chair. Aretha was taking in breath hard but none coming out and the old woman's fallen bosom rose higher and higher. A hissing noise in her throat like a snake about to strike. The air finally rushed back out and that's when she lost her religion. Called Pearl "a evil yellow heifer that ain't got no daddy" and starting calling down on Pearl's head curses shaded with the Lord's name. Then she yelled out Mr. Big John's name over and over, but how was he supposed to hear her two floors above the kitchen and probably asleep anyway?

Pearl stayed still up until Aretha's last conniption, until Aretha flopped on the big oak table face first in a plate of pound cake May Lois had been saving to take home. Then Pearl turned Aretha over, brushing the crumbs of cake off her mouth and chin.

4

These are the lessons Pearl remembers about a husband: There is nothing wrong with a poor man as long as he is sweet. As long as he will walk the miles barefooted to see you on Sunday evening, your only time off, his creaking brogans tied together by the laces and dangling from the fingers of his hand. Wait for you to finish feeding chickens and slopping hogs and say a grateful "Thank you, Pearl" for the pail of hot water you bring to him to wash the bottoms of his aching feet. As long as he doesn't ask about your father or mind your light brown skin and your stick-straight hair. Follows you around like you are Jesus Risen.

The next time Pearl showed up to church was six years later, the day of her marriage to Henry Collins. Folk didn't think Pearl would have the nerve to come back to church, even to get married. When Pearl walked into Red Mound the day of her wedding, wearing that white linen shirt waist and skirt—and a veil!—and escorted by Mr. Johnny Pinchard as she walked down the aisle, the people would have stopped in the middle of shouting Holy Ghost if there had been preaching that day.

Way past thirty and trying to marry Henry so soon cause she scared that mojo she working gone wear off if she didn't hurry up.

You know that satisfied look on Henry's face don't have nothing to do with Pearl's cooking. She might be bright-skinned with good hair, but that big butt of hers come straight from across the water.

I don't care if she do get married. She gone turn out just like her mama. Hear me, now.

Won't it Henry himself said he wouldn't be caught alive or dead with no bright yellow woman? That ain't right. You know his people liked to died. They them Siniglese niggers, ain't they?

Wait a minute, now, don't put the bad mouth on Henry. Henry put up with a lot. Ain't it Pearl done gone somewhere and brought back that damned hawk tied out back of the house?

Henry a brave man, you got to give him that. Most men be scared Pearl gone get mad one day and feed him something to make him lose his nature.

I tell you one thing, I wouldn't want no leftovers from Mr. Johnny's plate. Got the nerve to be walking that girl down the aisle.

Henry Collins, the man whom Pearl married. The man who saved for six months to give Pearl on their wedding day a silver-backed brush for the strange, dark corn silk on her head. The man who waited, back straight, by the altar while Mr. Johnny Junior walked Pearl down the aisle. The man who does not ask Pearl to work her mother's land with him, but throws off the covers of his side of the bed before dawn each morning except Sunday and strokes the heads of each of the three children before leaving; alone, he harnesses the mule. The man who feeds the strange hawk tied up out back, the beak stained from its meal. Who talks to the hawk in a mumbled language all his own, asking forgiveness for the gift of its talon. The man who saved the baby girl from dying.

No one wished the sickness on Pearl's last child, but there was a certain satisfaction to it all. After the grief she had caused on both the black and white sides of the railroad tracks and her silence in the face of it, at least she is not immune from bearing that grief herself. The sickness crept inside and one morning in spring, Annie Mae came down with a high fever and her eyeballs rolled up in the back of her head. She cried out for her mother and Pearl knew she wasn't taking Annie Mae with her to the Pinchard's kitchen or leaving her at home either, not this morning.

It was as if the dark skin of other two children, Rose and Brother Junior was armor against the sickness, that the girl who resembled Pearl the most must have been vulnerable somehow. Late at night, the measles crept into Annie Mae's mouth, pursed even in her sleep with a kiss for the trumpet her daddy had bought for Brother Junior but that Henry had taught the eager Annie Mae to play instead. "This is an angel's horn, boy," Henry insisted. "If you blow that God will come." Brother Junior gave Henry solemn gratitude then gave the battered trumpet to Annie Mae.

That spring morning Pearl woke up early with Henry. A pebble formed across the smooth surface of her mind and Pearl had dreamed of strange colors. She stood over Annie Mae's bed and saw the rash everywhere on Annie Mae's skin, the forehead hot enough to fry one of Mr. Johnny's breakfast eggs, but his breakfast now forgotten. She bathed Annie Mae in cool water every hour. Henry gave her his portion of meat to make a clear broth; as a child he was used to hunger, eating nothing but the feet and necks of birds his father discarded after taking the rest for himself. Henry is used to small sacrifices. Pearl spooned the broth into Annie Mae three times a day but the skin stayed hot and the rash wouldn't leave.

If women would tell their daughters about the pain, invasion in one's womb three-quarters of a year, the marks formed on one's waist, the flaps of skin never to tighten again, would there be any children? And if the rest was revealed, that one day you could stand above a creation wrought from your own blood, only to discover it was dust, surely the earth would be barren. Death come creeping in the room crouching in a corner, laughing. Think again, girl, that this child belongs to you.

The first morning Miss Lucy shows up at the door, whining. Where has Pearl been? Doesn't she know Mr. Johnny Junior gets cross when his breakfast isn't on the table and on time? Then threatening. Mr. Big John has been asking about Pearl. He's going to be angry. Then whining again.

The first night May Lois shows up. She's been promoted again and now she is crying. Miss Lucy be yelling today, did Pearl know that? Well, then, did Pearl know Miss Lucy done broke six of her own good china dishes trying to make one meal for Mr. Johnny and Mr. Big John and now she be taking that china out Pearl's wages?

The second morning, Pearl falls on creaking knees. She hasn't been to church since her wedding day but she prays every night by her bedside so she won't forget how. She prays and prays and prays the second day into night, falls asleep on her knees and dreams of thunder and the screaming of broken-legged hawks. A man chanting. Gabriel come down with his trumpet to play a muted song, mumbled praise muffled. Angel's feathers bloodied by God. The third morning Pearl awakes, her back aching. She smells soup bubbling on the stove. Her good Henry trying to cook the baby's last meal, trying to save his Pearl an hour's sleep. No matter, Pearl knows her child is dead. She has dreamed of blood, her womb has sighed its last. She should be crying but no matter, God's will be done. His will be done. His will be done. His will be done. She rambles through her basket; she will sew the prettiest dress to bury her baby in, one that Annie Mae would never wear if she was alive. Gathers. His will be done. Lace. His will be done. The lavender colors of sky. His will be done.

She hears Henry talking. "Drink this, baby. Drink it all up, now. That's right. Don't Daddy cook a good soup, better than your mama's?" Henry's rusty laugh and Annie Mae giggling, a dead child rising again. "That's right. That's Daddy's good girl." His will be done.

5

After Pearl quit the Pinchard's kitchen, saying Henry and her children needed her on the farm full-time, Mr. Big John just went downhill and gained more and more weight. Pearl seemed to be the only one who had kept him together but now Miss Lucy just didn't have the backbone to say no to Mr. Big John's sweet tooth or his demands for full meals six times a day, no matter how many lectures she heard from the doctor about Mr. Big John's diet. Mr. Big John was not to be denied and every other morning, he sent a wagon to Pearl's and Henry's house to pick up Pearl and Annie Mae and bring them to the Big House to spend the day with him in his room, listening to him read out of a big book to Pearl and the baby girl. He tried to intimidate Pearl into making her famous pound cake for him, too. Obviously Aretha couldn't come out of retirement, and bless her heart, May Lois had to be the worst cook God ever set down on earth. Won't she come back, even for Mr. Big John? No? Then Pearl was a heartless, cruel creature.

Pearl refused to cook, at least for Miss Lucy's kitchen and Mr. Big John's dessert plate, so Miss Lucy took to riding shotgun once a week when May Lois drove to Macon to pick up special cream cakes from the Italian bakery. Miss Lucy was the only one surprised that in less than six months after Pearl's quitting her kitchen, Mr. Big John died from some kind of attack.

Mr. Johnny got the house and pretty much every other business in town, but Mr. Big John had not forgotten to be generous to others as well. He left two hundred acres, a small house with hardwood floors, and a yearly stipend of five thousand dollars to Rosalie Driscoll, Pearl's mother, his "good and faithful servant, whose daughter, Pearl Driscoll, and son, John Thomas Driscoll, I have considerable affection for. In the event of Rosalie's death, the land and the house are to be passed down as Pearl sees fit as long as they remain in her family. The yearly stipend is to be split between Pearl and John Thomas until their deaths."

The problem was that Rosalie never had worked as a servant for Mr. Big John Pinchard or his mother and father, either; she'd never even been in the Pinchard Big House. At least to anyone's recollection, Rosalie never had worked a day when she alive, period—outside of her own small farm feeding a few chickens, some hogs, and milking the one cow. A woman that good-looking with a face and neck chiseled out of black stone, breaking a sweat and getting calluses on her fingertips for five dollars a week working for white folks? Not likely.

Mr. Johnny Junior wasn't bothered by the confusion of the will in the least, said it simply was proof that what folks had been saying about his daddy behind his back was wrong. Mr. Big John did not squeeze a dollar until the bird hollered after all.

6

There Pearl is, up on the wall there.

Now you don't hear me, you just seeing a picture of some old lady born over a hundred years ago.

Don't be fooled by that dress hanging long past her ankles.

Don't be fooled by them eyes turned gray in the middle, long hair plaited up close to her skull.

Yeah, her and her husband dead and gone but that one-legged hawk still tied up out back.

Stories about that woman up and down these dirt and paved roads. Mud running along the path since the time her waist was small.

She won't nothing but trouble. I'm telling you what I know.

That girl Pearl had a mojo strong.

RICHARD BUTNER

The Wounded

Richard Butner has published fiction, articles, and reviews in
Trampoline, Say . . . , RE: Arts and Letters, The North
Carolina Review of Books, When the Music's Over,
Wired, PC Magazine, Lady Churchill's Rosebud Wrist-
let, *and elsewhere. With John Kessel and Mark L. Van
Name, he co-edited* Intersections: The Sycamore Hill
Anthology *(1996), and he administers the Sycamore Hill
Writers' Conference with John Kessel. He holds a B.S. in
Electrical Engineering and an M.S. in Computer Engineer-
ing from North Carolina State University and lives in
Raleigh, North Carolina. This marks the first publication of
"The Wounded."*

It wasn't the wind or the unrelenting sun but rather the vastness of the waters of the sound that affected me most profoundly as I sat in the stern of the mail boat, waiting for my first glimpse of the islands. For two hours I sat in the heat, thankful at least that the breeze kept the black flies at bay, until finally the ruined lighthouse of Beacon Island faded into view to starboard. It was another hour before we reached the shores of Pilot Island, my destination. The whole scene was clouded by the diesel plumes billowing up from the engines. The mail boat captain dodged the black clouds when the wind shifted and blew them into the tiny cabin, but I didn't mind them. They were noxious, but I had smelled worse, and the only seat on the boat was near the engines.

The mail boat captain had been happy enough to take a dollar from me for the crossing, even though he shot me a suspicious look when I'd disclosed that I was neither a visiting hunter nor a fisherman come to take advantage of the unspoiled wildlife of the island. He said very little after I explained who I was, other than to grumble that I was "old for a student." I didn't offer a reply. Old I was compared to the other students at Black Mountain College. I never knew if I had been accepted there because I was the only person ever to apply to the place on the G.I. Bill, or because they thought that when a man is thirty-one and wants a college degree, he should be given the opportunity to get one.

As proof of my scholarship I gave the captain a quick glimpse into the olive-drab bag with the faded cross on the side that held my equipment. He saw my cameras and lenses, and I explained why I was headed to the island. I had come in search of unique subjects for my thesis. Most of the other students had stayed in the mountains as the semester wound to a close, fulfilling their work by designing shelters for the poor of Appalachia, casting ceramics, building furniture from bent plywood, staying safely within the shadows of the visionaries and eccentrics who taught at the college. I wanted to strike out for myself. I had an idea to try to hitchhike out West, filling up as many frames as I could while living by my wits in flatbed trucks and box-cars. My advisor, Crawley, barely older than me, counseled otherwise. "If you've tired of the mountains, then head to the sea. Head out across the water towards the desolation—or rather, the isolation—of Pilot Island. You'll find some pictures there."

Pilot Island had been a haven for pirates in the eighteenth century and a busy, if still treacherous, shipping port in the early nineteenth century. The pilots that gave the island its name would row out and guide freight vessels through the channels in the inlet bordered by Pilot Island to the north and Beacon Island to the south. But an especially powerful hurricane (in an endless series of hurricanes) had disturbed the inlet just after the War Between the States, shifting the bars and shoals around so that only the smallest fishing vessels could get through. Thus, a busy port at the mouth of a giant sound died back down to become a sleepy fishing village, untouched by the advances of the first half of the twentieth century. "Nowadays, at low tide, you can almost walk from Pilot Island to Beacon Island," Crawley had told me, concluding his geography lesson.

He helped me in more practical ways by giving an address where I could send a letter to arrange for passage on the mail boat. He sent one himself to set up room and board for me with a local family with whom he'd stayed on his one visit there. I set out with my rucksack, heavy with photographic gear, catching rides across the state, eating through my supply of peanut butter sandwiches and apples along the way. A logging truck took me all the way from the college to Goldsboro, and from there I caught a ride with a sullen youth in a '48 Studebaker to Beaufort, where a local fisherman took me the rest of the way. He was not headed to Pilot Island; he was merely going to fish in the sound from the docks. "Never been to Pilot Island," he had said, "and I never plan to go." He had been a laconic fellow the entire ride on the one-lane dirt road through the swamp, and I didn't question his views.

As we pulled up into the lagoon where the docks of Pilot Island spilled out into the silvery water, something splashed next to the left side of the boat very near me. I caught a glimpse of something like a manatee or perhaps a dolphin, although I was fairly certain that there were no manatees in the sound near Pilot Island. It was the kind of instant that made me think about a photograph, but by the time I'd registered the splashing sound and looked over, there was nothing but a flash of greenish white flesh that was gone long before I could pull out my camera. I looked back at the captain, who had noticed my interest, but he said nothing and continued guiding the boat slowly up to one of the docks.

Once I disembarked, it was fairly easy to get my bearings—there was only one strip of broken rocks that would have passed for a road on the mainland. This encircled the lagoon where the fishermen's boats were docked. Other paths radiated from this, but they were dusty foot trails, the fancier ones paved in broken oyster shells. Tucked back in the scrubby maritime forest lay the cottages and net houses, the cisterns and chicken pens. The farthermost arm of the lagoon ran out to the point of sand that jutted off into the inlet towards Beacon Island. Opposite that, to the north, the village dissipated into the sand dunes and the beach and the rolling waves of the Atlantic to the east, and the marshes bordering the sound to the west.

The mail boat docked just behind a community store, and it was here that I encountered the local accent for the first time. When I asked about the house of Captain Michael Brown, the clerk replied with "Do y'mean Moikel Brain?" It was a curious accent, as if it had been preserved from the time of the first English settlers here. "Take the road arraigned to the pint and look for the big woite house nair the shore." I could see why the poet Crawley had liked this place. Language itself was deformed here.

I found the Brown House with little trouble, pulling out and checking my light meter along the way just to get a feel for the exposure times necessary in the harsh sun. I passed no one on the road—not surprising, since the men would all be out in their boats fishing—and nodded at the few old women I saw rocking and fanning themselves on their front porches. The women, though, did not return my greetings.

The Brown House sat in a grove of twisted scrub pines, facing the inlet and Beacon Island beyond. "Mrs. Brain" answered the door. She accepted my payment in a manila envelope without even checking the contents and showed me to my room so that I could wash up after my trip. The house was larger than I expected—to the right of the stairs was an open door to the master bedroom, and upstairs there were no fewer than six bedrooms. Mrs. Brown confirmed that the house had once been an inn, built by her great-grandfather in the 1850s when the island bustled with life. The parlor in the front was furnished with a baby grand piano.

Mrs. Brown showed me to the bedroom closest to the upstairs bath, announcing it as her son's room.

"Will your son mind that I'm staying in his room?" I asked.

"Oh, no, he won't mind at all," she said with a wistful smile. "Our son died in the war."

"I'm sorry to hear that, ma'am. I'm a veteran myself."

"Stop," she said, holding up her hand. "I don't want to hear about it. You just get cleaned up after your long trip. There's clean towels by the sink."

With that she turned and descended the stairs.

I was tired from my travels but I hurried to wash up and prepare my equipment so that I could go to the docks and photograph the fishermen returning with the day's catch. I asked Mrs. Brown about a key to the house, so that I could come and go as I pleased, and she assured me that no one on the island locked their doors.

At the docks, I chose a telephoto lens so that I would be less obtrusive. The men gave me sidelong glances as they docked and unloaded their boats, but they seemed neither particularly friendly nor overtly hostile. Many did turn away from me when they saw my camera trained on them, so that their faces wouldn't be in the shot. They accomplished their work with a minimum of wasted motion, stowing their gear, unpacking the fish and crabs and lobsters, dealing in low voices with the fat cigar-smoking man who ran the seafood market which would buy the fish and ferry it to the mainland. I shot two rolls before deciding that I'd seen enough, and could better spend my time scouting out locations rather than expending film prematurely.

I ventured down several of the dirt pathways and shell-paved lanes that radiated outward from the main road, finding a greater variety of houses than I expected—everything from larger two-story homes, freshly white-washed, to small shacks that were barely more than lean-tos of wood and corrugated tin. Each house, though, had its own cistern for collecting rainwater, and many of the houses had obviously been built from timber salvaged from shipwrecks. There were even a few houses built out where the sandy ground faded into reedy marshland, poking up out of the muck on stilts.

I hiked northward out of the village, over the dunes and out onto the beach itself. Seagulls hovered over the roaring Atlantic, looking for prey. The beach itself was more pristine than any other I'd seen—littered with unbroken shells, completely uninhabited save for the scuttling crabs and the hovering gulls. It was only the remoteness of the island, I thought, that kept this place from becoming a tourist destination. I walked for an hour, hypnotized by the white sand and cool salt breeze, before turning and going back to the village.

On the Brown property I walked past the house and down to the inlet where a bare fringe of sand and rock bordered the waters. Here there were trees that had fallen over into the inlet, probably twisted down by the gales that frequently swept over the island. I sat on one that had been uprooted and now curved over into the water, and I gazed out across at Beacon Island. The collapsed lighthouse was the most prominent landmark, but from that distance I could also see the sunlight glinting off the tin roofs of the abandoned houses there, and the spidery black line of the docks.

As I got up to go back to the house, I noticed something in my peripheral vision. Farther along the shoreline, the carcass of a large fish, probably a sea bass, lay on the sand. Half its side had been eaten away to expose the white bones, probably by the Browns' dog or by one of the feral cats on the island, but its head and tail were intact. The dead eye of the fish pointed towards Beacon Island.

Back at the house I told Mrs. Brown where I'd been and she suggested several locations she thought worthy of "the art of photography." The salt marshes bordering the sound, and the scrub forests buffering the marshes from the sand dunes to the north of the village, all teemed with waterfowl and unusual plant life, according to her. She even offered use of Captain Brown's dinghy so that I could row up the shoreline and snap pictures using it as a platform.

"I'm more interested in the people of Pilot Island, Mrs. Brown," I said. "I want to capture what life here is really like, and what life on Beacon Island used to be like."

"Beacon Island? Well, there's nothing there, son. It's been deserted ever since the lighthouse fell. Nothing there but some tumbledown shacks and the last of the cats that haven't starved to death."

"Why, though? Why did they desert the island?"

"It was after a hurricane, a powerful one. Everybody on Beacon started getting sick. Maybe their cisterns got poisoned by something in the storm flood—nobody knows, really. This all happened when I was a little girl, of course."

"No one bothered to investigate? Wouldn't the state send over a doctor or a sheriff, at least?"

"The government doesn't care that we're floating way out here, child."

"What happens when someone gets sick around here?"

"Yaupon tea cures most ailments, and setting a bone or patching up a cut ain't too difficult. If somebody needs a surgeon, though, they have to take the mail boat to the mainland."

They were cut off out here, a few mounds of sand in the ocean.

Filling up the rolls of film I'd brought was easy, although I did have difficulty getting pictures of most of the older villagers. I did not take the Browns' dinghy out by myself, but I did go out with Captain Brown on his large fishing boat the next day. Two of the island teenage boys came with us to man the nets, to look for schools of jumping mullet, and to scoop up the crab pots. Neither seemed particularly interested in talking with me about my project or even about what life on the mainland was like. Brown, though, was interested in how someone as old as I managed to still be a college student, and I told him my story, both of how I came to Black Mountain, of how before that I'd been drafted at the advanced age of twenty-six, and of how before that I was happy to drive a dynamite truck in the mountains of North Carolina and Tennessee.

Life around the island seemed rough, but the inhabitants, while aloof, did not seem unhappy or even pitiful as did some of the poor I'd met in Appalachia, where I had seen enough hunger and disease already.

Crawley's lectures to students, whether they were studying poetry, architecture, photography, or painting, always started with the Rimbaud quote about the necessity of becoming a "seer." It was an important point, but it also loosened up the classes—Crawley, the one-eyed poet, talking about being a seer. Very funny. At thirty-one, though, I had seen enough. I had seen men lose both, not just one, of their eyes.

I had seen men lose all manner of things, including in too many cases their lives. Sometimes, though I was working to keep them alive until they could be delivered to the surgeons, death came as a more merciful option. I had seen men burned by napalm, men torn apart by bullets from Japanese and Soviet rifles, men hacked up by bayonets, men blown to bits by white-phosphorus mortar fire and grenades.

As a medical corpsman in an air ambulance with the Twenty-fourth Medical Battalion in Korea, I had seen all these things, flying up and back down the Yalu River between the pickup zones and the MASH units. It was where my interest in photography started, after I spent an hour in the field trying to hold the guts of a combat photographer together. He didn't make it—dead in the air—but his Nikon did. He knew he wasn't going to survive, even through the haze of morphine I'd administered. Fighting the drug, he reached up and clutched at my wrist as I turned to work on the other patient in the chopper, a sergeant with a bullet in his leg. The photographer gestured toward his rucksack with a limp claw of a hand.

"Take my picture," he'd said, his voice barely modulating his ragged breathing.

I complied—he had a lieutenant's bar, after all, and I was an enlisted specialist. By the time I set the camera down, the photographer's heart had stopped. After tending to the sergeant's leg, I slid back over next to the photographer and I held the dead man's hand until we landed.

I kept his Nikon M, filched some Kodacolor film from the quartermaster, and that's when my real training as a photographer began, months before I came back and enrolled at Black Mountain. I kept that stolen Nikon with me at all times, tucked in my medical kit, bringing it out to snap photos of the guys who I had helped to save. No more shots of the ones who went home tagged and bagged. Only the ones who got away with their lives.

I had seen enough ugliness, but even in the midst of that ugliness, I tried to record the beauty of life renewed.

On Pilot Island, I found a different kind of beauty. Captain Brown, after hearing my stories, only said, "There's a world full of evil out there, son." But I felt that he had a new respect for me, too.

We sailed over through the inlet and out into the Atlantic proper, going far enough out so that the crumbled lighthouse on Beacon Island was a speck on the horizon. The boys caught some mullet and drum in their nets. Off to the left I saw four boats congregating. We were close enough to where I could see that each boat was taking in netful after netful of fish.

"Why don't we head over there," I said, pointing. "Looks like they're making quite a haul today."

"Today and every day," Brown replied. "They're over there by the Hole. There's always plenty of fish there, feeding, and they're easy to catch. They also taste like Satan's own shoeleather. But there's a cannery in Beaufort that buys all that fish up and ships it overseas to folks who don't seem to mind the flavor. Nobody here will eat the fish caught near the Hole."

Back on shore, I photographed the other fishermen as they rowed back in from their nets and crab pots. I photographed the hunters as they marched back into town wreathed with duck carcasses, the children as they played hopscotch outside the one-room schoolhouse, the wives as they came to the general store to shop for provisions from the mainland and to gossip on the porch there. I found the Methodist church at the end of O'Neal Street. There was only a small cemetery adjoining, as most graves of the island were in private family plots near houses. I decided to return to photograph the church on Sunday, when the villagers would be dressed up in what they deemed their best clothes.

Saturday night I was sleepless with nausea. The fishmonger's wife had dropped in with an apple custard pie, and I feel certain this is what caused me to be so sick that night—neither of the Browns had eaten any. The noise of my retching in the upstairs bathroom was masked by the weather outside. It was not yet hurricane season, but a gale blew in and collided with a front from the mainland, dumping rain onto the island in freakish amounts. I finally fell asleep to the sound of the wind whistling in the shutters. When I awoke later in the night, the storm had passed. I looked out my window to see the house surrounded by floodwaters, a silver sheet in the light of the full moon. In the wake of the storm the island was quiet except for the croaking of the frogs in the distance.

I slept in that morning, undisturbed by the Browns. Evidently they were unconcerned about my mortal soul and felt no need to urge me to attend church services. The floodwaters had receded; I checked my gear and set off towards the church, hoping to at least catch the villagers as they left. As I walked around the lagoon I noticed that the harbor was almost as empty as it had been for the past two days. When I arrived, the church was not completely empty, but there were only a handful of the older women of the village there—none of the men. These women sat in the front pews and sang hymns a cappella, and weren't even aware when I peeked in the rear doors of the church. A quick dash back through the village confirmed that all of the paths and porches were devoid of life.

I used my longest lens as a telescope and pointed it at Beacon Island to discover what I already suspected I would see there—the abandoned docks no longer abandoned but in fact populated by the missing boats of Pilot Island. I decided that I would take Mrs. Brown up on her offer of the captain's dinghy, and soon I was pushing off from the lagoon into the inlet. The sea was calm as it sliced in between the two islands, but I still kept to the soundward side. After fifteen minutes of steady rowing, I reached the rotting docks of Beacon Island and tied up the dinghy amidst the other boats.

The town was as ruined as Mrs. Brown had portrayed it, although it was clear that most of the houses had at one time been much more splendid than the ones on Pilot Island. All, though, were caved in on themselves, like slowly deflating balloons.

As I walked from the docks to the center of the ruined town, the stench of rotting fish grew stronger.

The one building not in ruins was the church, roughly the same size as the Methodist church on the other island. I paused before mounting the steps, as on either side of the door, sitting on the wooden railings, were filthy gray pelicans. At first I had assumed them to be wooden carvings, but as I got closer I realized they were live birds. They made no move to fly away nor to attack me. I stepped back and squeezed off a quick shot of both of them flanking the doorway, then I put my camera away and crept between them and placed my ear against the door. As on Pilot Island, hymns were being sung, this time accompanied by a piano. I cracked the door and slid into the foyer. The fish smell permeated the church. I had smelled worse things.

Mrs. Brown sat at an upright piano at the far end of the church. She did not, as I had seen done at recitals back at Black Mountain, play with her forearms, or play with mallets, or play anything other than a strident hymn in a major key, as tuneful as the humid conditions allowed. The villagers all stood in their pews singing. It was all quite normal, except for the figure sprawled out on top of a sheet of oilcloth on the altar.

I had seen the navy's underwater demolition teams at work—the frogmen in their rubber suits, flippers, and goggles. On the altar was a frogman of a different kind. The figure there resembled nothing so much as a five-foot-tall frog, but the torso was tapered like that of a man, and the neck was delineated like that of a man too. Its head lolled to the side to face the audience, but its black eyes only stared, unblinking, off into space. From my vantage point at the rear of the church, I saw that its arms and legs still twitched.

My first instinct was to turn and run, and hope that the villagers hadn't seen me. Whatever their secret was, I felt certain that it was one that outsiders were not allowed to escape with. But I was transfixed by the creature at the other end of the aisle, and after a moment I realized that none of the villagers had come to restrain me. In fact, they all continued with their hymn singing as Mrs. Brown plunked along on the detuned piano. All but one—the cigar-smoking fishmonger—who turned and gave me a stare. He did not move to do anything, though, other than to tap the shoulder of Captain Brown, who sat next to him. It was Brown who slowly got up and walked around to the back, motioning me outside.

We stood out between the mute immobile pelicans. I had no idea what to say, where to start with questions. Brown lit a cigarette and paused before he spoke.

"They've been here as long as we have," Brown said. "The families that trace their line all the way back to the pirates that settled this strip of land remember tales of mermen from the deep washing up here.

"Usually it's just small things that float up out of the Hole. That's why the fish gather there—to eat the stuff. Every now and then something bigger comes out, like one of them," he said, gesturing towards the door of the church. "You ask me, I think we ought to seal up the Hole. Could be done with the proper explosives. But it's easy money for those who fish there.

"We're good Christian folks here, you understand. One of them washes up on shore, as this one did early this morning, dead or only half-dead, and we move services over here to Beacon Island . . . give it the only kind of funeral we know how before we bury it.

"So now you know the secret. Good luck convincing anyone on the mainland of it."

"Dead or half-dead?" I asked. "That one in there is still alive, isn't it?"

"Aye. There's nothing we can do for it. They can breathe in water and in air, but it's only a matter of time before this one breathes its last. No one's ever tried to patch up one of 'em that washed up half-alive. What would we do with a live merman? This one looks like it might've hit an unexploded depth charge or somethin'. There's lots of munitions floating around out there in the waters, thanks to the war."

"I have experience with the casualties of war," I said. "I know you do too. Let me help."

Many of the villagers protested when Brown and I returned to the church carrying his tackle boxes, and some murmured phrases like "blasphemy on top of blasphemy," when we marched up the aisle of the tiny church. I also heard the cigar-smoking man mutter something about how this would surely hurt the fishing. But Brown was respected in the community, and so the strange service broke up, and most of the women and men wandered outside, leaving Brown and me and a few of the oldest men. I set to working on what I found on the altar of that decaying church.

Who can define the depths of horror? I was a seer, and I had seen so many things—men with legs blown off by Chinese land mines, men who were nothing but a mass of burned flesh, men who cried out prayers and curses to God as their lives ebbed away. These horrors steeled me against what I dealt with that day, a creature slick with black blood, barely alive, whose webbed fingers curled slowly in mute pain. The gills on either side of its neck rippled slightly. The wide mouth set with slim rows of triangular teeth looked nothing but sinister, but its face was not built for expression—

all I could see was that its bulging black eyes had begun to cloud over, so I assumed there wasn't much time left. The wound was in its left side, a ragged hole that exposed what I assumed were its intestines. Using a straightened fishing hook as needle, and line as suture, I patched it up as best I could, tying off what appeared to be severed blood vessels and stitching up everything else.

As I worked it seemed to suck in air more quickly, more regularly, and its helpless twitching subsided. Its eyes seemed less cloudy. I had no idea whether I was saving its life or not, but I did know that I was staving the flow of the reeking black fluid that had oozed from its guts.

I was stitching up the main wound in its side, lost in my work, when its webbed hand thrust up and gripped my wrist. It rolled its head to face me, but its eyes . . . I had no idea how to interpret what I found there, no idea what it was trying to communicate. For all I knew, if it had all of its strength it would have reached up and clawed my eyes out with its talons. But that didn't matter at that moment. I slid my wrist through its slippery grasp until my hand clasped its hand. I could feel its pulse, slow but steady, pumping in the veins of its hand. There we were, brothers in arms, my tanned flesh against its grayish green skin. After a moment it released my hand and eased back down onto the altar. I tied off the stitches in its side and then asked for help from the other men. We gathered it up in the oilcloth, one man on each corner and two on the sides, and carried it out of the church. I left Brown's tackle box there at the altar but scooped up my camera as we left.

We marched it over the dune and out onto the wide shores of Beacon Island. We carried it out into the surf until the water was up past our knees. I signaled the other men to let go and Brown slid the oilcloth out from underneath the creature. I eased it down into the surf. The film on its glassy eyes lifted as it hit the water, and the gills on its neck ventilated rapidly. I was on my hands and knees in the surf, soaked, shoving it out to sea, but then I decided I had done all I could. I stood up, wiping my hands on the remaining patches of dry cloth on the back of my shirt. I ran to pick up the Nikon, checking the exposure and focus quickly.

I snapped a single picture of it as it flailed in the surf, trying to regain its strength. I wasn't sure what I was going to do with the negative once I developed it—I was almost certain that the men wouldn't let me off the island with it. But I had kept up my end of the bargain. I had taken the picture. Finally the creature lolled on its back and then curled underneath a crashing wave, and was gone. Ignoring the rest of the men, I packed up my gear and walked back to the boat.

ANDY DUNCAN

The Map to the Homes of the Stars

Andy Duncan published his first book, Beluthahatchie and Other Stories, *in 2000; it won the World Fantasy Award for Best Collection. The same year, his story "The Potawatomie Giant" won the World Fantasy Award for Best Short Fiction. In 2002, he won the Theodore Sturgeon Memorial Award and the Southeastern Science Fiction Achievement Award for his novella "The Chief Designer." He has also been a finalist for the Hugo, Nebula, and John W. Campbell Awards. His most recent stories have appeared in* Conjunctions 39: The New Wave Fabulists *and the anthologies* Mojo: Conjure Stories *and* The Silver Gryphon. *He holds an M.A. in English from North Carolina State University and an M.F.A. in fiction writing from the University of Alabama, where he is assistant director of Student Media. A native of South Carolina, Andy lives in Northport, Alabama with his wife, Sydney. "The Map to the Homes of the Stars" was first published in* Dying for It, *edited by Gardner Dozois.*

Last night, I heard it again. About eleven, I stood at the kitchen counter, slathered peanut butter onto a stale, cool slice of refrigerated raisin bread, and scanned months-old letters to the editor in an A section pulled at random from the overflow around the recycling bin. "Reader decries tobacco evils." "Economy sound, says N.C. banker." The little headlines give the otherwise routine letters such urgency, like telegraphed messages from some war-torn front where issues are being decided, where news is happening. "Arts funding called necessary." As I chewed my sandwich, I turned one-handed to the movie listings, just to reassure myself that everything I had skipped in the spring wasn't worth the trouble anyway, and then I heard a slowly approaching car.

We don't get much traffic on my street, a residential loop in a quiet neighborhood, and so even we single guys who don't have kids in the yard unconsciously register the sounds of each passing vehicle. But this was the fifth night in a row, and so I set down my sandwich and listened.

Tom used to identify each passing car, just for practice.

"Fairlane."

"Crown Victoria."

"Super Beetle."

This was back home, when we were as bored as two seventeen-year-olds could be.

"Even *I* can tell a Super Beetle," I said. I slugged my Mountain Dew and lowered the bottle to look with admiration at the neon green foam.

Tom frowned, picked up his feet, and rotated on the bench of the picnic table so that his back was to Highway 1.

Without thinking, I said, "Mind, you'll get splinters." I heard my mother speaking, and winced.

Now Tom looked straight ahead at the middle-school basketball court, where Cathy and her friends, but mostly Cathy (who barely knew us, but whose house was fourth on our daily route), were playing a pickup game, laughing and sweating and raking their long hair back from their foreheads. As each car passed behind him, he continued the litany.

"Jeep."

"Ford pickup."

"Charger."

I didn't know enough to catch him in an error, of course, but I have no doubt that he was right on the money, every time. I never learned cars; I learned other things, that year and the next fifteen years, to my surprise and exhilaration and shame, but I never learned cars, and so I am ill-equipped to stand in my kitchen and identify a car driving slowly past at eleven o'clock at night.

Not even when, about five minutes later, it gives me another chance, drives past again in the other direction, as if it had gotten as far as the next cul-de-sac, and turned around.

It passes so slowly that I am sure it is about to turn into someone's driveway, someone's, mine, but it hasn't, for five nights now it hasn't. I couldn't tell you if I had to precisely what make of car it is.

I could guess, though.

Maybe tonight, if, when, it passes by, I'll go to the front door and pull back the narrow dusty curtain that never gets pulled back except for Jehovah's Witnesses, and see for myself what make of car it is. See if I recognize it. But all I did last night, and the four nights before, was stand at my kitchen counter, fingertips black with old news, jaws Peter-Panned shut (for I am a creature of habit), stare unseeing at the piled-up sink, and trace in my head every long-gone stop on the map to the homes of the stars.

Even when all we had were bicycles, Tom and I spent most of our time together riding around town. We rode from convenience store to convenience store, Slim Jims in our pockets and folded comic books stuffed into the waistbands of our jeans. We never rode side by side or single file but in loopy serpentine patterns, roughly parallel, that weaved among trees and parked cars and water sprinklers. We had earnest and serious conversations that lasted for hours and were entirely shouted from bike to bike, never less than ten feet. Our paths intersected with hair-raising frequency, but we never ran into each other. At suppertime, we never actually said good-bye but veered off in different directions, continuing to holler at each other, one more joke that had to be told, one more snappy comeback to make, until the other voice had faded in the distance, and we realized we were riding alone, and talking to ourselves. I remember nothing of what we said to each other all those long afternoons, but I remember the rush of the wind past my ears, and the shirttail of my red jersey snapping behind me like a hound, and the slab of sidewalk that a big tree root thrust up beneath me in the last block before home, so that I could steer around it at the last second and feel terribly skillful, or use it as a launching ramp and stand up on the pedals and hang there, suspended, invincible, until the pavement caught up with my tires again.

Then we were sixteen and got our licenses. Tom's bicycle went into the corner of his room, festooned with clothes that weren't quite ready to wash yet; mine was hung on nails inside the garage, in a place of honor beside my older sister's red wagon and my late Uncle Clyde's homemade bamboo fishing poles. Tom had been studying *Consumer Reports* and *Car & Driver* and prowling dealerships for months, and with his father's help, he bought a used '78 Firebird, bright red exterior, black leather upholstery, cassette stereo, and a host of tire and engine features that Tom could rattle off like an auctioneer but that I never quite could remember afterward. Being a fan of old gangster movies, Tom called it his "getaway car." Tom and his dad got a great deal, because the getaway car had a dent in the side and its headlights were slightly cockeyed. "Makes it unique," Tom said. "We'll get those fixed right up," his dad said, and, of course, they never did. I inherited the car my father had driven on his mail route for years, a beige '72 Volkswagen Beetle that was missing its front passenger seat. My father had removed it so that he'd have an open place to put his mail. Now, like so many of my family's other theoretical belongings, the seat was "out there in the garage," a phrase to which my father invariably would add, "somewhere."

We always took Tom's car; Tom always drove.

We went to a lot of movies in Columbia and sometimes went on real trips, following the church van to Lake Junaluska or to Six Flags and enjoying a freedom of movement unique in the Methodist Youth Fellowship. But mostly we rode around town, looking—and *only* looking—at girls. We found out where they lived, and drove past their houses every day, hoping they might be outside, hoping to get a glimpse of them, but paying tribute in any case to all they had added to what we fancied as our dried-up and wasted and miserable lives.

"We need music," Tom said. "Take the wheel, will you, Jack?"

I reached across and steered while he turned and rummaged among the tapes in the backseat. I knew it was the closest I ever would come to driving Tom's car.

"In Hollywood," I said, "people on street corners sell maps to the stars' homes. Tourists buy the maps and drive around, hoping to see Clint Eastwood mowing his lawn, or something." I had never been to Hollywood, but I had learned about these maps the night before on *PM Magazine*.

"What do you want? You want Stones? You want Beatles? You want Aerosmith? What?"

"Mostly they just see high walls," I said, "and locked gates." I was proud to have detected this irony alone.

"We should go there," Tom said. "Just take off driving one day and *go*."

"Intersection coming up."

"Red light?"

"Green."

Tom continued to rummage. "Our map," he said, "exists only in our heads."

"That's where the girls exist, too," I said.

"Oh, no," Tom said, turning back around and taking the wheel just in time to drive through the intersection. "They're out there. Maybe not in this dink-ass town, but somewhere. They're real. We'll just never know them. That's all."

I had nothing to add to that, but I fully agreed with him. I had concluded, way back at thirteen, that I was doomed to a monastic life, and I rather wished I were Catholic so that I could take full advantage of it.

Monastic Methodists had nowhere to go; they just got gray and pudgy, and lived with their mothers. Tom pushed a tape into the deck; it snapped shut like a trap, and the speakers began to throb.

Lisa lived in a huge Tudor house of gray stone across the street from the fifteenth fairway. To our knowledge she did not play golf, but she was a runner, and on a fortunate evening we could meet her three or four times on the slow easy curves of Country Club Drive. She had a long stride and a steady rhythm and never looked winded, though she did maintain a look of thoughtful concentration and always seemed focused on the patch of asphalt just a few feet ahead, as if it were pacing her. At intersections, she jogged in place, looking around at the world in surprise, and was likely to smile and throw up a hand if we made so bold as to wave.

Tom especially admired Lisa because she took such good care of her car, a plum-colored late-model Corvette that she washed and waxed in her driveway every Saturday afternoon, beginning about one o'clock. For hours, she catered to her car's needs, stroking and rubbing it with hand towels and soft brushes, soaping and then rinsing, so that successive gentle tides foamed down the hood. Eventually, Lisa seemed to be lying face-to-face with herself across the gleaming purple hood, her palm pressed to the other Lisa's palm, hands moving together in lazy circles like the halfhearted sparring of lovers in August.

Crystal's house was low and brick, with a patio that stretched its whole length. From March through October, for hours each day, Crystal lay on this patio, working on her tan—"laying out," she would have called it. She must have tanned successive interior layers of her skin, because even in winter she was a dusky Amazonian bronze, a hue that matched her auburn hair, but made her white teeth a constant surprise. Frequent debates as we passed Crystal's house: Which bikini was best, the white or the yellow? Which position was best, faceup or facedown? What about the bottles and jars that crowded the dainty wrought-iron table at her elbow? Did those hold mere store-bought lotions, or were they brimful of Crystal's private skin-care recipes, gathered from donors willing and unwilling by the dark of the moon? Tom swore that once, when we drove past, he clearly saw amid the Coppertone jumble a half stick of butter and a bottle of Wesson oil.

Gabrielle lived out on the edge of town, technically within the city limits but really in the country, in a big old crossroads farmhouse with a deep porch mostly hidden by lattices of honeysuckle and wisteria. She lived with her grandparents, who couldn't get around so good anymore, and so usually it was Gabrielle who climbed the tall ladder and raked out the gutters, cleared the pecan limbs off the roof of the porch, scraped the shutters, and then painted them. She had long black hair that stretched nearly to the ragged hem of her denim shorts. She didn't tie her hair back when she worked, no matter how hot the day, and she was tall even without the ladder.

Natalie lived in a three-story wooden house with cardboard in two windows and with thickets of metal roosters and lightning rods up top. At school, she wore ancient black ankle-length dresses in all weathers, walked with her head down, and spoke to no one, not even when called upon in class, so that the teachers finally gave up. Her hair was an impenetrable mop that covered her face almost entirely. But she always smiled a tiny secret smile, and her chin beneath was sharp and delicate, and when she scampered down the hall, hugging the lockers, her skirts whispered generations of old chants and endearments. Natalie never came outside at all.

Cynthia's was the first house on the tour. Only two blocks from Tom's, it sat on the brink of a small and suspect pond, one that was about fifty feet across at its widest. No visible stream fed this pond or emptied it, and birds, swimmers, and fish all shunned it. The pond was a failure as a pond, but a marginal success as an investment, an "extra" that made a half-dozen nondescript brick ranch houses cost a bit more than their landlocked neighbors. Cynthia's house was distinguished by a big swingset that sat in the middle of the treeless yard. It was a swaybacked metal A-frame scavenged from the primary school. In all weathers, day and night, since her family moved to town when she was six, Cynthia could be found out there, swinging. The older she got, the higher she swung, the more reckless and joyful her sparkle and grin. When she was sixteen, tanned legs pumping in the afternoon sun, she regularly swung so high the chains went slack for a half-second at the top of the arc before she dropped.

"Zero gee," Tom said as we drove slowly past. Tom and I didn't swing anymore, ourselves; it made us nauseated.

Once a year Cynthia actually came out to the car to say hi. Each Christmas the people who lived on the pond, flush with their wise invest-ment, expressed their communal pride with a brilliant lighting display. For weeks everyone in town drove slowly, dutifully, and repeatedly around the pond and over its single bridge to see the thousands of white firefly lights that the people of the pond draped along porches and bushes and balus-trades, and stretched across wire frames to approximate Grinches and Magi. The reflection on the water was striking, undisturbed as it was by current or life. For hours each night, a single line of cars crept bumper-to-bumper across the bridge, past Santa-clad residents who handed out candy canes and filled a wicker basket with donations for the needy and for the electric company. Painted on a weatherbeaten sandwich board at the foot of the bridge was a bright red cursive dismissal: Thank You / Merry Christmas / Speed Limit 25.

At least once a night, Tom and I drove through this display, hoping to catch Cynthia on Santa duty. At least once a year, we got lucky.

"Hey there, little boys, want some candy?" She dropped a shimmering fistful into Tom's lap. "No, listen, take them, Dad said when I gave them all out I could come inside. I'm freezing my ass off out here. Oh, hi, Jack. So, where you guys headed?"

"Noplace," we said together.

She walked alongside Tom's Firebird, tugging down her beard to scratch her cheek. "Damn thing must be made of fiberglass. Hey, check out the Thompsons' house. Doesn't that second reindeer look just like he's humping Rudolf? I don't know *what* they were *thinking*. No? Well, it's clear as day from my room. Maybe I've just looked at it too long. When is Christ-mas, anyway? You guys don't know what it's like, all these goddamn lights, you can see them with your eyes closed. I've been sleeping over at Cheryl's where it's dark. Well, I reckon if I go past the end of the bridge, the trolls will get me. Yeah, right, big laugh there. See you later." Then, ducking her head in again: "You, too, Jack."

With the smoothness of practice, Tom and I snicked our mirrors into place (his the driver's side, mine the overhead) so that we could watch Cynthia's freezing ass walk away. Her Santa pants were baggy and sexless, but we watched until the four-wheel drive behind us honked and flashed its deer lights. By the time we drove down to the traffic circle and made the loop and got back in line again, Cynthia's place had been taken by her neighbor, Mr. Thompson.

"Merry Christmas, Tom, Jack," he said. "Y'all's names came up at choir practice the other day. We'd love to have you young fellas join us in the handbells. It's fun and you don't have to sing and it's a real ministry, too." He apologized for having run out of candy canes, and instead gave us a couple of three-by-five comic books about hell.

Tina's house always made us feel especially sophisticated, especially daring.

"Can you imagine?" Tom asked. "Can you imagine, just for a moment, what our parents would do?"

"No," I said, shaking my head. "No, I can't imagine."

"I think you should try. I think we both should try to envision this. That way we'll be prepared for anything in life, anything at all."

I cranked down the windowpane until it balked. "I don't even want to think about it," I said. I pressed the pane outward until it was back on track, then I lowered it the rest of the way.

"Oh, but you've *been* thinking about it, haven't you? You're the one that found out where she lived. You're the one that kept wanting me to drive past her house."

"It's the quickest route between Laura's and Kathleen's, that's all," I said. "But if it's such a terrible hardship, then you can go around the world instead, for all I care. You're the driver, I'm just sitting here."

He fidgeted, legs wide, left hand drumming the windowsill, fingertips of his right hand barely nudging the steering wheel. "Don't get me wrong, I think she's a babe. But this neighborhood, I don't know, it makes me nervous. I feel like everybody we pass is looking at us."

"Do what you like. I'm just sitting here," I said. I craned to see Tina's house as we drove around the corner.

Tina lived in what our parents and our friends and every other white person we knew, when they were feeling especially liberal, broad-minded and genteel, called the colored part of town. Tina's yard was colored all right: bright yellows, reds, oranges, and purples, bursting from a dozen flower beds. As so often when she wasn't at cheerleading practice, Tina knelt in the garden, a huge old beribboned hat—her grandmother's, maybe?—shading her striking, angular face. Her shoulders tightened, loosened, tightened again as she pressed something into place. Without moving her hands, she looked up at us as we passed. She smiled widely, and her lips mouthed the word "Hey."

Once we were around the corner, Tom gunned the engine.

"Uh-uh, no sir, hang it *up*," Tom said. "Not in my family, not in this town. Thousands of miles away, maybe. That might work. Oh, but then they'd want *photos*, wouldn't they? Damn. The other week, all my aunts were sitting around the kitchen table, complaining about their daughters-in-law. My son's wife is snotty, my son's wife is lazy, they aren't good mothers, they aren't treating our boys right, and so on and so on. Just giving 'em down the country, you know?"

"Uh-huh. I hear you."

"And I finally spoke up and said, 'Well, I know I'm never going to introduce y'all to any wife of *mine*, 'cause y'all sure won't like *her*, either."

"What'd they say to that?"

"They all laughed, and Aunt Leda said, 'Tom, don't you worry, 'cause you're the only boy in the family that's got any sense. We know we'll like *any* girl you pick out.' And then Aunt Emily added, 'Long as she isn't a black 'un!' And they all nodded—I mean, they were serious!"

After a long pause, he added, half to himself, "It's not as if I'm bringing *anybody* home, anyway—black or white or lavender."

"You bring me home with you sometimes," I said.

"Yeah, and they don't like *you* either," he said, and immediately cut me a wide-eyed look of mock horror that made me laugh out loud. "I'm kidding. You know they like you."

"Families always like me," I said. "Mamas especially. It's the daughters themselves that aren't real interested. And a mama's approval is the kiss of death. At this moment, I bet you, mamas all over town are saying, 'What about that nice boy *Jack*? He's so respectful, he goes to church, he makes such good grades,' and don't you know that makes those gals so hot they can't stand it."

Tom laughed and laughed.

"Oh, Jack!" I gasped. "Oh, Jack, your SAT score is so—so *big*!"

"Maybe you should forget the girls and date the *mamas*," Tom said. "You know, eliminate the middleman. Go right to the source."

"Eewww, that's crude." I clawed at the door as if trying to get out. "Help! Help! I'm in the clutches of a crude man!"

"Suppose Kathleen's home from Florida yet?"

"I dunno. Let's go see."

"Now you aren't starting to boss me around, are you?"

"I'm just sitting here."

He poked me repeatedly with his finger, making me giggle and twist around on the seat. " 'Cause I'll just put you out by the side of the road, you start bossing me."

"I'm not!" I gasped. "Quit! Uncle! Uncle! I'm not!"

"Well, all right, then."

On September 17, 1981, we turned the corner at the library and headed toward the high school, past the tennis courts. The setting sun made everything golden. Over the engine, we heard doubled and redoubled the muted grunts and soft swats and scuffs of impact: ball on racket, shoe on clay. The various players on the adjoining courts moved with such choreography that I felt a pang to join them.

"Is tennis anything like badminton?" I asked. "I used to be okay at badminton. My father and I would play it over the back fence, and the dogs would go wild."

"It's more expensive," Tom said. "Look, there she is. Right on time."

Anna, her back to us, was up ahead, walking slowly toward the parking lot on the sidewalk nearest me. Her racket was on one shoulder, a towel around her neck. Her skirt swayed as if she were walking much faster.

As we passed, I heard a strange sound: a single Road Runner beep. In the side mirror, tiny retreating Anna raised her free hand and waved. I turned to stare at Tom, who looked straight ahead.

"The *horn?*" I asked. "You honked the horn?"

"Well, you waved," he said. "I saw you."

I yanked my arm inside. The windblown hairs on my forearm tingled. "I wasn't waving. I was holding up my hand to feel the breeze."

"She waved at *you.*"

"Well, I didn't wave at *her,*" I said. "She waved because *you* honked."

"Okay," he said, turning into the parking lot. "She waved at both of us, then."

"She waved at *you.* I don't care, it doesn't matter. But she definitely waved at you."

"Are we fighting?" he asked. He reentered the street, turned back the way we had come. Anna was near, walking toward us.

"Course we're not fighting. Are you going to honk at her again?"

"Are you going to wave at her again?"

Anna looked behind her for traffic, stepped off the sidewalk, and darted across the street, into our lane, racket lifted like an Olympic torch.

"Look out!"

"What the hell?"

Tom hit the brakes. The passenger seat slid forward on its track, and my knees slammed the dash. Dozens of cassettes on the backseat cascaded onto the floor. Only a foot or two in front of the stopped car stood Anna, arms folded, one hip thrust out. She regarded us without expression, blew a large pink bubble that reached her nose and then collapsed back into her mouth.

"Hi, guys," she said.

Tom opened his door and stood, one foot on the pavement. "For crying out loud, Anna, are you okay? We could've killed you!"

"I was trying to flag you down," she said.

"What? Why?" Tom asked. "What for? Something wrong with the car?" I saw him swivel, and I knew that, out of sight, he was glancing toward the tires, the hood, the tailpipe.

"Nothing's wrong with the car, Tom," she said, chewing with half her mouth, arms still folded. "It's a really neat car. Whenever I see it I think, 'Damn, Tom must take mighty good care of that car.' I get a *lot* of chances to think that, Tom, 'cause every day you guys drive by my house at least twice, and whenever I leave tennis practice, you drive past me, and turn around in the lot, and drive past me *again*, and every time you do that I think, 'He takes mighty damn good care of that goddamn care just to drive past me all the fucking time.' "

Someone behind us honked and pulled around. A pickup truck driver, who threw us a bird.

"Do you ever *stop*? No. Say hi at school? Either of you? No. *Call* me? Shit." She shifted her weight to the other hip, unfolded her arms, whipped the towel from around her neck and swatted the hood with it. "So all I want to know is, just what's the *deal*? Tom? Jack? I see you in there, Jack, you can't hide. What's up, Jack? You tell me. Your chauffeur's catching flies out here."

Looking up at Anna, even though I half expected at any moment to be arrested for perversion or struck from behind by a truck or beaten to death with a tennis racket, purple waffle patterns scarring my corpse, I realized I had never felt such crazed exhilaration, not even that night on Bates Hill, when Tom passed a hundred and twenty. My knees didn't even hurt any more. The moment I realized this, naturally the feeling of exhilaration began to ebb, and so before I lost my resolve I slowly stuck my head out the window, smiled what I hoped was a smile, and called out: "Can we give you a lift, Anna?"

A station wagon swung past us with a honk. Anna looked at me, at Tom, at me again. She plucked her gum from her mouth, tossed it, looked down at the pavement and then up and then down again, much younger and almost shy. In a small voice, she said: "Yeah." She cleared her throat. "Yeah. Yes. That's . . . that's nice of you. Thank you."

I let her have my seat, of course. I got in the back, atop a shifting pile of cassettes and books and plastic boxes of lug nuts, but right behind her, close enough to smell her: not sweat, exactly, but salt and earth, like the smell of the beach before the tide comes in.

"Where to?" Tom asked.

"California," she said, and laughed, hands across her face. "Damn, Anna," she asked, "where did *that* come from? Oh, I don't know. Where are y'all going? I mean, wherever. Whenever. Let's just *go*, okay? Let's just . . . go."

We talked: School. Movies. Bands. Homework. Everything. Nothing. What else? Drove around. For hours.

Her ponytail was short but full, a single blond twist that she gathered up in one hand and lifted as she tilted her head forward. I thought she was looking at something on the floor, and I wondered for a second whether I had tracked something in.

"Jack?" she asked, head still forward. No one outside my family had made my name a question before. "Would you be a sweetie and rub my neck?"

The hum of tires, the zing of crickets, the shrill stream of air flowing through the crack that the passenger window never quite closed.

"Ma'am?"

"My neck. It's all stove up and tight from tennis. Would you rub the kinks out for me?"

"Sure," I said, too loudly and too quickly. My hands moved as slowly as in a nightmare. Twice I thought I had them nearly to her neck when I realized I was merely rehearsing the action in my head, so that I had it all to do over again. Tom shifted gears, slowed into a turn, sped up, shifted gears again, and I still hadn't touched her. My forearms were lifted; my hands were outstretched, palms down; my fingers were trembling. I must have looked like a mesmerist. You are sleepy, very sleepy. Which movie was it where the person in the front seat knew nothing about the clutching hands in the back? I could picture the driver's face as the hands crept closer: Christopher Lee, maybe? No: Donald Pleasence?

"Jack," she said. "Are you still awake back there?"

The car went into another turn, and I heard a soft murmur of complaint from the tires. Tom was speeding up.

My fingertips brushed the back of her neck. I yanked them back, then moved them forward again. This time I held them there, barely touching.

Her neck so smooth, so hot, slightly—damp? And what's *this*? Little hairs! Hairs as soft as a baby's head! No one ever had told me there would be hairs. . . .

"You'll have to rub harder than *that*, Jack." Still holding her hair aloft with her right hand, she reached up with her left and pressed my fingers into her neck. "Like that. Right—*there*. And there. Feel how tight that is?" She rotated her hand over mine, and trapped between her damp palm and her searing neck I did feel something both supple and taut. "Oooh, yeah, like that." She pulled her hand away, and I kept up the motions. "Oh, that feels good . . ."

The sun was truly down by now, and lighted houses scudded past. Those distinctive dormer windows—wasn't that Lisa's house? And, in the next block, wasn't that Kim's driveway?

We were following the route. We were passing all the homes of the stars.

Tom said nothing, but drove faster and faster. I kept rubbing, pressing, kneading, not having the faintest idea what I was doing but following the lead of Anna's sighs and murmurs. "Yeah, my shoulder there . . . Oh, this is wonderful. You'll have to stop this in about three hours, you know."

After about five minutes or ten or twenty, without looking up, she raised her left index finger and stabbed the dashboard. A tape came on. I don't remember which tape it was. I do remember that it played through both sides, and started over.

Tom was speeding. Each screeching turn threw us off balance. Where were the cops? Where was all the other traffic? We passed Jane's house, Tina's house. Streetlights strobed the car like an electrical storm. We passed Cynthia's house—hadn't we already? Beneath my hands, Anna's shoulders braced and rolled and braced again. I held on. My arms ached. Past the corner of my eye flashed a stop sign. My fingers kept working. Tom wrenched up the volume on the stereo. The bass line throbbed into my neck and shoulder blades, as if the car were reciprocating.

Gravel churned beneath us. "Damn," Tom muttered, and yanked the wheel, fighting to stay on the road. Anna snapped her head up, looked at him. I saw her profile against the radio dial.

"I want to drive," she said.

Tom put on the brakes, too swiftly. Atop a surging flood of gravel, the car jolted and shuddered to a standstill off the side of the road. The doors flew open, and both Tom and Anna leaped out. My exhilaration long gone, my arms aching, I felt trapped, suffocating. I snatched up the seat latch, levered forward the passenger seat, and stepped humpbacked and out of balance into the surprisingly cool night air. Over there was the Episcopal church, over there the Amoco station. We were only a few blocks from my house. My right hand stung; I had torn a nail on the seat latch. I slung it back and forth as Tom stepped around the car. Anna was already in the driver's seat.

"You want to sit in front?" Tom sounded hoarse.

"No," I said. "No, thanks. Listen, I think I'll, uh, I think I'll just call it a night. I'm nearly home anyway. I can, uh, I can walk from here. Y'know? It's not far. I can walk from here." I called out to Anna, leaning down and looking in: "I can walk from here." Her face was unreadable, but her eyes gleamed.

"Huh?" Tom said. It was like a grunt. He cleared his throat. "What do you mean, *walk*? It's early yet."

The car was still running. The exhaust blew over me in a cloud, made me dizzy. "No, really, you guys go on. I'm serious. I'll be fine. Go on, really. I'll see you later on."

"We could drop you off," Tom said. He spoke politely but awkwardly, as if we had never met. "Let's do that. We'll drop you off in your yard."

Anna revved the motor. It was too dark to see Tom's expression as he looked at her. Her fingers moved across the lighted instrument panel, pulled out the switch that started the emergency flashers, *ka-chink ka-chink ka-chink*, pushed it back again. "Cool," she said.

"I'll see you later," I said. "Okay? See you, Anna. Call me tomorrow," I said to Tom.

"Okay," he said. "I'll call you tomorrow."

"Okay," I said, not looking back. I waved a ridiculous cavalier wave, and stuck my hands in my pockets, trying to look nonchalant as I stumbled along the crumbling asphalt shoulder in the dark.

Behind me two doors slammed. I heard the car lurching back onto the highway, gravel spewing, and I heard it make a U-turn, away from town and toward the west, toward the lake, toward the woods. As the engine gunned, my shoulders twitched and I ducked my head, because I expected the screech of gears, but all I heard was steady and swift acceleration, first into second into third, as the Firebird sped away, into fourth, and then it was just me, walking.

They never came back.

Tom's parents got a couple of letters, a few postcards. California. They shared them with Anna's parents but no one else. "Tom wants everyone to know they're doing fine," that's all his mom and dad would say. But they didn't look reassured. Miss Sara down at the paper, who always professed to know a lot more than she wrote up in her column, told my father that she hadn't seen the mail herself, mind you, but she had *heard* from people who should *know* that the letters were strange, rambling things, not one *bit* like Tom, and the cards had postmarks that were simply, somehow, *wrong*. But who could predict, Miss Sara added, *when* postcards might arrive, or in *what* order. Why, sometimes they sit in the post office for *years*, and sometimes they never show up at *all*. Criminal, Miss Sara mourned, criminal.

Anna's parents got no mail at all.

I never did, either, except maybe one thing. I don't know that you could call it *mail*. No stamps, no postmark, no handwriting. It wasn't even in the mailbox. But it felt like mail to me.

It was lying on my front porch one morning—this was years later, not long after I got my own place, thought I was settled. At first I thought it was the paper, but no, as usual the paper was spiked down deep in the hedge. This was lying faceup and foursquare on the welcome mat. It was one of those Hollywood maps, showing where the stars can be found.

I spread it across the kitchen table and anchored it with the sugar bowl and a couple of iron owl-shaped trivets, because it was stiff and new and didn't want to lie flat. You know how maps are. It was bright white paper and mighty thick, too. I didn't know they made maps so thick anymore. I ran my index finger over sharp paper ridges and down straight paper canyons and looked for anyone I knew. No, Clint Eastwood wasn't there. Nor was anyone else whose movies I ever had seen at the mall. A lot of the names I just didn't recognize, but some I knew from cable, from the nostalgia channels.

I was pretty sure most of them were dead.

I searched the index for Tom's name, for Anna's. I didn't see them. I felt relieved. Sort of.

"California," I said aloud. Once it had been four jaunty syllables, up and down and up and down, a kid on a bicycle, going noplace. California. Now it was a series of low and urgent blasts, someone leaning on the horn, saying, come on, saying, hurry up, saying, you're not too late, not yet, not *yet*. California.

It's nearly eleven. I stand in the cool rush of the refrigerator door, forgetting what I came for, and strain to hear. The train is passing, a bit late, over behind the campus. My windows are open, so the air conditioning is pouring out into the yard and fat bugs are smacking themselves against the screen, but this way I can hear everything clearly. The rattle as my neighbor hauls down the garage door, secures everything for the night. On the other side, another neighbor trundles a trash can out to the curb, then plods back. I am standing at the kitchen counter now. Behind me the refrigerator door is swinging shut, or close enough. I hear a car coming.

The same car.

I move to the living room, to the front door. I part the curtain. The car is coming closer, but even more slowly than before. Nearly stopping. It must be in first gear by now. There was always that slight rattle, just within the threshold of hearing, when you put it in first gear. Yes. And the slightly cockeyed headlights, yes, and the dent in the side. I can't clearly see the interior even under the streetlight but it looks like two people in the front.

Two people? Or just one?

And then it's on the other side of the neighbor's hedge, and gone, but I still can hear the engine, and I know that it's going to turn, and come back.

My hand is on the doorknob. The map is in my pocket. The night air is surprisingly cool. I flip on the porch light as I step out, and I stand illuminated in a cloud of tiny beating wings, waiting for them to come back, come back and see me standing here, waiting, waiting, oh my God how long I've been waiting, I want to walk out there and stand in front of the car and make it stop, really I do, but I can't, I can't move, I'm trapped here, trapped in this place, trapped in this time, don't drive past again, I'm here, I'm ready, I wasn't then but now I am, really I am, please, please stop. Present or past, alive or dead, what does it matter, what did it ever matter? Please. Stop.

Please.

JAMES SALLIS

Under Construction

James Sallis gained early recognition as one of the most adventurous and literarily accomplished voices in science fiction; many of his early stories are collected in A Few Last Words. *His stories, poems, and essays have appeared in a variety of journals, including* The Georgia Review, Prairie Schooner, Transatlantic Review, The Magazine of Fantasy and Science Fiction, Alfred Hitchcock's Mystery Magazine, *and* American Poetry Review. *He has published several volumes of musicology, literary criticism, biography, and translation, as well as a series of crime novels featuring the detective Lew Griffin. He has been a finalist for the Anthony, Edgar, Nebula, Shamus, and Golden Dagger Awards. His most recent books are* Time's Hammers: Collected Stories, Ghost of a Flea, *a new Lew Griffin novel,* Chester Himes: A Life, *the novel* Cypress Grove, *and a collection of poetry translations,* My Tongue in Other Cheeks. *Raised in Helena, Arkansas, on the banks of the Mississippi River, Sallis now lives in Phoenix, Arizona, with his wife, Karyn. This marks the first publication of "Under Construction."*

They stood together there in the center of the room. The man rubbed thumb against fingers, feeling the grit of dust and refuse he'd bent to lift from the floor. Turning on one foot, the woman reached to brush the wall with her hands, then brought them to her face. There were smears of grayish white on the palms, from the paint.

"It's lovely," she said.

"One of a kind," the real estate agent, a Mr. Means, told them.

"But rather dear," the man said.

"You *could* look at it that way, I suppose. Have you been looking long? Seen what's out there? I'm assuming this is your first unit together." There was a gleam in his eyes. Surgically implanted, the man had heard. He had no idea if it were true. You were always hearing these things.

The woman nodded.

"And not just everyone can appreciate character like this. An exact reproduction, you know. Here," he said, "let me show you."

Taking the two short strides needed to reach the room's far side, he pulled back what appeared to be paneling on the wall but was in fact a curtain. Man and woman alike drew startled breaths.

A window!

"Fine touch, isn't it? From an artisan upstate. Best there is. They say he worked for years just to get the staining right. Glass looks like it's been up there ten, twenty years."

Down in the street, not in the street actually, but next to it, in a long, broad alley, workmen were erecting a wall. A dozen or more stood on line, passing rough-cut blocks of stone from hand to hand. The last man in line set a stone in place atop the wall. Then he moved to the rear of the line to wait his turn as the others shifted forward.

On the way here the man and woman had come across a construction crew lined up alongside streetcar tracks. The tracks went for several blocks and ended as abruptly as they'd begun. There were no indications of further construction, or of a streetcar.

"I'm also assuming," Mr. Means said, "that this would be short-term."

The woman looked first at the man, then towards the floor when he said "Of course."

"Different rates, you see. Long-term, now, that, you ever want to consider it, sometime in the future maybe, that one has teeth. But short-term, like I brought out to you on the wire, on that I can give you a sweet deal. *Good* numbers. Wouldn't even have to run them by my handler." He smiled. "Just so you know. Now, you take your time, look around all you want, get the feel of the place. I'll just stand over here, out of your way."

So saying, he took up position by the outside door. If someone came in, they might hang a coat on him without thinking. If anyone else could have got in here.

He owed this to her, owed it to himself, the man was thinking. If life couldn't have some specialness to it, something at the center that really mattered, how could it matter at all? He'd watched all his parents and all those around him, all his life, go on and on and without. Same schedule, same events, same thoughts and feelings day after day. A gray blur, like the air above. Until finally the blur seeped into you as well, and settled there.

"We'll take it," the man said.

"Oh, darling!"

Mr. Means nodded. "I hoped you'd realize how right it is for the two of you. Saw that right away, myself." A recorder appeared. He held it half at arm's length, peering. Fingers moved on the eye. "Short-term at—"

"Long-term," the man said.

The woman turned her head sharply to him.

"Long-term," Mr. Means said without missing a beat. "Of course. Now, for that, like I brought out to you, I have to go by the book, get approval from my handler." Light touch on the eye here, little more than a brush, longer one there. Then the smile: "Course, I never was much one for the books."

Finished, Mr. Means thumbed the recorder to display mode. The man looked it over and entered his code as Mr. Means glanced discreetly away.

"Welcome home," Mr. Means said, and went out the door.

When the man turned back, his wife (he'd have to start thinking of her that way now, he reminded himself) was gone. From the bathroom, that marvelous bathroom with crumbling plaster walls, broken tiles and rust stains, he heard the toilet flush. Mr. Means had shown them how the toilet used actual water, two gallons that got filtered, purified and recirculated again and again. There was a second flush as her clothes blew down into the vats for recycling. It sounded as though someone had held down adjacent keys on an accordion and tugged hard.

She came out after a moment and lay on the bed. Neither of them had thought to bring along new clothes; he'd have to go out later to purchase some. It had all happened so fast. But they'd heard about the apartment and rushed right over to see it. Now he'd signed away the equivalent of a full year's labor, enough to provide housing in the commons for the next ten.

Her dark hair lay long and loose on sheets that looked almost like cotton. When he sat beside her, one of the bed's bottom legs collapsed. The man and woman lurched together as though troughing a wave, and when they did, the other legs gave way as well. The man and woman laughed. With something that sounded very much like real joy.

"It's everything I could have imagined, darling," she said at length. "Everything. Oh, thank you!"

Maybe the old ways, some of them, *were* better, he told himself. Maybe we feel the way we do because we've lost all sense of tradition, all continuity. Maybe it's time for us to get some of that, what we can of it, back.

Periodically he woke to dial coffee or gruel from a console in the wall alongside the bed designed to look like an old radio. Once, he started from a dream of seas and dark skies and something coming towards him over the water.

He rose that time and stood by the window. Light had started up again by then. It swelled against the buildings, began enveloping them. Below in the alleyway he could see one of the workers peering over the top of the wall from within as the final bricks were set in place.

Later, when light had given way, had let go its hold again on buildings and sky, he lay awake still as she slept beside him. Cockroaches came out of the walls, following paths of inlaid wires, the same paths each time they appeared. Their eyes seemed to him to glow dully in the dark. He wondered if she knew they were mechanical.

GENE WOLFE

Houston, 1943

*Gene Wolfe is among the most accomplished and respected
authors in the history of science fiction. His* Book of the New
Sun *quartet of novels (*The Shadow of the Torturer, The
Claw of the Conciliator, The Sword of the Lictor, *and*
The Citadel of the Autarch*) is widely regarded as one of the
landmark achievements of modern fantastic literature. He
has continued the series, to equal acclaim, with the* Book of
the Long Sun *(*Nightside the Long Sun, Lake of the Long
Sun, Caldé of the Long Sun, *and* Exodus from the Long
Sun*) and the* Book of the Short Sun *(*On Blue's Waters,
In Green's Jungles, Return to the Whorl*). Among his
many other books are* The Fifth Head of Cerberus, Peace,
The Island of Doctor Death and Other Stories and Other
Stories, Free Live Free, Soldier of Arete, *and* There Are
Doors. *His most recent novel is* The Knight, *published by
Tor Books in 2004. He has won two Nebulas, three World
Fantasy Awards, and is an eight-time Hugo finalist. Born in
Brooklyn, raised in Houston, he lives with his wife in Bar-
rington, Illinois. "Houston, 1943" was first published in*
Tropical Chills, *edited by Tim Sullivan.*

The voice woke Roddie in the middle of the night. Or rather, it did not wake him at first. It seeped into his sleep, so that he dreamed he was at his desk in Poe School reading "The Murders in the Rue Morgue"; and through the open windows with smeared gray panes (the smear was to keep their shattered glass from cutting Mrs. Butcher and her class when the first Nazi bombs fell on the playground outside), and above the rising, fading hum of the big electric fan that shook its head forever *no, no, no* (because the room was so hot, boiling with the merciless Gulf heat that would endure not for days or weeks but for almost a year, a heat that soaked everything and that no fan could blow away), he heard his father's voice calling him.

His father was gone, as always except on Friday nights, on Saturdays, and on Sundays until evening, gone selling "systems" to defense plants. Roddie sat up in bed.

"Come."

He went to the window. His was a large bedroom in a small house that had only four rooms and a tiny bathroom; there were four windows at the side (facing Mrs. Smith's) and three at the rear. It was to one of the rear windows that he went.

A boy stood in the middle of the backyard, distinct in the moonlight. The boy was small and thin, almost frail; but his eyes caught the moonlight like a cat's eyes, and the moon filled them with a colorless glow. He waved, gesturing for Roddie to join him, silently saying that they must go somewhere together. The window was already thrown wide; Roddie unhooked the screen and climbed out, dropping four feet into his mother's fragrant bed of mint.

"Who are you?" he asked.

"Jim." The strange boy's voice was high and reedy, laced with an accent Roddie had never heard before. He had expected some neighborhood friend; this was a boy he did not know at all. The strange boy gripped him by the arm and pointed toward the crawl space beneath the house. His grasp was cold and damp, as if he had been groping after something lost in water.

"We'll get dirty."

The boy pointed again. At the edge of the shadow of the fig tree there was something Roddie took for a tarantula. He had seen many tarantulas, big, hairy spiders found lurking under boards or in firewood; this was the biggest ever, big enough to kill birds, something that only the largest did. It rose on five legs, ran swiftly to him, and climbed his pajama bottoms.

He slapped at it just as it reached his waist. Although it was as hard as his cast-iron clown bank, it seemed to slip for a moment, to lose its hold.

A moment more and it was climbing again, pinching the soft skin of his bare chest between sharp legs. He grasped it, felt its stiff hair and gouging nails, and knew he held a human hand. With all his strength, he flung it from him and heard it thump against the wall of the Jacobson's garage. In the shadow of the eaves, it fell softly to earth.

"Foul weather," Jim whispered. "'e don't like 'avin' 'is 'awser crossed. Better cut it."

Roddie said, "I'm going back inside."

He returned to the window, and the thin boy, Jim, followed him, not trying to stop him. "Better cut," Jim repeated.

Roddie raised the screen and pushed his head under it, put bare foot on the narrow white-painted finale that was the last board down the wall of the house.

There was a boy, another boy, sleeping in his bed. Roddie scrambled through the window, ran to the switch, and turned on light.

The other boy did not wake up or even stir. Roddie thought vaguely of offering to share the bed if the other boy—like Jim, perhaps—needed a place to sleep. He shook the other boy by the shoulder; his eyes opened at once, and he screamed.

Roddie heard his mother in the front bedroom, the click of the switch on her reading light, the patter of bare feet.

The boy in the bed screamed again, his eyes huge, his face empty of everything save fear. A thin line of spit ran from one corner of his mouth and wet his chin.

The door banged open. Roddie's mother flew in, her hair in curl papers, her pale face a study in terror and anger. "It's a dream, Roddie! Only a bad dream, see? Oh, that awful school! I'm right here. It's all right, Roddie— everything's all right." She hugged the blank-faced boy, crushing him against her breasts, rocking back and forth as she held him.

Icy fingers touched Roddie's shoulder. "Best cut, we 'ad. 'e'll be in main soon, if we don't. 'E'll be after 'e, but e might get 'er."

Baffled, Roddie backed away, out of the bedroom and into the little hallway. The phone rang as they passed; he jerked with fear, and at the sound of his mother's steps he followed Jim into the twilight of the big room that was living room and dining room together.

The phone rang again before his mother picked it up.

"Hello?

"Oh, good evening, Mrs. Smith. No, we're fine. Roddie had a nightmare.

"Really? In our yard?

"What did he look like? Do you think I should call the police?"

There were already past the hulking Crosley radio. " 'e'll be waitin at the back."

"*I'm* Roddie," Roddie said. It sounded false even to him as he said it, as false as the lies he told at times to get out of trouble. "Where we going?"

"Old man's."

The streets were hot, dark, and silent. They saw a single car on Old Spanish Trail, a black de Soto that hummed past them meditating upon secrets.

The old man's house looked like dozens Roddie passed every time he rode his bike to the Y, a tiny clapboard cottage with a sagging roof.

" 'E's 'ome," Jim said. "Open the door."

Roddie asked, "Shouldn't we knock?"

Jim made no reply; when Roddie looked around for him he was gone, and Roddie stood alone on the crooked little porch beside a rickety rocking chair. Tentatively, mostly because it seemed so silly to come way out here without doing anything, he knocked at the peeling door.

Someone inside laughed, a high, cracked cackling. "They hear. They hear. Sister, hear them!"

Somebody else moaned softly.

Roddie waited. And at last, when no one opened the door, he knocked again. This time a bell jangled inside the cottage, giving him the crazy feeling that he had pushed a button somehow instead of knocking, though he knew that he had knocked. He tried the knob, and it turned in his hand. There was a rattle and squeak as the latch crept back. The door seemed strangely heavy but swung ponderously away from him.

The interior of the cottage was a single room; even so it was smaller than his bedroom at home. A narrow cot stood in one corner, a commode with a broken seat in another.

In the center of the room, in place of a carpet or a rug, was a spreading pool of blood. It came from a black chicken hanging by its feet from the light fixture. The chicken's neck had been cut though its head was still attached. Its wings hung down as though to sweep up its own blood from the cracked boards of the floor.

Because both were so still, a second or more passed before Roddie saw the people. There were two, a shriveled old man with a beard as white as cotton, and a slender girl who to Roddie's unpracticed eyes appeared to be about nineteen. The old man was naked except for a long necklace of broken bones, the girl naked entirely. Designs had been traced upon their bodies in red and white—in places their sweat had made the designs run. The old man held a cracked leather strap with three brass bells sewn on it, and that and his beard made Roddie think of Santa Claus.

Roddie stepped into the room. "I'm really sorry. I didn't mean—"

The thing that had climbed his pajama bottoms in the backyard dropped onto his shoulder. As he grabbed for it, he felt it turn around like a dog lying down; its fingers closed on his neck.

He yelled; but the yell did not leave his lips as noise but as something else, a strong wild thing that he had never known he could make, as if the fingers around his throat had reshaped it, just as the those of Miss Smith (who lived next door with her widowed mother and taught art) could reshape the witless wax of his broken Crayolas into rearing horses and roaring flames. The wild thing smashed the lightbulb, casting tinkling shards all over the room, which at the same instant became pitch-dark. The strong wild thing vanished then, and something else dropped to the floor with a thud.

'Now 'ear me," rasped a voice at Roddie's ear. "Put down them 'ands, for they don't answer. 'E stand to."

It was no longer merely a hand, Roddie felt certain. Now there was an arm behind the hand, and a big man at the other end of the arm. He could sense the man's big body behind him and smell the big man's foul breath.

"Ask him, Doc!" It had to be the naked girl's voice. It was answered by a terrified mumble: "Jes', Marl, Jos'f . . ." The girl's voice again, clear and sweet: "Glory hand, you lead us! Petro man, you know the places, don' do you no good. Show us, and whatever you want, that you shall receive. Any-thin'. Doc an' me swear to it."

The hand was gone, and the man with it. Roddie would have bolted like a jackrabbit, but he misjudged the position of the door and ran full tilt into the wall instead—the crash of his body a whisper like a weary sigh. Aerial salutes burst orange and blue somewhere behind his eyes; he fell half-stunned.

"On thy feet! Stand to!"

He tried, but somehow fell again.

"Take 'im, Jim lad. Make 'im look."

There was a flare of light and the smell of sulfur—a match framed by the girl's disheveled hair. She held the match to the wick of a misshapen lit-tle candle, and it blazed and sputtered.

"Go on with you," Jim whispered. "You 'eard 'im."

"Okay," he said, floundering forward toward the girl and the light.

The hand lay on its back before her, darkly spattered with the chicken's blood. She placed the candle on its forefinger, shaping the greasy tallow to hold it there, and lit another from it. The dead chicken sprawled in its own gore now, a black isle rising from a crimson sea. Rod-die could smell the dust in its feathers over the sweet-salt tang of its blood.

Though the hand was gone, the big man's hand was on him, forcing him forward, forcing his head down.

Weakly, Doc said, "You take care, Sheba. Don' know what you got."

The fifth candle was burning. Sheba positioned it on the smallest finger and lifted the hand by the wrist. A new voice—the big man's voice—

boomed from the old man's mouth. "Look, 'e slut! In the blood pool. Mine!
MINE!"

Sheba peered down into the thickening blood. Roddie looked too, and
saw Sheba's face reflected there, startled and eager beside his own.

The cottage seemed to spin, though Roddie knew that it did not. He felt
that a long time had passed—not minutes or hours but months and years
and something larger. Jim and the big man were gone. He was alone except
for Sheba and Doc, and happy to be thus alone. Still holding the hand,
Sheba was snuffing out its candles, one by one.

"What you see, Sheba?"

"Li'l boy's face. White boy."

"That what he want, then. That one—got to be that special one."

As Roddie went through the doorway, he heard Sheba mutter, "He
gone get him."

It was black night still, but not quite night long before he reached South
Boulevard where he went to school. Doug, an older boy, was riding no-
hands down the street, folding papers and throwing them as he went. Roddie waved to Doug, but Doug paid no attention to him. Doug seldom did.

There were lights in the kitchen window already. The front door stood
open, and the living-room-dining-room was full of the morning smells of
coffee and bacon. The green enameled door to the kitchen swung both
ways—but not for Roddie, not today. He shoved against it hard with his
shoulder, but could move it barely an inch; the springs in its double hinges
seemed to have stiffened like cast iron.

"Mom!"

She had the radio on in the kitchen, as she always did. It was "The
Wide-Awake Hour" this early, drums and big brass horns that blew *ta-dah*,
ta-dah! Roddie usually liked "The Wide-Awake Hour."

"Mama!"

He could hear her moving around in the kitchen, the scrape of her spat-
ula on the bottom of the frying pan. But there was no reply.

Mysteriously, he felt that he was somehow in bed, bound in bed, only
dreaming that he stood helpless at the kitchen door; and after a moment or
two he went into his bedroom to see if he could find himself.

And did. He lay on his back in the bed, covered with a sheet, eyes closed, forehead beaded with sweat, even his arms beneath the sheet.

"Wake up," he said. "Hey, wake up."

The sleeping self did not stir.

Roddie knelt on the mattress beside it. He had never liked his face, with its chubby cheeks and insignificant mouth; but he had to admit that it was his face. He might have been looking into a mirror, except that his own mouth was closed, that of the sleeper slightly open. "Wake up!" he said again, and it seemed to him that the sleeper stirred.

He grabbed the sleeper's shoulders then and shook him. For an instant it seemed to him that his fingertips penetrated those shoulders ever so slightly. The sleeper opened his eyes and sat up, bumping him hard.

The sleeper could see him. He knew it because the sleeper recoiled just as he himself would have if he had bumped someone, and when he slid off the bed, the sleeper followed him with his eyes.

"Hello," Roddie said. "I'm you."

The sleeper did not answer, or even seem to understand.

"You're—"

His mother's voice interrupted him. "Get out of bed now, Roddie. You'll be late for school."

The sleeper only stared at her, and Roddie saw her face fall. "You're really sick, aren't you? Ever since last night."

Slowly, the sleeper nodded, his mouth still gaping.

"That does it. No school today—you're going to see Dr. Johnson. But first I'm going to take your temperature. Are you hungry?"

There was no reply. Roddie tugged at his mother's apron; but she only smoothed it absently as if it had been twitched by a breeze. Her eyes had filled with tears, and he was glad when she went back to the kitchen.

It was a long time before she returned with bacon, toast and two fried eggs, all of them cold. Roddie took a strip of bacon while his mother fed the sleeper like an infant, but he found he could not chew it, and it made him gag. He did not have the heart to follow them when his mother led the sleeper to the bus stop.

By then Boots had returned from her morning patrol of the neighborhood and lay, beautifully black-and-white, on the front porch, ever alert for strangers and food. In theory, Boots was Roddie's dog; in actuality, she was his father's, and both he and Boots knew it. But Boots was generally tolerant and even protective of him, and when it was not too hot she sometimes consented to chase the sticks and balls he threw for her. She only rolled her soulful brown eyes now when Roddie spoke to her When he patted her head, she snarled.

There were plenty of books in his room, but he discovered that it required all of his strength just to pull one from the shelf, and he let it fall to the floor. It was *Peter Pan* with wonderful colored illustrations; but he had read it before and the story seemed dull and stupid now, so that even turning the page took effort; it was as if the pages had become sheets of lead, heavier than the foil that he was supposed to save from his parents' cigarettes. After a time he realized that he was not thinking of the story at all but only of himself lying on the rug and turning the pages, invisible to everyone but Boots and the sleeper. He recalled seeing pages turn themselves when he and the sleeper had been one boy. He wondered who had been reading them, or at least looking at the pictures. Possibly it had been Jim, reading his books.

That's all right, Roddie thought. I don't care if you read them, just as long as you don't tear them up.

Jim had been able to see him, but where was Jim? He was not even sure he wanted to find Jim.

But Jim had not been the only one. The naked girl, Sheba, had seen his reflection. Then Sheba and Doc had said they were going to get him for the big man; but that was wrong, because the big man had been right there and could have taken him for himself if he had wanted to. Roddie poked among his toys, then lay down on his bed, feeling very tired.

The front door opened and closed, and Roddie went out to look. It was his father, carrying his suitcase as he always did, sweating as he always did in his navy blue business suit. Boots frisked around on the living room carpet, her stump of a tail wagging frantically. His father tossed his hat onto the floor lamp and did not see Roddie either.

It was boiling outside. It had seemed hot already in the house, but outside the sun struck like a blow, a heavy, burning weight that had to be carried like a sack of meal. Squinting up at the sun, Roddie decided it was already afternoon. Today was Friday, because that was the day his father came home. But his father never came home before noon—even on Friday—and anyway the sun was over the house at the end of the block. Or at least it looked that way.

A stinking orange diesel bus roared by on Mandell. There was a squeal of air brakes as it halted at the stop on the next corner. Roddie waited, then watched his mother and the sleeper walk slowly along Vassar and go up on the porch. His mother was wearing her best gray dress, the sleeper Roddie's own jeans and red-and-white striped pullover. Roddie was glad to see that his mother was no longer crying, although her face was grim as she went into the house, towing the sleeper behind her. Through the screen door, he heard his father say, "Oh. There you are."

Roddie went back onto the porch to listen. His mother was telling about taking the sleeper (whom to his disgust she called Roddie) to the doctor. The doctor had made an appointment for Roddie to see a specialist.

"I'll call him up," Roddie's father said. "I want to hear what he has to say about this." Like just about everybody, the doctor was a friend of his.

"Do you think we could go to the beach tonight?" his mother asked. "Do you have enough gas? I think the cool air might do Roddie good."

"Sure," his father answered. "Why not?" Because he was a salesman, his father had a "C" card.

Roddie left the porch, and in leaving it discovered that he could not hear his own footsteps. He stopped, stamped hard, and shuffled his feet; but there was no sound. He could make noise, though, he remembered—he had knocked on the peeling white door. He knocked on a fender of his father's black Plymouth and heard his knock crisp and clear.

That encouraged him so much that he skipped awhile despite the heat, though he knew that he would be tired and hot before he reached Old Spanish Trail. Whenever he could, he stopped in air-conditioned stores; the clerks could not see him either, or at least did not chase him out. That was good, he told himself; yet he would have given everything he owned to be chased out, to be seen and yelled at again.

The sun was under the phone wires when he found the cottage, so that he was afraid he would have to look for it in the dark. Yet instinct led him to

it, and he knew at once that it was the only place he wanted to be. Sheba
would look into a mirror, he thought. Girls were always looking at the mirror, always fixing their hair, as if anybody cared. Sheba would look, he
would put his face close by hers, and then she would see him. That would be
sufficient, he felt. If Sheba saw him, he knew that he would feel better; then
he would think of some way she could help him, and some way in which he
could tell her to.

"Ah," Jim's voice said. " 'Ere 'e are."

Jim was at his elbow, seeming to have come from noplace, a thin,
ragged boy with hair the color of sawdust and a bruise on one cheek.

"I have to go in there," Roddie told him. "I have to see Sheba." It was
not until he had said it that he realized it was really the other way around.

"Course 'e do." Jim grinned and nodded.

"Are you coming too?"

"Course I am."

Roddie pushed the door. It swung back even more slowly, even more
heavily, than before; but it swung, and he and Jim slipped inside.

The small room was crowded. Besides Doc and Sheba (Roddie had
been afraid she would not be there, and sighed with relief to see that she
was), there was a stiff old man with tobacco-stained whiskers, a thin woman
who seemed almost like a shadow, another boy, and Captain Hook. Roddie
recognized Captain Hook from his picture in *Peter Pan*, even though he was
handsome there and had nicer clothes. They do that for the pictures they put
in books, Roddie thought. They make everybody look nicer.

The shadowy woman stroked him. "Aren't you *pretty*."

Roddie shook his head violently. "No, I'm not!"

She laughed, a faint, thin sound Roddie remembered having heard at
night. "Well, *I* think so. Do you know what they're going to do here tonight? Do you go to church?"

Roddie shook his head again.

"That's a pity—it's so *useful*. Anyway, they are honoring us. It's a religious ceremony. 'Where two are gathered in my name—' "

The old man spat tobacco juice toward the toilet with the broken seat.
Jim said, "You was drawn, same as us, same as 'er and 'im. They got the
wrong 'un, but we was drawn all the same, and we'll 'ave slum out o' it."

The other boy had been lying naked on the narrow cot. Doc lifted him and laid him on the little red-covered table that now stood in the center of the crowded room. Slowly, muttering as if to himself, Doc placed various objects around him. They were mostly pieces of dead people and animals, Roddie decided. From time to time Sheba spoke in response to Doc's muttered prayers: "Oh, yes. Yes, yes. You know. *Arrivez!*"

The boy's feet were not tied, and Roddie wondered why he did not get up off the table when he saw the old butcher knife in Doc's hand, and the bright, new edge on its big blade. He tried to help the boy, but Captain Hook elbowed him out of the way.

Sheba had lit the candles of the hand again. She spread the boy's legs and placed it between them, then switched off the light. Other candles burned with blue flames near the walls of the room, though Roddie had not seen them until the light went out, big homemade candles with curling wicks.

"We'll get to 'e," Captain Hook growled. "Stand to."

Doc whispered a name Roddie did not know and raised the old knife above his head. It trembled with the thin hands that held it, so that blue candlelight danced along its edge; Roddie heard the faint rattle of Doc's necklace of bones.

"No!" Roddie shouted. The shadowy woman smoothed his hair as his mother sometimes did, and laughed at him.

Doc did not even hear them; Captain Hook's hand held his, and the old man's hands closed upon all three; the knife came down, splitting the boy's unprotected chest like a watermelon. Roddie turned away, retching, but Jim held him by the collar. "'Ere. 'E'll want it, if there's somat left for us."

And he did.

He knew it instantly, and had known it even before Jim told him. So it had been when his father had killed his pet duck—it had been awful to watch Donald die, his wings flapping uselessly and his white feathers dyed with his own blood. But once Donald was truly dead it had seemed to Roddie that there was no harm in eating him, though Roddie's parents could hardly touch a bite.

The shadowy woman whispered, "He was drugged, my darling. Believe me, he didn't feel a thing."

Roddie nodded absently. He was watching Captain Hook and the old man. For an instant the two big men stood eye to eye. When Captain Hook turned away, his face was twisted with rage. But turn away he did, and the old man smiled and bent over the dying boy.

"*Pig,*" the shadowy woman whispered.

For half a minute, the cottage was silent. Roddie could hear the hum of a mosquito roused by Doc from its post on the pull-string of the light. The candles filled the room with a smell like burning garbage.

Inch by inch, the scarlet hue of life vanished from the dying boy's clotting blood as the old man drank, leaving it a rusty brown; as more blood welled forth, he drank more. The shadowy woman made a tiny gesture of impatience, and there was black death in Captain Hook's eyes.

At last the old man straightened up, wiped his discolored beard on his sleeve and sauntered out of the cottage. At once Captain Hook took his place, drinking, it seemed to Roddie, even more greedily.

Sheba asked Doc, "Is he comin'?"

Doc shook his head and shrugged. Roddie whispered, "*Look at a mirror!*" but Sheba did not hear him,

"This a murder," Sheba murmured, "do they find out. You go to Huntsville, won't never see the outside again. You know?"

Captain Hook rose.

Instantly, Jim sprang toward the dying boy, but the shadowy woman tripped him expertly. He fell with a slight creak of the floorboards, and she bent over the blood as Captain Hook had.

All this Roddie saw only from a corner of his eye. He was watching Doc, suddenly metamorphosed, his back straight and his shoulders squared, his face somehow longer. With one hand he seized Sheba's throat and slammed her to the wall with a crash that threatened to bring it down. "'E slut! 'E stupid *slut!*" Sheba's mouth gaped wide. Her tongue protruded farther than Roddie would have believed possible, and her eyes seemed about to leap from their sockets. Doc shook her and dropped her to the floor.

"That was very *nice.*" The shadowy woman—no longer quite so shadowy as she had been—patted her lips. "I haven't had such a nice drink in a long time."

Jim was drinking eagerly now, though the new, bright blood had nearly ceased to flow.

"Stand to," Doc told Sheba, "I'll show 'e the lad we wants. On with thy slops." He had snatched a pair of old trousers from the foot of the cot and was thrusting his legs into them as he spoke.

Roddie put his mouth to Jim's ear. "That's the captain, isn't it? That's him. How did he do that?" Jim only pushed him away.

Sheba staggered to her feet, staring at Doc with fear-crazed eyes.

"There's a wench. I never minded drinkin' from the tar bucket." Doc tossed her a purple dress spotted with yellow flowers.

Jim wiped his lips on his forearm. "Course that's 'im. The blood let 'im. Woter 'e thinks?"

"Would it let me? . . ." Roddie could not find words for the thing he wanted to say.

"Jury-rig 'im 'e left behind 'e? Might, and there's any left."

Doc glanced toward Roddie. "Do it, lad. 'Andsomely, now."

"You can see me!" Roddie exclaimed.

Sheba was backing away, holding her purple dress in front of her. Her cheeks were streaked with tears, and Roddie felt sorry for her.

Jim said, "We 'ave to cut. Drink up."

Roddie still hesitated. "Where are we going?"

"Takin' 'e 'ome. We've need o' a lad, 'im and me do. But we 'ave to 'ave the other 'alf, twig?"

Doc took off his necklace of bones and held it out. "See 'em, lad?"

Roddie nodded.

"Know 'ose they be?"

"No, sir." Roddie shook his head.

"Mine, lad. Jim's and mine. 'E seen the 'and." Doc bent over Roddie exactly as if Roddie were a real person, and that made Roddie feel wonderful. " 'Ose 'and do it be, do 'e think?"

"Yours, sir."

"A likely lad! Oh, Jim, 'e's a promising 'un!"

Jim nodded. " 'E's that."

Doc crouched until his eyes were at Roddie's level. "They 'anged me in chains, lad. Now do 'e know?"

"No, sir," Roddie admitted.

"After 'e've 'anged, they tars thy remains, same as to tar the bottom of a boat."

Roddie nodded to show that he understood.

"And they wraps the 'ole in chains for to keep it together They hangs the 'ole wear it may do the most good. So I 'ung—long time it seemed to me. Me 'and was taken then, and various."

Roddie asked, "Did they hang Jim, too?"

"Oh, aye."

Jim said, "We want a Christian grave, we do, and 'e must give it to us. One for both."

"I will, honest," Roddie promised. "If you'll put me back together."

"Me own thought, lad." Doc smiled with satisfaction, then whirled to face Sheba. "And 'e, 'e wants treasure, wench, don't 'e?"

Sheba shook her head.

"*Wot!*" Doc laughed; it sounded almost as though two voices were laughing together, one shrill, one roaring.

"You let me go——" Sheba swallowed, edging toward the back door.

"Ah there, lass." Doc tossed the string of bones rattling onto the cot; with one swift stride he was before her, a hand against the door. "No rubies, lass, great as pigeon eggs? No gold? No em'ralds cut square, full o' green fire?"

Sheba shook her head. "I don't want them."

Doc laughed again. (Roddie wondered what the people next door thought, hearing that laugh.) "But we want 'e, lass. We must 'ave the lad, and 'e to 'elp us get 'im. Now drink, lad. No more nonsense, 'ear? Drink up!"

Roddie bent over the dying boy. For the first time, he truly noticed the boy's face; it was a little like his own, he decided, but not very much.

"*Drink!*"

Roddie discovered that he wanted to, that he was hungry and thirsty. Very thirsty. He tried to remember the last time that he had eaten, the last time he had drunk.

Jim said, " 'E don't like 'avin is 'awser crossed. Best be at it."

Roddie nodded, studying the blood. For a moment it seemed that all life had already been drawn from it, leaving it as dry and unappealing as so much dust. No: one single, shining drop remained, far down in the deep wound. He would have to put his lips against the edges of that wound, as if he were kissing it.

The dying boy's eyes opened, wandered vaguely, fastened on his. For a moment Roddie saw the dying boy and the boy saw him.

"Drink!"

Roddie lowered his head until he felt his lips smeared with the dead blood, extended his tongue; the dying boy's eyes rolled upward, no longer together, one drifting aside. Roddie shut his own, sought with his tongue for the drop and found it.

His father had given him a scrap of raw steak once. Though he had been so strongly attracted to the blood, he had supposed it would be like that—cold, wet, and nearly flavorless. It was hot instead; not hot like the sun, or his room by night, but hot like music sometimes, or like nothing else that he could think of, energizing and delightful.

"Main good, 'tis." Doc's hand dropped heavily on Roddie's shoulder, bigger and stronger than he would have imagined Doc's hand could be. "Now I wants 'e to do somat for me, 'ear? See 'em bones on the bunk? 'E're not asceered o' 'em?"

Roddie shook his head.

"There's a lad! Go lift em up."

Roddie did as he had been told, and Doc filled the little room with his strange laughter.

"Which way?" Sheba looked at Doc, and Doc at Roddie.

Roddie shrugged helplessly. "Just the beach, that's all. I can't drive."

"Wears the beach, lass?"

"They got two." Sheba was resentful, now that she was no longer terrified. "East Beach and West Beach." After a moment she added, "An' Stewart Beach."

"The closest 'un."

Another driver blew his horn behind them. Sheba punched down the long clutch pedal and shoved the old Ford into gear.

West Beach was practically deserted at this time of night, though a few die-hard fishermen still cast into the surf. The wind was rising, shaving grains of sand from the crests of dark dunes to carry across the road. To feel it, Roddie thrust his head from the rear window, just as Boots did whenever she rode on his mother's lap. Almost at once, he saw his father's black Plymouth coupe. *"There they are!"*

"Stop 'ere," Doc told Sheba. "Now, lad, 'ear me wile I gives 'e thy orders, and say 'em back after."

When he was finished, Roddie asked, "But will they see me?"

"Oh, aye. 'Tis 'ard, but 'e can do it, 'avin' drunk. By night, mind. By day 'e'd be sailin' into the wind, do 'e twig? Up anchor now."

Though Roddie tugged at the handle of the Ford's rear door, he could not move it; and at last, at Jim's urging, he slipped out through the window. They separated as soon as they had left the car, he going to his father's, Jim into the waves. As he had been directed, he climbed into the rumble seat.

He did not think that his parents would have seen him even if they could see him; they were staring at the horizon, at the faint orange glow there that was—as his father had told him on a previous occasion—a burning tanker. But the sleeper had seen him; the sleeper cared less for torpedoed ships even than Roddie himself. The sleeper stared vacantly at this and that, and now and then at Roddie. It seemed a long time before Jim called.

Or perhaps neither Roddie nor the sleeper had heard Jim at first. Jim's call was so faint, so much a part (it seemed) of the sighing of the night wind and the sobbing of the waves that it hardly seemed a voice at all.

Yet the sleeper heard it. He rose from his place between Roddie's mother and his father and walked down the sloping sand toward Jim. Roddie's mother stood too, but his father said, "He just wants to splash around a little. Let him alone." After a moment's hesitation, she sat down again.

Boots ran after the sleeper, then back to Roddie's father, a study in canine concern. "Keep an eye on him," his father said, and patted her head.

The sleeper hesitated at the edge of the water. Jim called to him; for a moment, as he listened to Jim's call, it seemed to Roddie that he saw a second vessel in the night, nearer than the burning tanker: a dark ship with raked masts and ragged sails.

Sheba had pulled the Ford off the road and onto the beach some distance away. She and Doc were sitting side by side on the sand in front of its bumper. Roddie remembered that people like them were not supposed to use the beach and wondered what would happen if the police came; perhaps the police did not care when the beach was so nearly empty.

Already, the gentle little in-shore waves were washing the sleeper's thighs. Roddie's father called, "Roddie! Come back here!" But the sleeper did not even look around.

Boots dashed out to him. Roddie noted the moment at which she could no longer wade and had to swim. She paddled in front of the sleeper, barking, lifted by the surf like a small, noisy boat.

Roddie's mother was on her feet. "I'll get him, Ray."

Boots had run back to his father, appealing far from mutely to that highest of all courts. "I'll do it," he said. He was pulling off his shoes and socks, rolling up his trouser legs.

Roddie looked for the sleeper again. He was hard to see, so far from the shore lights; but it seemed to Roddie that the waves had reached his neck. If Jim were still calling, Roddie could not hear him.

Roddie hunkered down in the rumble seat, thinking about the moment when he would have to make himself visible to his parents. It would come very soon now, and he was not sure he could do it. How did you make yourself visible? The only way he could think of was by jumping out of the bushes, but that was for when they were playing cowboys, he and Wes and John.

"Roddie! Roddie! Roddie!" His parents' voices sounded far away.

Raising his head, he saw them waist-high in surging waves. Boots was with them, or perhaps even farther out—her barking could hardly be heard above the pounding of the surf. He stood up, pretending he was pushing the bushes aside, cupped his hands around his mouth. *"Here I am, Mom!"*

They did not hear him, but perhaps that was only because it was so far. He tried to inflate his body, to render it real and substantial. *"HERE! Over here!"*

He could not quite hear what his mother said; but he saw her touch his father's arm and point, and his heart seemed to swell. He jumped up and down in the seat, shouting and waving. *"Here! Here! Here! IT'S ME!"*

His father had seen him and was splashing toward shore. His mother was ordering Boots to abandon the search, her faint "Here, Bootsie!" and the clap of her hands borne on the salt sea breeze. His father would be angry for a while; but when he was angry with Roddie he would not speak him, or even look at him. So that part would be all right.

His father shouted, "Roddie, are you still in the car?" and he strained to make himself visible again.

"Roddie, stand up!"

His mother was just coming out of the water. "Is he gone again, Ray?"

"No, he's hiding back there. He thinks that's very funny."

"Ray—"

"Let him alone. He and I are going to have a talk about this when we get home. Get the dog in the car. Make her stay on the floor." Soaked to the shirt pocket, angry and dripping, his father got behind the wheel.

Softly his mother asked, "Roddie, are you well now?"

Again that swelling in his chest. He answered, "Yes," and although she did not appear to see him, she smiled and took her place beside her husband. Boots came up panting and climbed in next to her feet.

Roddie slipped out of the rumble seat as the car began to move.

The road had shrunk until it was no more than a single lane surfaced with oyster shells. Roddie hated oyster shells, which snapped under the wheels of cars and trucks to release a choking white dust. He had rolled up his window, and he wished that Doc and Sheba would close theirs, too. But the car was much too hot for that; the sleeper's face was beaded with sweat. So was his; he had taken off his shirt, and he used it now to wipe his face. He thought of wiping the sleeper's as well but decided it would do no good. "Why can't I go back in?" he asked Jim.

"Couldn't nobody here," Jim said.

"Because of the car, you mean?"

Jim did not reply. He seemed to be studying the sleeper.

Doc had not spoken for a long while, making Roddie wonder if he was really Doc again. Now Sheba said, "We got to get some gas. You got any money?"

Doc only stared at her

"Ain' got none—don' look at me like that." After a moment she added, "Probably not no stations 'long this ol' road anyhow."

"'E's been 'ere. 'E told me."

"Only that one time, an' that 'bout a year ago."

"'E said they wouldn't know."

"Those police was back at the house? Don' think so. They Houston police anyway, ain' come out here. This here out in the county. They has to call the sheriff, get the sheriff to send them out a deputy."

The narrow road bent about a clump of moss-hung live oak to reveal a one-pump gas station. An elderly black man came out as Sheba pulled the old Ford up to the pump. "Evenin', folks. How many tonight?"

Sheba looked at Doc, but Doc said nothing. She said, "Fill it up."

Doc got out and walked into the station, a shack smaller even than the cottage. Roddie could not imagine what he was doing in there, and whatever it was made no noise. There was only the gurgle of gasoline from the hose and the singing of millions of frogs.

"That boy sick?"

Sheba nodded.

"You tell his mama, take him to the doctor."

"His mama gone," Sheba said. "I takin' care of him. We gone take him tomorrow, that why we need so much gas."

"That old man goin' to pay?"

Sheba nodded again. "He probably lookin' to buy some cut plug too. I tol' him you might have some."

The man hung up the hose and went into the station. Roddie heard a dull tap, as if someone had thumped a melon; then he saw a foot through the doorway, its toe pointed downward as though the man had lain down inside. After a minute or two, Doc came out and got back into the car. Sheba drove on.

They crossed a creek on a rattling wooden bridge, turned and turned again. The road lost its coat of oyster shells and became no more than a jolting track of red dirt. Roddie rolled his window down, but the car was moving so slowly now that the air coming through the window seemed only to add to the heat. Mosquitoes clustered on the sleeper's cheeks and neck, darkened his forehead until his hairline appeared to reach his eyebrows; from time to time he tried languidly to brush them away. Sheba waved a hand before her face as she drove.

A gator bellowed not far off, a noise not very different from the bellowing of a bull. "That's an alligator," Roddie said. "A real big one, too."

Jim said nothing.

Trees, bearded but dead, gave way to clearings that looked like meadows. Sheba stopped the car, pulled up the long handle of the emergency brake, and switched off the lights. "Road don' go no farther. They a boat over there, but it look like we got to pour the water out."

She and Doc left the car, and Roddie climbed over the front seat to follow them.

"Sheba, honey," Doc said, "what we doin' way out here?"

"This where he want to come," Sheba told him. She had hold of the half-sunken skiff's painter. "He'p me." Together they turned the skiff on its side, flooding the already-soft soil at their feet and revealing two oars and a rusty bailing can. "We should of bring a flashlight."

Doc said, "He want go to the cabin?"

Though a thin crescent moon had risen, Sheba's nod was next to invisible.

Roddie had been looking around for Captain Hook, but could not find him. While Doc and Sheba were putting the skiff back into the water, he went to the window of the car. "Is he still in there?"

Jim nodded.

Doc climbed onto the board seat in the middle of the skiff and took the oars. Sheba said, "Wait a minute, I got get the boy."

"We got a boy?"

"In the back, ain' you see? When the last you remember?"

"Back my house, offerin' up that white boy," Doc said. "We gone to throw him in?"

"This 'nother 'un," Sheba told him. She opened the car's rear door and took the sleeper by the hand; when he came out, Jim followed. All of them crowded into the skiff, Roddie and Jim slipping past Doc to the bow, the sleeper sitting in the stern beside Sheba.

"They here with us," Doc muttered. "I ain' move an' you ain' move, but this here boat move. You feel it?"

Sheba shook her head. "You don' remember 'bout that old man back at the gas station?"

"Isrul Caruthers? What 'bout him?"

Sheba cast off the painter. "Nothin'. Jus' I think maybe you kill him."

Doc shook his head, pulling at the oars. "I hope not. I know him ever since twenty-six."

Sheba said, "Then how come he don' know you?"

"He don'?"

"No, sir. He say, 'That ol' man goin' pay?' "

"He ain' Isrul, then," Doc said. "Isrul know me anytime, day or night."

"That good. How far now?"

"Jes' a bit. Mr. J.J. Randall, he build this place, only it be drier then. It flood here sometime, though, so he put it up on the big pilin's. I done the roof—that back when I work for him. Then the big storm come, and it be wet an' Mr. J.J. don' come no more. I use it ever since. Mr. J.J., he gone now."

Uninterested, Sheba said, "Uh-huh."

"You think I really kill him?" Doc asked.

"That man at the gas station? I don' know."

Something large slithered into the water at their approach.

"That li'l boy."

"Course you did."

Doc did not speak again. Their voices and the splash of his oars had quieted the frogs, so that it seemed to Roddie that he could hear the most minute noises, the most faraway sounds—cars and trucks and buses back in town, his mother calling him. He felt too that if he spoke, Doc and Sheba would hear him; but he did not want to speak to them and did not know what to say. He no longer believed that Captain Hook was somehow in Doc, and he wondered whether Jim still believed it.

Sheba said, "You want me row awhile? You mus' be gettin' tired."

Doc shook his head and continued to row. After a moment he chuckled, the stridulous merriment of an old man.

"What you laughin' at?" Sheba asked him.

"That Isrul Caruthers. He think I come way out here with a young gal, maybe I don' want nobody know. So he ask you if the old man pay." Doc chuckled again.

"Uh-huh. You goin' go to his funeral?"

"I s'pose," Doc said. "I know Isrul since twenty-six."

"You bes' not. The police gone be after you for killin that boy back in Houston. You don' remember, but the police be all over your place when we get back. That why we come out here."

Sheba was silent for a moment. "Maybe we could tell them we be out here together, somebody else use your house."

"Maybe. You know I never didn't mean for all this. Not killin' no li'l boy."

Sheba did not reply. In the silence, Roddie heard a faint, slow ticking, as though a grandfather's clock stood somewhere in the darkness beneath the trees, its hands raised in horror, its pendulum telling the hours of the salt marsh through which they rowed with more precision than the beating of Doc's oars.

"Used, I think they's way away," Doc said softly. "I try to make them hear me. I ever tell you 'bout Big Mike?"

"Huh-uh," Sheba said.

"That Big Mike, he be a panther, used to kill all the deers round hear, cows too. Mr. J.J., he hunt Big Mike many a time. One time he out hear huntin' quail, it gettin' dark, so Mr. J.J. and Jess start for home. Jess his bird dog."

Sheba said, "Uh-huh."

"Mr. J.J., he hear Big Mike holler, you know how they do? Like a woman that's scared, almos'. It sound like he way off, so Mr. J.J. don't pay it no mind. Jus 'bout then Jess give a holler, and Big Mike rear up in front of her. Mr. J.J. say he mus' of shot twice with that li'l bitty bird gun, 'cause there was empties in it after an' he been goin' loaded case Jess put up some birds comin' back. He don' remember a-tall. I ask do he hit Big Mike, and he say he don' know, he jus' glad he ain' hit Jess."

Sheba laughed softly. "Better be glad he don' shoot off his own foot."

"So then I say, Mr. J.J., how come Big Mike right there when you jus' hear him way off? An' he say, I think that big panther put his head right down at the dirt when he holler so I think he way off. He wait for me to come by, and if Jess ain' see him first, he kill me sure. Sheba, these what we been messin' with, I think they jus' the same. They be not no long ways away. They jus' be waitin' till we get a li'l closer."

"You think they still goin' give us that treasure?"

Softly, Jim said, "Aye," and Doc dropped one oar. Roddie had to cover his mouth to keep from laughing.

Sheba asked, "What the matter with you, old man?"

"Didn't you hear somethin'?"

Sheba shook her head. "I didn't hear nothin'."

"It behind me, closer to me than you," Doc muttered. He bent over the gunnel of the skiff, feeling with one hand in the dark water for the oar.

It was then that Roddie saw where the ticking came from. Something that seemed almost a sunken log was drifting slowly toward the skiff—toward Doc's groping hand—when nothing else in the water moved. The ticking came from that, the slow, slow beating of its heart.

Doc said, "Pull it out, Sheba. It back by you." He took his hand from the water.

Sheba thrust hers in, grasped the oar near the blade and swung the loom to him. "You keep on droppin' these, we never gone get there."

Doc glanced behind him. "We there now, don' you see?"

"I ain'—"

There was a scream from the darkness before them, a paean to hate and agony worthy of a damned soul charring in the flames of hell. Sheba froze, her mouth wide open, a hand upraised; the sleeper's eyes went wide, so that it appeared for a moment that he was about to wake. Doc continued to row, the slow beating of his oars unaltered.

Sheba gasped, "What the matter with you?"

"Nothin' the matter with me," Doc replied placidly.

"You hear some itty-bitty noise and drop the oar. You hear that and don' even look round again."

"'Cause I know what holler," Doc told her. "That be a li'l ol' bobcat. What you think, gal? It be Big Mike? Big Mike, he gone 'fore Mr. J.J."

Roddie had spotted the cabin, a black bulk against the less solid blackness of mere night; he pointed it out to Jim a minute or two before the side of the skiff scraped the little landing stage moored at the foot of its steps. The screamer yowled, a softer sound this time, and Roddie thought he caught a flash of green.

Doc shipped oars and pulled a kitchen match from his shirt pocket. Striking it on his thumbnail, he held it up so that its flare of blue and yellow drove the night into sudden retreat. A large black cat arched its back at the top of the cabin steps, glaring at them through a single green eye.

"Not even no bobcat." Doc chuckled. "Jus' a li'l pussycat got lost out hear, maybe throwed out somebody's car." Tossing the match into the water, he rose and stepped onto the stage. "Now pass me that rope, gal, so I can tie the boat up, and don' talk no more 'bout who scared and who ain'."

As though in a dream, the sleeper followed Sheba out of the skiff. Roddie saw the hungry way in which Jim eyed him.

Sheba was looking at him too. "We gon' do it tonight?"

Doc jerked his half hitches tight and grasped the sleeper's arm without replying, leading him up the rotting steps. The cat spat at them, then moved aside.

Jim said, "This won't be like town. 'I'm an me, an' 'e. That's all there be."

"You said you wanted both parts of me," Roddie protested.

"Said we needed both." Jim grinned as he followed Sheba up the steps, slipping through the doorway just as she closed the door.

Roddie heard it shut, and the rattle of its old-fashioned latch. For half a minute or more he stood on the little landing stage, wondering whether Doc and Sheba would open for him if he knocked, as they had back at the cottage. Light poured from the wide windows of the cabin; Doc had struck another match and lit a candle, or perhaps a lantern of some kind.

Something moved uneasily in the water. Roddie watched it a moment, then went up the steps and caught the cat by the loose skin at the back of its neck. It yowled and clawed, but its claws seemed no more than feathers stroking Roddie's arms. He tried to quiet it, then decided that its cries and frantic movements might actually be helpful.

It liked the water even less than it liked Roddie, wailing and splashing as he pushed it under.

The cabin door flew open. Looking up, Roddie saw Doc with a rifle in his hands. Captain Hook stood behind him, his hand upon Doc's shoulder. Roddie let go of the cat, which scrambled back onto the stage. Fire flashed from the muzzle of the rifle—the report struck Roddie's ears like a blow. The cat shrieked with pain, and with a backhanded swipe Roddie knocked it into the water again.

Apparently satisfied, Doc shut the door.

The big gator was coming, swimming with astonishing speed; even the slow tick of its heart sounded faster. Roddie helped the wounded cat onto the stage and urged it up the steps. He had wondered vaguely whether the gator would have difficulty in getting up onto the floating stage; it took it with a rush, its body propelled by a powerful stroke of its tail. It was larger than Roddie would have guessed, eight feet long at least and as thick through as one of the empty drums buoying the stage.

Bleeding and frantic, the cat scrambled up the cabin door. Roddie pounded on the rough planks with his fists. Inside, he heard Sheba say, "They here." The door swung open again.

The gator's charge knocked her down like a tenpin. With a sinuosity that seemed almost that of a python, it turned. Sheba screamed as its jaws closed on her body.

The rifle was leaning in a corner, and both Doc and Roddie scrambled for it. Roddie had fired a twenty-two in a shooting gallery once; he knew that rifles had safeties, buttons to keep them from working. Captain Hook's curved iron hand pierced his cheek, knocking out a milk tooth—he was jerked backward like a hooked fish. The sleeper yelled, hands grabbing his empty face.

It seemed to Roddie that Sheba should be dead, and yet she screamed and struggled, clutching the edge of the doorway. Doc had the rifle at his shoulder. With two fast motions, he pulled its lever down and shoved it up again; *klu-klux-klan*, whispered the mechanism. He fired, the noise of the shot deafening in the little cabin.

" 'E bleedin' bugger!" Something slammed against Roddie's temple. The cabin seemed to spin around him, tossed upon wild seas as though it were really the cabin of ship; he saw Doc's necklace of bones and the mummified hand beside a kerosene lamp on a greasy table before Doc fired again and a sweep of the gator's tail knocked the table to kindling. The lamp's glass chimney shattered. Kerosene splashed the floor. For an instant it was only a spilled liquid, darkening the boards like so much water; but flames raced after it.

" 'Ere," Jim shouted. "Take 'em quick." He thrust the hand and the necklace at Roddie. An empty cartridge case flew before his face. At point-blank range, Doc fired at the gator's head. Sheba still screamed, her long black hair blazing.

The hand wriggled drily in Roddie's grasp like a spider; instinctively, he flung it and the bones out of the closest window.

At once the hook vanished from his cheek. Faintly, as if an unseen artist had traced their pictures in the smoke, he saw Captain Hook and Jim back toward the flames. The captain's hard face and Jim's haunted eyes seemed far away—old, half-forgotten things lost in the reality of the present.

"Rest in peace," Roddie told them. He had remembered that it was the thing you were supposed to say over dead people. He swallowed. "You're sailors, and this's the way they bury them in the water." He could see them still, see the fire licking at their legs. "In peace in the name of God and Jesus and the Holy Ghost and—and Mary (Mary was his mother's name) and everybody."

They were gone. Roddie put his hand to his cheek. It hurt, but he could feel no blood.

The sleeper was standing up, his blank eyes wild. Roddie ran at him, trying to drive himself back into the sleeper's body by main force. The sleeper's face changed, briefly, as though from a shadow cast by the flames. Roddie grabbed him, shouting and coughing, and pushed him toward the doorway, past Doc, over Sheba and the still-living gator, the sleeper stumbling on the gator's moving, armored back, tumbling headlong down the steps and hitting the landing stage with a bang.

Roddie leaped after him, landed lightly and picked himself up, and turned to look back at the cabin. Doc had the barrel of his rifle between the gator's jaws, prying, and Roddie thought that was the bravest thing he had ever seen.

The whole cabin crackled a thousand times louder than wood in a barbecue; a moment afterward, its roof fell. There was a ball of flame and a great *whoosh!* followed by a cloud of sparks. Roddie pulled the sleeper away from the heat and forced him into the skiff. The black cat was crouched in the prow. It licked its side and stared at Roddie as he made the sleeper sit down and take the oars. "I understand all this now," Roddie said as he cast off. "Row, won't you?"

He was forced to guide the sleeper's arms through the first three strokes; after that the sleeper rowed on without coaching, though even more slowly than Doc, and much more clumsily.

"It's a bad dream I'm having," Roddie told him as the skiff moved sluggishly away from the firelight and reentered the realm of night.

The sleeper did not speak.

"You know the cat in back of you? It's in a story by Edgar Allan Poe. Jim was from one called *Treasure Island,* and Captain Hook and the alligator are from *Peter Pan.* This is a nightmare, that's all."

It seemed to Roddie that the sleeper shook his head, though in the flickering light it was hard to be sure. Roddie said, "I think that when we come back together, we'll wake up."

He waited for some reaction, but the sleeper rowed on; and whenever Roddie tried to return to him, his face became that of the dead boy whose blood Roddie had drunk.

This through an endless dark to which there came no day.

JAMES L. CAMBIAS

See My King All Dressed in Red

James L. Cambias was a finalist for the 2001 James Tiptree, Jr. Memorial Award for his short story "A Diagram of Rapture;" he was also a finalist for the 2001 John W. Campbell Award for Best New Writer. A native of New Orleans, he currently lives in Deerfield, Massachusetts, with his wife and children. This marks the first publication of "See My King All Dressed in Red."

Having the meeting at their house was the logical thing to do, but Steve was still nervous as six o'clock approached. He had gotten home early to do some cleaning, and had spent more than an hour obsessively rearranging the hand towels in the downstairs bathroom. When he tried to tidy up in the kitchen, Ron ordered him out, brandishing a wooden spoon menacingly. "Don't make me burn the rice!"

So it was with some relief that Steve heard the doorbell ring ten minutes early. He opened the door and led their guest inside.

"Dave, this is my partner, Ron Foley. Ron, this is Dave Butler."

Ron came to the kitchen door in his apron to shake hands. "Dinner's just ready. I hope you like gumbo."

"It sounds super. Steve here was telling me you're some cook."

Ron reappeared with a steaming bowl of rice. "Blame my upbringing. In New Orleans we had a kind of proprietary attitude about food, kind of the way the English think they own literature."

"I've been to England; very nice people there. Very polite."

Ron brought out the big pot of gumbo. "Dinner's on. Something to drink? We've got a nice Gascon white open, or beer."

"Can I have some iced tea?"

"I'll get you some," said Steve before Ron could answer. "Just a little wine for me, please."

They sat down to plates piled with rice and covered with green sludgy-looking gumbo. Ron dug into his hungrily, but Steve noticed that Dave was picking suspiciously at his.

"I thought gumbo had chicken in it," he said.

"Sometimes," said Ron. "There's a whole spectrum of different varieties: chicken gumbo, seafood gumbo, even vegetarian gumbo—gombe aux herbes. This is crabmeat and oysters."

"Dave, why don't you tell Ron about the project?"

"Sure," said Dave, setting down his fork. "This is something we're all very excited about in Orlando. We want to put on a genuine, authentic, old-fashioned New Orleans Mardi Gras parade in the park. I'm one of the people doing research, and Steve here tells me that you've got a really high-quality collection of Mardi Gras material."

"Well, it's not just mine. There's a big refugee community here in Atlanta, and we've managed to put together a little museum of our own things and some rescued items. Not just Mardi Gras stuff—we've got a whole New Orleans archive, photos, music, everything."

"Super! It's mostly visuals I'm interested in, of course, material for our artists and designers to work with when they create the floats and costumes. I'd like to see what you've got."

When they finished with dinner, Steve did the dishes while Ron hunted through the closets and scrapbooks, and Dave flipped through the books and photo albums, occasionally running his hand scanner over a page. Ron kept up a running lecture, all about Carnival, its Christian and pagan roots, the history of Mardi Gras in New Orleans, and things he remembered from growing up.

"Well, this has been really helpful,' said Dave when the clock read midnight and his third disk was full. "I'm sure the designers will find lots of ideas in what I've got here. Oh, and the dinner was super."

"Are you giving Ron any kind of consulting fee?" asked Steve.

"Oh, sure. The standard rate is a thousand a day, and all our contributors get a free pass to the opening. That should be about a year from now."

They said their good-byes, then Steve started getting ready for bed. He glanced back into the living room to see Ron sitting on the sofa flipping through one of the photo albums.

"Coming to bed? It's late."

"In a minute. I was just looking at some old pictures of a cute guy in a pirate costume. You had so much hair back then!"

"And you were so skinny. That was a long time ago."

Steve Koenig's first Mardi Gras was in 2017. He was a sophomore at the University of Wisconsin, had come out to his friends, but hadn't yet worked up the courage to tell his parents. The Lesbian-Gay-Bisexual-Transsexual

Center was putting together a van trip down to New Orleans that year and it sounded like fun, so Steve got himself an injection of immunobooster nanobots at the campus clinic, made himself a fake ID, and cashed the check his grandmother had sent him for Christmas.

He spent sixteen hours riding in the van between a freshman with a liter bottle of vodka who passed out before they even reached Illinois, and a pale bi Goth girl who claimed to be a vampire. There were three other guys on the van besides Steve and the unconscious freshman, but two of them were a solid couple planning to marry after graduation, and the third was a sixth-year senior with sweaty palms whom Steve had learned to avoid about thirty minutes after coming out.

They had a motel room reserved, out past the New Orleans airport—a beige and anonymous place which catered to truck drivers fifty-one weeks of the year and drunk college kids at Mardi Gras. Twenty yards west of their parking space the lot ended at the levee, and the pounding of pile-drivers was a nonstop dance beat as the Army Corps of Engineers constantly built up New Orleans's defenses against the water.

Not that Steve spent a lot of time in the room. They got in at 3:00 A.M. Saturday morning, unrolled their sleeping bags, and crashed until noon. They ate brunch at a Burger King and drove the van downtown, but after that Steve hardly saw his traveling companions.

He was surprised at how normal things were. Somehow he expected the entire city to be in costume, dancing around drunk in the streets. The bars in the French Quarter were busy, but the streets were open to traffic and there were plenty of locals going about their usual Saturday shopping and work. It was easy to tell the natives, because they were all bundled up in ski jackets and scarves against the sixty-degree weather.

Since he didn't have the money or the stamina to stay drunk until Tuesday, Steve wound up doing a lot of walking around. His guidebook said the center of gay life in the city was on the downriver side of the French Quarter, so he drifted that way, hoping vaguely to meet his soul mate, or have wild sexual adventures, or some combination of the two. As it happened, he met Ron Foley.

He was following Bourbon Street away from downtown, passing first through blocks of strip clubs and gift shops, then restaurants and gay bars, until he came to a residential section.

"Hey! Show us your dick!"

He looked up. A party was under way in a big old house across the street. A dozen gay men of various ages were crowded onto the balcony, holding drinks and waving strings of beads at him. Steve looked up and down the street in confusion.

"Come on, show us your dick!" yelled one of them, a cute guy who looked to be about Steve's age.

Steve felt himself blushing. "Why should I?" he called back.

"Show! Your! Dick! Show! Your! Dick!" the men on the balcony started chanting, waving fistfuls of beads.

He blushed even more, hesitated, looked around once again, and then opened his jeans and waved it at them. The balcony burst out in cheering, and Steve was pelted with beads and little plastic toys. He zipped himself up again and started to walk on.

"Good job! Come on up and have a drink!" the cute boy called down.

So Steve crossed the street and was buzzed through the steel security gate on the courtyard, and soon found himself on the balcony with the others, a glass of Champagne and orange juice in his hand.

"I'm Ron," said the cute guy.

"I'm Steve." And that was that.

Around dinnertime eight of them went off in one car to get chicken; Ron and Steve squeezed in together under the hatchback. Ron was playing tour guide, pointing out buildings and places as they passed—the gilded baroque spire of a church, the monument to Robert E. Lee, a mule cart selling "Roman Chewing Candy," a sculpture garden in front of an office building. Steve was more aware of how their bodies were pressed together.

The fried chicken was greasy and good, and afterwards they found a place along St. Charles Avenue to wait for the parade that night. The parade was late in coming, but Ron explained that was standard. "I've been going to Carnival parades since I was six, and none of them started on time." They passed the time trading life stories, and by the time the first floats came in sight Steve hardly cared.

He spent the next three days with Ron, making only one run back to the motel to pick up his stuff and leave a note for the others. Ron had a place of his own, a skinny turquoise shotgun-style house near the Tulane campus furnished in a mix of student salvage and some elegant pieces inherited from his great-grandmother. In the mornings they lolled about in bed, in the afternoons they toured the city, and at night they went to parades and parties.

On Mardi Gras day Ron dressed up in a fabulous blue Napoleonic military uniform and helped Steve improvise a pirate costume out of torn jeans, a billowy linen shirt, and a red bandana. "We can be Jackson and Lafitte," he said, and then spent the streetcar ride to the parade route describing the Battle of New Orleans.

They walked about twelve miles that day, all the way from Napoleon Avenue to the Quarter and back. Near Louisiana Avenue they met Ron's uncle and aunt (Mickey and Minnie Mouse) and their three little girls (fairy princess, leopard and Red Riding Hood). The family was set up for a long siege, with lawn chairs, coolers and a little roll-up television to watch between parades. "We're waiting for float ninety-eight in Crescent City," Ron's aunt explained. "A guy who goes fishing with my brother's on it and he promised to save lots of throws for the girls."

Halfway to Canal Street they stopped at a party given by the parents of a boy Ron had gone to high school with. "I think that's why people here stay in touch with old friends and obscure relatives," Ron explained. "One of them might own a house along St. Charles." At Lee Circle they saw two drunk women get into a fistfight over a gold-painted coconut from the Zulu parade. Steve was astounded to see the black men on the Zulu floats were wearing blackface makeup and wigs. "It's traditional," said Ron, as if that explained it. In the French Quarter they pushed through the amazing crowd on Bourbon Street and watched the transvestite costume contest. They necked in public and got nothing but good-natured whoops from passersby.

They got back to Ron's place about eight that night, hungry, footsore and drunk, but not too exhausted to make love before collapsing. In the morning Ron drove Steve out to the motel, barely making it in time to catch the van back to Wisconsin.

He was eating ramen in his dorm room when his phone peeped. It was Ron. They talked for six hours.

Ron got off the plane from Orlando looking haggard.

"How was it?" asked Steve, taking Ron's bag for him.

"I'll tell you later. I don't want to start ranting in the airport. Let's get out of here—I want a drink and some food that doesn't come with a toy."

Ron was unusually quiet all the way home, and mixed himself a Bloody Mary as soon as they were in the apartment. "God, there are times I wish I was an alcoholic."

Steve warmed up some leftover pad Thai, and Ron finished his third Bloody Mary with dinner.

"So," said Steve at last. "How was it?"

"It was bad. I mean, I had expected them to change things, dumb them down, commercialize them. I'm not stupid. It's Disney World, not the Smithsonian. But—Steve, they got every single fucking thing wrong! All that time I spent with that little weasel Dave, showing him all my books, all my photos, all my old doubloons and throws, taking him through the museum—I might as well have been talking to Walt Disney's corpse."

"What did they do wrong?"

"Everything. To start with, Disney's Quasimodo's Mardi Gras Carnival (tm)"—Ron traced a little circle in the air—"runs every day except Sundays, January through October. None of this Catholic mumbo-jumbo about stopping during Lent or anything, you understand. The floats were just horrible—self-propelled wedding cakes like something out of the Rose Bowl parade, nothing like real Carnival floats. And they didn't throw anything, not even beads. I guess that would mean too much cleanup afterwards. Just a bunch of trademarked characters standing and waving as the floats moved by at a brisk pace. There were women in hoopskirts marching along between them, and clowns, for some reason. A band performing all your favorite cartoon soundtrack hits. One float had an oobie-doo chorus singing some kind of lobotomized arrangement of 'Mardi Gras Mambo.'

The king of the parade is Quasimodo (tm), and I'll bet Victor Hugo is just as pissed as I am."

"Did they use any of the things you showed them?"

"Here and there I could see little fossil traces of something that had survived the focus groups and the marketing teams. There was a guy dressed as an Indian, which I guess is their nod to the Wild Tchoupitoulas. He was white, of course."

"You couldn't expect them to do a real Mardi Gras," said Steve.

"I know, but it was all so wrong. Everyone was sober, sexless, smiling and well-behaved. There were no little boys risking death under the floats for a string of plastic beads. No high school girls pulling up their shirts to get a gold-painted coconut. No drunk civic leaders trying to stay on their horses."

"Well, it's over now. You survived your free weekend vacation."

"I should have stayed home. I knew I should have." Ron made himself another drink. "You know what really bothers me? It came to me on the plane. From now on, that's what people will think of as Mardi Gras. In twenty years there'll be nobody who remembers what it was like in New Orleans at all, and the Disney version will reign supreme."

For the next year or so, things seemed to be back to normal. Steve spent his days selling Oriental rugs and logged a lot of miles on the Atlanta expressways dropping off carpets at tract mansions after work. Ron had a job with a construction company, turning run-down old malls into New Urbanist subdivisions full of optical fibers, nanotechnology, and espresso machines. In the evenings he would sit at home drinking Bloody Marys and making elaborate animated drawings on his computer. Steve looked over his shoulder once as he worked: it was a view of New Orleans, surrounded by huge flood-control walls and locks to keep the water out. Within the barrier, the city was crisscrossed by canals, and tiny gondolas floated past the Superdome.

Steve got home one evening in February of 2024 to find Ron surprisingly cheerful and active. There was a pot of jambalaya simmering on the stove, and Ron greeted Steve with a big smile, a peck on the cheek, and a cold bottle of Corona. "Let's go to Mardi Gras."

Steve looked at him in alarm. "Ron? Are you okay?"

"Of course." He saw the concerned look on Steve's face and laughed. "No, I'm not going crazy. I saw it on the Net; some people are putting together a final farewell celebration in New Orleans. This is going to be the real deal, not that sappy sentimental celebrity-fest they had after the flood. We're all going down to New Orleans and have the wildest party the world has ever seen. Think about it! A whole empty city to have fun in! No blood monitors, no designated drivers, no police cameras, no indecent-exposure laws, no nothing! The true spirit of Carnival—a day of sacred madness and debauchery!"

"Ron, it's not going to be like it was. The city is abandoned. There's no electricity or fresh water or anything. It's probably full of vagrants and gangs and stuff. Most of it's under five meters of water."

"A lot of the older sections are only partially flooded. Bienville picked a good spot to build on. And with ten thousand people coming in to have fun it'll be as safe as anyplace else."

"Where will you stay?"

"Wherever I want! Maybe I'll sleep in the Delgado Museum, or Gallier Hall. Or take over a floor of the Fairmont Hotel. Always wanted to stay there. As you say, the city's empty. Are you coming?"

"I don't know. I've got work, and—"

"Oh, forget about work. You've got vacation days. Isis can fill in for you. Come on, it'll be great! Just like that first time! Please?"

Two weeks later they left Atlanta with the Friday evening tide of traffic, angling southwest through the empty part of Alabama. Steve's car was a little hydrogen-electric hybrid made for city driving, and it was slightly terrifying when the triple-trailer trucks went rumbling past them in the darkness, the suction of their passage threatening to drag the little plastic car along like a piece of debris.

At midnight they pulled into a truck stop in Slidell to figure out how to approach the sunken city. Ron had his computer unrolled on the table, and had loaded up the latest topographic maps and coastal navigation charts. "The roads are bound to be blocked. There's only four ways into the city anyway, so you could seal it off with maybe a dozen state troopers."

"You think they know about this?" asked Steve.

"Of course! If a couple of guys in Atlanta heard about it, I'm sure the state police did, too."

"Won't they try to shut it down, then?"

"I don't think so. The police were always pretty cool at Mardi Gras. As long as you didn't get into any fights or bug other people, they were willing to look the other way. They're probably going to try to keep people out of New Orleans, but it'd be really hard to go in and arrest everyone. How do you search a whole city?"

"And what do you do with them once you arrest them?" said Steve thoughtfully.

"Exactly. No cop wants to haul ten thousand drunks across fifty kilometers of swamp. It sounds like a boat would be our best option. Maybe a canoe. You've been canoeing, right?"

"Yeah, up in Minnesota. But we don't have a canoe."

"We can get one. The stores here are probably sold out, but I bet we could find one in Meridian or Mobile or someplace."

"Y'all trying to get to New Orleans?"

They looked up, startled. Across the aisle a brick-shaped man in a faded Tulane sweatshirt was grinning at them.

"Well—maybe we are," said Ron.

The man laughed. "Well, maybe I've got a boat, and maybe I'd be willing to take y'all across the lake. Interested?"

"Sure. How much are you charging?"

"A hundred bucks for each of you. Round trip if you can find me."

Ron glanced at Steve, then back to the man. "Okay. Where's your boat and when do we leave?"

"Right now. I don't want to get caught out on the lake in daylight. That's my truck outside, with the trailer; follow me down to Fort Macomb and we'll put the boat in the water. You'll be in the city by dawn."

The man with the boat gave his name as "Dr. Doug." His boat was a twelve-foot bass boat with a flat bottom and a square prow, stocked with two coolers of beer, a GPS unit, a chrome-plated .45 automatic, a radar detector and an eight-piece box of fried chicken.

Ron and Steve helped him launch the boat at a drowned shell road near Fort Macomb. The night was chilly, but Steve had his old parka, made for

Wisconsin winters, and Ron was wearing his Russian navy overcoat and thermal underwear. Dr. Doug had on a camouflage hunting jumpsuit and kept himself fueled with beer.

They stayed away from open water, hugging the shore to where the old flood-control gates stretched across the old mouth of Lake Pontchartrain. The support towers loomed in the darkness, black monoliths ten stories high lit only by the blinking red safety lights on top.

"Look at that!" yelled Ron. "The Corps of Engineers' greatest triumph. The Maginot Line of flood control! By the time these things were finished, the river had already broken through at Destrehan and not even the Corps could put it back in its old bed. What a waste."

"Were you boys here for the evacuation?"

"No, we were up in Atlanta," said Ron. Steve could hear the slight note of bitterness.

"It was a hell of a sight. A quarter-million people trying to get out ahead of Hurricane Veronica. The bridges were all packed; they had all the lanes switched to outbound traffic. I was on I-10 over the spillway when some old idiot's car broke down. About twenty of us got together and just pitched it over the rail. The National Guard was taking people out by helicopter, and the navy had hovercrafts taking people across the lake. Everything that could float was carrying people—even some of those gambling riverboats that never left the dock from the day they were built were chugging up to Baton Rouge. The troops tried to keep down the looting, but toward the end there weren't enough of them to stop it. I was with a group that went back to Charity Hospital afterwards, and it was picked clean."

"They could have saved it," said Ron. "With enough money the floodwalls could have been ready in time. The feds blew all the disaster fund on saving important places like Baltimore and Miami. Louisiana couldn't afford it—especially with half the state already underwater."

"Well, it must have been a tough choice," Dr. Doug said affably. "I mean, if you have to choose between saving New York and saving New Orleans, which one do you pick?"

"I have no argument with that," said Ron. Steve gave a little sigh and huddled into his parka. "New York, Boston, Washington—no argument at all with saving them. Those are major cities and centers of finance and gov-

ernment and culture. But Tampa? Orlando? They saved Disney World and
let New Orleans sink! A city of a million people with three hundred years of
history should be more important than a place inhabited by cartoon characters! If I could do it I'd blow up the seawalls and let all of Florida drown."

All that night Dr. Doug followed the line of the unfinished floodwall
through what had been the eastern half of New Orleans. He had to go
slowly for fear of hitting a submerged house or one of the many dead trees.
The night was dark and beautifully clear. The Milky Way stretched across
the sky ahead of them, and Jupiter gleamed brightly in the west above
Orion. Steve had a brief memory of standing outside on a freezing winter
night in Wisconsin while his grandfather tried to teach him the constella-
tions. A crescent moon was rising behind them as the boat passed the monument sticking out of the water where Jackson and Lafitte had battled the
British.

"Do you come down here often?" Ron asked Dr. Doug.

"Now and then. The fishing's good. A lot of people come here to go
scuba diving. They bring up all kinds of stuff."

Once in the old river channel, Dr. Doug relaxed a bit and opened
another can of beer. The sky began to turn from black to purple as the stars
disappeared. Ahead they could see the towers of the city, first as dark sil-
houettes against the brightening sky, and then suddenly luminous gold as
the rays of the sun struck them.

Now that he could see to navigate, Dr. Doug piloted the boat into the
city proper. "How do you like the breakwater?" he asked, pointing at a long
line of rubble and twisted steel running from the twin span of the bridge to
the double line of buildings that marked Canal Street. "Used to be the convention center, but the hurricane wiped it out. This end is the Aquarium and
the Hilton Hotel. There's a passage here at the foot of Canal Street—did
you see the CNN footage of the storm surge rushing up the street? This is
where it broke through."

He steered between the shattered remains of the Aquarium and the collapsed Hilton, then up Canal Street. For a moment, Steve felt like he was
aboard one of Ron's little animated gondolas. It was surprising how many
of the buildings were intact, although the water was lapping at the second-
story windowsills. The Mariott Hotel tower had toppled over, covering a

block in rubble, but most of the older buildings had survived. Everything was covered by vines.

"So where's the party at?" Ron asked aloud.

"The Quarter." Dr. Doug piloted the boat along what had once been Chartres Street towards the spires of the cathedral.

The French Quarter had suffered considerably. Many of the older buildings of stucco and brick had simply dissolved into heaps of mud, while termites and plants were hard at work on those which remained. Here and there Steve could see rusted iron balconies or even old furniture hidden by kudzu and Spanish moss. He couldn't imagine how they could even find a place to leave the boat, much less room for thousands of people to gather.

He got his answer when the little boat entered Jackson Square. At first Steve couldn't imagine what the big square building on the downriver side of the square could be; it certainly hadn't been there when he'd met Ron. It was long and windowless, painted red on the lower portion and turquoise on the upper floors. Then he saw the wheelhouse and smokestack at one end and realized it was a ship—a huge, boxy container ship, evidently tossed into the Quarter by the storm surge of Hurricane Veronica. It had plowed completely through the Pontalba building and the Presbytère, just missing the cathedral, to sit beached with its stern atop the Café du Monde and its bow on the other side of Bourbon Street.

Close to a hundred boats—sailboats, cabin cruisers, a fishing boat, motorboats, and dozens of skiffs and canoes—were moored along the waterline of the beached ship, and from the deck came the sounds of music and cheering. Dr. Doug found a spot to tie up, and the three of them climbed a terrifying rope ladder up to the deck.

The party was a weird mix of things all happening at once. At one end of the long deck, in the shadow of the wheelhouse, there were nostalgic middle-aged white men and women, sipping beers, sharing food around and looking out ruefully at the drowned city. About a hundred kids, mostly college age but a few suspiciously young looking, were raving down in the main cargo deck, where the steel walls and a huge amp system created enough vibration to make Steve's eyeballs ache. A couple of dozen tough-looking black men in fantastic Indian costumes were passing around blunts inside an empty cargo container amidships and showing off their handguns.

An old Cajun man assisted by a small army of relatives was making alligator gumbo in a set of cut-down oil drums, with two dead alligators waiting to be skinned and butchered lying on the deck. And at the bow of the ship there were twenty gay men putting on their annual costume contest as if nothing had changed.

Ron was in his element. From the moment they climbed over the side he was dashing from one group to another with a big delighted grin on his face. He pressed a beer into Steve's hand, compared recipes with the man cooking the alligator, scored some assorted pills from a rave girl wearing nothing but glitter, and got masks for the two of them from a big pile on the deck.

Steve downed the beer, swallowed a pill, and let his rational self take the weekend off. He later remembered the next few days as a series of disconnected images, some real, some he hoped were just hallucinations. Eating gumbo with his fingers because there were no spoons on the entire ship. A man wearing a huge fake penis that dragged on the ground. Necking with Ron on the bridge of the ship as the sun set. Fireworks. Dancing on the cargo deck in a packed mass of people. An oiled muscle boy dressed as Snow White. The men dressed as Indians firing their guns at the night sky. The old Cajun man frying a turkey. A fistfight between two men in matching bird costumes that ended with their white feathers all bloodstained. Opening the door of a cargo container and seeing nothing inside but writhing naked bodies. Tossing showers of golden doubloons into the water. Gondolas filled with singing courtesans drifting past. Telling a person dressed as the moon the names of the stars. An ape in flames running along the deck.

Most of the kids and hangers-on drifted away at the end of the weekend, so that on Fat Tuesday itself only two dozen people were left camping in cargo containers on the deck of the ship. By a kind of unspoken popular acclaim, the elderly Cajun man reigned as King that day, in a maroon satin costume and a platinum blond Prince Valiant wig. He sat atop one of the containers and tossed beads to the others, then led everyone in a toast, followed by a speech which Steve couldn't understand at all, but which he and everyone else applauded with great enthusiasm. At midnight the handful remaining toasted the end of Carnival with the last of the beer, and then huddled for shelter on the cargo deck as a rainstorm came.

Steve and Ron rode back to Slidell the next morning with Dr. Doug and a teenage girl who slept the whole way.

It didn't work.

For the first couple of weeks after they got back, Ron was his old self— clever, passionate, happy and interesting. He went on a cooking binge, making jambalaya and pompano en papillote and alligator soup and bread pudding and muffaletta sandwiches and crawfish bisque and brown cabbage until Steve's pants started to get tight in the waist.

But by the time they had been home a month, Ron began to get moody and silent again, and one day in the middle of April he disappeared. Steve was moderately concerned when Ron didn't come home from work, then he was angry with Ron for not calling, then he was terrified that something had happened. At midnight he called the police. "He's six hours late, and I've called all our friends and he doesn't answer his phone and I don't know what to do."

The cop's voice was professionally calm and reassuring, but her training couldn't quite hide the boredom at having to deal with yet another couple asking her to referee their breakup. She told Steve that nobody answering Ron's description had been admitted to any Metro Atlanta hospitals, nor was he in jail. "If he doesn't turn up by noon tomorrow, call me back and we'll start a Missing Persons trace."

The next three days were torture for Steve. He stayed home, eating ramen at intervals and never letting the phone ring more than once. When Ron was officially missing, the police did a location trace on his pocket phone which turned up nothing. "He's probably pulled the batteries," the detective explained to Steve. "That's a good sign."

"Why?"

"See, suicides want to be found, so they leave the phone on. And most crooks are still dumb enough to try stealing the phone. Pulling the batteries means he did this on purpose."

On the fourth day he got a padded mailer from Ron, postmarked Jackson, Mississippi. His phone, credit cards and bank cards were inside, along with a note on motel stationery.

Dear Steve,
I'm sorry, but I have to go back. Please forgive me. I love you.

                                                                    Ron

Just outside Gonzales Steve found an old gas station just inside the line of new seawalls, with a sign reading N.O. & Bayou Tours. He hired a boat and a pilot named Jolie who looked about sixteen and had a terrifying-looking automatic shotgun slung over her Hello Kitty T-shirt. When Jolie found out why he was going to New Orleans she was terribly sympathetic and spent more than an hour recounting her own man troubles, which involved cheating, arson, and tense political infighting on the Prom Committee.

They cruised down the Mississippi and entered the flooded streets of New Orleans at Audubon Park. Now that spring had come, the city was a mass of greenery, and water hyacinths made the open water look like a neatly mowed lawn.

Ron's old house seemed like the first place to search, but getting there proved more difficult than Steve had expected. Even with Jolie's GPS unit there was no way to be sure which of the overgrown masses of rotting wood was which. Not that it mattered—the only way Ron could be living in his old house would be if he had grown gills.

"What now?" asked Jolie.

Steve pulled out the list he had made. "Try the Delgado Museum next. Know where that is?"

"Oh, yeah. I went there a lot right after the flood. People was going diving, looking for those diamond egg things from Russia. Then a snapping turtle bit one guy's hand off, and some woman got killed by a alligator, and they quit coming."

The museum was structurally intact, half above water and covered with vines. It made a very attractive ruin, and they circled it several times but saw no sign of life.

They headed downtown after that, passing the collapsed bulk of the

Superdome, and the statue of Robert E. Lee walking on the water. From there they motored up St. Charles Avenue to Gallier Hall, but found nothing there either. It was getting to be late afternoon, and the sky was turning cloudy.

"I got to tell you, if your boyfriend's hiding we ain't gonna find him."

"I know. There's one more place I'd like to look. Can you find the Fairmont Hotel?"

They cruised through the narrow streets of the old business district, between crumbling skyscrapers. Both the huge One Shell Square tower and the nearby St. Charles Place building had collapsed into masses of rusting steel and shattered marble skin. The older buildings seemed to be decaying more gracefully. The Fairmont looked no different from the others at first. Vines had covered the lower floors, and tattered curtains flapped in the breeze from broken windows.

Steve borrowed Jolie's binoculars and scanned the lower floors carefully. If Ron was in the hotel, he wouldn't be too low for fear of high waves and alligators; at the same time, he wouldn't want to climb too many stairs. A section on the fourth floor had intact windows, and—yes!—what looked like an improvised chimney sticking out of one.

"You think he's in there?"

"I don't know. *Ron!!*" He waited a moment, then cupped his hands around his mouth and bellowed. *"Ron Foley! It's me, Steve!"*

No answer. The curtains in one window twitched a little, but that was all.

"Could you steer over there so I can climb in one of the windows?"

"I could but I ain't gonna do it. There's some funny people living here. If that ain't your boyfriend, you might get shot or cut up or something."

"I just want to talk to him."

"Well, whoever's in there don't want to talk to you. It's getting late and the wind's picking up. We're going."

"Ron!!" Steve shouted one last time. The only answer was the flutter of frightened pigeons on a ledge. The curtains didn't stir again. "Okay, let's get going."

That was the end of it, or nearly. That fall Steve met a very nice older man while delivering a carpet, and moved in with him just before Christmas.

What with the change of address it was nearly Easter when the card arrived.

It was postmarked Baton Rouge, with a date sometime in February. The card was a yellowed picture postcard of the luxurious Fairmont Hotel, and the message was "Happy Mardi Gras." There was no signature. Steve thought about throwing it away, but wound up tucking it into one of the scrapbooks, next to a picture of Ron dressed as King Tut. He looked at the photos for a while, then put it away.

SCOTT EDELMAN

My Life Is Good

Scott Edelman is a four-time finalist for the Hugo Award for Best Editor. He was the founding editor of the magazine Science Fiction Age *and is currently editor-in-chief of* Science Fiction Weekly *(http://www.scifi.com/sfw). His novel* The Gift *was published in 1990, and his stories have appeared in numerous magazines and anthologies, including* The Twilight Zone, Weirdbook, Pulphouse, Fantasy Book, MetaHorror, Moon Shots, Mars Probes *and* Once Upon a Galaxy. *A collection of his short fiction,* These Words Are Haunted, *was published in 2001 by Wildside Press. This marks the first publication of "My Life is Good."*

Last night I saw Randy Newman on the time machine, with some smart, rich New York Jews. I still had hours to go in my shift, and was already at that familiar point in my day where I was so sick of his smug face as to worry that I wouldn't be able to find the stomach to see it through.

Since The Visitors had come, this mind-numbing study of each vapid moment of Newman's life was a daily irritant for me, and up until then it had been another typically boring evening. The time machine had been bringing me only scenes that I had already witnessed before, recapping a life dedicated to mocking the privilege that had molded it, but the tableau that this time confronted me on the screen was new to me.

I waved a hand to dim the subbasement lights so I could make out his features more clearly on the tiny window to the past. Newman was smiling, but dressed as he was, I don't see how it was possible for him to maintain that grin. He wore a plaid suit that could only have been bought at a store that catered to unsuccessful used car salesmen and the most insecure of television evangelists. The tie that strangled his fleshy jowls was a chaotic patchwork quilt of overlapping Confederate flags. This garish ensemble was out of character for the man I'd unfortunately come to know, and on top of that seemed completely wrong for its intended audience.

Perhaps he thought he was being funny. I'd learned right at the beginning of this that being funny had always been one of Newman's greatest problems. Or rather, *thinking* himself funny had been, when in fact he'd been far from it. The man on whom The Visitors had me waste so much of my time spying was literally addicted to satire, a flavor I despised, and I had no further patience for his uncontrollable habit.

But this outfit, this setting, seemed more than the usual idiocy; things were too off-kilter, even for him. For one thing, during all the hours I'd put in studying the man, I'd never before caught him willingly in a suit and tie, garish or otherwise. One of the other things I'd learned quickly was that when he'd lived, Newman had not been a formal sort of man, and was unlikely to have kept that unflickering smile when trapped in such a getup.

The picture made little sense to me. At first I thought that the time machine had captured Newman at a costume party of some sort, but since the rest of the crowd that milled about him in the oak-paneled ballroom had forgotten their costumes, I cast that theory aside.

The women dressed as rich women did in that not-so-long-ago time by the calendar but which the arrival of The Visitors had now made inconceivably distant. They were statuesque in their jewels and furs, and the plastic surgery which gave them the appearance of youth and firmness had obviously been obtained from the best, for their scars were barely visible. The men did not bother to trouble themselves over their physical appearance. Their doughy forms were stuffed into dark wool suits, and they'd already had too many drinks. They laughed too loud. A few of them had checkbooks in their hands, and one was already pressing a folded donation into Newman's breast pocket with fat knuckles.

I'd long been looking back to keep my eye on Newman, but I'd never before seen anything like this. It worried me, but not so much that I was yet willing to alert The Visitors upstairs and have to look into those saucer eyes again. My worries were still more about the future than the past. My hopes were that it was the machinery, rather than the timestream, that was askew. I called Pall, the technician, and had him examine the equipment. He was happy for the chance to be in the room while the time machine was operating, because The Visitors did not give him much opportunity to do so. They trusted me, and me alone, to be a witness to Randy Newman's life.

Unfortunately, Pall found no hardware problems. The troubling picture was real. Something had happened that had never happened before. I let Pall continue to huddle with me before the small screen, Visitors be damned.

"What do you make of it?" I said. "I've never seen anything like this before. Look at his face. Look at those eyes. It's as if those aren't the same eyes. He's changed somehow."

We watched the normally awkward Newman move through the crowd as if he had been born to it, shaking hands, clapping the men on their backs like brothers, kissing the women on their cheeks until they flushed, and collecting more checks in the process.

"Is there any way we can hear what they're saying?" I asked. "As soon as this scene started, the sound crashed."

"There's too much static," said Pall. "I don't know why. But why don't we try this? Let's detach the focus from Newman himself. Unlock the gaze and let the machine's point of view wander. Maybe that will show us something."

I manipulated the controls to stop targeting Newman, the maker of my weary days. The image slid from him sluggishly, and shifted to let us see glimpses of the rest of the room. At first there seemed no answer to the mystery there. A bustling wet bar. A coat rack. A buffet table overflowing with bowls of jumbo shrimp, decorated with an ice sculpture of Huey Long, a man whose profile I would not have recognized without having been forced to study him thanks to Newman.

But then we both saw a tall poster, ten feet high, filled by Newman's face. Pall didn't know enough of my mission to react, but the sight made me dizzy. I was stunned to see that above the smiling photo were the words:

EVERY MAN A KING

Below the photo, in large red, white and blue type, was written:

A NEWMAN FOR A NEW DAY
RANDY NEWMAN FOR PRESIDENT

"Something has gone terribly, terribly wrong," I said. My gut inflamed at what this meant my next step would have to be. Those eyes. I would have to suffer them again. "I'm going to have to tell them."

"You lucky bastard," Pall whispered.

His words pushed me back from the screen. I'd had enough of Newman for this day or any other day.

"You can have my luck," I said coldly, immediately regretting the tone I took with Pall. It wasn't his fault. The blame rested entirely with The Visitors. "You can't possibly know how sick and insignificant I feel when I have to face them."

"But you realize what this means, don't you? This must be what they were waiting for all along. This must be what this project is all about. You *are* a lucky bastard."

And then Pall, in a voice washed with awe, uttered the words I never thought I'd live to hear.

"They're going to have to send you back."

2 | *The World Isn't Fair*

I once thought I had a life of my own, but now I only have his. Randy Newman's. A minor American singer-songwriter with a voice like a tortured cat and a heart like a pumice stone whose tunes were more smirk than sincerity.

Maybe I was only fooling myself about that life business, though. Before it all changed, I'd been lost in the world of theoretical physics, stepping beyond that arena only to do what I had to do to stay there, and as little as possible beyond that. So perhaps maybe I never really had any life at all. Maybe living Newman's life vicariously for twelve hours a day is better than having none at all.

But upon reflection, I don't really think so.

Until The Visitors came in their shower of blood and thunder and set me to the task, I'd spared no time for popular music. Other people may have needed it to give their lives meaning, but I had the more basic poetry of the quark. I was deaf to song, and not entirely by choice, either, but rather by constitution. As I studied particles dancing just beyond the edge of perception, the songs the singers sang were unintelligible to me.

Randy Newman, with whom I've been ordered to spend my days, created the most unintelligible of them all. With his uncle Alfred scoring Hollywood movies and winning Oscars in the process, Randy Newman was born to make music. Instead, he only made noise.

The fact that he'd been able to garner any fame at all is as senseless as the songs themselves. He had the superior attitude of the frat boy, without the substance to back it up. He sang that "Short People" had no reason to live, but he meant us to understand that he really didn't mean it. "I Love L.A.," he wrote, but from the words, who could really tell? He called southerners rednecks, but didn't seem to mean it in a pejorative way, and wanted license to call African-Americans niggers in the name of his supposed art. Why did he think people would want to struggle to unravel meaning and intent from a song, when all they were seeking was a distraction? Give me a song that is what it presents itself to be, with no ambiguity. There is enough mystery in the world without adding more.

No wonder that when The Visitors summoned me to set me to my task, the difficulty of my research was almost overwhelming, because in this century, Newman's musical corpus seemed as dead as his physical one.

Regardless of my difficulties or distaste, I could not protest, only submit. After the day that they announced themselves and gave that first terrifying proof of their power, no one dared question The Visitors. Whatever they wanted, they got. With their inarguable supremacy, they could have plucked the treasures of Earth.

Luckily for the world, they didn't want much.

Unfortunately for me, one of the few things they did want . . . was me.

I didn't know why. I still don't. I was as far from suitable for the assignment as it is possible for one human to get. When I was taken from the university and told by my government that henceforth I would be using a time machine given us by their alien technology to peer into the past, I was ecstatic. I thought that everything my life had been headed towards was about to be fulfilled. I'd finally arrived at the fruition of my impossible dreams. But it turned out that none of my physics training was to mean anything. They could have grabbed any semicomatose couch potato, thumbs thickened from wrestling with the remote control, for all the manipulation I ever had to do of the device they gave us. I was to watch the pictures of Randy Newman as they paraded by, and report on any anomalies.

The promise I'd thought the universe had kept had instead been broken. I lived my days in pain, as if in the grip of a disease.

I could never tell them that. I'd decided I'd rather live. They wanted me, and so they had to have me. But though I'd suffered in silence, that suffering still raced through my mind as I waited to tell them the news of the aberration. I tried to avoid meeting with them, did my best to share the information with them over a holo, but they forced me to stop before I could tell them what I had found.

They wanted to see me in person.

I did not like the way I could look into those large, liquid eyes and see myself looking back. Their gaze made me feel as if they were able to read my mind. I am not a paranoid man, and yet they were able to make me feel like one, and I did not want to have to stand there and let them see again how stupid I felt wasting my life this way for them. I could barely hide my discomfort from Pall and the others I was assigned to work with, so how could I hope to hide it from them?

But I had no other choice.

As I sped inside the high-speed elevator from the subbasement that housed the project to where The Visitors dwelled on the skyscraper's top floor, I wondered if Pall could possibly have been right. Was this what we all had been waiting for? Would it really cause me to be sent back in time?

As the doors began to open and reveal a place I dreaded, all those thoughts emptied from my mind. What was left was fear. That fear grew when I saw their tall, attenuated forms and realized that though I'd never before seen more than one of them at a time in person, there stood two. So something out of the ordinary had indeed occurred, and they already knew it. They stood at opposite ends of the large, windowless room. The elevator that left me dead center of the room recessed into the floor, placing me pinned between them in the dimness.

I could not tell the two Visitors apart. They had no distinguishing features to individualize them. No difference in eye color, nor scars, nor variation in tone of voice. Seeing them this way made me wonder about my past visits to the top floor, whether either of these had been the one I had seen my few luckless times before, and in fact, whether their sameness now meant I had never seen any Visitor more than once, but had only thought so.

I stayed silent until they spoke, not due to any conscious decision to show respect but rather because, this time as always, their presence left me speechless.

"You have news to report," said one, sliding closer.

"I do not understand why, but the subject is not who he once was." So great was my anger at Randy Newman for wasting my life this way that I did not like to say his name aloud, particularly in front of The Visitors, who would surely hear my contempt. I spoke to them formally because that was the only way I was able to bring myself to speak at all. "Something has changed about the past. I have looked at this moment before, and each time all was always as it always was, but now he is no longer a man who writes music. The timestream has altered. He appears to have entered politics."

"That is . . . not good," said the other, taking its own fluid steps closer to me.

"He must be . . . protected," said the first.

"But he's in the past," I said. "How could he be in need of protection? What's happened has happened."

Said one, its voice becoming louder as it approached, "What's happened has not happened yet."

Said the other, "What's happened never really happened."

"You're speaking in riddles. What does that mean? Is the past truly fluid? Has the past put the present in danger? Will this alteration catch up with us here? Tell me, please. Is something terrible going to happen to our timeline if he is allowed to become president? Am I going to the past to protect our future?"

I was rambling on, verging on hysteria as the distance between us shrank. I was going to say more, but then they were suddenly upon me, and words were no longer a part of my palette.

"You must fix this," said one.

"Go now," said the other. "Put it back as it was."

One of The Visitors reached out a hand towards me. I shrieked as the elongated fingers grew near. I started babbling, speaking as I'd never dared to speak before, questioning them out of a greater terror than I'd ever known.

"Why?" I shouted. "Why do you care? Why have I been doing this? Why does it matter to you?"

My questions would have horrified Pall. In challenging The Visitors, I was risking everything, including my own life. But with a Visitor about to lay hands upon me, all propriety had fled.

"Just go," said the other, answering my frustrated questions by beginning to reach for me as well.

When their flesh touched mine, an explosive energy coursed through me, blinding me, and they, the skyscraper, and all of the world I knew, were gone. For I had come unstuck in time.

3 | *Mama Told Me Not to Come*

I popped back into existence on the twenty-seventh floor observation deck of the Louisiana State Capitol, a setting which on its own merits told me that this was an earlier century than my own. I felt a sense of freedom to be back in a time before The Visitors had razed such buildings to the ground to get our attention, but it was only a momentary emotion. I knew I was not truly out of their reach, and could not pause to enjoy this place. I had to get on with it.

I blinked into the morning sun and admired the Mississippi as it rolled towards the Gulf of Mexico. Louisiana's state capitol building, when it still stood, had been the tallest of such buildings, which was a good thing, for it meant that the structure contained enough square footage for The Visitors to have found a spot in which to have me appear that would not attract attention.

I'd had no time to prepare for this trip. Luckily, The Visitors had prepared for me. My tunic was gone, replaced by a finely woven suit that could easily allow me to pass as a member of this century's elite. As I stood there, the wind had a different feel to it that morning, and when I touched a hand to my head to figure out why, I discovered that my shaggy hair had also been altered. It was now closely cropped in a style I loathed. I could only hope that when at the end of all this nonsense I was allowed to return to my own time, my hair would return as well.

My physical shell wasn't the only thing that had been made right for this time. How else would I know without a doubt the spot on which I stood? How else would I know instinctively that I was hundreds of feet above Baton Rouge, and that if I walked mere yards to the south, I could look down on the grave of Huey P. Long, the former governor of Louisiana, felled by an assassin's bullet to then be musically commemorated by Randy Newman? As I walked along the deck so I could study where the martyr was buried, I felt as if I belonged here, and I realized that The Visitors had filled me with enough of the essence of the time and place to pass as one of them.

And then I realized something else. I was not alone.

I did not at first recognize the man who was leaning against the rails. My approach took me up to him as he stood with his back turned, and that was a side of him that the time machine, focused on telling me his story as it was, had never let me witness. As I drew to the right side of him, could see him there with his eyes closed, I was momentarily stunned. Randy Newman, whom I had known up until then only as an historical figure on the flat screen of a time machine, was before me as a living, breathing man. And I once more cursed The Visitors and mourned the loss of those I would have chosen to see on my first excursion back in time—Galileo, swearing that the Earth still moved; a young Einstein, still working at the Swiss patent office; my parents, before they'd met, before the thought of me had even entered their lives; my own self, paradoxes be damned.

Newman's head was bowed, and beneath the halo of his graying curls, he seemed lost in prayer. His forehead rested against the fleshy fingertips of his clasped hands. What was he praying for? To be the next president?

Even though almost everything I had seen of him during my long hours with the timescreen had offended me, this offended me more. And not just because I was the first human to travel through time, and I was trapped having to pay attention to *this*. But because I knew who he was supposed to be, and this was not it. I preferred to think of who we are as immutable. He was supposed to be mocking governors, not being one, and certainly not one on the road to the White House. From all I'd learned of him, from the clowning deviousness of his songs, I knew he was a buffoon, not a statesman. Maybe that would be good enough for Louisiana, but not for the rest of the country. That must be why The Visitors wanted him stopped, why this fracture in the timeline had to be extinguished. If Newman could not be turned from this path, something bad would come of this, or why else would The Visitors have expended so much effort? Maybe, if allowed to proceed unchanged, this timeline could ripple forward to catch up with our own, and end the present as we know it.

Randy Newman had to be stopped.

The Visitors had given me information, but not a plan on how to use it. Standing there, staring at him, I was frozen. How do I begin to change the universe? Better that they'd sent someone else. Someone who was a strategist, or a private detective. Someone who did not hate Randy Newman so much. Someone who could see what had to be done.

Yet I had to get through this somehow. Without that, I knew that there was no getting back to my own time.

Newman opened his eyes, but kept his head bowed against the early morning sun, and took a moment to survey his city. He lived. He breathed. I was still startled to behold him. I could not take my gaze off him until he started to turn his head in my direction, and I lowered my own before he spotted my hungry attention. I shifted my look to Huey Long's grave, and quietly said a little prayer, but it was not the one Newman thought.

"I'm usually the only one who feels a need to take in the view this early in the morning," he said. His voice seemed friendly, in tones that were now familiar echoes to me, but there was a wariness to it as well.

"You're not the only one who feels the need to commune with the governor, Governor," I said.

I was startled to discover that The Visitors had not only altered my brain and my body but also my voice. When I spoke, it was with a lazy Southern drawl. I bid him a good morning, just to hear myself speak, and then laughed softly at the sound of it. He didn't seem to take it amiss.

He nodded towards the sacred spot hundreds of feet below.

"They would like to laugh at him, you know," he said. "Laugh at us. Let them, I say. So he was a cracker. Well, I'm a cracker, too. From the sound of it, so are you. But he bound the people together like no one else before or since."

He laughed.

"Look at me. I'm getting goddamned maudlin on you. But that isn't just a metaphor. Why, do you know that you can't get from one end of the state to the other without passing over at least a half a dozen of the one hundred and eleven bridges he built us. And the roads! The son of a bitch added over twenty-three hundred miles of them. In 1931 alone, the state of Louisiana employed ten percent of the workers involved in building roads nationwide. Man, what I would give for the power to do that. He was a unifier, in more ways than one."

"You'll get no argument here, Governor."

"I like the man. Without him, Louisiana wouldn't be what it is today."

"With your love of Louisiana, I don't see why you'd want to leave it. I don't see how a man of your temperament could stand the air of Washington."

"I couldn't leave Louisiana behind, no matter where I end up. It's in me. But, you see, there's so much more that I can do, not just for the people of my state but for my country as a whole. The world isn't fair. I'm just doing my best to make it so. And that's a job I just can't do from Louisiana."

I was suddenly startled to realize that I liked him better this way. It's as if that part of him that was inside-out had been burned away, leaving what was pure and true and honest. And at least this way he wasn't singing and writing any more of those sarcastic songs.

I was tempted to leave him this way. He could surely do no more harm to the world than his other self had with his endless cynicism. But I knew that the aliens wouldn't see it my way.

"But why? Why do it? Why care enough to make that sacrifice?"

He leaned in close to me, and whispered. "Now, you wouldn't happen to be a reporter, would you?"

"I'm just a fellow southerner, like yourself."

"Then come with me."

I followed him inside, where two bodyguards were surprised to see me with the governor. The four of us took the elevator down to the first-floor executive corridor between the House and Senate chambers.

"This is where they got him," he said. His voice quivered as he pointed at the spot. "If they hadn't gunned him down, he'd have been president for sure. So since he can't make it, I will have to be president in his place."

Newman was silent for a moment as he stared at the site of Huey Long's assassination, and then his face hardened.

"When I was a small boy, my mother often took me to get ice cream. Ice cream can be a very powerful motivator for a small boy. If only it wasn't."

He scratched his full stomach and laughed ruefully.

"One day, we went to one of those one-man ice cream wagons," he said. He spoke as if he was not there, as if he was not chatting up a potential contributor. He was far away, traveling in the only time machine most of us ever know. "There were signs on the side. One side of the cart was meant for whites, and the other side was for colored. You don't look quite old enough to have ever seen such signs yourself. Two black children were already being helped there when I arrived. The man turned from them the instant I appeared, and ignored them both. I didn't think it fair, but I did let it happen. Because I wanted the ice cream, you see. We all want the ice cream. Only—we can't always be allowed to have it. Or else, life isn't fair."

"But why did it have to be politics? Why not choose music? After all, both of your uncles . . ."

"When has a song ever changed the world?" He hesitated then, and looked at me oddly. He took a step back, and glanced at his beefy guards. "You seem to know an awful lot about me and my family."

"No, I assure you, I don't." I'd sent the wrong message, but I had no idea how or why. "No more than any other proud Louisianan, Governor."

Newman stared down with wide eyes at the spot on which he stood, where an earlier governor had fallen, and blanched.

"Oh, no," I said, realizing where his thoughts were heading. "I would never do such a thing. Please don't think that."

But he did. And as he started to shout for help, I turned and ran.

I heard shouts, followed by a gunshot. Then another. I have no idea whether it was the bodyguards who fired or some other good Samaritan. This was Louisiana; undoubtedly half of the building was armed.

I felt no pain, but I must have been hit, for the world faded away and I thought, *How meaningless, to die, here, for this.*

4 | *Good Old Boys*

I returned to myself not yet dead on a blazing summer day, the only relief from the heat being the cool ice cream melting down a stick onto my fingers. I winced under the assault of the sun directly overhead, my eyes and mind still back in the damp cavern of the Louisiana State Capitol. I had no memory of purchasing an ice cream bar, and no hunger that would have caused me to do so. I had only an anxiety that caused my temples to pulse with the tension of it. I tilted my hand so the drips would hit the dusty pavement instead of running down my shirt cuff.

I was in yet another past, one even more distant from my own time.

Randy Newman's past.

I looked around for the ice cream cart that I knew had to still be near. That's why The Visitors had not yet brought me back. My first excursion had been for information only. There was still work to be done. The wagon was half a block away, surrounded by children. From this distance, I could pretend that it did not bear the signs marked White and Colored. Not only had he told me about it in his time, mere minutes ago that were impossibly still decades in the future, but I had been forced to listen to him sing about it in my time. Over many months, The Visitors had insisted that I listen to that part of his oeuvre and all else. I moved closer to see what was to come.

An elderly woman walked by, dragging behind her a small cross-eyed boy. She sneered in disdain at my sticky hand. The boy looked at me with one eye and away with the other, and from his split stare I realized it was Newman. The painful operations to fix those eyes would not come until later.

As the woman tugged him along, it became clear to me that he hadn't been looking at me at all, but rather at the melting confection in my hand. He wanted it very badly. A chill went through me at that desire, for I knew then with a certainty that not only was this boy a young Randy Newman but that this was the pivotal day as well.

Still holding her hand, he skipped slightly ahead of the woman so that he was pulling her along instead of the reverse. He pointed at the ice cream wagon, and the pleading began. Even with the weight of this event heavy on my heart, I could not help but smile. The young were always able, whatever their time. It didn't take too much pouting to get her to acquiesce, and she reached into her purse to find a coin. She planted herself where she stood and watched as he skipped down the street to the cart. I dropped my ice cream bar to the pavement, and muttered to make the action seem accidental. I needed a reason to pull near, and so I grimaced and looked at the cart as if deciding whether to buy a replacement. The Visitors had made an actor out of me.

I moved closer to young Newman, his nose as yet unbroken by all the things that would come later, and watched as he stepped up behind two small black girls, only to be shooed by the jeering vendor around to the other side of the cart. I stepped up behind him and watched as one of his eyes read the sign that said Whites and the other seemed to study the two girls who had just been abandoned by the server.

"They were here first," said Newman in a high-pitched voice.

The server coughed.

"Don't tell me how to run my business, son," he said. "What'll it be?"

Newman turned and looked at me. Well, *half* looked at me. I was an adult, and he hoped that I would solve this for him. But I could do nothing. Yet.

"Mister, you saw it," he squeaked, his voice a whistle. "They were here first."

I grunted. What was I to tell him there, with others still listening? That life wasn't fair? It wasn't time for that. He would learn that soon enough himself.

"Well?" asked the ice cream man, seeming to take joy in Newman's discomfort.

The boy shifted his stance, turning his back on the girls, as if that was the only way he could find within himself the ability to place an order. He looked at the coin that had been dropped in his hand.

"Do you want an ice cream or not?" said the man.

"I do, I do, only—"

"Only what?"

Newman bit his lip and, unable to speak his order aloud, pointed to a picture printed on the side of the cart. The man thrust it in his hand through mist from the dry ice and then looked at me, the two girls still ignored. I quickly got a bar to replace the one I had dropped.

Newman had not yet gotten too far, his relative still a short distance away. I quickened my steps to catch up with him, trying at the same time to look casual about it for anyone who might be watching, as if I'd just happened to approach him on the way to somewhere else.

"*E pluribus unum,*" I said to him.

"What was that, mister?" he said, blinking, unsure I was talking to him.

"*E pluribus unum.* It's a phrase the founding fathers decided to put on our money. It was stamped on the coin you just gave the man. It means, 'Out of many, one.' One people, all the same and equal. Because that's what the founders envisioned this country to be."

Newman stuck out his lower lip, his ice cream momentarily forgotten.

"Someone should make it be that way, then. Someone should change things so that they're the way they're supposed to be. If I were president—"

"Oh, no," I said. "Not president. If I were the sort of lad who wanted to make a difference in the world, a president would be the last thing I'd be. Presidents don't really change things."

"Well, who does then?"

"No, definitely not," I said. "Not politics. Politics is definitely not the way to go."

"Well, what then?" he demanded petulantly, snapping at his ice cream bar in frustration. "What am I supposed to do?"

He looked back at the wagon where the seller, without a smile, was still attending to the first of the little black girls.

"You know who really changes the world?" I said. "Writers. Particularly writers of—"

"Randy! Come over here this instant!"

A stern voice cut me off, and I looked up to see the woman striding towards me, holding her purse as if ready to use it like a weapon.

"Get away from my boy this instant! You, sir, are being far too familiar!"

I stumbled away, having run out of time.

"Remember, Randy," I cried out. "Remember what I told you. You must remember that."

I walked swiftly away, the woman continuing to stride past the boy so she could further hector me. I raced around a corner to escape her and found the hot street suddenly gone, for I discovered myself cloaked in the cool dark of a New York City hotel ballroom.

5 | *Maybe I'm Doing It Wrong*

I realized that I was back in the same room that with its fractured glimpse of Randy Newman had begun my trip through time. And not only was it the same room—I sensed that it was also the same crystal of time that had held that catalytic fund-raiser. The South was behind me now, if the South could ever truly be said to be behind me as long as I was forced to focus on Randy Newman. Perhaps Pall was up ahead in the future, watching me now, studying the moment to see how things were going as I had once watched, peering into the past to see if the timeline had changed. There was no way for me to tell; I could not return his gaze. But at the same time I felt reassured by seeing around me in person the same dark wood paneling that I had once watched—or rather, would watch in the future—on the compact screen of the time machine.

As my eyes adjusted to the dim room, I was relieved to see that the walls had no posters blaring of a presidential run. People were squeezed into ragged rows of chairs that faced an empty podium. I saw neither furs nor pinstripes around me, nothing that smacked of the elite fund-raising crowd that had been there earlier. (Or was that later?) The crowd contained T-shirts and long hair, scraggly beards and a general sense of poor hygiene. The rich had been replaced, and now I was surrounded by an army of songwriters.

Newman came into the room then, and he, thank God, looked the way I remembered him. A blinding Hawaiian shirt draped his gut, and he had the sardonic twinkle in his eyes that I had come to expect. I did not realize that I'd been holding my breath until I sighed. I'd done it. This is how that earlier scene was obviously meant to be. A crowd of songwriters gathered to hear from the songwriters' songwriter. (He obviously wasn't, and never would be, a lay audience's songwriter.) My words had nudged him in the right direction. It was over.

He stepped behind the podium to applause. He smiled as a few attendees started to whistle and hoot, waved and smiled at someone he spotted in the front row, and began before the sound that had greeted him had stopped.

"I love you sons of bitches," he said, and the room filled with laughter. It felt good. Things were right again. *I sure don't love you, you son of a bitch*, I thought.

I leaned back against the wall behind me, and waited to be returned to my own time. My own life. I'd soon be back to it. It was a miserable life, but it was my own. Maybe now that the puzzle of Newman's life had been put back the way it should be, now that my mission was over and I had accomplished what The Visitors had intended, they would leave me alone. I would be freed from the bondage of studying a man I did not like on the screen of a time machine I envied. I don't often pray, but I prayed then to be taken from this place, as I was taken from the Louisiana State Capitol, as I was plucked from the hot summer streets of an even more distant past.

Instead, when I opened my eyes I was still trapped listening to the buffoon talk. What more did The Visitors want of me? Why did they want me to undergo more of this suffering?

"You're the only ones to pay attention to what really matters in this world," continued Newman. "Others may waste their days delineating the mundane, wasted lives of college professors, but only you know that there are galaxies being born right next door, and that somewhere there are civilizations being snuffed out as galaxies die. I am home here, with the only people who understand me. The hell with the talented myopics who can only write stories of things that are thrust under their noses, when the issues that matter can best be described with metaphors that don't yet exist, that we can only imagine—aliens and planet-hopping rocket ships and time machines. You know who the real audience is for my novels? You are. I'm so proud to be one of you."

He paused, choked with emotion. It appeared that there was more he wanted to say, but could not. He returned his index cards to his pocket, and could only repeat:

"I love you sons of bitches."

I was dazed by his confusing words. What did his ramblings mean? Why was a tunesmith talking to his peers about novels and time machines? Randy Newman had never written a novel in his life. As far as I was concerned, he had barely written songs.

I was the only one who seemed bothered by any of this; the audience ate up every word. Looking at them more closely, I could see that some of their T-shirts bore pictures of scientific formulae, others had spacecraft, and the faces of aliens looked out at me with visages much like The Visitors themselves. I raced to the closest audience member and grabbed a booklet from his hand. Newman's face was on the cover of the pamphlet, but by the words that accompanied the caricature, I could tell that this wasn't the gathering of songwriters I'd originally thought it to be. Instead, this was a science fiction convention! That was the reason I was still trapped here, pinned to the past by my pain.

I'd only been half-right. My message had gotten through to him as a child, but I had been interrupted before I'd been able to deliver the whole of it. I screamed my frustration to the world, but by the time the audience turned from Newman to me to see what had caused the commotion, I was no longer there to be seen.

6 | *Last Night I Had a Dream*

A square of moonlight hit the boy's face as he drooled against the pillow, dreaming of . . . of what? That's what this was all about, wasn't it? I sat uncomfortably on the other side of young Randy Newman's dim bedroom, contorted in a chair meant for a child. Looking at him, with his smooth face and his mussed hair, the boy did not look like someone destined to cause me pain, seemed indistinguishable from any other sleeping child, but there was potential in him I had to derail. A potential for what, I did not know. But he had become fractured from what the universe had originally planned for him, and it was up to me to set his life back within the groove before disaster struck.

Gazing at him, I could not tell, now that I was back once more in the deeper past, whether this moment was a time before or after the incident at the ice cream wagon, or even, perhaps, some other timeline entirely.

It struck me that this was one of the few times I'd ever seen him without his glasses. He appeared peaceful and serene.

I don't think I've ever felt such hate.

If he were to die right then, I thought, I would be far better off, and so would the world. He would never then grow into the man who would make music that was more curse than song, and would never attract the attention of The Visitors. I would never be sitting there where The Visitors had put me, a place where I had no right to be, hoping to be freed from this. Perhaps that was the way to solve this, by ending the matter entirely rather than trying to reinvent him. It seemed the far easier way to stop whatever disaster they meant to prevent.

Those thoughts fled when I heard the murmur of a voice, and I tensed, fearful that the approaching sound was his mother creeping up the stairs. But then I realized that what I was actually hearing was a low humming, as of someone preparing to sing. It scared me, until I realized that the vibrations were coming from my own throat. Then it no longer scared me.

It petrified me.

I have never been a person with an inclination to song, another reason why the whole assignment has been so painful for me. During my commutes, I always chose talk radio of any kind over music of any flavor. Yes, I understood music scientifically, the relationship of one note to the next, the effect they are supposed to have on the listener, how music can make emotions rise and fall, but I find no pleasure there, nor a true empathy for the pleasure it causes in others. If you were to tell me that music was a hoax, I would think, "Ah, yes, finally they tell me the truth," and believe you.

Yet here I was, readying myself in a dark room to sing a small boy some sort of reverse lullaby. Instead of putting him to sleep, I was to wake him to a new potential.

Without even knowing what was to come next, I found myself singing the opening verses of "This Land Is Your Land." Surprisingly, I didn't sound half bad. In addition to everything else The Visitors had given me for this journey, a decent voice seemed to have gone with the package.

Little Randy Newman awoke halfway through, and I continued on to the final verse that is rarely sung, the one that rails against the private ownership of land. He rubbed his eyes as he looked at me, but did not say a word. So I told him about Woody Guthrie, and the various causes he championed, and how he'd had inscribed along the edges of his guitar the phrase, "This Machine Kills Fascists."

I sang songs to him from times that had come before him, but also times that had not yet occurred, though it was doubtful he'd see the difference. I sang him Joe Hill's "Casey Jones—The Union Scab," followed with "I Dreamed I Saw Joe Hill," and sketched in the effect they both had on the beginnings of the American labor movement. His eye grew wide as I told him the story of student protesters shot by the National Guard, and sang Neil Young's "Ohio." I told him of the civil rights movement and how "We Shall Overcome" helped power it. I told him about the antiwar efforts of John Lennon and sang "Give Peace a Chance." I sang "The Times They Are a-Changin'," but I don't know that he got the full effect, because the voice The Visitors had given me was better than Bob Dylan's. I did my best to let him see how people paid more attention to songwriters than they did to politicians or novelists. That much I could give him. The cynicism that would put him back the way he'd been still had to come from within.

When he finally spoke, it was to say, "I'm still asleep now, you know, mister." His voice was insistent as he pushed out his bottom lip. "I think it's time I had a different dream."

He closed his eyes. Searching for another song, I found nothing. I had run through them all. I waited there until he opened his eyes again and glared at me.

"Go away," he said.

I would have liked nothing better. But the choice was not my own. I would not know I was ready to leave until I was gone.

"Just remember what I told you tonight, Randy," I said. "Remember what the martyred Joe Hill said. He wrote that a songwriter is the only kind of writer that has meaning in this world. He wrote, 'A pamphlet, no matter how good, is never read more than once. But a song is learned by heart and repeated over and—'"

The door opened suddenly, cutting me off with a shaft of blinding light. His mother stepped into the room and moved towards her son, his arms flung over his face.

"What is it, dear?" she said. "I thought I heard you cry out."

I tried to slip out behind her into the hallway, but the floor creaked beneath my heels, and she turned to see me.

"You!" she shouted. "You're that man who was bothering us yesterday!"

It was only then that I realized I was in the same timestream I had visited earlier.

"I can explain," I said weakly as I backed away, then said nothing more. The Visitors had filled me with knowledge, but had not given me the words to deal with this.

She raced from the room, but did not look afraid.

"Now you'd really better go," said Newman. That smug look on his face reminded me once again why I hated him so.

"Just remember," I said. "Please."

There was no way to explain to him that that was the only way I'd ever get home.

I slipped out a window and dropped to the yard below. As I limped along the quiet street, a shotgun exploded behind me. After a life without violence, gunshots were chasing me for the second time that day. Between the blasts I heard a high-pitched voice shout, "Mother, no!" and then all went black.

One way or another, I prayed for it to end. I no longer cared how.

7 | *The World Isn't Fair*

So silent was my pop back into existence in my own time beside Pall that at first he did not even realize that I had returned. I was at his elbow as he stared at the time machine, and on the screen I caught a glimpse of myself vanishing from the dark street just as bullets breezed through the spot I had just been inhabiting. The picture then vanished to be replaced by static. Pall cursed at the blizzard and backed from the screen, and only noticed I was there as he bumped into me. Turning, his cursing increased. He lifted me up in a bear hug as I complained.

"You did it!" he said. "You traveled through time."

"Yes," I said, reaching out to touch my world of now, the chairs, the walls, the blank time machine before us, almost as if I thought they would all be quickly taken away from me again. "I traveled through time."

"I witnessed it," he said quietly. "All of it. They let me see you. What was it like?"

"I don't know," I said quietly.

Pall shook his head.

"I can't accept that. You were the first human to go backwards in time. I know you. I know what that must mean to you. You must feel *something*."

I looked inside myself, and all I saw were things I needed to forget. What I felt could not be expressed in words without driving me insane. Even thinking them as abstract emotions was difficult enough, but to make them concrete . . .

All my life I had wondered if such a thing as what I had just accomplished was possible. If it were possible, I would surely be the man to figure that out. There were so many things I wanted to see and do on such a voyage into history, so many precious moments I wanted to collect.

To have it handed to me in this way, like spare change tossed to a beggar, that made it worthless. And to be led around the past on a leash for as insignificant a reason as Randy Newman, that made the whole thing even more insulting still. Some pain was not meant to be endured.

So all I could say was, "I feel . . . nothing."

And then hope to forget.

The interference on the screen faded, and there was Newman again, as he had been all those months before, as he had come to haunt my dreams. There he was as a young boy watching his uncle Alfred conducting an orchestra on a sound stage as snippets of film flickered above them. There he was meeting his first wife, and then later writing a song about their marriage dying, and yet later again writing another about how stupid he felt to be still loving her after all. There he was, losing an Academy Award, which pleased me. All the pieces came together into the cynical mosaic of his life as it always had.

I had succeeded. I had saved the world from whatever great unknown it was The Visitors had foreseen. Maybe they would now let it end.

"So what was that all about, anyway?" asked Pall. "Did you save the world? What was he going to do as president? Did you avert a nuclear war?"

I sat in the chair that had owned me for too long.

"I don't think they'll ever tell us."

I hoped that it was over. Now that all was well within the time stream, perhaps I would not ever have to watch Randy Newman again. I reached behind the machine, unplugged it from the wall, and sighed.

It was a good sigh.

That was when the voice in my head said, "Turn it back on."

8 | *That's Why I Love Mankind*

My life is good.

At least I, unlike many others since The Visitors have come, have a life. I must be thankful for that.

I have grown used to spending my days as I do. The pain of it is duller than when I started my vigil. It has become bearable. I accept that though I have watched him be born, watched him live, and watched him die, I will be forever deaf to all he does. Even as I wince at it, I accept that I must be his eternal witness.

I have grown to know the rhythms of Randy Newman's life as well as I know the pulse of my own blood, the music of my own lungs. I watch constantly, and when an aspect of his life goes awry, when he jumps the track of his enforced destiny and creates something other than those infantile songs of his, I can sense the disturbance immediately. And almost before I can alert The Visitors to what needs to be done, I am gone, sent back by them again to set things right.

I have seen him become a short-order cook, a comic book artist, a television weatherman, a vagrant, a schoolteacher, a radio DJ, and more, and each time I have put him gently—and sometimes not so gently—back in his place.

I have been doing it for years now, and I still do not know why. I have asked The Visitors and have been given only silence. So I no longer ask. I try to find comfort in Pall's belief that I have saved the world many times over, but I gain no solace from that. I cannot be sure of that. I can be sure of only one thing.

I once had a dream, but now only have dreams of him.

I was going to be the one who would figure out how to unravel time, only I have instead found myself knotted in it. I was a man who liked his music straight and honest, if forced to have a choice in music at all. I was a man with little use for irony, and yet Randy Newman serves me a portion every day, mocking slavery, making fun of the homeless, and meaning neither. Or so he says.

How ironic that the last person on Earth who should be doing this job is the very one forced to do it.

How . . . ironic.

As that thought began to gel, another thought intruded on my own:

"Come to us," it said.

I slumped in my soul and went to join The Visitors. It never got any easier. I was terrified to see, when the doors opened around me and the elevator slipped back into the floor, that this time there were a dozen of them. Never before had I seen more than two at a time, such as when I was launched on my first mission, and the ones that followed. As far as I knew, no human had ever seen more than two at once. I tried again, petrified, to distinguish them one from the other, looking for scratches, discolorations, differences in appearance of any body part. I hoped that their increased number could help me find distinctions. But they could have been stamped out by a machine, so identical was their flesh. It was hopeless.

"Do you know why we have called you?" one said.

I could not speak, could not even shake my head.

"We thought perhaps you already understood," said a second.

"It is time," said a third. Or maybe it was the voice of the first speaker again. I could not be sure. Their intonations were so similar that they could have been speaking with one voice.

"It is time," one of them said again.

"Time?" I asked, my voice a dull croak. But even before I finished spitting out that single short syllable, I already knew what they meant. They intended, at last, to explain it all.

"Then tell me," I whispered. "Why, then?"

After years of sparse and cryptic sentences, the words came this time in a torrent, first from one, then another. So many words after so long a time. I try to avoid attributing emotions to aliens, but now it was as if they were as excited that this time had come as I was. I looked quickly from one to the next, trying to keep track of who was speaking, but soon their voices melded together so that I did not know which of them had spoken. The unleashed sentences came barreling out of them so rapidly that what I heard carried the qualities of an uninterrupted soliloquy.

"We thought you were smarter than this, little one," they said. "Don't you perceive it? Don't you yet see the truth? You know, you were on the verge of figuring it all out when we called for you. You were so close to the answer, so close that you almost thought it yourself. You should not have to ask us why. You will undoubtedly figure it all out on your own soon."

I feared for a moment that they were dismissing me. If they had brought me this close to the brink only to leave me dangling, if they intended to send me back to the time machine with no answer, I did not think I could survive it. If this moment was just meant to be a malicious tease, I doubted that I could live much beyond the day. I needed to know.

"Do not worry. We will be the ones to tell you so that we can see your face as it happens. Think back. What was it that you were thinking when we summoned you? Do you not recall it? You were thinking that you were the last person on Earth who should be doing this job. Well, you are right. You meant it as a metaphor, but it is true . . . literally."

I grew dizzy, and flung out an arm, but there was nowhere to support myself in the bare room.

"And we would know. You see, we have come to love irony. Irony, we have discovered, is the most delicious of all emotions, a thing we have learned well in our travels throughout the universe. It is our hunt for the highest degree of irony that put you in charge of this project these many years, and it is irony that has left you there."

"You're saying I am here precisely because I shouldn't be?" The anger in my voice for the first time overcame my fear. "That I am the most unfit candidate for the job, and you know it? So you're torturing me deliberately? You mean you crossed a galaxy for that? What kind of creatures are you? You came up with a stupid project designed to be the opposite of who I am just to watch me wriggle?"

"You must not call Randy Newman stupid!"

The sound in my head was deafening, and I fell to my knees. Their words continued to bombard me, each one opening a new wound.

"Do not pride yourself in thinking that it was you who came first. This wasn't designed around you, it was Newman, first, last, and always, and it is you who were chosen around him. It is this project that takes precedence. Why is it that you think we came here? Do you think that Earth's sunsets are more beautiful than the ones on other planets, or that your air smells sweeter, or that your goods are worth our export? Actually, we can see that you *do* think that. But that is not so. We come here for one reason, and that reason is Randy Newman. Without him, do you think that we would bother to keep Earth alive? No, without him, Earth would be a ball of ash. We have seen the universe entire, and we know that Earth produces the most flavorful taste of all, for he is the king of irony. You are engaged in the only thing worth doing on this planet, which is keeping his life on track, so that he can continue to produce that delicacy."

"But I thought you were trying to prevent him from going astray because of something horrible he might do, not to protect the things that he did do."

"You hoped that you were saving your planet from a nuclear holocaust? We would not care if your entire race save one went up in flames. No, we needed you to keep the shifting timeline on track, to make sure that nothing occurred that would keep Randy Newman from blossoming in all the fullness of his spirit. He sees life as it truly is. He is the only one of your entire species. As for you, there is only one reason why you and your exacerbated frustrations are involved, a reason you were close to realizing on your own. You were chosen because of your potential, because now the story of your life is as full of irony as any of Randy Newman's songs. It's all very simple, you see."

I could not speak for the horror washing over me. I covered my ears so I would not hear the judgment that they were about to deliver, so I could avoid the summation of my life, but their words seeped through my fingers anyway, and drove straight to the core of my brain.

"We want you to hurt like we do."

BRET LOTT

Rose

Bret Lott's most recent novel is Forgiveness; *he is also the author of the novels* A Stranger's House, Jewel *(an Oprah Winfrey Book Club selection)*, Reed's Beach, *and* The Hunt Club, *the collections* A Dream of Old Leaves *and* How to Get Home, *and a memoir*, Fathers, Sons, and Brothers. *His short stories and essays have been widely anthologized and have appeared in such journals as* The Yale Review, The Iowa Review, Gettysburg Review, Story, *and* The Southern Review. *He holds an M.F.A. from the University of Massachusetts, where he studied with the late James Baldwin. Born in Los Angeles, Lott lives with his wife and sons in Charleston, South Carolina, where he is professor of English and writer in residence at the College of Charleston.* "Rose" *was first published in* Shenandoah.

—for Mr. Faulkner, with all respect.

I

Once she was dead, there would be more stories. She knew that, knew how the contemptible commoners of this town thrived on what they could say of her, Miss Emily Grierson. This was a festering town, festered with the grand and luxurious nothingness of small lives that lent them the time, plenty of it, to tell themselves and the dark of humid evenings filled with the stagnant decayed nothingness of their own lives tales of her not true, not true, but true because they would tell them to each other, and believe them.

Of course she had killed him. Someday they would know that. But the truth they would never divine. Given all the years of a base and fallen town's life, they could not know the truth: the depth of her love.

She pulled through her hair the engraved sterling brush, black now with tarnish so that his monogram could no longer be read, just as she had each evening since she had given him the comb, this brush, and the other of his toilet articles. Her gift to him that night.

Each night since that night she had brushed her hair before going to bed, hair iron gray now with the passing of years, the same iron gray as her father's when he, too, died so very many years before. Even before she had met the man with whom she had lain, the man she had murdered. Each night, as this night, she brushed her hair by light of the lamp's rose shade as calmly and serenely as she had when, once the man she had lain with was dead, she had risen from the evening summer sheets heavy with the depravity of this life, this town, to find upon the seat of her gown, pure pure white, the small red smudge of red that signaled her the pain she had felt in their sanctification was indeed real. Then she had simply gone to the dressing table and seated herself upon the chair, its rich burgundy velvet that night thick and rare in its feel, now this night the chair worn smooth to a slick dull red from the years she had sat here each night since.

How many nights? she wondered. Was it last night, when she had lain with him and killed him? A week ago, a fortnight? Or years, decades?

Now?

They would tell stories of her because of the man, dead all these years, in the bed behind her. He would be found out, she knew, with her own passing when the townspeople would break in to her home to find her. They would find his body in the new nightclothes given to him that night upon which she had killed him, him fused into his nightclothes and the bedclothes that had not been changed since that evening a fortnight, decades, moments ago, his flesh no longer flesh but part of the real of this room, as real as the layer of dust on his suit folded neatly over the cane chair at the foot of the bed, on the dresser his tie, his celluloid collar. As real as flesh and bone and love all fused into the sheets, in just the same way lies were fused into the air about this hungry decrepit peasant town filling now, even as she pulled the brush through her hair as every night, with stories about her.

Let them, she thought. Let them all, in the ugly alchemy of the cracker mind, spawn their bastard lies of her. She knew the truth, knew enough truth to fill the grave, enough to land her in the great bald cold hereafter by dint and force of the truth of love and love and love, love past what any of them could imagine. Then, when each of them met the nothing end of their nothing lives, she would be there on the other side of the muddy disconsolate river of death, and they would see her upon the opposite shore, see she'd crossed pristine and glistening and dressed in pure pure white to the cold bald great hereafter. Then each one of the townspeople, the cretins, who had lived upon lies they would tell about her, Miss Emily Grierson, lies savored like a dog savors a bone gnawed to nothing, these crackers would then cry to her for salvation as they themselves tried to cross the disconsolate river, only to find themselves quickly, surely drawn with the ugly weight of their lies of her to the slick silted bottom of the river, their impotent cries to her for salvation and her requisite silence in answer the last reckoning to the truth they would have before their lungs filled with muddy water of the difference between themselves and her that had stood between them their entire living lives: she was of legitimate blood; they were of empty.

2

They were dogs, she knew, every townsman save perhaps the Negro, her boy all these years, the boy now an old man who came and had come and would come with the market basket every few evenings, who swept the kitchen, and the pantry, the hall and parlor, as well as the room in which she now slept.

She did not sleep in this room, this room only a place she visited each night, first to lie down beside the dead man for a moment as best to recapture in the fleshless smile he held and fleshless arms drawn to his throat as if in embrace the beginning of love she'd encountered that night, and next to brush her hair at the dressing table as she had the night love had in fact begun.

She did not sleep in this room, but in a room far more significant than any of these crackers would ever know, could ever know. She slept in the room off the hall downstairs, the room in which, she had been told by her father, her mother had died in childbirth. She herself had been all of her years the only proof positive her mother had ever lived, no pictures, no por-traits, not even a moment of clothing or smell or a single strand of perhaps iron gray hair of her mother's own any evidence her mother had ever existed, save for the words given to her by her father: *Your mother passed in childbirth, giving me you*, he had said to her only once, the day of her fifth birthday, when only then it had occurred to her to ask. He spoke of it not again, ever. Not even her name.

She'd had the Negro move her father's articles from his bedroom the day after she had killed the man and into the downstairs room, the birthing room and passing room, the furniture as big and ungainly as the new secret she held inside her bedroom, the Negro, young then, wrestling the mattress and headboard and footboard and night table and dresser along the dark wood walls of the upstairs hall and down the staircase and into the room.

And she had the Negro as well keep her larder full, her pantry filled so that she might eat, and eat, both to hide and to nourish, his trips in with the market basket those days daily pilgrimages, so that even he would not know.

The Negro, she had seen in his eyes when he'd deduced the truth of what had occurred that singular night that would and had and did become every night of her life, was without duty to any but her and her father. A boy born to know his own caste, she knew, born like herself into the life before the War that ended the old life and its way of settling with only the bloodshed of birth who one was upon the face of the earth. The Negro was a boy she could—and this was the horrible miracle, after an entire life lived here in this town rent not with the emancipation of the Negro but a town rent, irreparably torn asunder, by the emancipation of the Cracker to become the rulers of this hamlet, the aldermen and mayors and exactors of tax of a generation that did not know its place, that had forgotten the precious gift of a time when order had reigned as it ought to reign, in observance of lineage and standing—the horrible miracle was that now and all these many years it had been only the Negro, unblinking servile Tobe, she could trust.

He had seen things, she knew, and had been trustworthy, had been a good Negro who knew not to let eyes meet and who knew not to question purchases made at the druggist's and who knew not to question as well the smell that had blossomed days after a night that would be the night of all nights in her life.

All nights, save for one. A night even the Negro did not know of, a night beyond reckoning of any sort.

Let the town tell its stories. She had stories of her own.

3

Of the night four weeks and five days after the purchase of the arsenic from the druggist, writ across the package beneath the skull and crossbones the words "For rats" in the druggist's hand himself. By then the smell from her bedroom was blossoming horrid and full and genuine, Miss Emily seated on the cracked leather of the parlor's furniture mornings and evenings and afternoons while she ate, and while she stared at the crayon portrait of her father upon its tarnished gilt easel before the fireplace, her father with his iron gray hair, his mouth closed tight, eyes bright with bearing.

The eyes of a vigorous man. The eyes of a man of will and power.

The eyes of a man who had driven away any suitor who might have delivered her from his eyes, and hence the eyes of a man who kept from her the love she so desired. Until the man in the bedroom upstairs had arrived upon her front porch a year after her father's death.

While the smell blossomed from the room upstairs—could it have been this afternoon? A lifetime ago?—she spent those days in the parlor bearing the stench in the same way she had borne the temper of her father who had threatened the horsewhip to men who, of a Sunday evening, had made their intentions evident with their appearance at the door of this house, this same squarish house with its balconies and cupolas and spires, still elegant despite the loss of its white paint in blisters popped and peeling back as the man's flesh blistered and popped, left to rot. But the street that had once been the most select of the entire town had grown indigent with itself for all the bearing these new low-slung spireless sheds could hold, sheds that had crept up on her own poised home like the men who had crept up that midnight four weeks and five days after the purchase of the arsenic from the druggist.

She'd spied the men from her window in this room, where she repaired once the day had been spent before her father's portrait, the lamp no longer lit for the dark in which she wanted to sit with her love growing, the man only newly dead then, the smell inside this room a rank blossom too huge and significant and powerless to keep her from staying here in this dark.

Four weeks and five days after the arsenic purchase, the town believing, she knew, the poison was meant for her, her own suicide a kind of expected gift these dullards wanted as a means to give themselves the self-assured nod, to say among themselves, We knew it. We knew she was crazy after having been jilted by the man.

But neither had she been jilted nor was she crazy. She knew, of course, he'd meant to jilt her, but she'd allowed instead the arsenic for him, spooned that afternoon into the bottom of the lead crystal glass in which she poured out bourbon for him once their consecration had been made that night. She hadn't even risen from their bed, only leaned to the small table beside her, where she had put the glass and decanter in which her father had kept the bourbon all these years, then watched the man smile at her in the kind of smile that betrayed a man's lust sated and his escape begun.

Then his smile twisted into itself, the arsenic quick and swift and blind in its affections, and she had reached to him, taken the glass from him before he might drop it and spoil these sheets, desecrate them with alcohol when they had been so blessed with the beginning of love only moments before, the two still beneath these sheets as all who have loved with a love as deep as she had begun to know ought still to be. Then his eyes cinched shut with the force and grandeur of a poison meting out its purpose whether for rats or for lovers, and his hands went to his throat, his mouth an O of lovely pain, beautiful and thrilling and exquisite pain, his mouth the same mouth only minutes before she had met with her own lips.

She had watched him die, then brushed her hair.

She watched the men down in her yard that night four weeks and five days after the purchase, watched men look furtively to left and right, each slung over his shoulder a sack as if of seed, each man reaching into the bag like a sower and throwing handfuls to the ground beside her house, at the foundation.

Lime. It was lime they were spreading in the ridiculous belief, she imagined, that somewhere on the premises a rat or dog or some such had died, herself too much the crazy woman to know or care to dispel of the dead animal and its offenses.

Here was a story she could tell of them: they were fools, all of them. The smell had come from here, where she sat watching them work as though they might not be detected. She had seen them here, where love had begun, while they tried as best and stupidly to break down love's fiber and being with a handful of lime thrown along the foundation of this house. As if that might kill love.

She relit the rose-shaded lamp then, and seated herself before the window to signal those who would look up at her she knew who they were, knew why they were here, knew their place. She knew.

One of the elect down there, his hand inside his bag of lime for another handful of lies to spread, turned slowly to her at this window, in this rose-hued light, and then another man came to the first and just as slowly looked up at her in this light as well. The men then moved away from the house, disappeared into the shadows of the locusts that lined the street, the town's elect vanquished as simply and easily as making her presence known, the smell that had drawn them here in the belief they might end it, that sad gift from the man no longer a man but a vessel, a vessel only for love, still just as horrid and full and powerless as it would ever be.

She had sent the signal: *I know who you are, and you know who I am. And you cannot kill the love I know.*

4

She could tell the story of her courtship, so very misunderstood by all, a courtship begun with the negation of all possibility of courtship and hence love, driven away by dint and force of fatherhood.

So that when the contract for the paving of the town's sidewalks was let a year after the death of her father, and the Yankee foreman had knocked on her door of an afternoon to ask smiling after a glass of lemonade, she knew she'd found the sound and shroudless agency of the love she sought. Though he wore a waistcoat and collar and tie, cuffed starched sleeves and herringbone trousers, a straw boater atop his head—every indication of his affluence and enterprise—still his face and hands were tanned for the overseeing of the Negroes hard at work with pick and shovel on the street beyond the shadow of the locusts, the color of his skin betraying the quality of sun-drenched toil his job entailed; the solid line of his shoulders and the way that line traced its own vigor gave her to believe he might be enough to hold on to in order to find what she needed; and the color of his eyes, a green so very near and yet so very distant from the green of her father's— gilt green, mordant green—gave her no choice but to see her father, with his horsewhip and temper, there in this Yankee's eyes.

It was then the man winked at her, in that most impudent and improvident blink of an eye something passing from him into her, a cutting shard of possibility, a dagger of prospect, the notion already taking shape in her mind of the agency of love he was to become.

A Yankee. A glorified day laborer. A man so shameless, so arrant as to seek refreshment from a single woman of her bearing, and to wink. Her father would have already made good on his threats with the horsewhip at so vulgar a gesture.

And her father was dead.

There followed the evening visits after his hours in the sun, his arrival

at her front door for all this base and common town to see fodder for more
and more stories that would give these dullards life with the telling of them.
Sunday afternoons the two rode drenched in the same broad daylight that
had perverted his skin to the brown it had become, rode in his yellow-
wheeled buggy led by twin bays through the streets of town, her chin high,
eyes lighting on no one as they circled the streets, the man's black cigar
burning in the glorious and putrid way her own father's had evenings at the
dining room table, her food when a child the drenched black and acrid taste
of the air as she ate it, a little girl growing and growing toward a resolve to
find love that would discover its reward in the man she rode beside, a man
with skin too tanned and eyes too near her father's green, that resolve to find
love eclipsing the impropriety of their affair, and the impropriety of the man
himself.

There followed too his proposal, in secret yet there in the parlor in full
view of the portrait of her father on its gilt easel tarnishing even then, a proposal not for marriage but for fornication, though he'd used the word "love"
upon her, his hands touching her in what she knew was a feigned passion
places she had herself only allowed her own hands to touch.

He did not know what love was, she'd known then and knew it now and
knew it all along, his impassioned passionless touch proof enough of his
ordination as the one by whom she would find love. He touched her, and
though she'd allowed herself small protests at his touching there, and there,
and there, she'd found in herself no rising passion at all. Only that resolve:
to find love.

Then, as she had known they would, like flitting moths drawn to a
flame that would in a moment's touch burn them to ash and air, the town
revealed its own ill-bred blood in the impropriety of its admonishment, the
town's elect, she had no doubts, sending the Baptist preacher to her door.

The preacher—a dull man, a simple man—let himself in past the
Negro one afternoon near a year after she and the Yankee had first been seen
together, dispatched no doubt to warn her of indiscretions known to all. She
found him seated in the dull afternoon light of the parlor, saw him stand
dully as she entered, saw him hold his black hat in both dull hands, his dull
eyes daring to meet her own and hold hers, as though the cloth of his voca-
tion were enough to have earned the right to let eyes meet.

She'd held her head high, listened what seemed a lifetime to empty nothings spewed from his mouth like the stagnant decay of evenings in which stories were to be told of her and had been told. She stared at him, head held high, until finally the dull man looked down, his eyes broken by her own.

That was when she turned to the door, drew it open, and made threat to him, on her lips a newfound power, a prayer as old and dangerous and full of horrible promise as the oaths she had heard her father make all her years of possible courtship, oath drawn from the Word and in full ordination of the Christ who oversaw them all—*And when he had made a scourge of small cords, he drove them all out of the temple*, she heard herself say, *and the sheep, and the oxen; and poured out the changers' money, and overthrew the tables*, and felt the instantaneous black joy of such words and knowledge and being, a joy she knew her father himself must have known with each driving of a suitor from their door of a Sunday evening.

The preacher, dull eyes open wide, bovine in his look of genuine low birth for its surprise and awe and terror all at once, was at once gone, stumbling down the stairs off the front porch of the house that was now hers, and not her father's.

Yet still the town would not recognize its place: next came her cousins from Arkansas, dispatched, she would learn, by the wife of the preacher to spend with her days and nights filled with these harpies' presence speaking to her of Grierson lineage and birth and bearing, when only she knew how close she was to finding love, to knowing it, to letting it grow into itself as she had dreamed it might from the moment the idea of love had been given her, and given only once, words ever in her ear and heart and mind, words drenched with the black acrid air of his cigars, drenched in the threat of the horsewhip, drenched in the eyes of power and vigor staring down to her from his portrait across the vast abyss of empty days between her father's death and the appearance of the Yankee: *Your mother passed in childbirth*, came her father's words across the broad expanse of all her days until then, *giving me you.*

The cousins had only left once she'd agreed to end the indiscretion of seeing the Yankee.

She could tell the dullards of this town the story of the courtship that had landed her where she had wanted to be, in the arms of a man as near to her father and as distant as the farthest star. But they would not understand, neither the courtship nor the truth behind fact.

They could not understand the depth of her love.

A courtship none of them would understand, ending as arranged with the appearance of the Yankee at her kitchen door three days after the cousins had left, the Negro admitting the Yankee and then disappearing, leaving the man to find her in the parlor, where she awaited, dressed in an evening gown of pure pure white.

Thus began the night that was to be all the nights of her life.

All nights, save for one.

5

She finished now as she did each night with the brush, and turned it over in her hand, scrutinized with her ancient eyes the sterling silver back for the monogram, the tarnish there a kind of black map to the depth of love she had wanted to begin through him, and had begun.

There was the Yankee's monogram, thin lines curled upon themselves like her own ancient fingers curled upon themselves: *HB*.

Homer Barron, his name had been, Homer Barron, she recalled, and smiled at a name lost each day to the memory of her own life's passing only to be found each night in these same and serpentine black lines in black silver and in the fusion of flesh and bedclothes and nightclothes in the bed behind her, this skeleton and its fleshless grin drawn tight in a new and perfect fleshless smile the same each night, every night.

She stood from the chair, placed his brush upon the dresser, and turned, smiled down in answer to the man, this Yankee, whose name even as she turned was already leaving her, as vague as the outline of her head on the pillow beside his own so ravaged and peaceful with his accomplished decay.

Once she was dead, she knew, there would be stories, even more, and they would make of the outline, and perhaps the iron gray strands of her hair she knew must lie there upon the pillow something larger than it was. Let them, she thought. Let their belief this man and his wiles and her love scorned be the lie they would tell to each other once she was gone. Let them believe she was crazy.

Because there was another story. There was the truth.

She dimmed the rose-shaded lamp as she did each night, and pulled the bedroom door closed behind her, locked it as she did each night with the key she kept on the white ribbon round her neck, then placed a hand to the dark wood of the hall, the feel of the cold walls as close to the feel of a tomb as she might imagine, and then she was at the stairs, descending them one at a time for the age upon her, and for the love she had borne with such regal ease all these years.

The entire world was of empty blood, she knew, only she of legitimate.

Then she was downstairs, and in the hall, all by no more light than a midnight might allow, and now she was at the door to her room, the one in which she slept. The one in which her mother had birthed, and had passed.

Her own room now.

She turned the knob, admitted herself into the room and saw in the darkness the white of her bed, the black of the dresser, and the round shape above it that was her lamp, this one rose as well but glass, and she struck a match from the holder beside the lamp, lit it, let the room grow with this rose hue, this warm and reckoning light, then knelt to the bed that had been her father's, the bed in which her mother had birthed her, and in which her mother had died.

A bed of love, she believed, not because of what her father and mother had made here but because of what her mother had given here, the perfect love she herself had joined her mother in knowing now all these years, the perfect gift she had received upon execution of the covenant she had made with herself, a covenant to find love.

Kneeling, she reached as she did each night beneath the bed, reached and reached, reached as if the loosed board beneath the bed might have of its own accord mended itself, might have made itself whole in a kind of horrible miracle she could not predict but believed might have happened each night she reached for it and could not find it, and then she felt the board's edge, the gap between it and the next, and with one curled finger levered the single board up, all this without seeing it for the rote pilgrimage the search had become all these years. She lifted the board, reached beneath it to touch

the corner of the cardboard box, then inched her finger along its side to find
the ribbon with which the box had been tied a night so very long ago, a night
just last night, a night now upon her.

Her fingers took hold the ribbon and box, slipped it up between the
boards, and she pulled it to her until here it was, the square dress box at her
knees as mottled and decayed with age as her own hands, the white ribbon
the color of parchment, passion finally upon her and rising as new and as
ancient as the gift inside she had given herself: love. Here was the only passion worth finding, the only passion worth touching. No other passion
existed, save for that rising in her as it rose every night since she had placed
the gift here, in the mottled and decayed and beribboned dress box she
held.

Slowly, carefully she stood, the box in her hands as though it were the
crown of life it was, and laid it on the bed, this bed she and her mother
shared in their purpose and design as procreators of the line of legitimate
blood. Carefully, gently, she set the dress box on the bed as she set it each
night, as every night, even as on the night she herself, Miss Emily Grierson,
had borne the child, a night spent alone in this bed and pushing, her body fat
with the food she had eaten both to nourish this love and to hide its proof
from the Negro, herself the one to remove the bloodied bedclothes and burn
them in the cellar furnace, the smoke they might produce evidence further
to an ignorant town, a fallen world, that she was crazy for burning the furnace that spring morning, as they would tell one another and believe for the
telling of it, her fingernails that selfsame night she'd burned the bedclothes
digging so deeply into the headboard above her they bled with blood the
same red as on the seat of her gown the evening she had made this child with
the nameless Yankee who might well have been her father for the mordant,
gilt green of his eyes, her silent and extravagant screams at the relentless
pressure below only extravagant in the expanse of her mind as she swallowed them down to nothing in blood red resolve to find what love is,
screams made silent by bearing and heritage and a father with eyes so pitiless
and cold she did not know nor want to know what the sound of her own
voice in rage and blood-filled resolve might sound like.

It was resolve that mattered, the resolve to find love. Not the luxury and
pity of a self-indulgent scream.

Gently, slowly, she untied the ribbon as she did each night, slowly, carefully, she lifted free the lid.

There it had been, would be, and was now: the child she had made, nes-
tled inside the gown that had bore the red smudge of red, that red the first-
fruit of the child's birth, her beginning of love, though the gown had
become the night she had borne the child brilliant with blood, drenched in it,
only to become this night as every night she could recall the powerless and
caustic brown of old blood.

A baby, withered into the essence of gristle and bone, brown too with
blood, its ribs and arms and legs fused into the gown, collapsed into themselves to become the real of the room itself, its skull with its fleshless grin,
empty eyes, teeth not yet teeth waiting to form, all here for her to take in and
take up as she had each night, and as she would.

Her child. Love. Love so precious she could not, would not allow its
presence felt in so fallen a world as the one she now inhabited, a world rent
with emancipation into chaos, a world loosed of its reign of history and
order and lineage left to wander dully into the void of all time and eternity.

Here was the depth of love the contemptible commoners of this town
could not know: the burden of a family's history in a vulgar world that
would shrug history aside, history settled as it was that night and this and
those to come always and only with the bloodshed of birth.

She lifted the baby in its once-white nest as she did each night, weight-
less always in her arms as though history were not the crushing weight it
always was, held it close this last moment before she would return the baby
to its place hidden from the indigence of this town, her baby's dignity—the
whole of her class's history—retained with the secret of its presence kept.

Rose, she whispered now, the name she had given the child the moment
after its advent and the moment, before its death, that single stranded
moment between both when, mouth open in its only inhale and set to
scream, the baby ready to hear herself for the first time upon the face of this
world, Miss Emily Grierson strangled her, set her free for the great cold bald
hereafter ahead of her, so that as the child made her way across the muddy
disconsolate river of death she would have a name, and so a history: *Rose*,
she whispered again.

Rose. Her mother's name, she believed then and now and on to the end of all belief, the end of all time, the end of a history placed squarely on the backs of those worthy enough to bear it, those with the resolve to bear it.

Rose. Her mother's name, she believed, though she had never heard it spoken, never knew a name existed.

MARK L. VAN NAME

Boar Lake

Mark L. Van Name has published fiction in a variety of magazines and anthologies, including Asimov's Science Fiction, When the Music's Over, Full Spectrum 3, Armageddon, Foreign Legions, *and* The Year's Best Science Fiction. *He has also written or co-written over a thousand computer-related articles. He was co-editor, with John Kessel and Richard Butner, of* Intersections: The Sycamore Hill Anthology. *Having grown up in Florida, he lives in Raleigh, North Carolina, with his wife and children. This marks the first publication of "Boar Lake."*

Jim Morrison was the only one whose fire wasn't lit by the time the boom box reached that old classic. Jackson offered me the joint, but I waved him off. The sensimilla he grew in his little garden in the forest was powerful stuff, and I was already feeling no pain. Hilly took it from him.

"Don't you think you've had enough?" I said.

"Christ, Kevin, lay off. I've had less than you."

"Yeah, but I'm not the one who's pregnant."

"Our only mistake, if you ask me." Hilly smiled at me, dragged on the joint, and passed it to Karen. "What are you afraid of, anyway? I've been clean the entire five months, and it's not like one joint is going to ruin the baby. We're here to mourn, and mourning requires dope."

"All right, all right, I'm sorry. Just trying to be a good father and all."

"Maybe he wants the baby to be a Republican," David said. He and Hilly stared in mock horror at each other, then at me.

"I don't know, Kevin," she said. Hilly's face caught the glow of the setting sun and she looked sixteen again, just as she was when I first saw her at Boar Lake twenty years ago. "Maybe you're the Republican." She faced Jackson. "They took him, Jackson, they took my husband!" She made the sign of the cross with her fingers. "He's a Republican pod person!" She glanced at the bottle of Wild Turkey beside her. "Don't they melt if they get wet? Isn't that right?"

"No, Hilly," I said.

"Yeah, that's right." She grabbed the bottle and stood.

"Hilly, come on, not the whiskey. I'll stink for hours."

Before I could get up she poured some of the booze on me and ran away, laughing. I took off after her, waving good-bye to the gang as I ran.

I caught her in less than fifty yards. I had always been the faster runner, and now she was carrying extra weight. I hugged her and smeared my wet clothes and hair all over her. We both laughed and she made a few halfhearted attempts to escape. After a few seconds even those efforts stopped and she held me tightly.

Jackson and David cuddled a few feet back from the fire, Jackson's ponytail a hair scarf around David's neck. Karen, as always, sat alone. In the over fifteen years we had been running into one another at the lake, she had always been alone. She spoke so rarely we knew almost nothing about her. I caught Hilly also watching her, and I knew we were thinking the same things. Was Karen straight or gay? Single or married? How old was she? What did she do for a living? As it had so many times before, years of frustrated nosiness clawed at me, but I kept quiet and focused on Hilly, who was looking up at me.

"Why in the hell do they have to do it?" she asked.

"I don't know. You can't stop the government. Our parents couldn't stop it in '68, and we can't stop it now." The harvest moon was sneaking onto the stage of the sky, its reflection shining in the water like the edge of a glowing Frisbee. The fading light of the sun and the edge of moonlight caressed the still water. "Let's go join the others. Who knows when we'll see them again?"

Hilly grabbed my hand and we walked slowly back. The night was not cool enough for a fire, but Jackson had insisted. "You need a fire to keep a vigil," he had said. Nobody had argued, but we all stayed well back from the fire, and we kept it low.

As we sat on our blanket, Jackson spoke. "I always figured the Park Service was one of the last great places to hide. And a twenty-acre lake in the middle of Ocala National Forest?" He laughed. "Hell, it was perfect. When I bought my trailer and moved in, I thought I'd finally won. I could do anything and be anything out here, and that was my victory." He shook his head slowly. "Some victory."

David whispered in Jackson's ear.

Jackson smiled. "Yeah, you're right. At least we're still together."

I noticed the name patch, ranger insignia, and epaulets were missing from Jackson's shirt. He disdained most of the things the Park Service gave him, but he always wore one of the shirts. He said he liked having his name over his heart and, besides, they were cheap and durable. "Jackson, what happened to your shirt?"

"Finally spotted it, eh? Did you ever see that old TV show, *Branded*?" He stood. "Chuck Connors gets unfairly drummed out of the army, and they rip off his patches and break his sword." He held up his trip pointer, which he used on his infrequent tours of the area for the rare tourists who managed to get lost enough to find Boar Lake. It was bent in the middle, the top half dangling like a broken bone. "David and I went through that ceremony earlier tonight."

"But you haven't been fired, just reassigned."

"Yeah, but if I'd had any guts I would have fought this more, or quit, or something. Remember the show's theme song, 'scorned as a man who ran'? Well, that's me. I ran from fighting this, from fighting anything, too damned afraid I'd lose my job and have to go back to the real world." He paused and took a long drag on the joint.

David shifted slightly away from him. "You're not alone," he said. "Nobody fought it much. What are you supposed to do about navy target practice missiles? Practice? What kind of practice is it to sit ten miles offshore and blow up trees a hundred miles away? What a stupid idea that is!" Karen sat up and took the joint from Jackson. She stared at David as he continued. "The government's always let the military blow shit up, right? But the places were always in the desert or on some pissant Pacific island where no Americans lived. So why do they have to blow up a lake in the middle of a United States National Forest? Our lake?"

Hilly's eyes blazed. "Have you ever seen the photos of those 'pissant' islands before and after our practice sessions? Have you ever seen the pictures of the people who lived on those islands? We relocated those people to places they'd never even heard of, and sometimes we put them right back on islands so radioactive that over half the people died. Christ, we lost a refuge; they lost their homes."

David's face softened. "You're right, of course. I'm sorry. I guess that, in a way, we're starting to have to pay now. We're running out of places to blow up. I just hate to lose this place, that's all." He took the joint from Karen, smiled at Hilly, and handed it to her. "Yell at me anytime I'm a jerk like that, okay?"

"Sure. No problem." Hilly took a hit, snuffed out the roach, and handed it to Jackson. He stuffed it in his pocket and moved nearer to David.

Karen leaned against the tree and closed her eyes. Hilly and I lay down, my head on her shoulder. She played lightly with my hair.

The Doors finished, but no one moved to put in another CD. Over the curve of Hilly's breasts and stomach I watched the rising moon. The lake glowed and the stars glittered in the clear Florida night. The sounds of life played a low symphony. Crickets chittered and frogs bellowed. Mosquitoes buzzed only feet away, waiting for our repellent to wear off. Occasionally a fish or bird splashed in the water. The wind sang in the pines, its voice a high moan of satisfaction. The fire's dying embers crackled. Birds flapped and fluttered and sang sweet, barely audible songs to one another.

Tomorrow, troops would seal the area.

I felt the din of life as if it were a favorite old sweater wrapped around me. I wondered if the frogs and crickets, like people who knew the missiles were coming and had only twenty minutes to live, were making more desperate love, or singing finer, final songs. Did the wind blow harder, or the fish swim with greater joy, in the face of the incoming shells? I listened again and willed it to be so.

I held Hilly tighter and snaked one of my legs between hers. We had met here when we were sixteen. We lost our virginity together here. We decided here what to do at the end of our trial separation. We had even come here early this year, in late April, when we were sure we wanted a child. We had watched Jackson's hair grow from above his ears to below his waist, from dark brown to salt-and-pepper. We had filled many drives with fanciful speculations about Karen's real life.

The frogs and crickets and birds and wind played on. I wrapped myself more tightly around Hilly. She looked at me and smiled.

I stood. "I've gotten about as morose as I can stand to be. This may be a wake, but a wake is also a party. Let's do something. Enough of this sitting around and moping!"

"Like what?" asked David.

"I don't know. Anything. Something."

Jackson threw his broken pointer into the air and cried, "Eureka!" With a bow and a flourish of his arm he withdrew from his shirt pocket a key ring. "The good ship Jackson is ready to sail!"

I grabbed the keys and headed for the lake, Jackson close behind me. I yelled as I ran, "Last one to the raft has to shove off!"

Jackson kept the raft tied to a small pier at the tip of the snout of Boar Lake. The end of his trailer was just beyond the mooring, under the lake's snout and in front of its mouth. Our fire and the open camping area were around the lake's curve, under its chin. For most of the rest of its perimeter the lake was surrounded by the forest; the only exception was a small, roped-off swimming area in front of the campground. Jackson owned the raft, and he let only a few of us use it. He told inquisitive tourists that we were Park Ranger ecology deputies on water analysis assignments.

Jackson beat me to the raft by two steps and was not even breathing hard. He held up the padlock while I fumbled with the keys. Karen came in third, with David right behind her. He was covered with dirt and griping about tripping being foul play. Karen laughed and bounded onto the raft; David followed her. I opened the lock as Hilly hit the shore, a distant last.

"I'll push off for you," I said. "You go ahead and get aboard."

"Kevin! One more time: I'm not broken, sick, injured, incompetent, or helpless. I'm just pregnant. I'll push off the damn raft, so get your ass on it. Now!"

"Right." I stepped onto the raft. "Getting aboard." The raft was a square of treated pine planks about ten feet on a side that sat on a base of empty, sealed oil barrels. The top of an old marker buoy was nailed to the floor in the center. A long pushing pole and four oars were stuck through the marker and tied to it. It looked like a miniature Eiffel Tower run through with gigantic spears. David and Jackson leaned against the tower. Karen sat on the edge of the raft.

Once we were far enough from shore for Jackson to use the pole, I helped Hilly get aboard. When she was comfortably seated, Jackson started pushing for the center.

In a few minutes we reached water that was too deep for the pole, so Jackson and David pulled the oars from the tower. A few cockroaches skittered from under the marker, and I moved away from them, closer to the edge of the raft.

"Christ, Kevin," Hilly said, "they're only roaches." One started in my direction and she flicked it with her fingers back toward the center of the raft. After a few seconds of exploration all the roaches returned there, apparently as unhappy to be out with us as I was to be with them. I took the oar Jackson handed me. Hilly grabbed hers and joined me on my side, while David moved to the opposite side to row with Karen.

"What about you?" David asked Jackson. "How are you going to earn your pay?"

Jackson stepped to the center of the raft and leaned against the tower. He rested one foot on a crossbeam halfway up it. The slight wind ruffled the unbuttoned flaps of his ranger shirt. He looked like a cross between Smoky the Bear and King Kong. "I shall navigate, command, and all that stuff." He took a step up the marker and raised his hand to shield his eyes. "All clear ahead."

With a little grumbling we all began rowing. After a few strokes Hilly and I found our rhythm and were able to work without getting in one another's way. Jackson stayed at his perch, lost in his thoughts and surveillance of the lake. I was sure I could hear the roaches under the tower, no doubt planning some disgusting assault. My shirt soaked with sweat and clung to me. I warmed up slowly as we rowed. No one spoke. We could not quite manage to row in sync, but the raft was moving well enough that we quit trying. Our oars sliced the water in slow alternation: ours, then David's and Karen's, then ours, then theirs, a steady rhythm of disturbed air and lightly splashing water. The raft spun lazily from the mismatched strokes as we moved across the lake. The water's surface was smooth gray velvet. The shore faded to blackness as the shadows from the trees engulfed it. The only visible light onshore was the orange glow from our fire's embers as they reflected off the walls of Jackson's trailer. We moved through blackness in an arc of moonlight, Jackson a lazy Charon in a Disney version of the journey of the dead.

Not long after my arms began to tire, Jackson spoke. "Enough. We're here."

Hilly seemed eager to row more. "Where? How can you tell? This spot doesn't look any different from that one over there, or the one a few feet ahead of us."

"Does it matter?" Jackson stepped off the marker and waved his arm. "Look around. The shore is black everywhere, so we have to be close to the middle of the lake. Besides, you guys were losing the pace, so I figured you were getting a little tired."

Hilly sighed and handed her oar to Jackson. We all followed suit. He tied them to the tower, then sat with David. Hilly and I lay down, my arm under her neck and her head resting against my shoulder. I heard Karen move and noticed that she, too, was lying down.

David coughed slightly. "I wanted to tell you all that I'm really going to miss this place, all of you—ah, you know."

We murmured in agreement, but no one spoke. I kissed Hilly's forehead and held her tighter. The silence was broken only by the slow pattern of our breathing, the occasional flurry of activity by the roaches under the tower, and the gentle splashes of small fish. The sounds of shore, the crickets and the frogs and the wind through the trees, were barely a whisper out on the lake. I rested my head against Hilly's and closed my eyes. I tried to recall all our times here, to memorize the lake, my friends, the raft . . . everything. I wanted to lose nothing, to keep it all in my head, to tell our child, to somehow keep Boar Lake alive by caring about it.

I must have dozed, because I jerked suddenly awake. I was sure I had heard something odd, something wrong, but I could not figure out what. I looked around the raft. Karen was still lying on the opposite side. Jackson and David were leaning against the marker. Hilly's eyes were open, and she was smiling at me.

I listened harder, mentally cataloguing the sounds, checking for something out of place: the roaches moving, our breathing, slight breezes blowing through the trees, the frogs bellowing. All were sounds I had heard before. I gave up and rested my head again.

And raised it almost instantly. How could I so clearly hear the frogs? Moments earlier, I could barely hear them. I was sure we were drifting a little, but no part of the shore seemed particularly closer than before, no piece of land emerged from the shadows. No one else seemed to notice, however, so I tried again to relax. I cursed myself for smoking so much dope.

The sound from the crickets joined the noise from the frogs. The wind grew louder, too, sounding now as if it were whistling through branches a few yards away. The volume of all the sounds rose smoothly but quickly. I sat up and saw that Jackson, too, was looking around. He stared at me. "Do you hear? . . ."

I nodded. Hilly sat up. "Me, too," she said.

Karen and David turned to face us and nodded. We all crawled to the center of the raft and bunched together against the tower and the oars and the pole. I grabbed the pole, glad to have something solid to hold on to.

The sounds grew louder and louder. More and more fish splashed in the water. Frogs croaked enthusiastically, and crickets played on. The wind blew harder, whipping branches back and forth. The tempo picked up as the volume rose. The noise reached the level of a normal conversation, and kept on going. The roaches crawled from under the buoy and ran to the raft's edge. Their flight sounded like the footsteps of a class full of children racing to recess. I wanted to scratch at myself, to claw away the bugs that surely had to be right on top of me to be so loud, but there was nothing.

The noise began to hurt my ears, and I covered them with my hands. I felt like I was sitting three feet in front of the main speakers at an Offspring concert gone back to nature. Each individual frog, fish, cricket, roach— every living thing around us—roared at once, a thousand thousand proclamations screamed in unison. The sounds rushed upward until I began to fear for my hearing, until my head hurt, and then they held. Like a million electric guitarists refusing to release the last chord at the end of a million solos, the din held. We all had our hands to our ears. We were looking frantically around, trying to understand, wondering how we could get away.

A roach scuttled toward me from the edge of the raft, then fell onto its side suddenly. An amber teardrop of light rose slowly from it. I shook my head and looked again. Now three roaches were down, and silky yellow lights wafted upward from all of them. I nudged Hilly and Karen and pointed. Hilly grabbed Jackson. We all pointed and nodded, everyone glad the others could also see. The noise still hurt and I quickly covered my ears again with my hands. The other roaches on the raft quickly fell, until we could see none standing. The shimmering amber tears, each no bigger than the roach beneath it, drifted to the sky.

Bugs rained on us from above the raft, small tears heading upward from the insect bodies falling onto us.

Bits of glowing amber appeared all over the lake, some hovering just above the water's surface, others swaying higher in the air, at first only a few and then hundreds. The population of lights grew by leaps and bounds, a frantic geometric progression of yellow tears. All had the same shape, though they ranged in size from ones much smaller than the roaches to some as large as my forearm. More and more of them rose above Boar Lake, each floating slowly upward like all the others.

As more lights joined the rush the sounds of life quieted slightly. I took my hands from my ears, the noise no longer painful.

The first tears rose from shore. Down low, small ones illuminated the grass and shallow water. Much higher, huge ones, amber drops as big as my legs, ascended from some of the tallest pines. By the gleam of the floating amber we could clearly see the shore, Jackson's trailer, the camp area, our cars, everything. In terror, I looked at Hilly. I stared at her face and shoulders and chest and stomach. No lights, no yellow. I released a breath I hadn't realized I'd been holding. I looked back toward the shore.

Amber bathed all of Boar Lake, the lights a blanket of glowing yellow, so many around us and above us that we could not distinguish their edges. The sounds lowered to a whisper. The lights continued their upward flight as the sounds diminished. As each glowing tear cleared the tallest of the trees it picked up speed and raced out of sight.

Soon I could hear nothing save the sounds of our breathing. No more yellow came from the shore. The last flock of amber tears reached the top of the trees and rushed to the moon and the stars and then vanished. Silence enclosed us. Hilly cradled her face in her hands. Karen stared straight ahead, her mouth slightly open. David and Jackson looked away, their expressions lost to me.

A slight breeze still blew, but no branches rustled. Dead roaches and mosquitoes carpeted the raft. Fish corpses floated on the flat surface of the water. The moon and the stars still shone on Boar Lake, but the light was cold and distant.

JACK MCDEVITT

The Mission

Jack McDevitt's first novel, The Hercules Text, *won the 1986 Philip K. Dick Special Award, and the Locus Award for Best First Novel. A revised edition has been published, with his second novel,* A Talent for War, *in* Hello Out There. *He won the 1992 Universitat Politecnica de Cataluña prize for his novella "Ships in the Night," the Darrell Award for* Eternity Road, *the 2001 Southeastern Science Fiction Achievement Award for his novel* Deepsix, *and the 2000 Phoenix Award for his body of work. McDevitt is a multiple Hugo and Nebula Award finalist. His other novels are* The Engines of God, Ancient Shores, Moonfall, Infinity Beach, Chindi, Omega, *and the recent* Polaris. *His short fiction was collected in* Standard Candles. *He lives with his wife, Maureen, in Brunswick, Georgia. This marks the first publication of "The Mission."*

They were looking down on a dust storm racing across the Martian surface when the transmission came in. "Columbia, we are losing control of the situation here. The plague is everywhere. I don't know how much longer we can keep the station open. Abort and return."

Status lamps blinked in the darkened cockpit. Alice looked at him, her eyes dark and troubled, but for a long time nobody said anything.

"Tommy." The distant voice lost its impersonal tone. "We'll try to stay with this until we get you back—" And the transmission exploded in a burst of static.

Tommy glanced around at the others. "What do you think?" he asked.

Frank stared at the radio. "Make the landing. We can't go back without making the landing."

Alice nodded, but her face was a mask. "Yes. Do it."

Tommy took a deep breath. Below them the storm swirled across the lower latitudes.

"It came in over there, over the woods." Uncle Harold pointed east. "Just off to the left of Harpie's place. And it came right past where we're standing now and touched ground maybe there, near the old hangar. It kept going, of course, because it was hell-bent, fastest thing I ever saw, all lit up.

"You never saw an airplane, I guess, did you? They pulled them all out of here during the early days of the plague. Don't know where they sent them. North, I guess, where it wasn't so bad at first. Well, they're really something, especially at night. And they used to come in here all the time. Air force jets landing and taking off. But *this* one, it wasn't really an airplane at all. It was a rocket, and they kept it up on the station. In orbit, and when the Mars mission came back and the station was empty, it was the only way they could get home. Somebody's left it for them."

"Because," said Tommy, "everything was shut down by then."

"That's right. The Death had been running eight months and there just wasn't nobody left."

Tommy looked the length of the old runway, tracing the glide path from the woods on the east past Harpie's, past the crumbling hangars and maintenance buildings that everybody said were haunted, past the place where they sat their horses. On into the night. The sky was cold and damp and threatening.

"It was a night like this," Uncle Harold said. "Chilled. Rain just beginning to fall."

He imagined it coming in, full of light, the three astronauts inside, feeling for the ground like they weren't sure it was there.

"Why'd they come here to land, Uncle Harold?" Tommy had heard bits and pieces of the story before, how it had come to Warner-Robbins, and how people had ridden out from the town and the astronauts had gotten out and just walked away and nobody ever saw them again. But it had never meant much to him until he actually came to live in Warner-Robbins a few days before. After his mother died. And he came out here to see the place where the lander came down.

"Nobody really knows, Tommy," said Uncle Harold. "I mean, they just rolled to a stop. Well, they didn't exactly *roll*. They sort of bounced up and down a lot and busted a wing and they finally swung around and tipped over."

"Did it catch fire?"

"No. It just laid out there in the dark like a big dead bird."

"And the astronauts—?"

"Well, like I said, they got out, the three of them—"

"What happened to the fourth? Mrs. Taylor said there were four on the mission."

"That's what the books say, but only *three* got out. And they walked off north. Toward Macon."

"Macon's a long way. Why'd you let them do it?"

"I didn't let them do it, Tommy. They pretty much done it on their own. Horace Kittern and Mack Willoughby, they rode after them. Asked whether they was hurt. Whether they could do anything. But the astronauts, they never slowed down, just waved and said everything was fine. Said they'd be back later for the lander. I thought at the time maybe they were afraid of us. Afraid we were infected."

"And they really never came back?"

"Nope. Never seen 'em again."

"How about up in Macon?"

"Wasn't nobody *in* Macon by then. Macon went early."

"The whole town?"

"Far as we know."

Tommy imagined them walking into the night. Into the rain.

Uncle Harold was riding Montie. The horse was cold. It breathed out a cloud of frost and he patted the animal's flank. "Tommy, I wasn't as old as you at the time. Wasn't nothin' I could do. Or anybody else."

Tommy shifted his weight. Poke stirred under him, and a cold wind blew down out of the trees. Across the old airfield. It began to rain. "What happened to the lander?" he asked.

Harold turned Montie around. Started for home. "What happened to the lander?" he said, as if the question puzzled him. "Let's go back to the house and I'll show you."

He was glad to get into the barn and out of the wind. They unsaddled the horses, gave them water, and closed them up in their stalls. Then Uncle Harold picked up the lantern and led him to the back door where they kept the equipment. "There." He pointed to a plow.

"And *there*." A spade.

"And here." A yoke for the team.

"And over here." Braces for the wagon. "We used some of the Teflon to wire the main house. For insulation."

Tommy didn't understand at first. And Uncle Harold kept right on going. "You can still see the tiles. They're from the outside of the lander. We used them to line the smelter down at Jimmy's. And the town freezer that used to be over at Bobby Joe's place but that we moved to Hazlett's after Bobby Joe died. They were put on the outside of refrigerators from one end of town to the other. Saved energy at a time when we hardly had any.

"They salvaged the computers and kept them going for a while, as long as somebody thought they'd be useful. Turned out they didn't really need computers anymore.

"We took the radios. The kids. I got one, but it wasn't no use because there wasn't anything on it except an Atlanta station where they just kept playing the same music and asking whether there was anybody out there until we got into January and I guess it got too cold. They stopped broadcasting and we never heard from them again.

"One of the fuel pumps runs the water system at your uncle Tim's. They took something off the wings that helped keep the town generators going for a while. And the chairs. They're scattered around. Pete Baydecker's got one. It's the most comfortable chair I've ever sat in—" He seemed to run down, like a clock that needed to be wound.

"You just took it *apart*?" Tommy asked. "And used it to make stuff?" He remembered the legend, recalling vividly in that moment Mrs. Taylor's description of what it must have been like as the astronauts, three Americans and a Russian, had neared Mars, and they heard the news, that a virus had broken loose at home, was killing everyone.

"And eventually their radios must have gone quiet." She had said the words and Tommy had imagined himself with them out in the cold dark night between the worlds, a million miles from the ground.

"You have to understand what it was like then," Uncle Harold was saying. He opened the door that would take them across to the house. "We were caught with no power, except what we could produce ourselves. One night the lights and the TVs just went out. They came back on long enough for us to go to bed. But it got cold during the night and we all had to go down and sleep by the fire.

"What ran the lights also ran the tractors and the milking machines and the combines. And suddenly none of it was there anymore. They had all that equipment but they didn't have gas to make it run."

"You could have gotten other people to help you."

Uncle Harold shook his head. "The plague was everywhere. There was nowhere to go. Nobody to help. People were scared to leave town. You never seen anything like the way people behaved when a stranger came up the road. They were bad times. We were lucky to survive."

He turned the lantern out, signaling that it was time to go into the house. Candles burned brightly in the windows. But Tommy didn't move. "You took *everything*? And melted it down?"

"I didn't. The town did. Everything we had went, Tommy. The pickups and the cars that nobody had any use for anymore, and the tractors, and the lander. We needed raw materials to keep alive. I can tell you, Tommy, it was a near thing. We had our hands full just getting through the winter. People died. Half of Warner-Robbins died. Not from the plague. Thank God it never came here. But people died from exposure and sheer exhaustion. We'd forgotten how to live without supermarkets and electricity. But we survived.

"For six years we even managed to light the town. I have to tell you, the people here saw the lander as a God-given miracle."

Tommy felt his heart beat.

"Frank and Alice must know what happened." Uncle Harold sounded guilty. Sounded as if he knew he'd done something wrong.

Tommy looked back at his footprints in the soft earth, watched the rain pooling in them. "Frank doesn't know that," he said. His voice felt strange. "It wasn't right."

"It's what we had to do."

"And Alice doesn't know it either."

Frank and Alice had befriended him after he arrived last week. After Mom died, Tommy had locked onto the lander as if it were part of the world he'd left behind. As if it were connected with his mother and the life over in Milledgeville, which hadn't been as lucky as Warner-Robbins. And Uncle Harold had seen an opportunity to distract him, had talked to him about the Mars mission, had shown him pictures of the *Columbia*, photographs of it under construction and later docked to the space station, and artists' drawings of it in Martian skies. He'd asked whether the astronauts had landed on Mars.

Nobody knew.

He was aware of that, of course, but he asked the question anyway. It was required, somehow. Part of the ceremony. *"Did they ever get to the ground?"* It seemed not right that they had gone all the way out there and not gone down to the surface. So he and Alice and Frank had invented their game, had taken the *Columbia* to Mars, listened to the terrible news, orbited the planet, and landed.

They walked across the red sands and sometimes they found turtles and sometimes lizards and once they even found tall red-skinned natives with saucer eyes who'd chased them while they yelped and ran for their lives.

"Frank and Alice," said Harold, "probably never asked about the lander. It's no secret that it kept us all going. There's not a house or a farm that doesn't have a piece of it out in its barn, or holding its windows together, or keeping its furnace running. You want the lander, son? It's all around you."

They were racing above the southern hemisphere, gazing down on an ocher desert that stretched out forever when Tommy raised the question. "Yeah," said Frank. "I knew that."

Mars vanished, and Tommy looked with dismay at his copilot.

"Sure. Everybody here knows. Right, Alice? We've got some pieces of it in our kitchen. Or is it the furnace? I forget."

They were in the living room at Alice's house and suddenly Tommy could smell the oil lamps. Without moving, Alice pointed to a cushion on the sofa. It was old and worn and black, but it was soft like leather except that it *wasn't* leather. "*That* came out of the lander," she said. "My ma wants to toss it because she says it doesn't look right. But Pa won't hear of it."

Tommy stared at them. "You knew? All this time you knew what they did?"

"What's the big deal?" Frank asked. "It's no secret. *Everybody* knows."

"They should have kept it," said Tommy. "They should have taken care of it."

"It was out on the runway." Alice was getting annoyed. "It would have rusted out. What difference does it make?"

And Tommy couldn't explain. They should have kept it because one day we'll be going back. Because it was part of something important and you don't just tear things like that apart to make hoes and rakes. Because they didn't know whether the astronauts would come back or not and suppose they had?

Alice was the tallest of the three. She had a dark complexion and dark eyes and a quick smile. And she tried to tell him he was making too much of it, that what else would you do with a wreck sitting in the middle of the runway? That they just flat out needed the metal.

They didn't play the Mars game anymore after that. And a couple of days later Alice tried to kiss him but he didn't let her.

The freeze came early. Tommy helped with the horses, chopped firewood, brought in water, and occasionally took the wagon over to Rob's feed store to pick up supplies.

They had a few books in the house, some novels that he read over and over, *David Copperfield* and *Northanger Abbey* and one that he didn't understand about the end of the Civil War. There was a history of the United States, which everybody pretended still existed out there somewhere, and a Bible, a book on needlecraft that had belonged to Aunt Emma, and the book that Tommy especially liked, a big volume called *Galaxies*, with lots of pictures.

They'd had only a Bible at his mother's house and he hadn't even realized there *were* other books until Uncle Harold had come after Ma's death and brought him here.

He understood that the galaxies were very far, and that the *Columbia* could never have reached them. But he liked to imagine going out to them anyhow, taking a right turn at Mars, and snuggling warm and happy in the cockpit while he watched the stars grow in number and size.

Columbia is still up there. Docked at the station. And on nights when it's clear, you can see it, a bright light in the south that never moves, that keeps its place while the stars race past.

Out of reach now. Forever.

We should have saved the lander.

He rode out on Poke one night close to Christmas, back to the place where he'd sat with Uncle Harold. It was unseasonably warm, the stars were bright, and there was no moon in the sky. The station sparkled in its accustomed place, above the old interstate.

Uncle Harold didn't like him riding out here alone after dark. Minutes after he'd left, he heard the outside kitchen door slam and knew his uncle had missed him, knew he'd follow pretty soon.

He looked back toward the east and watched the lander drop slowly out of the sky, brighter than any star. Brighter even than the station. It had four lights, one on each wingtip, one on its belly, and one atop the tail. He didn't really know whether that had been so, and nobody he'd asked knew either. But it didn't matter. That was the way he imagined it, so it had become the only truth there was.

It came in slow and the lights were visible the whole time. A few people rode out of town to see what was happening. He could hear them talking and asking one another whether help was coming at last. From the government.

The lander dropped down through the night, and the blaze of its lights silhouetted Uncle Harold, coming easy on Monty. Its engines roared and the wings waggled slightly as a burst of rain hit them. The airstrip lay open and clear before the descending spacecraft.

Tommy inched up in his saddle so he could see better. Poke dug at a piece of sod with his front hoof.

It touched down and rolled along the runway, maybe jouncing a bit because it was coming too fast and braking too hard.

The riders watched it slow and tip over and stop. For a long time nothing happened. A few of the horsemen approached and hatches popped open. The lights went off, first the ones on the wingtips, and then the others. Three astronauts climbed out and stood looking around.

"You okay, Tommy?" Uncle Harold was still riding slow.

There were tears in the boy's eyes. "You shouldn't have taken it apart," he said.

His uncle came up alongside him, clamped a big hand down on his shoulder, and squeezed. "Tommy, it's time to let it go."

Tommy just sat his horse.

Uncle Harold nodded. "You warm enough, son?"

"You think they did the right thing. That makes you just as bad."

"Why is it so important? That the lander was broken up?"

"Because of where it's been. Because maybe we can go back one day. Because we *need* it." Tommy was trying to keep his voice level, to keep the strangled sounds out of it.

Harold held out a kerchief, and waited while the boy took it and blew his nose and wiped his eyes. "Tommy, people here did what they had to. I'm not saying we wouldn't have made it otherwise, but the rest of the world was dead, as far as we knew. Everything that would give us an edge, we had to use."

"Not the lander. That's what takes us back."

Harold looked up at the sky. At the station. "No," he said, "it's not the lander. We can make a new one when the time comes. What we have to have, what we absolutely cannot do without, is *you*. And Alice. And Frank." He pulled his collar up around his neck. The temperature was starting to drop. "We survived, boy. *That's* what matters. First things first."

Tommy was silent.

"We *will* go back. Maybe *you* will. But you've got to be alive to do it."

"No. It's not going to happen."

Harold pulled his scarf up around his face. His gaze moved past Tommy and fastened on the house. They could see the glow of the oil lamp in the living room. He tugged gently on Tommy's reins and started back. Tommy pressed Poke's flank and followed.

They were both looking at the sky. "Which one's Mars?" Harold asked. Tommy showed him.

"Duller than I thought," he said.

Poke picked up the pace and they trotted at a leisurely clip beneath the stars.

MARIAN CARCACHE

The Moon and the Stars

Marian Carcache has published fiction and articles in Shenandoah, Mississippi Quarterly, The Chattahoochee Review,
Belles' Letters: Contemporary Stories by Alabama
Women, *and elsewhere. An opera based on her short story
"Under the Arbor" premiered in 1992 and was televised on PBS
in 1993; the opera was nominated for a regional Emmy and
was a finalist at the International Festival of Film and Television in 1995. A native of Russell County, Alabama, Marian
holds an M.A. in hispanic studies and a Ph.D. in literature
from Auburn University, where she is currently an instructor.
She lives in Auburn with her son, John-David. This marks the
first publication of "The Moon and the Stars."*

The first time John Starbuck Lumiere saw Lily Paris, she was swinging on a crescent moon inside a bar off Bourbon Street called the Pearl Palace. John had counted his french fries at the Dairy Queen earlier that day and found that there were twenty-seven. Later, in traffic, he got behind a Blue Bird school bus, number 27. When Lily came down off the moon to take a break, he mustered the courage and started a conversation with her, during which he learned that she was twenty-seven years old. A strong believer in signs and wonders, John Starbuck was then convinced that Lily was the woman Fate had designated for him.

Years later, Johnny Paris, the son of John Starbuck and Lily, found a framed photograph of his mama, a picture she had given John Starbuck soon after they met. It was a picture of Lily at work, riding her moon, and was inscribed "To John Starbuck—my lucky star—Love, Lily." In the photo, Lily was sitting in the curve of her crescent, wearing a skimpy wizard's costume that showed her pretty legs to great advantage, and she was flashing a pearly smile that was, at once, both flirtatious and shy. Lily was actually swinging on the moon, but whenever Johnny tried to piece together the fragmented information he had gathered about his past, for some reason, he thought of his mama straddling the moon, riding it through the night sky as if it were a white stallion.

Unlike most people, he had the advantage of never knowing his parents and could, therefore, imagine them the way he wanted them to be. By the time Johnny was born, his daddy was long gone. Nobody really knew where or why, but popular opinion around Bourbon Street was that Lily's mama, a still-pretty old lady named Delphine, who knew roots, had "fixed" him. Most people figured he was dead. After all, he had left Lily a little too heavy to keep her job swinging on the moon at the Pearl Palace. It wasn't uncommon to hear speculation that John Starbuck was at the bottom of the bay, sleeping with the fishes.

Since Lily bled to death giving birth to him, and everyone else who knew what happened was afraid of Delphine, Johnny had no way of finding the truth. And John Starbuck never even knew he had a living son. Only the old lady knew what really happened, the old lady and a servant who saw and overheard things in Delphine's house that made even her mostly Haitian blood run cold. She heard the old lady cut a deal with Lily: "Let him go," Delphine had said, "and he lives. Try to keep him, and I put a curse on him worse than Satan's Own could imagine. Not just on him, but on every poor soul who shares an ounce of blood from his bloodline."

Lily had seen the damage her mother could do. She had seen the handsome unfaithful men of some of Delphine's wealthy female clients transform overnight into bloated froglike creatures. She had seen beautiful women drawn irresistibly to liver-lipped men who seemed to have been formed from flour paste, but had been fortunate enough to afford Delphine's services. And worst of all, she had seen what could happen to stunning young women who agreed to be the kept lovers of the husbands of wealthy termagants with money enough to buy Delphine's strongest curse. A beautiful goddess could transmogrify into the face of death within a week. And in all of these cases, Delphine had had only a business interest. Lily shuddered at the thought of what her mother might come up with when her own personal interests were involved.

So Lily, who knew roots herself, though not as well as her mother, let John Starbuck go with every intention of strengthening her own powers, hexing the old lady into oblivion, and rejoining her lover at a later date. She pleaded for one more week with John Starbuck, promising that after that week, she would not even mention his name again. The old lady, briefly remembering the passion of her own youth, reluctantly agreed, and Lily began her own brand of magic: the infiltration of his senses.

Knowing that John drank many cups of his favorite chicory coffee each day, Lily built a ritual around coffee drinking so that she became inextricably connected with it in John Starbuck's mind. She made his coffee strong and then added thick, sweetened condensed milk, teasing him that she had sweetened it with her own love juices. She knew by the look in his eyes that he half believed her, and that he'd never drink coffee again without remembering the taste of her love.

Lily easily coaxed her lover into Electric Eddie's tattoo parlor, where they both submitted to the needle of the man whose reputation as an artist often took second place to the stories about the framed samples of tattooed human skin that decorated the walls of his shop. Some said he took them from corpses; others told that he bought them from living former clients, now down on their luck. Having grown up in Delphine's house, Lily was not easily made squeamish, so she found such stories more fascinating than horrifying. And John Starbuck was so deeply in Lily's thrall by now that he hardly felt the needle, let alone the sublime horror of being in a seedy back alley in a room papered with human flesh. All that his conscious mind could acknowledge was that he was being tattooed with a lily, the symbol of his love. He never noticed that it was the same lily Eddie used in most of his Jesus designs because, this time, instead of superimposing it on a cross or making it appear to grow out of a bleeding heart, Eddie put it inside a crescent moon, and etched it forever on John Starbuck's inner thigh. For herself, Lily chose a small star, a simple enough design, that she had put on the tender flesh of her left breast—right above her heart.

The sense of hearing gave Lily the most trouble. She had to think of the one sound of the many noises John would hear every day that she could count on to make him not just think of her, but think of her so strongly that he smelled, tasted, felt her. For three days, she fretted over the sense of sound before the obvious became clear to her: the heartbeat, her own, John Starbuck's, that of their unborn child. On that third day, she began the great performance of listening to heartbeats. Her tears ran down John's chest as she listened to his marvelous heart and wondered how many months would pass before she lay so close to him again. She listened to his heart beating calmly as he held her. She listened to it beat more and more rapidly as he desired her. She heard it almost burst as he loved her, and then grow calm again as he fell asleep holding her. But even more important to her quest was when, having satisfied himself with her breasts, he rested his head on her heart and listened to the sound he could never forget. And then the crowning moment: when he moved his head downward and listened for a while to the heartbeat of the child inside her.

Their usual lovemaking included the use of oils and incenses. Lily created mood with scented candles and incense. She massaged her lover's tired shoulders with the essential oils of aromatic plants. And as she worked with the fragrances she knew to be ruled by Venus—patchouli, bergamot, ylang-ylang—she called on the goddess of Love to keep John true to her until she could get rid of the curse of Delphine and be with him forever. But on her final night with John, she went even further. She bought and stole and begged for roses until she had enough to make a blanket of rose petals to lead her lover to by the light of the midnight moon. She knew her efforts had been rewarded as their bodies pressed and bruised the tender petals. The sweet odor of rose came in waves, and it seemed to Lily that she and John Starbuck left the ground momentarily and floated like the scent of the rose petals on the dewy midnight breeze. And it also seemed to Lily that every time the sweet wave of rose washed over them, the baby kicked, as if he smelled it too.

By the time her week was up, Lily knew she had succeeded. She knew she was part of John Starbuck Lumiere's being now, had invaded his heart and mind and soul, his very blood, like a virus. When he went away to find a place to wait in for her to join him, far away from Delphine and her blacker magic, he was no longer just John Starbuck; he was Lily, too.

The old lady found him when Lily died. When she sent the Haitian to tell him that Lily had bled to death giving birth to a stillborn baby, his heart broke, his mind unraveled, his soul dried up. He returned to New Orleans in a daze and wept on Lily's grave. So grief-stricken was he that he took the old woman's word that the baby had died and been buried, unnamed, in the coffin with its mother. Then he left New Orleans, numb, never knowing that he was leaving behind a living son whom Lily had called Johnny the one time she had held him before she died. Never knowing that he was leaving their baby to be brought up by Delphine, the root doctor.

All he did know was that every time he smelled roses or tasted coffee or saw the lily tattooed on his thigh, his broken heart shattered into tinier pieces. Finally, to escape the pain brought on by the beating of his own heart, he willed it to stop. A derelict, searching for food or treasure in garbage cans, found John frozen in an alley on a hot, muggy morning in Baton Rouge. He was buried by the city, not as John Starbuck Lumiere but simply as John Doe. The coroner's report identified him only as a vagrant with a distinguishing mark: a tattoo of a star under his left nipple.

KELLY LINK

The Specialist's Hat

Kelly Link won the James Tiptree Jr. Award in 1997 for her story "Travels with the Snow Queen" and the Nebula Award in 2002 for her story "Louise's Ghost." "The Specialist's Hat" won the World Fantasy Award in 1999. Her debut collection, Stranger Things Happen, *was named a* Village Voice *Favorite and a* Salon *Book of the Year. Kelly is the editor of* Trampoline, *an anthology of original fiction. Her most recent stories have appeared in* The Dark, Conjunctions 39: The New Wave Fabulists *and* McSweeny's Mammoth Treasury of Thrilling Tales. *She holds an M.F.A. in creative writing from the University of North Carolina at Greensboro and now lives in Northampton, Massachusetts, with her husband, author Gavin J. Grant, with whom she co-edits the ʒine* Lady Churchill's Rosebud Wristlet. *Beginning in 2003, she and Gavin are co-editors of the fantasy half of* The Year's Best Fantasy and Horror. *"The Specialist's Hat" was first published in* Event Horizon.

"When you're Dead," Samantha says, "you don't have to brush your teeth. . . ."

"When you're Dead," Claire says, "you live in a box, and it's always dark, but you're not ever afraid."

Claire and Samantha are identical twins. Their combined age is twenty years, four months, and six days. Claire is better at being Dead than Samantha.

The baby-sitter yawns, covering up her mouth with a long white hand. "I said to brush your teeth and that it's time for bed," she says. She sits crosslegged on the flowered bedspread between them. She has been teaching them a card game called Pounce, which involves three decks of cards, one for each of them. Samantha's deck is missing the Jack of Spades and the Two of Hearts, and Claire keeps on cheating. The baby-sitter wins anyway. There are still flecks of dried shaving cream and toilet paper on her arms. It is hard to tell how old she is—at first they thought she must be a grown-up, but now she hardly looks older than them. Samantha has forgotten the baby-sitter's name.

Claire's face is stubborn. "When you're Dead," she says, "you stay up all night long."

"When you're dead," the baby-sitter snaps, "it's always very cold and damp, and you have to be very, very quiet or else the Specialist will get you."

"This house is haunted," Claire says.

"I know it is," the baby-sitter says. "I used to live here."

Something is creeping up the stairs,
Something is standing outside the door,
Something is sobbing, sobbing in the dark;
Something is sighing across the floor.

Claire and Samantha are spending the summer with their father, in the house called Eight Chimneys. Their mother is dead. She has been dead for exactly 282 days.

Their father is writing a history of Eight Chimneys, and of the poet, Charles Cheatham Rash, who lived here at the turn of the century, and who ran away to sea when he was thirteen and returned when he was thirty-eight. He married, fathered a child, wrote three volumes of bad, obscure poetry and an even worse and more obscure novel, *The One Who Is Watching Me Through the Window*, before disappearing again in 1907, this time for good. Samantha and Claire's father says that some of the poetry is actually quite readable, and at least the novel isn't very long.

When Samantha asked him why he was writing about Rash, he replied that no one else had, and why didn't she and Samantha go play outside. When she pointed out that she was Samantha, he just scowled and said how could he be expected to tell them apart when they both wore blue jeans and flannel shirts, and why couldn't one of them dress all in green and the other in pink?

Claire and Samantha prefer to play inside. Eight Chimneys is as big as a castle, but dustier and darker than Samantha imagines a castle would be. There are more sofas (there are eighteen sofas), more china shepherdesses with chipped fingers (six shepherdesses, thirteen chipped fingers), fewer suits of armor (one pair of gauntlets). No moat (zero moats).

The house is open to the public, and during the day, people—families—driving along the Blue Ridge Parkway will stop to tour the grounds and the first story; the third story belongs to Claire and Samantha. Sometimes they play explorers, and sometimes they follow the caretaker as he gives tours to visitors. After a few weeks, they have memorized his lecture, and they mouth it along with him. They help him sell postcards and copies of Rash's poetry to the tourist families who come into the little gift shop.

When the mothers smile at them, and say how sweet they are, they stare back and don't say anything at all. The dim light in the house makes the mothers look pale and flickery and tired. They leave Eight Chimneys, mothers and families, looking not quite as real as they did before they paid their admissions, and of course Claire and Samantha will never see them again, so maybe they aren't real. Better to stay inside the house, they want to tell the families, and if you must leave, then go straight to your cars.

The caretaker says the woods aren't safe.

Their father stays in the library on the second story all morning, typing, and in the afternoon he takes long walks. He takes his pocket recorder along with him, and a hip flask of Gentleman Jack, but not Samantha and Claire.

The caretaker of Eight Chimneys is Mr. Coeslak. His left leg is noticeably shorter than his right. He wears one stacked heel. Short black hairs grow out of his ears and his nostrils and there is no hair at all on top of his head, but he's given Samantha and Claire permission to explore the whole of the house. It was Mr. Coeslak who told them that there are copperheads in the woods, and that the house is haunted. He says they are all, ghosts and snakes, a pretty bad-tempered lot, and Samantha and Claire should stick to the marked trails, and stay out of the attic.

Mr. Coeslak can tell the twins apart, even if their father can't; Claire's eyes are grey, like a cat's fur, he says, but Samantha's are *gray*, like the ocean when it has been raining.

Samantha and Claire went walking in the woods on the second day that they were at Eight Chimneys. They saw something. Samantha thought it was a woman, but Claire said it was a snake. The staircase that goes up to the attic has been locked. They peeked through the keyhole, but it was too dark to see anything.

And so he had a wife, and they say she was real pretty. There was another man who wanted to go with her, and first she wouldn't, because she was afraid of her husband, and then she did. Her husband found out, and they say he killed a snake and got some of this snake's blood and put it in some whiskey and gave it to her. He had learned this from an island man who had been on a ship with him. And in about six months snakes created in her and they got between her meat and the skin. And they say you could just see them running up and down her legs. They say she was just hollow to the top of her body, and it kept on like that till she died. Now my daddy said he saw it.

—An Oral History of Eight Chimneys

Eight Chimneys is over two hundred years old. It is named for the eight chimneys, which are each big enough that Samantha and Claire can both fit in one fireplace. The chimneys are red brick, and on each floor there are eight fireplaces, making a total of twenty-four. Samantha imagines the chimney stacks stretching like stout red tree trunks, all the way up through the slate roof of the house. Beside each fireplace is a heavy black firedog, and a set of wrought-iron pokers shaped like snakes. Claire and Samantha pretend to duel with the snake-pokers before the fireplace in their bedroom on the third floor. Wind rises up the back of the chimney. When they stick their faces in, they can feel the air rushing damply upward, like a river. The flue smells old and sooty and wet, like stones from a river.

Their bedroom was once the nursery. They sleep together in a poster bed that resembles a ship with four masts. It smells of mothballs, and Claire kicks in her sleep. Charles Cheatham Rash slept here when he was a little boy, and also his daughter. She disappeared when her father did. It might have been gambling debts. They may have moved to New Orleans. She was fourteen years old, Mr. Coeslak said. What was her name? Claire asked. What happened to her mother? Samantha wanted to know. Mr. Coeslak closed his eyes in an almost wink. Mrs. Rash had died the year before her husband and daughter disappeared, he said, of a mysterious wasting disease. He can't remember the name of the poor little girl, he said.

Eight Chimneys has exactly one hundred windows, all still with the original wavery panes of handblown glass. With so many windows, Samantha thinks, Eight Chimneys should always be full of light, but instead the trees press close against the house, so that the rooms on the first and second story—even the third-story rooms—are green and dim, as if Samantha and Claire are living deep under the sea. This is the light that makes the tourists into ghosts. In the morning, and again towards evening, a fog settles in around the house. Sometimes it is grey like Claire's eyes, and sometimes it is gray, like Samantha's eyes.

I met a woman in the wood,
Her lips were two red snakes.

She smiled at me, her eyes were lewd
And burning like a fire.

A few nights ago, the wind was sighing in the nursery chimney. Their father had already tucked them in, and turned off the light. Claire dared Samantha to stick her head into the fireplace, in the dark, and so she did. The cold, wet air licked at her face, and it almost sounded like voices talking low, muttering. She couldn't quite make out what they were saying.

Their father has mostly ignored Claire and Samantha since they arrived at Eight Chimneys. He never mentions their mother. One evening they heard him shouting in the library, and when they came downstairs, there was a large sticky stain on the desk, where a glass of whiskey had been knocked over. It was looking at me, he said, through the window. It had orange eyes.

Samantha and Claire refrained from pointing out that the library is on the second story.

At night, their father's breath has been sweet from drinking, and he is spending more and more time in the woods, and less in the library. At dinner, usually hot dogs and baked beans from a can, which they eat off paper plates in the first floor dining room, beneath the Austrian chandelier (which has exactly 632 leaded crystals shaped like teardrops) their father recites the poetry of Charles Cheatham Rash, which neither Samantha nor Claire cares for.

He has been reading the ship diaries that Rash kept, and he says that he has discovered proof in them that Rash's most famous poem, "The Specialist's Hat," is not a poem at all, and in any case, Rash didn't write it. It is something that one of the men on the whaler used to say, to conjure up a whale. Rash simply copied it down and stuck an end on it and said it was his.

The man was from Mulatuppu, which is a place neither Samantha nor Claire has ever heard of. Their father says that the man was supposed to be some sort of magician, but he drowned shortly before Rash came back to Eight Chimneys. Their father says that the other sailors wanted to throw the magician's chest overboard, but Rash persuaded them to let him keep it until he could be put ashore, with the chest, off the coast of North Carolina.

The specialist's hat makes a noise like an agouti;
The specialist's hat makes a noise like a collared peccary;
The specialist's hat makes a noise like a white-lipped peccary;
The specialist's hat makes a noise like a tapir;
The specialist's hat makes a noise like a rabbit;
The specialist's hat makes a noise like a squirrel;
The specialist's hat makes a noise like a curassow;
The specialist's hat moans like a whale in the water;
The specialist's hat moans like the wind in my wife's hair;
The specialist's hat makes a noise like a snake;
I have hung the hat of the specialist upon my wall.

The reason that Claire and Samantha have a baby-sitter is that their father met a woman in the woods. He is going to see her tonight, and they are going to have a picnic supper and look at the stars. This is the time of year when the Perseids can be seen, falling across the sky on clear nights. Their father said that he has been walking with the woman every afternoon. She is a distant relation of Rash, and besides, he said, he needs a night off and some grown-up conversation.

Mr. Coeslak won't stay in the house after dark, but he agreed to find someone to look after Samantha and Claire. Then their father couldn't find Mr. Coeslak, but the baby-sitter showed up precisely at seven o'clock. The baby-sitter, whose name neither twin quite caught, wears a blue cotton dress with short floaty sleeves. Both Samantha and Claire think she is pretty in an old-fashioned sort of way.

They were in the library with their father, looking up Mulatuppu in the red leather atlas, when she arrived. She didn't knock on the front door, she simply walked in and then up the stairs, as if she knew where to find them.

Their father kissed them good-bye, a hasty smack, told them to be good and he would take them into town on the weekend to see the Disney film. They went to the window to watch as he walked into the woods. Already, it was getting dark, and there were fireflies, tiny yellow-hot sparks in the air. When their father had entirely disappeared into the trees, they turned around and stared at the baby-sitter instead. She raised one eyebrow. "Well," she said. "What sort of games do you like to play?"

Widdershins around the chimneys,
once, twice, again.
The spokes click like a clock on the bicycle;
they tick down the days of the life of a man.

First they played Go Fish, and then they played Crazy Eights, and then they made the baby-sitter into a mummy by putting shaving cream from their father's bathroom on her arms and legs, and wrapping her in toilet paper. She is the best baby-sitter they have ever had.

At nine-thirty, she tried to put them to bed. Neither Claire nor Samantha wanted to go to bed, so they began to play the Dead game. The Dead game is a let's-pretend that they have been playing every day for 274 days now, but never in front of their father or any other adult. When they are Dead, they are allowed to do anything they want to. They can even fly by jumping off the nursery beds, and just waving their arms. Someday this will work, if they practice hard enough.

The Dead game has three rules.

One. Numbers are significant. The twins keep a list of important numbers in a green address book that belonged to their mother. Mr. Coeslak's tour has been a good source of significant amounts and tallies: they are writing a tragical history of numbers.

Two. The twins don't play the Dead game in front of grown-ups. They have been summing up the baby-sitter, and have decided that she doesn't count. They tell her the rules.

Three is the best and most important rule. When you are Dead, you don't have to be afraid of anything. Samantha and Claire aren't sure who the Specialist is, but they aren't afraid of him.

To become Dead, they hold their breath while counting to thirty-five, which is as high as their mother got, not counting a few days.

"You never lived here," Claire says. "Mr. Coeslak lives here."

"Not at night," says the baby-sitter. "This was my bedroom when I was little."

"Really?" Samantha says. Claire says, "Prove it."

The baby-sitter gives Samantha and Claire a look, as if she is measuring them: how old; how smart; how brave; how tall. Then she nods. The wind is in the flue, and in the dim nursery light they can see the milky strands of fog seeping out of the fireplace. "Go stand in the chimney," she instructs them. "Stick your hand as far up as you can, and there is a little hole on the left side, with a key in it."

Samantha looks at Claire, who says, "Go ahead." Claire is fifteen minutes and some few uncounted seconds older than Samantha, and therefore gets to tell Samantha what to do. Samantha remembers the muttering voices and then reminds herself that she is Dead. She goes over to the fireplace and ducks inside.

When Samantha stands up in the chimney, she can only see the very edge of the room. She can see the fringe of the mothy blue rug, and one bed leg, and beside it, Claire's foot, swinging back and forth like a metronome. Claire's shoelace has come undone, and there is a band-aid on her ankle. It all looks very pleasant and peaceful from inside the chimney, like a dream, and for a moment, she almost wishes she didn't have to be Dead. But it's safer, really.

She sticks her left hand up as far as she can reach, trailing it along the crumbly wall, until she feels an indentation. She thinks about spiders and severed fingers, and rusty razor blades, and then she reaches inside. She keeps her eyes lowered, focused on the corner of the room and Claire's twitchy foot.

Inside the hole, there is a tiny cold key, its teeth facing outward. She pulls it out, and ducks back into the room. "She wasn't lying," she tells Claire.

"Of course I wasn't lying," the baby-sitter says. "When you're Dead, you're not allowed to tell lies."

"Unless you want to," Claire says.

Dreary and dreadful beats the sea at the shore.
Ghastly and dripping is the mist at the door.
The clock in the hall is chiming one, two, three, four.
The morning comes not, no, never, no more.

Samantha and Claire have gone to camp for three weeks every summer since they were seven. This year their father didn't ask them if they wanted to go back, and after discussing it, they decided that it was just as well. They didn't want to have to explain to all their friends how they were half orphans now. They are used to being envied, because they are identical twins. They don't want to be pitiful.

It has not even been a year, but Samantha realizes that she is forgetting what her mother looked like. Not her mother's face so much as the way she smelled, which was something like dry hay and something like Chanel No. 5, and like something else too. She can't remember whether her mother had gray eyes, like her, or grey eyes, like Claire. She doesn't dream about her mother anymore, but she does dream about Prince Charming, a bay whom she once rode in the horse show at her camp. In the dream, Prince Charming did not smell like a horse at all. He smelled like Chanel No. 5. When she is Dead, she can have all the horses she wants, and they all smell like Chanel No. 5.

"Where does the key go to?" Samantha says.

The baby-sitter holds out her hand. "To the attic. You don't really need it, but taking the stairs is easier than the chimney. At least the first time."

"Aren't you going to make us go to bed?" Claire says.

The baby-sitter ignores Claire. "My father used to lock me in the attic when I was little, but I didn't mind. There was a bicycle up there and I used to ride it around and around the chimneys until my mother let me out again. Do you know how to ride a bicycle?"

"Of course," Claire says.

"If you ride fast enough, the Specialist can't catch you."

"What's the Specialist?" Samantha says. Bicycles are okay, but horses can go faster.

"The Specialist wears a hat," says the baby-sitter. "The hat makes noises."

She doesn't say anything else.

When you're dead, the grass is greener
Over your grave. The wind is keener.
Your eyes sink in, your flesh decays. You
Grow accustomed to slowness; expect delays.

The attic is somehow bigger and lonelier than Samantha and Claire thought it would be. The baby-sitter's key opens the locked door at the end of the hallway. Behind the door is a narrow set of stairs. She waves them ahead and upwards.

It isn't as dark in the attic as they had imagined. The oaks that block the light and make the first three stories so dim and green and mysterious during the day don't reach all the way up. Extravagant moonlight, dusty and pale, streams in the angled dormer windows. It lights the length of the attic, which is wide enough to hold a softball game in, and lined with trunks where Samantha imagines people could sit, could be hiding and watching. The ceiling slopes down, impaled upon the eight thickwaisted chimney stacks. The chimneys seem too alive, somehow, to be contained in this empty, neglected place; they thrust almost angrily through the roof and attic floor. In the moonlight they look like they are breathing. "They're so beautiful," she says.

"Which chimney is the nursery chimney?" Claire says.

The baby-sitter points to the nearest righthand stack. "That one," she says. "It runs up through the ballroom on the first floor, the library, the nursery."

Hanging from a nail on the nursery chimney is a long, black object. It looks lumpy and heavy, as if it were full of things. The baby-sitter takes it down, twirls it on her finger. There are holes in the black thing, and it whistles mournfully as she spins it. "The Specialist's hat," she says.

"That doesn't look like a hat," says Claire. "It doesn't look like anything at all." She goes to look through the boxes and trunks that are stacked against the far wall.

"It's a special hat," the baby-sitter says. "It's not supposed to look like anything. But it can sound like anything you can imagine. My father made it."

"Our father writes books," Samantha says.

"My father did too." The baby-sitter hangs the hat back on the nail. It curls blackly against the chimney. Samantha stares at it. It nickers at her. "He was a bad poet, but he was worse at magic."

Last summer, Samantha wished more than anything that she could have a horse. She thought she would have given up anything for one—even being a twin was not as good as having a horse. She still doesn't have a horse, but she doesn't have a mother either, and she can't help wondering if it's her fault. The hat nickers again, or maybe it is the wind in the chimney.

"What happened to him?" Claire asks.

"After he made the hat, the Specialist came and took him away. I hid in the nursery chimney while it was looking for him, and it didn't find me."

"Weren't you scared?"

There is a clattering, shivering, clicking noise. Claire has found the baby-sitter's bike and is dragging it towards them by the handlebars. The baby-sitter shrugs. "Rule number three," she says.

Claire snatches the hat off the nail. "I'm the Specialist!" she says, putting the hat on her head. It falls over her eyes, the floppy shapeless brim sewn with little asymmetrical buttons that flash and catch at the moonlight like teeth. Samantha looks again, and sees that they are teeth. Without counting, she suddenly knows that there are exactly fifty-two teeth on the hat, and that they are the teeth of agoutis, of curassows, of white-lipped peccaries, and of the wife of Charles Cheatham Rash. The chimneys are moaning, and Claire's voice booms hollowly beneath the hat. "Run away, or I'll catch you. I'll eat you!"

Samantha and the baby-sitter run away, laughing as Claire mounts the rusty, noisy bicycle and pedals madly after them. She rings the bicycle bell as she rides, and the Specialist's hat bobs up and down on her head. It spits like a cat. The bell is shrill and thin, and the bike wails and shrieks. It leans first towards the right and then to the left. Claire's knobby knees stick out on either side like makeshift counterweights.

Claire weaves in and out between the chimneys, chasing Samantha and the baby-sitter. Samantha is slow, turning to look behind. As Claire approaches, she keeps one hand on the handlebars and stretches the other hand out towards Samantha. Just as she is about to grab Samantha, the baby-sitter turns back and plucks the hat off Claire's head.

"Shit!" the baby-sitter says, and drops it. There is a drop of blood forming on the fleshy part of the baby-sitter's hand, black in the moonlight, where the Specialist's hat has bitten her.

Claire dismounts, giggling. Samantha watches as the Specialist's hat rolls away. It picks up speed, veering across the attic floor, and disappears, thumping down the stairs. "Go get it," Claire says. "You can be the Specialist this time."

"No," the baby-sitter says, sucking at her palm. "It's time for bed."

When they go down the stairs, there is no sign of the Specialist's hat. They brush their teeth, climb into the ship-bed, and pull the covers up to their necks. The baby-sitter sits between their feet. "When you're Dead," Samantha says, "do you still get tired and have to go to sleep? Do you have dreams?"

"When you're Dead," the baby-sitter says, "everything's a lot easier. You don't have to do anything that you don't want to. You don't have to have a name, you don't have to remember. You don't even have to breathe."

She shows them exactly what she means.

When she has time to think about it, (and now she has all the time in the world to think) Samantha realizes with a small pang that she is now stuck indefinitely between ten and eleven years old, stuck with Claire and the baby-sitter. She considers this. The number 10 is pleasing and round, like a beach ball, but all in all, it hasn't been an easy year. She wonders what 11 would have been like. Sharper, like needles maybe. She has chosen to be Dead, instead. She hopes that she's made the right decision. She wonders if her mother would have decided to be Dead, instead of dead, if she could have.

Last year they were learning fractions in school, when her mother died. Fractions remind Samantha of herds of wild horses, piebalds and pintos and palominos. There are so many of them, and they are, well, fractious and unruly. Just when you think you have one under control, it throws up its head and tosses you off. Claire's favorite number is 4, which she says is a tall, skinny boy. Samantha doesn't care for boys that much. She likes numbers. Take the number 8 for instance, which can be more than one thing at once. Looked at one way, 8 looks like a bent woman with curvy hair. But if you lay it down on its side, it looks like a snake curled with its tail in its mouth. This is sort of like the difference between being Dead, and being dead. Maybe when Samantha is tired of one, she will try the other.

On the lawn, under the oak trees, she hears someone calling her name. Samantha climbs out of bed and goes to the nursery window. She looks out through the wavy glass. It's Mr. Coeslak. "Samantha, Claire!" he calls up to her. "Are you all right? Is your father there?" Samantha can almost see the moonlight shining through him. "They're always locking me in the tool-room. Goddamn spooky things," he says. "Are you there, Samantha? Claire? Girls?"

The baby-sitter comes and stands beside Samantha. The baby-sitter puts her finger to her lip. Claire's eyes glitter at them from the dark bed. Samantha doesn't say anything, but she waves at Mr. Coeslak. The baby-sitter waves too. Maybe he can see them waving, because after a little while he stops shouting and goes away. "Be careful," the baby-sitter says. "*He'll* be coming soon. It will be coming soon."

She takes Samantha's hand, and leads her back to the bed, where Claire is waiting. They sit and wait. Time passes, but they don't get tired, they don't get any older.

Who's there?
Just air.

The front door opens on the first floor, and Samantha, Claire, and the baby-sitter can hear someone creeping, creeping up the stairs. "Be quiet," the baby-sitter says. "It's the Specialist."

Samantha and Claire are quiet. The nursery is dark and the wind crackles like a fire in the fireplace.

"Claire, Samantha, Samantha, Claire?" The Specialist's voice is blurry and wet. It sounds like their father's voice, but that's because the hat can imitate any noise, any voice. "Are you still awake?"

"Quick," the baby-sitter says. "It's time to go up to the attic and hide."

Claire and Samantha slip out from under the covers and dress quickly and silently. They follow her. Without speech, without breathing, she pulls them into the safety of the chimney. It is too dark to see, but they understand the baby-sitter perfectly when she mouths the word *Up*. She goes first, so they can see where the fingerholds are, the bricks that jut out for their feet. Then Claire. Samantha watches her sister's foot ascend like smoke, the shoelace still untied.

"Claire? Samantha? Goddamn it, you're scaring me. Where are you?" The Specialist is standing just outside the half-open door. "Samantha? I think I've been bitten by something. I think I've been bitten by a goddamn snake." Samantha hesitates for only a second. Then she is climbing up, up, up the nursery chimney.

BUD WEBSTER

Christus Destitutus

Bud Webster has published fiction in numerous magazines and anthologies, including Analog Science Fiction, Drums Around the Fire, New Dominions, *and* Interzone. *His poem "The Ballad of Kansas McGriff" won first place in the National Hobo Association Rendezvous 2000 Poetry Contest. His work has been reprinted in* The Year's Best Fantasy and Horror. *He has also contributed articles about fantastic literature to the* New York Review of Science Fiction, The Magazine of Fantasy and Science Fiction, *and* Supernatural Fiction Writers, *published by Gale, as well as a quarterly column in* Chronicle. *He lives in Richmond, Virginia. This marks the first publication of "Christus Destitutus."*

Jesus lay dying in a five-dollar flop. Dark against the sheets, his face and hands were marked and bent by every day of his seventy years; his thin body barely made a dent in the old mattress.

None of the beds in the shelter's clinic were empty. There was no shortage of old men too poor for the hospitals or for whom there was simply no room elsewhere. Once, he had tended the hopeless old men in these beds; now he was just one more of them.

"Yeshua bar-Yosef." The voice was lifeless; the words a statement, not a question. It was his birth name; no one had called him that for two thousand years.

He opened his eyes.

"Oh," he said, "it's you. What are you doing here?"

The old man glanced down the aisle to the desk where Vic sat. If the floor supervisor had heard the voices, he gave no sign. The words weren't English—weren't any earthly tongue—but it wouldn't matter anyway; there was always the low murmur of voices here. Some patients prayed, some babbled, or cried out in pain; if you were here long enough, you got used to it.

He wouldn't see the angel standing over the old man's bed.

"I am here for you," the angel said.

"Yeah, well, I didn't call for you. Go away."

"It is not permitted."

"By who? Him? Screw Him," the old man said hotly. "It's not His life. It never was. Leave me alone, Uriel."

"It does not have to be your time."

"Bullshit. It's been my time for the past twenty centuries. It's *always* been my time. Go away and let me die in peace."

"It is not permitted. You know this."

The old man sighed; his lungs crackled, and it turned into a coughing fit.

" 'Angelic compassion,' " he finally managed. "You're inhuman. You can't know."

"What can I not know?"

"What your compassion is for, that's what. What a joke." The old man reached for a chipped mug on the table next to the bed. The messenger watched, but did nothing to help.

The cup shook as he tried to lift it to his lips, spilling water on the worn blanket.

"Here, Pete. Lemme help ya." The supervisor, alarmed by the old man's coughing, had hurried over. He cranked the head of the bed to a sitting position and held the cup so the old man could drink. "You okay now? You want me to call Father Nicholas?"

"Nah, Vic. I'm as okay as I can be, I guess. Thanks."

"Hey, 's awright. You'd do th' same." Patting the old man's hand, he returned the cup to the little table and walked back to his desk.

"That, Uriel. *That's* compassion. That's *humanity*." He shook his head against the pillow. "I pity you, all of you, because you'll never know."

The Messenger said nothing.

"They've had many names for you. Cherubim, Seraphim, Principalities, all those dancing-on-the-head-of-a-pin names. You know what name fits you the best? Aliens. Strangers. You don't touch humanity at any given point, did you know that? You don't love, don't hate, eat, fart, or fuck. You've been given dominion over humanity since the very beginning, and you haven't had the slightest idea in all that time what you were dealing with." The old man chuckled. "No wonder the human race is so screwed up."

"It is our lot. There is no justification, no explanation. It just is."

"Why, Daddy?" the old man replied in a high, quavery voice. Then, much lower, " 'Because, that's why.' What a crock."

The Messenger blinked. "You blaspheme."

"Then take your goddamn flaming sword and run my ass out of the goddamn garden, Uriel. Who has better reason to blaspheme?"

"It is not permitted."

"Yeah, right, I don't have a fucking permit. So sue me."

Both were silent for a few moments. Finally, the old man spoke.

"You really want to know why, Messenger?"

The angel shrugged. "Perhaps."

"You were there at Golgotha."

"I was there."

"Then you saw what happened. Didn't it ever occur to you to ask why? Shit, He destroyed Sodom. He let Joshua bring down Jericho by blowing rams' horns. He gave it to Moses to part the Red Sea. Did you ever stop to wonder why He didn't just bring me down off that goddamn cross once He'd made His point?" The sound the old man made might have been a laugh.

" 'Goddamn cross' is right," he went on. "He turned His back on me. I took the sins of the whole world on my bleeding shoulders because it was His Will, and He turned His almighty back on me because I made Him want to puke. *He left me there to die alone*, Uriel! He abandoned me because I did what he put before me to do, because He couldn't stand to see what He'd made me become." A tear leaked from the corner of one eye.

"Why did He do that? It was all His idea, His . . . *Plan*. I did what I was supposed to do. Hell, even *Judas* did what he was supposed to do." He turned his blazing eyes on the Messenger. "And where is the thirteenth Disciple now, Uriel?" he asked softly. "What tree in hell bears his name and sorrow?"

The Messenger gazed down at the old man, but showed no signs of feeling.

"It is not for us to know—" it began.

"It was for *me* to know, goddamn it! I was His 'only begotten son,' or had you forgotten that?"

"I forget nothing."

The old man sank back against the pillow.

"Leave me the hell alone, Uriel. You can't do anything for me and I can't do anything for you."

The angel looked around impassively, then said, "There are humans present. This is no concern of theirs."

"The hell you say."

"We must not attract undue attention."

"Then fix it! You're the frigging supernatural entity here, you want this to be private, *you* do something about it. Take us to Limbo or someplace. I don't care, as long as I can get Vic's attention if I need to."

"To take you out of this reality would be pointless. I am to stay with you until your death, and my time is limited. However, as of now, none can hear us."

"Try to imagine how comforting that is," the old man said, voice thick with irony.

There was a palpable silence; then the Messenger spoke. "You have confused us with this manifestation. After almost two millennia, why did you choose this time and place?"

"I needed time to think. Time to cool off. I stayed dead a long time, Uriel." The old man sighed. "Time goes by fast when you're having fun. After nineteen hundred years or so, give or take a decade, I decided to try again, on my own."

"You deliberately chose an anonymous path when your Second Coming would have been celebrated. Most of humanity would have followed you."

The old man shook his head. "I didn't want that. I wanted to see if I could make it work without all the church stuff, just by being what I could be." He picked idly at the thin, worn blanket. "I wanted friends, not followers. I helped a lot of people in small ways. It turned out I had a real talent for healing—how's that for irony, Messenger?—and I went all over the place. I worked in hospitals, rode with rescue squads, I was even an army corpsman. Hell, I've been here almost twenty years. I just wanted to help." He shrugged and the sheets whispered against his thin back. "It's all I ever wanted to do.

"It seemed to work. People got better, were grateful. They passed along the favors to others, donated time and money to the shelter, made the world a slightly better place than it might have been otherwise.

"I've lived a lot longer this time, too. And you know the best part, Uriel? Nobody will come along after I'm dead this time to piss in it so they like the taste. No Crusades in my name, no Inquisition, no pogroms. No 'ethnic cleansing.' If He really had wanted to do this thing right, He'd have gathered an army of 'unnecessary manifestations' and set us loose all over the world. But then," he continued wearily, "there wouldn't have been a Big Book with His name in it and all those ludicrous stories."

"You avoid the question."

"I'm under no obligation to answer it. I've paid those dues. Look," he continued, "He came to me when I was just a kid. I was smart enough to have attracted some attention with the rabbis, and I asked a lot of questions that some of them weren't comfortable with. God gave me a vision one night, and promised me a lot of things—immortality, the ability to really help people, whatever it would take for His Plan to work." He shook his head. "I said yes. What did I know? I was just a kid."

"That was then. What of now?"

"Okay. You want reasons?" the old man asked quietly. "Renewal. Recompense. Requital. Restitution." With each word his voice grew stronger. "Release. Rectification. Revenge. Resurrection." Then, softer: "Redemption."

"Is this proper?"

"You ask stupid questions, Uriel, and insult both our intelligence. Vic!" he called out to the supervisor. "Ask God about 'proper,' Uriel. Was it 'proper' for Him to go off in a sulk because he didn't like the way His experiment turned out? Because He couldn't handle the enormity of what he'd done?" He struggled to raise himself. "Job. That poor bastard didn't know how well off he was. *Vic!*"

Vic hurried over. "Whaddaya need, Pete?"

"I gotta piss, man. Can you get me to the can?"

"Yeah, sure." He helped the old man sit up, then put his arm across the bony shoulders and half carried him to the bathroom. The Messenger looked on disinterestedly.

After seating the old man on the toilet, Vic said, "Now, you call me when you need me. Don't try an' make it back by y'self, okay?"

"Okay, Vic. I'll call you if I need you." He smiled wanly as Vic left.

The flow from the old man's bladder was slow and painful; he didn't have to look to know it was tinged with blood.

The Messenger appeared in front of him.

"Oh, this is a good one, all right," the old man muttered. "Uriel in the urinal. What are you doing here, Messenger?"

Something about the angel's bearing betrayed uncertainty.

"You left after your resurrection. We watched you walk away from your Disciples, leaving them frightened and puzzled, full of questions. You did nothing to answer those questions."

"That was Paul's job, and he was welcome to it. Hell, he wrote most of the New Testament and let the rest of them take the credit—or the blame. I just wanted out." He leaned his head back against the wall. "I'd had enough of the cult, enough of the adoration and the praise. It's not what I wanted, ever."

"You went to hell."

"Heh. Yeah, I went *all* to hell." He closed his eyes. "I was furious. I wanted to kick ass and take names. I couldn't take it out on the poor bastards who hung me up. They didn't know what they were doing. So, I harrowed hell."

"The marks remain. The gates have not been rebuilt."

"Yeah, well. Milton was impressed. What's your point, Uriel?"

"Where did you get such power?"

The old man glared. "I had it. Not that I wanted it. When I let Him . . . recruit me, He charged me like a battery. There was plenty left."

"Even after He had abandoned you?"

"Look, He set all kinds of shit in motion that day. Earthquakes, an eclipse, storms. It doesn't just dissipate. Once you manifest on the physical plane, you have to deal with physical laws. How much power do you think it takes to rise after three days? Just because He turned away doesn't mean He turned it off like some kind of heavenly circuit breaker."

"You could have used the power to search for Him."

"And then what? Reasoned with Him? Begged Him to take me back? Beat the living shit out of Him?" The old man reached behind himself and flushed. His hand trembled. "What you are to Humanity, He is to me; there's no common point for discussion." Eyes closed, he slumped wearily against the back of the toilet.

"Ah, God, I'm so tired . . . so fucking tired. Why are you here, Messenger? I didn't ask for you."

The angel was silent for several minutes. "There is an imbalance. It must be corrected."

"What kind of imbalance?" the old man asked dully.

"An impermissible one. One that concerns the entirety of humanity."

"Great. Well," he said after a moment, "what? C'mon, I'm old and tired, and I just want to die and have done with it. What's so important?"

"You were wrong."

"Wrong about what?"

"Your crucifixion and its consequences."

The old man's eyes opened, and he turned to focus on the other's face.

"What are you telling me, Messenger?"

The angel stared at him with cold eyes. "Are you so arrogant that you believe He turned His back on you alone? He deserted all of us."

"I don't understand. All's right with the world, isn't it? Doesn't that mean God's in His heaven?"

"Your jest is meaningless and out of place."

"Yeah, well, you guys were never known for your sense of humor. Explain yourself."

"My statement was clear. God has abandoned His throne. There is no existing physical or metaphysical plane that we have not searched. He went where none of us could follow."

The old man stared as the enormity of this sank in. He passed a shaking hand over his eyes.

"This . . . you can't be serious. You can't have looked everywhere, not everywhere."

"We have. Our search was systematic and complete. There is no place in existence in which God can be found. He is gone."

A look of sick horror passed over the old man's face. "When? When did He leave?"

"Is it important? He is gone."

"*When*, goddamn it?"

"Golgotha."

"Golgotha! But . . . the souls in heaven. Are they gone, too? Did he at least pull the plug and let them go?"

"He did not. The souls remain."

"But without Him, with just you there, they couldn't survive. Not and stay sane."

"They have survived. They are not . . . whole."

"Oh . . . oh, my . . ." There were no words to express what the old man felt. He raised his head, tears now falling freely. "What about hell?"

"All mad, demons and lost souls alike."

"Purgatory?"

"All mad."

"Even limbo? Even the righteous heathen? And . . . Oh, God, the children! Even the children?"

"Mad. There was no one," the angel said, "capable of maintaining their sanity after He left. Do you understand?" The angel stared at the old man. "Do you understand all that this means?"

Eyes again closed, the old man nodded his head. "They have no one to guide them, no one to help them make sense of what's happened. Their 'Heavenly Father,' the one who made all the promises, isn't there to counsel them, to make them safe." Hopelessly, he looked at the angel. "Do they know that they've been abandoned?"

"How could they not know? God is gone."

"And you . . . you waited *two thousand years* to tell me this?"

"Our time does not pass as yours. Our search was extensive, it required much more time than that." The angel's voice was ice. "It passed no more quickly for those who are lost."

"How long?" the old man said between clenched teeth. "How long has it been for them?"

"Eternity."

Jesus wept. Slumped against a toilet in a New York shelter for the homeless, his thin body wracked with sobs, he wept for the souls of the dead; lost now, lost always, lost forever.

"Do you understand all that this means?" the angel repeated.

"*Yes*, goddamn it, I know! He walked out on the whole human race, walked out on all His promises, and plans, and against His sworn word. I *know* what it means." His head sagged against his chest. "Just let me die and get it over with. I'm tired."

"You do *not* understand. God is gone. His place must not remain empty."

The words sank in slowly. Jesus raised his head, eyes wide with shock. "What?"

The angel looked at him without emotion. "You spoke of compassion. You said that you pitied us, that we would never know what it meant. You were wrong."

The old man said nothing; he just stared.

"Those who are lost, those who will come, need guidance. We cannot give it. They cannot give it to themselves. There is only you. We can no longer allow them to suffer."

"No! It's too much! I've *earned* dying, damn it!"

"You will take His place."

"I said no! I won't do it!"

The angel looked down at the old man with cold eyes: burning cold, inhuman eyes.

"I will tell you as I once told Ezra. Go weigh for me the weight of fire, or measure for me a blast of wind, or call back for me the day that is past. Can you do these things?"

The old man's voice shook with helpless rage. "You know I can't! I never could! I wasn't born with power, He wasn't my Father!" He tried to bring himself under control, but his hands and head shook as if palsied, and his face was as blotched as the tiles beneath his bare feet.

"I was given this choice once before, Messenger, and I took it even though I knew it would kill me. This time I'm refusing the cup!" His voice became petulant. "You can't make me do it, you son of a bitch!"

"You had choice in Gethsemane. Here and now, you do not. I am not here to bring you back, or to coax you, but to tell you what will be." The air around the angel grew bright and hot as it spoke. "You will die. You will ascend. You will take the throne. There is nothing else. God is gone, and you have no choice."

"Bastard . . . bastard . . ." The ancient voice was whisper thin now, cracked and broken like spun glass. "Let me die. . . ."

"Yes." The angel placed a hand on Jesus' brow.

And the old man's hands stopped shaking; his head fell back against the wall; his worn body sagged slowly in place; and he died.

Back at his desk, Vic grew worried. Pete had been in the toilet a long time, and there was no sound. Not wanting to disturb the other patients, he got up and hurried around to make sure everything was okay. He tapped softly on the door.

"Yo, Pete. You need help?" There was no answer. "Pete!" he said louder.

Alarmed, he eased the door open just far enough to look in; he didn't want to embarrass the old man if he'd just fallen asleep on the john.

What he saw made him curse softly and rush to the old man's side. He felt the thin wrist, then turned and rushed out of the bathroom and down the hall where Father Nicholas's room was. He returned moments later with the priest behind him.

"I couldn't find a pulse, Padre. Oh, jeez, what a way to go. . . ." His voice was thick with grief; the old man had been well loved.

Father Nicholas checked for a pulse, then closed the eyes and began Last Rites. Vic stood to one side, unashamed tears on his cheeks.

The priest finished the sacrament, then went to phone for an ambulance. Vic followed, his eyes pleading for comfort, for sense.

"Why'd he hafta die in *there*, Padre? Why'd he hafta go in the can?"

The priest patted Vic's shoulder. "I know, I know. It's a bad place to end, especially for a man like Pete. But it's okay, Vic." He turned to look one last time at the body sprawled on the toilet. "It's okay. He's with God now."

DON WEBB

Ool Athag

Don Webb has published fiction and poetry in a wide variety of magazines, including Asimov's Science Fiction, Realms of Fantasy, Science Fiction Age, Interzone, Century, Deathrealm, *and* The Third Alternative. *His books include* Uncle Ovid's Exercise Book, A Spell for the Fulfillment of Desire, The Explanation and Other Good Advice, The Double: An Investigation, Anubis on Guard: The Selected Poetry of Don Webb, Essential Saltes: An Experiment, *and* Endless Honeymoon. *He lives with his wife in Austin, Texas. This marks the first publication of "Ool Athag."*

For Guiniviere

Even the most skilled of dreamers could not tell Ferin what was revealed at Ool Athag. They said that the name was too old, and that as such, it must lie so deeply in the Dreamworld that human dreamers surely could not make the journey past the Seas Which Bleed and the Mountains Who Sing, but Ferin, who had once been wholly of the waking world, had seized upon the name of Ool Athag and resolved to go there and see what was shown. Despite the warnings of dreamers whose skill was a thing of legend, Ferin decided to pursue the quest.

He left his city, which was poised on the gap between the waking world and the Dreamworld, and moved wholly into the world of Dream, forsaking the waking world. He traveled by violet mist that is kind to dreamers who know no fear, and will carry them far beyond where their puny will could take them. He came at last to a village known as Nandinoor, a place of tiny twisting streets laid out in the shape of a character from an alphabet used by no human race.

Nor were the men of Nandinoor wholly human either. In the most general outline, in a candlelit room they would pass for human. That their brats had tails, and their wives short stumpy wings was of no matter. Such things are common in the Dreamworld, where time favors the mixed and the impure. The village was prosperous in the trade of false books and the exporting of heresies to the Thousand Worlds. The village reeked of the ink of octopi and the attar of a phosphorescent rose that induces dreaming, for these are the chief ingredient for the inks for their scrolls. Ferin, who knew much of the cults and creeds of the waking world, soon found employment there. He spent a hundred years creating false faiths to spread in the world so that he might earn the opalescent coins made from dragon's scales that were the currency of the village of Nandinoor.

When his bag was full of coins he knocked at the door of the three sages' home, and paying a great fee was told all they knew of Ool Athag.

The youngest sage was of much human blood, that only the slight horns that peeked from his graying hair and his eyes the color of copper, told of his Otherness.

"Ool Athag," said the sage, "is a town by the lake of the Sun and the Moon. It appears only when the moon is dark and clouds hide the sun, for it holds secrets that are too frightening for the sun to look on, and if the sun caught a glimpse of them, he would flee our sky, as happened years ago before the coming of human dreamers. If you travel east past the Mountains Who Sing, and wait for the darkness of the sun and moon, you will find Ool Athag. It is not a popular spot for human dreamers, for there they learn their true place in the universe, and this knowledge makes them grow small like gnats, whereupon the santh bird of the lake devours them. But perhaps such is a happy death. Who can say?"

The second sage had skin the color of tarnished silver, and when it spoke Ferin's skin itched and his mouth tasted rusty iron. It told that Ool Athag was long ago taken away.

"Ool Athag," said the sage, "was a theater, where the Mao Games were played every fourteen years. Those who knew the ancient tongues and could pass an examination of the meaning of the two and seventy masks of darkness, were allowed to watch the Games; although even watching the Games was said to be dangerous as the excitement thereof could often drive souls from their bodies. But the Emperor Purpus of the Shining Shield had attacked the town of Monat and burned down the theater. And yet it was said by those who traveled beyond the Mountains Who Sing that the ruins of the theater may be found, and that placing one's ear to the ashy timbers one could still hear the Mao Games, and if one lay in the ruins for nine nights, one might dream of them, and go mad. Perhaps with the madness of poets, or perhaps merely mad like those of the waking world who dream of returning to the Dreamworld. Who can say?"

The third sage did not appear to be a living creature at all, but a mass of metal half the size of a man's chest. The metal rocked softly back and forth, and Ferin heard its words in his mind. This disturbed him not, for he was an experienced dreamer, but the words themselves disturbed him greatly.

"Ool Athag," went the words, "was a human like yourself. He longed to found a dynasty in the kingdom of Zmonat, by a lake called Sun and Moon. He knew that the race that dwelt there was old and tired and that it longed to return to its own space in the Thousand Worlds. So he led his army against the city and the old race threw open the doors and died gladly upon the swords of Ool Athag's army, and the streets ran cobalt blue with their blood. But Ool Athag was not content to merely wear the strangely shaped crown of his kingdom, he sought to possess their knowledge as well as their land, for he was a fool such as you. He listened to their singing scrolls, and drank their bottled books, and grew wise with strange lore. He found out all and everything about the Dreamworld, and the Lands Beyond, and the Thousand Worlds, and the waking world from whence he had come. He knew the name of each star—not the name that men or Kanree call the star but the name the star calls itself. He called his people together and spent three days and three nights telling them all and everything. And they rose up against him, cursing his name for removing all their illusions and they tore his skin from his body, and wrote down all that he had said, so that they might forget. They made a pact among themselves to never meet again, so that they would never be tempted to speak one with the other of what they had learned, and they disappeared to all the corners of all the worlds, where they die in silence and poverty. But the accursed scroll still remains, for such runes of truth cannot be unwritten, and every thousand years, a fool such as yourself finds the scroll and reads it, and journeys back to his own world, but there he cuts his tongue out, knowing that it would bring the end to all things to tell such truths. You have learned of Ool Athag, and this is more than any in your world know. Go back there, and be happy, and trouble not the past, for the past does not forgive. But perhaps the name has hooked you like a fish, and you cannot escape. Who can say?"

Ferin bowed deeply to the three sages and spent a year in drinking and whoring, afraid to seek Ool Athag, but slowly his curiosity rose. The stories that the three sages had told him could not all be true, so perhaps all were false, created to hide their ignorance, or perhaps to hide a great treasure that they drew their wisdom from.

So he hired men, or such as pass for men in the village of Nandinoor, and he set off for the east. They crossed the cold desert, although frost stole ears and fingers from some of them. They entered into the parched foothills, and some died of thirst, and others were carried off in the night by quiet flying things that smelled of cinnamon and made tiny purring sounds like cats.

With four of his men, Ferin reached the shore, and they deserted him, for they would not look upon the Seas Which Bleed. He came into a small seaport, where only aged men dwelled, and these old folk were silent, communicating only with hand signs, or with writing in letters Ferin knew not. Ferin had a hard time making his desires known, and when at last they understood that he wished to travel to Ool Athag, they drew back and were afraid. But one of them, by far the oldest, signed that he would take Ferin across the sea, for he was greatly old and knew that Death herself would find him soon. So in a ship made of the light bones of some vast sea creature and bearing sails of a somber purple, Ferin sailed east.

At first he thought that the way the sun shone redly upon the water at its rising had given the seas their name, but he came to see its secret after eleven days of journeying.

The sea began to shimmer and the ancient sailor tied a black band over his eyes that he would not see it. He handed a band to Ferin, but Ferin was too drawn by the early visions. The ancient sailor held the wheel still. Images began to form in the water, of places far away. These were scenes of strife, battles and wars, dragons feasting on humans, humans fighting moon beasts, humans fighting Kanree, but mainly humans fighting humans. Battle after battle, and as the figures shown in the sea would bleed, their blood seemed to rise to the surface of the water. Ferin could smell the blood and grew sick of it, and still the ship sailed on.

Once the scene was of a siege where men killed wizened figures who kept themselves completely cloaked, yet bled deep blue blood. Ferin wondered if he was watching the scenes of which the eldest sage spoke. He hoped that it was not true, for that was the story that he feared most, and still the ship sailed on.

But the next morning, the scenes began to change, and he began to see battles in the waking world. At first he watched these with great interest for they showed many marvels of ancient warfare, and many things the historians had gotten wrong. Whole empires, fighting styles, weapons that no one had guessed of in his time, and still the ship sailed on for days of these battles.

But the scenes lost their charm and historical fascination, as they neared his own time. He saw how mankind had grown fiercer and more cruel, and how the weapons of war created newer and more cruel hurts. He wanted to turn away from these scenes, yet some part of him realized that he had made a bargain with the obscene gods of the sea, for seeing the earlier scenes, he had to watch these. And still the ship sailed on.

The scenes grew into battles involving his nation and his time, and he saw such things as man should not see. And still the ship sailed on.

Then the sea showed him scenes that he had known in the waking world, the scenes that he had turned his back on, because of their guilt and horror. These were the scenes that had made him take up the art of a dreamer. These were the scenes that had led to him to wine and strange drugs. These were the scenes that he had sold much to think of never again. And the ship sailed on.

The next day there was only one scene. It showed Ferin cutting the throat of the ancient sailor while he slept, and drinking the old one's thin blood. The sea became the sea again and the smell of blood vanished from the air. Within the hour, the old sailor began sniffing the air and smiled and removed his blindfold. He smiled at Ferin and Ferin at him, and they ate the cheese and olives that were the ship's store, and drank of the springwater from the skins.

That night the wind stopped.

When the sun rose, they found the sea full of seaweed, and not a breeze stirred. The old sailor got out the vessel's oars, but neither he nor Ferin could make any progress in the weed-filled water. It was the same the next day.

And the next.

And the next.

First the water ran out, then the food. The old sailor and Ferin began watching each other, as they pretended to fish, or to fire arrows at the birds that circled the small boat. Both knew that their arrows fell short, both saw that nothing disturbed their lines. But age was the old man's undoing, and Ferin cut his throat as he lay sleeping, just as he had seen in the sea. Ferin drank of the watery blood of the old man.

The next day, the sea was clear and the winds strong.

Ferin made good progress and when he saw landsign, he tossed the old man's body into the sea, and cursed the gods of the sea. One of the birds flew low, and he thought its call was a sort of laugh. The beaches were red, and the sand sharp and cutting. He pulled the bone ship ashore and went into the forest to search for food or men.

He found some berries and mushrooms and other things that hunger made him brave enough to try. After he had fed and found a small sweet rivulet from which to drink he returned to the beach and found the bone boat was sailing swiftly away—a strong breeze carried it to the west, but he could see no one sailing it.

He tried his magical arts to summon the violet mist, or to conjure some spirit that might carry him, but he was too far from the spirits he knew, or perhaps they could not cross the evil seas, for none answered his call. He set out to the east, farther inland, and none stopped him, but at night he would hear a roar like a tiger.

After some days of journeying, the land began to rise and grow more wild, so he hoped that he was nearing the Mountains Who Sing. His heart gave a great leap one morning when he could smell meat roasting, and he began running like a wild man toward the smell.

He came upon a crude village in a small clearing.

A burly woodsman split logs in front of a wooden cabin. He hailed Ferin.

"Stop friend, we don't see many men here."

Ferin came forward and begged something to eat. The woodsman took him inside and introduced him to his wife and comely daughters. There was roast pig and a home-brewed ale, and song and good cheer.

That night one of the daughters came to Ferin's bed, and the next day the woodsman begged him to stay. He needed help to tend his little farm, to hunt and gather, to sell wood and hides. Few humans dwelt here, because of the wood's evil reputation. But Ferin told him of his desire to see Ool Athag.

The woodsman said that in his grandfather's time, a group of men and Kanree had come looking to see Ool Athag, and that they had been turned into owls for their presumption. He asked Ferin to remain.

Ferin stayed for two more nights. On each night another of the woodsman's daughters gave herself to him, and on the last night the youngest daughter promised Ferin afterward (amidst many tears) that she would never eat an owl again. The woodsman packed goat cheese, and bread made from nut flour and a jug of the home-brewed ale for Ferin, but the woodsman's wife spat upon him and cursed him and told him that he did not know what a great fool he was to leave behind such good things for the promise of Ool Athag, which, she added, did not exist at all.

Within a day's hiking he came to the Mountains Who Sing. As he climbed their slopes he heard the wind singing to itself through the leaves of the aspens, and he decided that such had been the source of the name. But that night things grew very still, and there was no wind, nor song of birds, nor the flying of the creatures peculiar to the Dreamworld. As the moon rose, Ferin saw the cliff face, near where he had camped, put forth a mouth like a woman with sensuous red lips. The cliff sang to him of his many failed romances, of women he had abandoned and families he had ruined, and of a dancer who killed herself for him. He tried to cover his ears, but the song found its way to his ears nonetheless.

The second night when he was far along the trail into the mountains, the boulders sang to him of the many times his friends had tricked him (both in the waking world and the Dreamworld), and how many ruses and cons had been worked on him because of his trust. The boulders sang with his father's mouth, and sported his father's beard.

The third night as he sheltered himself amidst the snows of a high pass, the icicles sang to him with the mouth of the woman who taught him the art of dreaming. The icicles sang of the lies that his teachers had taught him, and that his religious and moral instructors had taught him, and that princes and government leaders had told him.

The fourth night as he had begun his descent into a rocky desert, but could see a great lake on the horizon, the rocks and gravel grew many tiny mouths with blue lips. The many mouths sang of the Great Lie that was Ool Athag, and of the fools that died of the desert or were poisoned by the waters of the lake while seeking the lie.

On the fifth night as he lay in the foothills, a great granite dome grew lips that were Ferin's own lips and sang him the saddest song of all—the song of What Might Have Been.

He journeyed through the black desert till he came upon the great lake of a poisonous blue, that stretched like a sea. He made his way around the shore until he came to some squares of stone, that he decided must have been foundations.

Could this be what was left of Ool Athag? Had he journeyed so far and long for this?

He camped on the ruins for a day and a night, and he asked the spirits there to let him know if this was Ool Athag.

He waited another night and day, but no answer came from the spirits, so, full of tears and loneliness, he began to leave.

He tripped on a small metal canister lying half-buried in the black sand.

He pried it up and upended it. Within was a scroll written on a flimsy piece of yellow paper. It was a mere fourteen verses.

After he had read them, he thought.

They made all things clear.

They showed him the quest of Ool Athag for knowledge, and what that knowledge was. They showed him how the theater had changed the world by its simple masques. They showed him how those, who built a city on the theater's ruins, were unequipped for the knowledge that came to them in dreams, and how they shrank like gnats.

The verses showed him how all of these things were true and none of these things were true, and how they stood as a symbol for a certain knowledge, and what that knowledge was.

The verses, if meditated upon, revealed all the truths of all the worlds.

For fourteen days with neither sleep nor food, Ferin meditated on the verses. He knew all things. Such knowledge came with racking pain and utter ecstasy, with mind-numbing boredom and curiosity that could cut through steel. It was all and everything that he sought in the Dreamworld, and he felt that it was time to return to the waking world, and share what he had learned with the race of man.

Such returns are easy for one possessed of such great knowledge. Ferin found himself walking along a certain road in the city of New Orleans.

New Orleans is one of the cities that sits at the edge of the Dreamworld, and Ferin had come there seeking certain gateways.

Although hundreds of years had passed in the Dreamworld, Ferin found but little time had passed here. The city was afire with a strange sect, recently arrived there, and with a blush Ferin recognized his own work from long ago in Nandinoor.

Ferin walked down the street, and into the French Quarter where his studio lay. There he began painting. He painted all the allegories that his mind had been filled with, he painted the truth about Life and Death, he painted the Secrets of Magic and Art, he painted the truth of falsehood and the falsehood of truth, he painted the why-for of games and the games of why-for. He assembled, in a dizzying year, all that mankind did not know.

He threw open his studio, and called all the art collectors in the city.

They came and looked. They spoke little. They bought nothing.

Day after day passed, and no one bought a single canvas, and Ferin became silent. After a while no one even came to the studio, and one night Ferin left it, with its doors open to the elements.

He was very quiet as he slipped out of the city. Perhaps he returned to the Dreamworld.

Who can say?

In days the studio was rented anew, and the owners threw the various canvases that showed Truth into the trash.

There's no market for such things.

MICHAEL BISHOP

The Yukio Mishima Cultural Association of Kudzu Valley, Georgia

Michael Bishop has written over two dozen books of fiction and poetry, a body of work that stands among the most admired and influential in modern science fiction and fantasy literature. His 1982 novel No Enemy but Time *won the Nebula Award; his 1994 Locus Award–winning novel* Brittle Innings *is widely regarded as one of the finest works of contemporary American fantasy. His 1981 story "The Quickening" also received a Nebula Award, and his story "Dogs' Lives" was included in* Best American Short Stories 1985. *He has won the Rhysling Award for poetry, received four Locus Awards for fiction and editing, and garnered multiple nominations for the Hugo Award, the World Fantasy Award, and the Townsend Prize for Best Book of Fiction by a Georgia Writer. His most recent books include the poetry collection* Time Pieces; *the fiction collections* Blue Kansas Sky *and* Brighten to Incandescence; *two mystery novels,* Would It Kill You to Smile? *and* Muskrat Courage, *both written with Paul Di Filippo and published under the pseudonym Philip Lawson; and the as-yet unpublished novel* An Owl at the Crucifixion. *His recent short fiction has appeared in* The

Silver Gryphon *and* After O'Connor: Contemporary Georgia Stories. *Bishop lives with his wife, Jeri, in Pine Mountain, Georgia, where he is at work on a young-adult novel. "The Yukio Mishima Cultural Association of Kudzu Valley, Georgia" was first published in* Basilisk, *edited by Ellen Kushner.*

I am a new resident of Kudzu Valley, Georgia. After losing my teaching position at the state university, I came to Kudzu Valley to 1) steep myself in bitterness, 2) find solace in the rural life, 3) lead the local inhabitants out of their charming but dissolute provincialism, and 4) gain, during my exile, sufficient inner resolve and outside support to browbeat the villainous provost into reinstating me as an instructor in the comparative literature section of the English Department, preferably with clauses in my contract granting me back pay, a private office in the *old*, and hence more prestigious, wing of Park Hall, and damages for "the untoward suffering wreaked upon Mr. M. by an unfeeling bureaucracy." That's how I envision it. Quite.

You see, I was turned out because my last highest degree—a master's with a thesis entitled "Mather Biles: His Role in the Introduction of the Heroic Couplet from England to the American Colonies"—is from the state university, and the provost has declared that, in the interests of catholicity and cosmopolitanism, not to mention that of upgrading the educational milieu of the campus, no one who has earned his last highest degree from our institution may hold forth in its lecture rooms. A taboo, if you like, against "intellectual incest." There are exceptions to this primitive ruling, of course, but I was not one of them.

Here in Kudzu Valley, then, I intend to devote myself to Purpose No. 1 (see above) for no less than two but no more than three months; to Purpose No. 2 for all that time from the end of my bitter steeping to my triumphant return to the comp. lit. division; to Purpose No. 3 whenever the occasion should present itself; and to Purpose No. 4 coterminously with my observance of each of the other three purposes hereinbefore noted. Since I am single and living in a house willed to me off the top of a distant cousin's cancerous skull ("This town's been dying even longer than I have," it's reported this old woman—one Clarabelle Musgrove Sims—told her physi-

cian toward the last; "I intend to transfuse it by my dying"), I should be able
to devote myself to these various enterprises without significant let.

OCTOBER 23

My self-imposed durance of bitter steeping has lasted four months
rather than three, and, upon inquiry, I have passed off my solitariness as a
period of meditative acclimatization. Then Mrs. Bernard Bligh Brumblelo—the foremost social lioness in town, and, as she has told me over the
telephone, "a dear friend of your beloved, departed cousin Clarabelle"—
invites me to an evening tea. I accept, not because I am overfond of either
tea or Mrs. Bernard Bligh Brumblelo, but because attending this affair will
offer me a nice possibility of fulfilling Purpose No. 3.

Others at the get-together in the old woman's starkly modern, all-
electric home are Ruby and Clarence Unfug (of Unfug's electric), the gro-
ceryman Spurgeon Creed, Lisbeth and Q. B. Meacham (of Kudzu Valley
Drugs), the plumber and electrician Augustus Houseriser, the kindergarten
teacher Lonnie Pederson and her husband Tom, who works for Valley Poul-
try Processing, and, surprisingly, at least to me, the black woman preacher
Fontessa Boddie. We are perfunctorily introduced. Tea and hot apple cider
are served.

An insufficient number of chairs forces us to stand on Mrs. Brumblelo's
pepper-and-salt shag carpet shifting our teacups and canapés from hand to
hand and getting in, I'm afraid, nary a bite. We discuss, in turn, these four
topics while our hostess putters in the kitchen: 1) The ill health of Kudzu
Valley businesses, 2) flagging attendance at the community's two churches,
3) the almost inevitable prospect of the valley's inundation when the state
legislature approves the construction, above us, of a new dam, and 4) public
apathy in the face of these several threats to the general welfare.

"But," says Mrs. Brumblelo when she at last emerges from the kitchen,
"I asked you here not simply to rehash Kudzu Valley's problems—since our
mayor and police department will do nothing—but to acquaint you all with
Clarabelle's young cousin, Mr. M., who has only recently moved among us."

At last we put behind us the wearying catalogue of topics (see above)
that has preempted all other discussion the last thirty or forty minutes, and I

am paid heed to. "What do you do," Augustus Houseriser wants to know. "Nothing," I say, "at present." Everyone considers this. "What *did* you do?" Fontessa Boddie asks, savioress of the untenable moment. I tell them about the comp. lit. section of the English Department at the state university. Says Clarence Unfug, "What—exactly, you know—is this *comp. lit.* business?" I chuckle appreciatively at the way he has made the abbreviation— all inadvertently, of course—sound like a footnote in Latin. Then I say, "It's a discipline whose purpose is to discover significant relationships among different works of literature, across the barriers of both language and time." Petite Lonnie Pederson, whose husband, Tom's, dewlaps are wagging (I suppose) much in the manner of his preprocessed turkeys', says with a hint of endearing pique, "For instance, Mr. M.?" "Well," I oblige, "one of the graduate students in our section has just composed a paper detailing the similarities between the works of the French writer Proust and the Japanese novelist Yukio Mishima." "Oh, I just *love* Proust," says Mrs. Brumblelo, who is a female litterateur manqué as well as a lioness long since manifest (one wall is lined with Reader's Digest Condensed Books); "he's so *soporific*." But neither she nor anyone else there has heard of Yukio Mishima, and Mrs. Brumblelo asks me to write the name down for her on the back of a napkin. In the meantime, I tell the group about Mishima's melodramatic suicide in 1970, discoursing a bit on the meaning and the various techniques of *seppuku* and explaining as best I can—most of this, really, is out of my field of greatest expertise, Early American Literature—why a writer at the height of his powers would do such a repellent thing. Even the laconic Spurgeon Creed is subtly animated during my lecture: both erubescent earlobes, obscenely pink pendulums, begin to tick. The Unfugs are openmouthed, the Meachams quietly stupefied. How rewarding it is to fulfill Purpose No. 3.

Fontessa Boddie says, "He died that horrible way to protest the road his country was goin' down?"

I incline my head in assent.

"That's very interesting," says Mrs. Bernard Bligh Brumblelo; "that's very interesting." While saying good night to us at the very stroke of ten (I am the last one out the door), she now and again mumbles, as if to fix the words in her memory, *"Yukio Mishima, Yukio Mishima, Yukio . . . "* A foreboding follows me outside, sniveling to itself as forebodings are wont to do.

OCTOBER 25

Two days later I receive this note from the lioness:

Kudʒu Valley is committing suicide by default, Mr. M., and the old saviors of private pride, religion, community spirit, and free enterprise have failed us. In telephone consultations with the Unfugs, Fontessa Boddie, the Meachams, the Pedersons, Spurgeon Creed, and Augustus Houseriser I put forth the idea of a Yukio Mishima Cultural Association to help us draw back from the abyss. Everyone agreed that this was a wonderful idea, and I now have the pleasure of informing you, dear Mr. M., that we have unanimously appointed you our chairperson.

NOVEMBER 9

I am *not* delighted. Nevertheless, I have complied with the unanimous request of the social "elite" of Kudzu Valley. If not I, who would have undertaken the chairing of this association, ill conceived and incongruous as it may well be? One must accept his responsibilities and run with the ball— even if the ball comes, so to speak, from out of left field. This is a sentiment that national leaders from Valley Forge to Chappaquiddick and beyond have frequently endorsed, because of its soundness. It *was* I, after all, who put Mrs. Brumblelo on to Mishima, and palpable good may yet derive from a society devoted to the life and works of a foreign author.

As Fontessa Boddie put it in an organizational assembly in the gymnasium of the Kudzu Valley Elementary School two nights ago, "We been kickin' aroun' ole Joel Chandler Harris for too long, folks."

Present at this assembly, somewhat amazingly, were a hundred ten people, only two hundred or so short of the population of the entire town and surrounding community. My first official acts as chairperson were to gavel this assembly to order and to preside over the ensuing discussions. The most heated of these involved the name of our society, since Berle Maunder, the owner of the builders' supply store on East Broadway, expressed some concern that our acronym might spawn confusion among outsiders. He even suggested that we follow the Japanese practice of placing the surname first, the given name second, in order to avoid any possible confusion.

Seated to my right at the head of the table, Mrs. Brumblelo had the final word: "There is no chapter of that *other* group in Kudzu Valley, Mr. Maunder, and since this one is solely for residents of our immediate area, I see no reason to yield up our original choice. In any case, think how much better we will be able to remember the initials of our own association."

NOVEMBER 12 TO DECEMBER 2

I have been putting up "Who is Yukio Mishima?" posters in public places. These are expensive black-light posters, ordered from Atlanta. In them Yukio Mishima is naked but for a loincloth, his hands and feet are bound, and his body is pierced with many cruel-looking arrows. This is the pose of a Western saint, I am told, in whom the Oriental novelist was interested; I don't know which saint, however, since none of this falls within my area of greatest expertise. The posters are eye-catching, in a shoddy sensationalist way. I have put them up in the post office, the laundromat, the Greyhound stopover depot, two service station garages, and the lobby of the Farmers and Merchants Bank of Kudzu Valley.

There are no bookstores or newsstands in Kudzu Valley. The Variety Five and Dime has a solitary spin-around rack with a number of books in it, but most of these titles are by either Dale Evans or Pat Boone.

From the proper New York distributor I order copies of Mishima's final work, the tetralogy that he called *The Sea of Fertility*. In a mere three weeks the books have arrived, and Clarence and Ruby Unfug agree to display the novels in the window of Unfug's Electric. Ruby and Clarence are true to their word. One fine rural Monday morning I go by their shop and see copies of *Spring Snow*, *Runaway Horses*, *The Temple of Dawn*, and *The Decay of the Angel* in the front window—right there among the propane space heaters, the air conditioners, the gas and electric water heaters, the portable fans, the toasters, the microwave ovens, and the automatic can openers.

The Unfugs, inside, wave at me enthusiastically. Business is brisk. As I stand on the sidewalk wondering what has happened to derail so thoroughly the fulfillment of Purpose No. 4 on my list of top-priority endeavors, a black teenager comes out of the Unfugs' with an armful of books. "Hey, man," he says, and goes on up the street. Kudzu Valley overflows with goodwill these days, and I realize that Mrs. Bernard Brumblelo and the other intellectually, if not otherwise, disadvantaged inhabitants of this backwater community *like* me. Such an illumination is unnerving: I put one hand on the Unfugs' well-scrubbed plate-glass window.

How am I going to tell these people that never in my life have I read an entire work by Yukio Mishima? How am I going to impress upon them that I don't intend to, either?

DECEMBER 14

In the Atlanta *Constitution* one morning I read,

> *The legislature has approved funds to complete construction of the Cusseta Dam above Kudzu Valley. Little resistance to this plan is expected from residents of the area.*
>
> *"Those affected will be generously and swiftly reimbursed," said state senator Ira Weems late yesterday, "and the recreational opportunities which will be available after the dam has been built may reverse the economic slump they've been experiencing down there."*

This means I will be paid for Clarabelle Musgrove Sims's house. This means I will inherit, indirectly, to a cash legacy. Go back to square one, I tell myself, in order that you may fulfill Purpose No. 4; all the others are behind you, after all, and in Purpose No. 3 you have succeeded too well, too well. . . .

JANUARY 3, 1976

Yukio Mishima to Donald Keene, as quoted in the About the Author section of each of the four volumes of his tetralogy: "The title, *The Sea of Fertility*, is intended to suggest the arid sea of the moon that belies its name. Or I might say that it superimposes the image of cosmic nihilism on that of the fertile sea."

Fontessa Boddie has been canvassing Kudzu Valley, taking subscriptions for the construction of a new church. At the moment, Kudzu Valley has a Baptist church and a Methodist church; it does not have a church of Cosmic Nihilism. Fontessa Boddie has been collecting funds in order that we may build a First Cosmic Nihilist Church right here in the Valley—this she does in the face of adverse and probably prohibitive news out of the capital. Fontessa Boddie, formerly a freelancer, intends to be the more-or-less permanent minister of this new church.

I gave her two dollars.

MARCH 26

It has got out of hand, this business; it has got monstrously out of hand. When I go by the elementary school during recess periods, the children in the schoolyard are dueling with bamboo staves, practicing karate, or meditating like Hosso Buddhists in front of the teeter-totters and monkey bars. Black and white alike, they all cry *kendo!* or they all say their ineffable Buddhist prayers.

Construction on Fontessa Boddie's First Cosmic Nihilist Church is nearing completion, and the Methodist and Baptist ministers have publicly abjured their respective Protestant denominations in favor of membership in Miss Boddie's fold.

At night it is possible to go to the elementary school and hear both children and adults read reports on Mishima-related topics. One evening, when I could no longer abide the haunted silence of Clarabelle Musgrove Sims's wallpapered parlor, I took me to this school and heard these papers:

1. "Takamori Saigo: The Last Samurai?"
2. "Ichikawa's *Enjo*: Mishima into Film"
3. "The Influence of Lady Murasaki on Yukio Mishima"
4. "Masculinity and Homosexuality in Mishima's *Forbidden Colors*"
5. "The Meiji Era and Contemporary Japan"
6. "*Spring Snow*: Kiyoaki Matsugae as a Romantic Analogue of the Author"
7. "*Seppuku*: The Death of an Honorable Man"

Most of these papers, I am certain, were improperly footnoted, and the children did not project their voices well.

Yesterday, in the bank, a complete stranger asked me if I knew that both Mishima and Proust had been influenced by Ruskin; this stranger was a farmer in a railroadman's striped coveralls, and he gave me to understand that he had recently written the comp. lit. section of the English Department at the state university for "any additional, you know, information you got on ole Mishima." I left without cashing my check. But for the cornucopian goodwill of the citizenry, I could almost believe myself once again in an academic environment. No, that overstates the case—but clearly the advent of the Yukio Mishima Cultural Association has led these people into unbecoming extremes of behavior.

It has all got out of hand, this business; it has all got monstrously out of hand.

Last night, for instance, that paradigmatic observer of the proprieties, Mrs. Bernard Bligh Brumblelo, drops in on me at 10:17 P.M. without so much as a telephone call for warning. First, still clad in my Edgar Allan Poe dressing gown, I must make tea for her. Then in the parlor I have to entertain her while trying, in the interests of modesty, to keep my knees together. Mrs. Brumblelo notices nothing amiss; she does not even recognize the indecorousness of her own untimely visit, so far has the general insanity progressed.

"Did you know that before he actually committed *seppuku*," Mrs. Brumblelo says, her thin face elongating into a distorted oval, "Yukio"—of late she has taken to calling him Yukio—"told an American friend that he didn't know what he would write upon the completion of his tetralogy, and that he was afraid. Did you know that, Mr. M.?"

"No," I say.

"Oh, let me read it to you. I have it right here." Mrs. Brumblelo takes a magazine clipping out of her purse. It trembles in her hands. " 'What are you afraid of?' " she read. " 'It's just a big book, after all.' That's his American friend asking him, you see, Mr. M., and this is what Yukio replied: 'Yes, I don't know. I'm afraid, and I really don't know why.' So touching, so touching, it's an absolute revelation to me, Mr. M., it truly, truly is." Mrs. Brumblelo's transparently violet eyes fill up with tears; with an embroidered handkerchief she daubs at these tears, and the veins in her haggard old face open up to me an appalling anatomy primer.

To make matters even more unpleasant, after Mrs. Brumblelo has left, I have a dream in which Clarabelle Musgrove Sims slips into my bedchamber—the room she insisted on dying in, by the way—and urges me to drink water from the top of a human skull. "Quite rejuvenating," she says, "if you put your mind to it." I have always been put off by non sequiturs, and for this reason I awake in either a tepid or a moderately coolish sweat, my confusion permits no accurate discrimination. This whole business, I must reiterate, has got monstrously out of hand.

APRIL 3

I receive a formal invitation bearing upon it a monogram resembling a golden butterfly afloat: a large *B* with two smaller *B*'s overlapping each other inside it.

> *Dear Mr. M.:*
>
> *The members of the Yukio Mishima Cultural Association of Kudzu Valley, Georgia, and environs, herewith invite you to commit* seppuku *with us on the last day of April, at two o'clock in the afternoon, on the lawn of the U.S. Post Office building. This event will serve as 1) quite a dramatic protest against the unfeeling pragmatism of our state bureaucracy, 2) an irrevocable farewell to our conciliatory and apathetic pasts, 3) a fulfillment of your cousin Clarabelle Musgrove Sims's dying wishes (indirectly, you know) and 4) a heartfelt homage to Yukio Mishima, who has saved us by his example.*
>
> *We have also agreed among ourselves that as chairperson of our association you, Mr. M., ought by rights to have the opportunity to precede the remainder of us in the commission of these several purposes. That honor, should you desire it, is yours.*
>
> *Yours in Yukio,*
> *Mrs. Bernard Bligh Brumblelo*
>
> RSVP

I am enraged. The fools. The country simpletons. The redneck louts aspiring to be literary. Across my dead cousin's parlor I hurl a decorative china plate, which breaks on the fireplace grating and shatters into a diversified population of accusatory shards.

Later, more calm, I send regrets.

JUNE 1

Yesterday afternoon everybody in Kudzu Valley, Georgia, with the exception only of children under the age of six and a single responsible adult, committed *seppuku* on the lawn of the U.S. Post Office building. This morning's Atlanta *Constitution*, in a story run under the byline of Sybyl Celeste, reports that the ceremony was "lovely."

My hands tremble. The trembling surface of my coffee, in a hand-painted china cup, returns to me a disconcerting image of a man whose purposes are unfulfilled. By this premeditated treachery, you see, Mrs. Bernard Bligh Brumblelo and all the conspiring others have made me the sole adult inhabitant of their anemic, tumbledown, backwater community.

I have become Kudzu Valley, Georgia. Dear, dear God, what am I supposed to *do*?

MICHAEL SWANWICK

The Last Geek

*Michael Swanwick won the Hugo Award for Best Short Story
in 1999, 2000, and 2002, and for Best Novelette in 2003. He
has also received the 1994 World Fantasy Award for his story
"Radio Waves," the Nebula Award for his novel* Stations of
the Tide *(1990), and the Theodore Sturgeon Award for his
story "The Edge of the World" (1989). His other novels
include* In the Drift, Vacuum Flowers, The Iron Dragon's
Daughter, Jack Faust, *and* Bones of the Earth; *his stories
have been collected in* Gravity's Angels, A Geography of
Unknown Lands, Slow Dancing Through Time, Moon
Dogs, Puck Aleshire's Abeecedary, *and* Tales of Old
Earth. *His influential essays "A User's Guide to the Post-
moderns" and "'In the Tradition . . . '" were published as*
The Postmodern Archipelago *in 1997. He lives with his
wife in Philadelphia. This marks the first publication of
"The Last Geek."*

He is met at the airport by an overtall grad student with bad skin. The grad student is nervous. He's working toward a degree in Elvis Studies and is convinced that he is the worst possible choice for the job. He'll bungle it. He'll say all the wrong things. He won't be able to identify the man among the crush of travelers when he gets off the plane.

But the geek is unmistakable. A short, plump man with ginger hair, he has a sad, pink, ageless face. He could be thirty-seven. He could be seventy-three. He wears a sports jacket with no tie and matching white belt and shoes. Though the airport is thronged, he stands apart. He is in the crowd, but not of it.

"Sir!" The grad student jabs a graceless hand in his direction. He turns slowly, the way movie stars do, and unfolds the sweetest of smiles beneath the kindliest of wisdom-crinkled eyes. His speech is melodious. Somehow they are in the car. Somehow everything is all right.

There is a fruit basket waiting for the geek in his hotel room. Pristine in cellophane, it contains, in addition to the astonishing apples and oranges and pears, two small bottles of spring water, three foil-wrapped wedges of cheese, and a narrow box of gourmet crackers.

With the unthinking reflexes of the constant traveler, he snaps on the television set and immediately tunes it out. He hangs up his jacket in the bathroom and turns on the shower at its hottest setting so the room will fill up with steam and gentle out the wrinkles. Then he unpacks his bag, neatly filling the bureau drawers, shirt by shirt and shorts by shorts.

He takes off his shoes, but leaves his socks on.

Finally he removes the flask from its elastic pocket in the suitcase and carries it and an apple out onto the balcony. The night is warm and a strange city lies glittering at his feet. Behind him, the television laughs and screams, a familiar presence, the nomad's home and family.

There is a chair on the balcony. He sits in it, and puts his stockinged feet up on the rail. He unscrews the top of the flask. He takes a sip. Jack Daniels.

He stares off into the night and thinks thoughts that are his and his alone.

He is eating a modest breakfast from the buffet in the lobby restaurant when the grad student reappears in the slipstream of a woman who pushes eagerly past the other diners. She is an academic, and dresses as one, but with a pashmina scarf thrown loosely over her shoulders and angular silver earrings to assert her individuality. She has a sharp and lively face. White teeth put a crisp bite into her smile when he rises to greet her. She glides into a chair at his table with the assurance of a woman who belongs there.

She is Professor Djuna Bloom and she is the head of the Department of Southern Culture at the university that has paid to bring him here. It's an honor to meet him at last and there are just a few details to go over about his appearance today so that everything goes smoothly. The words tumble out one after another, but so briskly and clearly enunciated that they do not seem rushed.

He nods at everything she says. "Foah the sun," he says when she comments on the Panama hat that rests on an empty chair alongside him. "As you can see, I have fair skin."

The department head is charmed.

Now she touches the back of his hand. She's actually *flirting* with him. The grad student (still there!) recalls first the legendarily easy way carnies have had with women and then old departmental gossip about Professor Bloom and a certain married faculty couple. To his intense embarrassment, he finds himself scowling and blushing.

After a tour of the campus, the geek is feted at a luncheon in the chancellor's mansion. The chancellor has a cook, but not a very good one. The food is dreadfully ordinary. Vegetables are boiled until they're limp, a roast cooked until it's brown. But the plates and silver are genuinely old, and the dining room is Victorian in the very best sense. It's a pleasure merely sitting in it.

"It must be wonderful," says Professor Martelli of Social Sciences, "to have a budget robust enough to fly in guest speakers." It is her long-standing opinion that Southern Culture is a subdivision of anthropology, and as such properly belongs within her department.

"I *think*, Rebecca," says Professor Bloom testily, "that you'll find . . ." Voices lift from every corner, objecting, pleading, calling for reconciliation. The chancellor half rises from his chair.

A sudden chiming of spoon on crystal cuts through the voices and silences them. They turn to see their guest smiling gently at them.

"Watch this." He breathes upon the spoon, polishes it with his napkin, breathes upon it again. He places the bowl upon his nose, slides it downward, releases the handle.

As if by magic, the spoon hangs from the tip of his nose.

Delighted laughter fills the room. Even the chancellor laughs. Even Rebecca Martelli laughs.

He nods, removes the spoon from his nose, and returns to his food.

After the meal, the geek goes back to his hotel for a nap. Then the long-suffering grad student ferries him back to campus for an informal chat with the Senior Honors Seminar for the department's most promising undergrads.

"It's a dying profession," he tells them. "I mean that quite literally. I've lost so many dear friends to death. Now I'm the last practitioner of my . . . peculiar profession"—he pauses while they chuckle—"and when I'm gone, it won't be revived, any more than you're ever going to see Minoan bull-leapers again. I am a revenant of a vanished way of life."

Because this is a closed seminar, he is free to tell them things that will not be touched on in his public presentation tonight. He talks about the kootch dancers and what they did with boiled eggs. He discusses the folk cures for syphilis that were still being practiced in his youth, and their appalling effects. Then he tells a story about the tattooed lady and what she charged amorous suitors twenty dollars to see that is so raw it makes Dr. Petri, the seminar leader, laugh like a horse.

Wiping tears from his eyes, Dr. Petri exclaims that this, *this* is why he went into teaching in the first place!

There is a light supper at a local restaurant alone with Professor Bloom, who insists he call her Djuna. Afterwards, she leads him across campus to Vanderbilt Hall, where the department holds a sherry reception. There are crackers and a wheel of blue cheese and they drink out of tiny little glasses from what the undergraduates jokingly call the Hereditary Bottle because no one can remember when it was first opened and it isn't near empty yet.

The geek stands holding a glass, with his other hand in his pocket, perfectly at ease. The purpose of the party is to allow the students to interact with him informally. Most can't. The teachers cluster about him so tightly that only the most aggressive students are able to worm their way into that tight knot of conversation and score an acknowledged remark off of him. Even the shyest undergrad, however, even Debbie Harcourt, who wears thick glasses and ugly dresses and walks about in a perpetual cringe, can feel the calm aura of authority that radiates from him. It's simple charisma. Some people have it. The rest flock about those lucky few.

The presentation is an enormous success. Every seat in the auditorium is filled and in defiance of all fire regulations there are people sitting in the aisles and standing, arms folded, against the back wall. When the geek appears, his soft voice is picked up by the microphones and permeates the room.

"Good evening," he says. "How y'all doing?"

They applaud warmly.

He begins with a little autobiography, talking about his impoverished rural childhood and how he ran away to join first a forty-miler, then a full-fledged tent show. When he explains how some of the games of chance are rigged so that nobody can win, mouths open into astonished circles throughout the audience. He is too much the gentleman to use the term "sucker," but many of those present realize that that's exactly what they've been.

He talks about traveling around the Old South by rail. His stories evoke a kinder, gentler era, a time without haste and worry, one filled with simpler pleasures and a hunger for wonder that a carnival could perfectly fulfill.

But then he turns to the question of racial prejudice. "Oh, it was awful," he says. "You have no idea." He tells of the time he witnessed a lynching. The audience listens in a silence so profound that when somebody coughs, half of them *jump*. It's a harrowing story. It makes their hair stand on end.

"And they brought their children along to see," he concludes. "Their children!" He shakes his head sadly. "For all the very real problems we have today, it's a miracle that things aren't worse."

The hours fly by. He finishes up with an exploration of the deeper significance of his profession. He quotes Derrida. He quotes Barzun. He quotes Rousseau. The audience is in his hands.

Finally, the dean of Admissions comes out from backstage carrying a live chicken. Grinning, the dean holds it out to the geek, who solemnly accepts it. He strokes the bird's feathers, calming it, hypnotizing it. He holds the creature up before his eyes.

Then he bites off its head.

The audience roars. Their applause swells as he walks offstage with a modest little wave. The students are on their feet, clapping and stamping as if they were at a basketball game. The sound is thunderous. After only the slightest of pauses, the chancellor, deans, and dignitaries seated in the front row also stand, making the ovation universal.

Backstage, Djuna hands him an envelope with his honorarium check, which he places in an inside pocket of his jacket. Impetuously, she darts forward and plants a chaste peck on his cheek. The grad student, tears in eyes, seizes his hand and pumps it up and down.

Then it's back to his hotel room, alone. In the morning, he'll catch a plane for his next appearance. He is the last of his breed, as American as John Wayne or Buzz Aldrin, a solitary man perhaps, as all great men are, a living cultural treasure and an acknowledged national icon. But when the applause dies down, there's nothing but the night, the road ahead and one more gig. He's alone again with silence and his own thoughts.

DANIEL WALLACE

Slippered Feet

Daniel Wallace is the author of the novels Big Fish, Ray in Reverse, *and* The Watermelon King. Big Fish *was filmed by director Tim Burton. A native of Alabama, Daniel lives in Chapel Hill, North Carolina, with his wife and children. "Slippered Feet" was first published in* The Massachusetts Review.

We tried to learn the language, Eva and I. We bought a book and tapes and three or four days a week a couple of months before the trip we listened and read and asked each other questions. We worked on increasing our vocabulary.

In the morning, for instance, at breakfast, Eva would say "Pass the milk, please," or rather simply "Milk," and then she would point to it and I would say "Here is the milk, Eva." And she would say "Thank you, Robert," and I would say "Think nothing of it."

Learning a new language at our age was a challenge, but it was also fun. It made us feel like kids again, studying together for the final exam. That's where we met, Eva and I, at college, back East, reading Chaucer on the steps in front of the library. But that was some time ago, more like history than any kind of real memory. We were both retired: Eva from teaching grammar school, me from management. I mean we had the time now, and so we tried to learn a new word every day.

At night after dinner we'd listen to the voice on tape and repeat after it. It was the same man, the same voice, night after night. We would drag our slippered feet into the living room, and with the tape player on the coffee table before us we would say what he said in just the way he said it. Or tried to: he gave us very little time to respond. There was only so much blank space before he went on to the next question or Useful Expression ("How much is this?" "How long before the next train arrives?") and only rarely was their a sufficient pause allowed, a *reasonable* pause allowed in which we could speak without stumbling. The tapes irritated me a little bit, but we did the best we could. We tried to learn one Useful Expression every evening.

There was progress, a notable progress with both of us. But women, I've heard, are naturals with this kind of thing, and Eva was no exception. She was always a few vocabulary words ahead of me. She had the better accent. She was a bit more keen on learning. Still, it surprised me how one night not long after we'd begun with these sessions, when Eva claimed to have actually dreamed the language. Said she dreamed in the words of the language.

I've never seen her so excited, telling me about it.

She was at breakfast in the dream, she told me, she was at breakfast downstairs in the morning room, which was no different in the dream, she said, than it was in real life: there was the same small round maplewood table we sit at every morning, the same wicker chairs; the window framed a view of the same old patch of pine. Even the same squirrels were there, in her dream, the same squirrels I've threatened to maim and kill and eat with my hands on more occasions than I can remember. All this was the same, and Eva was speaking the language. She said "Pass the milk, please," and "Butter, please," and "Is there a way out of here?"—straight from the book, all of it, nothing special.

But the man she was speaking to wasn't me. I wasn't the man in her dream. The person she was speaking to, the person facing her on the other side of the table, was the man on the tape. Rather, it was to the voice of the man on the tape that was there; she couldn't actually see him, she said. All her questions were answered—the milk was passed, the butter, too—but by no one she could see in the dream. It was just his voice, the sound of his voice in her dream.

I didn't believe her, of course. Though I'd heard of this kind of thing happening before, I knew that there was no way she could have attained this level of—what? *linguistic intimacy*, I think they call it—in such a short time; *I* hadn't, at any rate, and we were both shooting par on this language thing. She wasn't that much better than me. What I thought was this, and I told her: I said she probably hadn't had the dream she thought she'd had. I said that she hadn't been studying the language long enough for her to have such a dream. What I did say is that it was quite possible that she had *dreamed* she dreamed the dream in the language—which is quite some difference.

Eva listened patiently, nodding when I made my main points, smiling. Then she kind of laughed.

"I think it's funny," she said, "that anyone would try to tell anyone else what they did and didn't dream. Granted, you sleep beside me, and we do spend almost every minute of our waking lives together, since you retired. And though you seem to have a knowledge superior to mine on most things, especially on those things you know nothing about, I must tell you, now: you cannot, and never will tell me what I did and what I did not dream. It's absurd."

Well, this surprised me, coming from Eva. Usually she dreams about flying through shopping malls on her father's back, or being outside in the front yard without any clothes on—harmless, meaningless dreams. I had never said anything about them before. But now I had, and I saw that she had a point: I should stay out of her mind while she was sleeping.

"You're absolutely correct, Eva," I said. "I had no right, I was out of line and I'm sorry."

But I still don't believe you, I thought.

If the inside of her head was private, so mine could be too.

" 'A garden spot,' " I read to Eva the next evening, " 'one of the very last on earth.' " This was from one of the many books we had purchased about the place. There was a picture of a group of black-haired children lapping up water from a stream. Behind them, in the distance, were the famous Kotomanzi forests, near the eastern ridge of the island country. I showed the picture to Eva, and she nodded, smiled.

"Nice," she said.

We never had or wanted children, but we have always enjoyed looking at pictures which have children in them.

" 'It is a country of hills, bridges and streams,' " I read, " 'where the past becomes present, and where the present remains fixed in the past.' What now?" I said. "What do you think *that* means?" I asked her. " 'Where the present remains fixed in the past?' That's impossible. That's impossible, isn't it? The present is *now*, the past is *then*. How can it be now and then at the same time?"

"It's a guidebook, Robert."

"I know what it is," I said. "I know it's a guidebook."

"Sometimes they exaggerate," she said.

"And lie," I said. "Sometimes they just flat-out lie. And it doesn't mention anything about the future. But I suppose the future is past as well. Or maybe it just never happens."

But Eva wasn't listening to me. This was after dinner, and she was fooling with the tape. Even though it was hardly past eight, she had changed into her nightgown and slippers—a habit of hers. I looked at her, trying to remember how beautiful she had been as a young woman—which was quite an exercise, I must say, for those days were a part of history as well. She had been beautiful, of course, a great beauty, finely wrought, a porcelain, elegant beauty. But she had not aged as gracefully as I might have hoped, or, I'm sure, as she would have liked to. She had become *old*, painfully, obviously old. She had reached that age where every bit of her that wasn't made of bone began to fall away from her body, as if gravity were exerting a special pressure on it, and she just wasn't built to take such pressure: she was slender, but when she moved pieces of her shook, her arms and legs, and when she slept she looked dead—dead! In the middle of the night I've opened my eyes and thought, Here I am, sleeping with a dead woman! But it was just what the pillow had done to her soft face, and the way her mouth hung open, and the general lifelessness of everything in the middle of the night.

She isn't dead, I thought. She is my wife. We've been married for thirty-five years, and I love her.

Still, I wished she had turned out to look different.

I wish she had stayed pretty.

"Ready?" she said. "Tonight's lesson is on what to do in case of an emergency."

"Ready," I said, and she hit the Play button, and the man's voice filled the room.

Tonight, as he did every night, the man said the sentences much too fast. It was almost impossible to say "My wallet was stolen, can you help me?" before he proceeded with "I think I'm bleeding, call an ambulance." Eva didn't seem to be having as much trouble with him as I was: she was poised like a swimmer on a platform, ready to dive, except that she was on the edge of the sofa, intent, listening, almost trembling she was so stiff.

Looking at her like this I completely forgot to listen to the next Useful Expression.

"Play that back," I said. "I didn't quite get that."

She glanced at me, I thought, with an expression of both amusement and irritation.

"With pleasure," she said.

So she rewound the tape, and the man said, "I have been wandering this road for three days. I need a glass of water."

I stared at the translation in our books.

"Stop the tape," I said.

"What?"

"Stop the tape, please, Eva. Now."

She sighed, and somewhat reluctantly hit the Off button.

"What is it, Robert?" she said. "We only have a little more to go for tonight."

"Did you hear what he just said?" I asked her. "Did you hear what he wants us to learn? 'I have been wandering this road for three days. I need a glass of water.' Now, why in the world would we need to learn that? What kind of Useful Expression is that? 'Wandering this road for three days . . .' Who's going to be wandering a road? We're going to get a guide, for heaven sakes."

"It's a primitive country in many ways," she said. "You can never tell what might happen. Their priests still perform magic. You read that, didn't you? The prime minister himself is a priest, Robert. What happens if our guide gets mixed up in some voodoolike ritual and dies on a day trip? What happens if we have to fend for ourselves after that? Under the circumstances," she said, "I think it might be wise to memorize everything he says."

"Okay," I said, sort of throwing up my hands. "Hit Play."

"May I sleep with your wife?" came the voice.

"This is ridiculous!" I said, standing.

"It's a custom, Robert!" she said, calling after me. But I had had enough for the night. I went upstairs to read, and to sleep, listening to the sound of their voices below.

Learning the language had been Eva's idea—a good one, I thought at the time. When we decided we wanted to see a part of the world, neither of us wanted to become your typical American tourist—especially of the old, ocean-liner kind—and so I suppose that was why I agreed so readily to the tapes and books. It would distinguish us. It would make us, in some way, new—I mean young, or like the young, open-minded. You hear so much about old age all your life that by the time you get to it the only thing that's a surprise is the truth of all you've heard, all the infirmities and strange failures, all the bones in your body becoming tight and dry. Old age is an old story. It is, more than anything, ugly, plain and simple, and the work comes from trying to see past these things. But it's like being deprived of most of your vocabulary.

We were trying to escape the cliché.

I mean we tried to learn the language.

"How late did you stay up last night?" I asked Eva the next morning in the breakfast room. She was frying an egg, humming a strange tune. I had never heard it before. Then I recognized it: it was the music which introduced the Useful Expression section of the tapes.

"Oh, I don't know," she said. "I didn't notice. Not too late."

"I guess you got pretty far ahead of me," I said.

"Not really," she said. "I went back. I just listened to his voice."

"What?"

"I reviewed," she said, smiling at me over her shoulder.

She brought me my egg, humming her little tune. She hummed with the quivering voice of an older woman. It sounded as if she was in pain and it irked me.

"Eva," I said. "Please stop humming."

"As you wish, dear."

She stopped humming, but she still seemed to be in a good humor: I could tell she was humming inside. Even her arm, as she reached for the butter, did so with a singsongy kind of grace, as if it were dancing. Her flesh shook. In that moment I pitied in a profound way all women who lived to be old: so few of them stayed together. So few of them were easy to look at. Most of them, I thought at that moment, are like junky antiques, attic-bound. But even my pity, which I felt radiating from me, did not affect her mood.

"You seem cheerful today," I said.

"I had another dream," she said. "Would you like to hear about it?"

"Not particularly," I said.

I wouldn't give her the satisfaction.

"What about the dream I dreamed I dreamed?" she said, and laughed.

I set my fork and knife down on the plate.

"What's so funny, Eva?"

"Oh," she said. "Things. This and that. You know."

Then she picked up her eggs with her fingers, and stuffed them in her mouth.

"For God's sake Eva. What—"

"Like they do in the islands," she said.

"I see," I said.

But I didn't. I didn't see anything at all but my old, tired wife, eating breakfast with her hands.

Over the next few days a change took place in Eva, a change I would at the time ascribe to fragility, to the brain of an aging woman losing balance and making a fall. She smiled a great deal, and hummed, and time and again I would find her in the living room, sitting in a chair, staring at nothing. "Eva," I would say, and she would blush, stammer, and rush into the kitchen, as if I had embarrassed her. Through the kitchen door, if I pressed my ear close enough to it, I could hear her giggling like a little girl.

Our trip was only a few weeks away now; everything had been arranged. Our itinerary, along with our plane tickets, had arrived, and I kept them in a dresser drawer beneath a pair of black socks. We were all set, and I for one was looking forward to the change.

But as Eva's sickness—and it was a sickness—progressed, I felt uncertain about the voyage. Was it wise to leave home now, I wondered, to go so far away, into strange and perhaps dangerous country, as Eva was falling apart?

She gave me odd looks.

Every night before bed she said, "Bostandurasi-silamingo," which is the island word for "Sweet dreams."

"Good night, Eva," I said.

The odd thing was, she seemed happy. She seemed so happy, and acted so absurdly girlish, it was sad. It was very, very sad.

And yet we continued our evening sessions. After dinner she would rush into the living room, set up the tape player, and call for me to join her.

"Sahashi is ready," she said. "Come on!"

"Sahashi?" I asked her, and laughed. "Who in God's name is Sahashi?"

I felt a little cruel for laughing, and touched her on the shoulder to make up for it. I felt so sorry for her.

"Sahashi," she said, "is the voice. I was looking through the manual and came upon his name. Isn't it a pretty name, Robert: Sahashi?"

"It's probably something like Frank or Elmer in their language," I said. "But yes, it has a ring to it."

"He's thirty-seven years old!" she said. "Doesn't he sound older?"

"They give his age?" I said.

"Let's start," she said.

And so we did. His voice began. We listened. My heart, however, wasn't in it, and as Sahashi spoke and Eva spoke back to him—she had such a knack for languages—all I could do was watch her old eyes sparkle and shine. She was looking forward to this trip even more than I. For the last week she had been reading all she could about the islands, their history and culture, and from time to time would catch her breath, and if I were in the room would read to me, ". . . At night in the country the darkness is as deep as velvet, and a low fog, a thick mist covers all roads. It is the mist that reminds one of heat rising from the jungle floor, of history and prehistory, of the ancient animals who once roamed these volcanic islands, some of which are said to still exist." The words made her eyes grow wide, and some nights, long after I'd gone to sleep, she would be up reading, licking her fingers, turning another dry page.

Suddenly Eva hit the machine with the palm of her hand, shutting it off.

"You're not listening!" she said. "You're not *listening*, Robert. Why aren't you listening to Sahashi?"

"I . . . my mind was elsewhere, Eva."

"Why," she said, stuttering in a queer rage, "that's the most inconsiderate thing I've ever heard! I can't believe you! Sahashi has gone out of his way to help us with this language, and you—your mind is elsewhere! You're such an oaf, Robert! I don't know what to say, I—I don't want to talk about it anymore. So please leave us. Please leave us alone."

"What?"

"Please leave the room. *Now*, Robert."

I did. I did as Eva told me to.

But as of that moment, the trip was off.

There have been times, a number of them over the years, when I wished that Eva and I had gone to the trouble of having children. If we'd had children when we'd thought about it, thirty-five years ago, they would be grown now, and I could call one of them up and say, Your mother isn't well. For some time now she has been acting strangely. What do you think I should do?

I needed advice then—I still do—and I wished I had a son or a daughter who could give it to me.

Because Eva took a plunge. I'd seen it coming, of course, I knew she wasn't right for a long time, but when she finally took the plunge and was lost to me, I had nowhere to go, no one to turn to.

The night she asked me to leave the room I went upstairs and prepared for bed. I opened my sock drawer and stared at the plane tickets we'd never use, read the names of the places we'd never see. The forests of the Kotomanzi, the bridges, the little black-haired children drinking water from the streams. I'd been looking forward to taking a few pictures, maybe even turning it into a slide show, and was wondering what Eva would do when I broke the news to her—when I heard laughter coming from the living room downstairs. It wasn't just Eva, either. There was a man laughing, too.

"Eva?" I said, coming to bottom of the stairs. "Is everything okay?"

I peered around the corner and saw her wiping a tear from her eye, and breathing deeply after her last fit of laughter.

"Oh, Robert," she said. "Did we disturb you? It's just that Sahashi was telling me some jokes. Tape Six," she said, "is all about the native sense of humor. You have to listen to this. Sit down. I'll play it back.

"Now listen," she said, after she had found the right place.

And I listened. But not a word of what I heard coming from the little black box made sense to me. Oh, I did pick out some sounds I thought I recognized—"banana," he said at one point—but I was lost as far as any real meaning went.

When the "joke" was over Eva collapsed into another frenzy of laughter, while I stood there, uncomprehending.

"Eva," I said, walking toward her. "I think we need to talk."

"I know what you're going to say," she said.

"You do?"

If she knew I supposed she wasn't as sick as I thought she was. Maybe, I thought, there was some hope.

"You don't get it, do you?"

"No," I said. "I don't understand why you've—"

"It's in the way he tells it, really, isn't it? I mean, you can't *talk* about a joke, can you? You either get it or you don't. I'm sorry, Robert."

"Come to bed, Eva."

"In a minute," she said. "He's got one about a traveling salesman he says I *have* to hear before bed."

"A traveling salesman?" I said. "In the islands?"

"Some things," she said, "are universal." She stood and kissed me on the cheek. "Bostandurasi-silamingo," she said. "Taskedashi. Mabarareta! Good night!"

Though I have hoped for one, there is no happy ending for Eva and me. There is not even an ending. We simply go on.

When I told Eva, the morning after her scene in the living room, that we would not be going on our trip, she took it much worse than even I had imagined she would. I was ready for another scene, for a tantrum, but she didn't say a word. She didn't even ask why. She just looked at me for a moment, excused herself from table and went upstairs, where she was up there for most of the day. I didn't bother her, of course. I wanted to give her time to accept the disappointment, and when she came downstairs later that day, almost six hours later, I thought she had. The small, sad smile she gave me seemed to say that she was resigned to my decision.

"Eva," I said. "I don't mean to say that we'll never go. Just not for a while. Not until we get our own lives in order."

She smiled again, and went about preparing dinner.

"Eva," I said. "I know how badly you wanted to go. But I did too. I really did. I'm not happy about what's happened either. I just wish you would say something."

"Tastandi," she said. "Sta kustandi rina-ste."

"What's that mean?" I said. " 'All's well?' "

"*Tastandi!*" she screamed. *"Sta kustandi rina-ste!"*

Then she broke down crying and ran into the living room, and though I followed her she was too fast, and by the time I reached her she already had the tape deck out and on.

"Taskete," Sahashi said. "Las nastashi. Las nastashi."

"Las nastashi," she said. "Las nastashi."

And so on.

Spring came, then summer.

It's January now, and the streets are covered with snow. It's too cold to do anything but sit inside and study, to listen to these tapes. Sahashi still irritates me—he doesn't work with me the way he works with Eva—but I am trying to keep up with her, it's important to me, now that she seems to have forgotten English completely. I don't think she's forgotten it, though. I think she just refuses to speak it anymore.

As hard as I work, though, as much as I study, Eva seems to be just that far ahead, and I can only understand about 10 percent of everything she says to me. And I can't bring myself to eat with my hands, and Eva laughs at me because of it.

What happened? How is it things turn out the way they do? Eva is old and ugly. We are, both of us, closer to the end of our lives than to the beginning. Sometimes I wish I had never met her. But now she is all I have. I have to learn how to talk all over again. Every night she calls to me, and I drag my slippered feet into the living room, and we sit there, the two of us, listening to that man. And though I wish I was better at this sort of thing, and that one day, soon, I might be able to speak with her, I wonder: When I finally do learn, what will I say? What words will I strike her with in this new language? How, dear Eva, will we begin?

KALAMU YA SALAAM

Alabama

New Orleans editor, writer, and filmmaker Kalamu ya Salaam is founder of Neo-Griot, a black writers' workshop (text, recordings and video); cofounder of Runagate Multimedia publishing company; leader of the WordBand, a poetry performance ensemble; and moderator of e-Drum, a listserv for black writers and diverse supporters of their literature. His latest book is the anthology 360° A Revolution of Black Poets *(Black Words Press). Salaam's latest spoken-word CD is* My Story, My Song. *His background includes thirteen years as editor of* The Black Collegian *magazine and a five-year member of the Free Southern Theatre. He is the codirector of Students at the Center, a writing program in the public schools of New Orleans. Salaam can be reached at* kalamu@aol.com. *This marks the first publication of "Alabama."*

I

it is late in december 1998, the weather is uncharacteristically warm. there is much that is wrong. an old man has killed himself.

if he had been an airplane and fell from the sky, the forensic engineers might have diagnosed: metal fatigue—the quality of structural breakdown when the weariness caused by the ravages of time destroy an object's physical ability to bear the weight of existence. but this fellow was not a passenger jet. he was just a chestnut-colored, elderly african-american who everyone said looked remarkably good for his age.

his eyesight was fit enough—without glasses he could drive day or night. and he would step two flights of steps rather than wait on a slow elevator. he was sensible about his diet and walked two miles every morning to keep his weight down. plus, any day of the week, he could outbowl his son. No, his age was not a problem.

so what was so disastrous in his life that the permanent solution of suicide was the action of choice to deal with whatever temporary problem he was confronting?

we are not sure what exactly was wrong, but we do know that when he resolved to end it, he was watching television. got up and said something to his wife, who was in the kitchen. shortly thereafter went into his backyard with a gun in his hand—no one in the house saw him go outside. but what if they had? could they have stopped him? probably not. at best they may have been able to momentarily postpone the inevitable, but eventually life turns cold. or we are deluged with the dreariness of chilly rains. and we die.

what did the slow-moving man think as he descended the steps into the backyard? indeed, did he think, or was his mind blank with certainty?

his body died there, but was he already dead in spirit? does it matter what happens to the body, once the spirit has been broken? this is a story about death.

2

i have often thought about those stark black-and-white photographs of lynching scenes. we know what happened to the lynchee, but what happened to all the lynchers? the ones standing around. some smiling into an unhidden camera—look, you can see that these people know that a photograph is documenting them. a number of them are looking at the camera full on, challenging the lens to capture something human in the grisly scene. a significant number are children, young boys and girls, leering.

i have heard stories of whites who were repulsed by those death scenes. those who were changed forever by witnessing a lynching, hearing about a lynching, backing away from their parents come back home chatting about the nigger who got what he deserved. okay. but what I want to know is what happened to the lynchers who did not back away. those who took in the murder scene as acceptable. later on in life, how did they raise their children? do they have flashbacks of lynchings—occasionally? often? never?

does watching a man or woman die a violent death diminish the person who enjoys the spectacle? can one revel in the fascinating flame of a human on fire and afterwards remain emotionally balanced? and what about memory, does the extreme violence of mob murder involuntarily replay years later triggered by scenes such as o.j. maintaining he did not slice nicole's throat or wesley snipes on the silver screen bigger than life kissing a white woman who favors irma singletary, your daughter's friend who divorced a black man after he beat her one night and she refused to press charges against him the next morning?

in many of those garish photographs there are a lot of people standing around. I wonder how many among those audiences are alive today, driving america's streets and buying christmas gifts?

3

richard hammonds was a handsome man. he was moderately intelligent. could work hard but really didn't like to exert his body to the point of sweating. believe it or not what he was really good at was leatherwork. give him a piece of leather and his tools and he could make anything from shoes to hats and everything in between. and he would do it well, so well that a number of people have been buried wearing shoes richard had made—their family knew how proud the deceased had been of richard's handicraft, so that's what the corpse wore at the funeral.

for example, brother james sweet—his name was actually james anthony johnson but, with a twinkle in his eye, he would raise his left hand, flashing his ruby-and-diamond pinkie ring, graciously tip his ever-present gray stetson, and, in his trademark rumbling baritone, request that you call him "james sweet, bra-thaaa jaaaames sweee-eat, cause i'm always good to womens, treats children with kindness and is a friend to the end with all my brothers"—well, brother sweet had instructed everyone of concern in his immediate family to bury him in his favorite oxblood loafers that richard had hooked up especially for sweet. there were no shoes more comfortable anywhere in the world and he, sweets, which was the acceptable short form of brother sweet, certainly didn't want to be stepping around heaven with anything uncomfortable on his bunioned feet (nor, likewise, running through hell, if it came to that—and he would wink to let you know that he didn't think it would come to that). of course, at a funeral you don't usually see the feet of the recently departed but that was not the point.

the point is that people were really pleased with richard hammonds's handiwork. unfortunately, in terms of a stable income, although richard hammonds excelled at making leather goods, what he actually loved to do was watch and wager on the ponies. and since he lived in new orleans and the fairgrounds racetrack was convenient, well, during racing season, which seemed to be almost year-round, richard spent many an afternoon cheering on a two-year-old filly while his workbench went unused.

fortunately, richard hammonds seldom wagered more than he could afford to lose and on occasion won much more than he had gambled for the month. however, winning at the racetrack was uncertain. no matter what betting system he used, richard could never accurately predict when he would win big or how long a losing streak would maintain its grip on his wallet.

routinely, richard would do enough leatherwork to pay the house note and give eileen an allotment to buy food and then it was off to the races. needless to say, had eileen not worked as a seamstress at haspel's factory in the seventh ward, this would have been an unworkable arrangement.

but richard hammonds didn't drink more than a beer now and then, went to mass every sunday morning, and was moderately faithful, so what could have been a precarious and intemperate social situation settled into a predictable and manageable state of affairs until richard was wobbling home one october evening—he had had a very good day and had indulged in a few drinks at mule's, in fact, he had even bought a round for the guys and stashed a small bundle in his hip pocket for eileen and still had in his inside jacket pocket enough money to pay for every bill he could think of.

when the police stopped richard his explanations of who he was, where he had come from, where he was going and how he came to have so much cash weren't sufficient to please the two officers who were looking for a middle-aged colored man who had robbed and raped a woman over in midcity.

we do not have to go into any details. the focus of this story is not on the beating, the injustice of his subsequent death, or even the condemning of the two police officers. remember, we are concerned with death, and the question is: when, if ever, did richard know he was going to die and what was his reaction, or more precisely, what were his thoughts about that awful fact, if indeed he ever realized the imminence of his demise?

4

everybody, sooner or later, thinks about dying. for many african-americans there is even a morbid twist on this universal reflection on the inevitability of mortality. for us, it is not just a question of when we will die but also a more thorny question, a question we seldom would admit publicly but one that at some occasion or another consumes us in private: would i be better off dead? if you had been reared black in pre-60s white america, sooner or later, you probably looked that thought in the eye.

however, the universality of death thoughts notwithstanding, there is a big difference between abstract speculation about the eventuality of death and the far more difficult task of confronting the stale breath of death as it fouls the air in front your nose. death is nothing to fuck with. indeed, actually facing certain death can make you shit on yourself, particularly if death not only surprises you but also perversely gives you a moment to think about crossing the great divide. like when a lover in the throes of getting it on, sincerely announces through clenched teeth that they are about to come, you respond as any sensible person would by doing harder, or faster, or stronger, or more tenderly, more intensely, more whatever, you increase the pressure and help usher that moment, well, when it's death coming what do we do, do we rush to it, or do we withdraw from it? don't answer too soon. think of all the people you have heard of who died as a result of being someplace they really shouldn't have been, being involved in some situation they should never have encountered, at the hands of someone whom they should never have been near. think about how often we die other than a natural death—and then again, what death is not natural, because isn't it part of human nature to die, and to kill?

richard never expected to die on that day, especially since he had just experienced the good fortune of a twenty-to-one long shot paying off on a fifty-dollar bet. even when the tandem took turns trying to beat a confession out of him, even after his jaw was broken and he could only moan and shake his head, even then richard still didn't think of death. he was too busy dealing with pain. when they put the gun in his mouth, he perversely thought, "go 'head, pull the trigger, that would be better than getting beat like this," but even then, richard didn't really expect to die. he just wanted the beating to be over and if it took death to end it, well, he was feeling so bad he thought that death might be preferable. yet, richard didn't really think he was going to die. in fact, as is the case with so many of us, richard died before he realized they were going to kill him.

we blacks wonder about fate and destiny, justice and karma. sometimes there seems that there is no god, or rather if there is a god then he is capricious with a macabre sense of humor—we grant him humor because to think of god without humor would be to concede that we are at the mercy of a monster who enjoys literally tormenting us to death.

which brings up another question, would we procreate if it were not so pleasurable? if sex didn't feel good, would we bother with conceiving children? for many of us the answer is obvious; of course we wouldn't. that's why birth control was created—to protect us from disease and children, to make it possible for us to enjoy the pleasure of sexual procreation with none of the responsibilities of child rearing. which means that the drive to have children may in fact not be as strong as we have been led to believe, or maybe, it's simply that in modern times we have been conditioned to think only of ourselves—the personal pleasures. but the question i really want to raise is this: what if death were pleasurable, would we end ourselves? what if it felt really good to die—not just calming but totally pleasurable?

of course, richard was not thinking any of these sorts of questions as the two officers smashed in richard's face. Formal philosophy is a task engaged in by those for whom survival is not a pressing issue.

5

every age, every people, every society has an ethos—a defining spirit. and this spirit expresses itself in sometimes odd and fascinating ways. for much of the twentieth century the ethos of african-americans was one of contemplating the future with a certain optimism. why else march through the streets of birmingham, alabama, and sing "we shall overcome" to bull connor, a man who was not known for any appreciation of music?

the birmingham of bull connor was just about half a century ago. during that period when bombs regularly sounded throughout birmingham and the deep south, if you go back and look at the pictures of black people of that era when they posed for a portrait, especially if they were college educated, you will invariably spy among the men what i call the classic negro pose of hand to chin in contemplation. a variation is one temple of a pair of glasses held close to or between the lips; then there is the pipe firmly grasped, not to mention the college diploma held to the side of the head like a sweetheart—

these are iconic images of optimistic negroes, images that capture the ethos of their era.

today, the hand has moved from the chin. We no longer pose in contemplative ways, what is cropping up more and more is the hand to the crown of the head, not in a woe-is-me posture but more like: damn, this is some deep shit we're in.

unconsciously, during a recent photo shoot, i ended up in that pose. when the picture was published i was mildly surprised, i did not remember adopting that look of serious concern. but just because i don't remember it does not mean that it didn't happen. clearly it happened. there is my unsmiling portrait. and i see that pose more and more, particularly when i look at the publicity shots of writers. we are children of production—we are shaped and influenced, even when unconscious of it, by the prevailing ethos. a lot of us look like we are gravely weighing the upsides and downsides of both life and death.

and when people tell you how much they like that photo, then that tells you just how much the photo reflects our current contemplation of death. In those photographs rarely are we smiling. our eyes are wide open. we are not dreamy-eyed romantics. we are not lost in meditation. we are looking at death. the disintegration of our communities, the fissure of our social structures, the absence of lasting interpersonal relationships, the proliferation of age and gender alienation. the death of a people.

and when i took my photo it was supposed to be a happy occasion. but obviously the myth of the happy negro is long gone.

6

i wonder when the old man put the gun to his head did he hold his head with his free hand?

7

richard couldn't put his hands to his head because his hands were hand-cuffed behind him.

8

which story seems more plausible: the old man or richard? Is it not odd that by piling up details and framing the story in a believable context it is relatively easy to believe that richard hammonds actually died as a result of a police beating and shooting in the late '50s in new orleans? And that the old man seems to be a metaphor. But an old man (whose name I don't want to reveal because it would add nothing to our story) actually killed himself during the christmas holidays (of course I speculate and fictionalize a lot of the old man's story, but the suicide actually happened) and the story of richard hammonds is totally fictitious except for the cops who killed him—cops did kill negroes in new orleans.

9

the old man and richard hammonds had gone to high school together, and gone to bars together, making merry, drinking and acting mindlessly stupid on a couple of occasions. they had double dated a couple of times, and had once even engaged in sex with the same woman (at different times, months apart, but the same woman nonetheless—she remembers the old man as the better lover because he was more tender, seemed more sincere.

————

(there had been this untalked-about but often expressed rivalry between richard and the old man. close friends are often bound by both love and jealousy, so there was nothing unusual about them being attracted to the same woman. but remember richard was the handsome one. he was also glib, perhaps because he learned how to hold back his feelings. he could talk a woman into bed, or more likely the back of a studebaker—richard's father worked as a pullman porter and made nice money for a colored man and had bought a car but was often not in town to enjoy the car, and richard, though he didn't personally have much money, did have access to the car. anyway, richard never thought about what the women he bedded in the backseat thought about before, during or after he bedded them. after all it was just a moment's pleasure.

(but the old man, well, he was a young man then, he thought about how others felt about him a lot, and though he fucked mildred, it was not because she was available but because he was really, really moved by mildred and told her so. told her, "girl you moves me."

("I do?" she was used to men wanting to sex her, but not to men admitting that they were deeply affected by her.

("yes, you does," and he twirled her at that moment—they were dancing and he was whispering in her ear, dancing in a little new orleans nite club, to a song on the jukebox—he twirled her. and smiled. and she had never been twirled quite like this gracefully dancing young man twirled her. and when she reversed the twirl and spun back into his arms, he momentarily paused and said, "i wish i could dance with you all night.")

the old man had not been angling to get her in bed, he was just genuinely enjoying her company. he liked to dance. she liked to dance. they were having a good time. and when somehow they ended up making love on the sofa in her front room that night while her sister and her sister's children soundly (he hoped) slept two rooms away, he had been a little nervous at first.

her softness felt so good, before he knew it, a little cry caught in his throat. he was trying to be quiet, but goodness and quiet sometimes do not go together. i mean, you know how good it hurts to hold it in? well the possibility that the sound of your lovemaking will disturb and awaken others nearby, that anxiety about discovery adds to the covert enjoyment. so, instead of surfacing upward through his throat, the cry was redirected down into his chest, but it bounced back and was about to pop audibly out of his mouth. mildred felt that sound about to pour forth like a coocoo clock gone haywire, and with the mischief that only a woman can summon she cupped one hand tightly over his mouth and with her other hand reached down and gently squeezed his testicles.

ya boy liked to died. he shuddered. he couldn't breathe. her hand tightly covered his mouth and partially blocked his nose. and he was coming like mad. and he moaned a stifled moan, air yo-yoing back in forth between the back of his mouth atop his throat and the near bursting constriction of his chest. finally, he wheezed gusts of exhales out of his distended nostrils, which flared like those of a race horse heaving after a superfast lap. and then he cried out and tried to call back the sound all at the same time. and that was followed with another terrible quake. in a semiconscious state, he lay helpless, wrapped up in the murmured laughter of mildred's playful passion.

but he didn't hear her soft, soft laughter. he didn't hear anything. he was totally out of it. he was struggling to catch his breath, in fact had almost slipped off the large couch—if her legs had not clamped around him so firmly, he would have tumbled to the floor. after that he didn't distinctly remember anything until he woke up the next morning, at home, in his own bed and didn't know how he got there. he must have walked home or something, but all he could remember was her softness, her touch, his lengthy orgasm (he had never come that long before), and the way her legs held him when he almost fell over. you can easily forget a short walk home, but there are some experiences that are so sharply etched in the memory of your flesh, those encounters you never forget.

a couple of days later when richard asked the old man about mildred, whether they had done it, the old man had said, "no, we just had a good time dancing and i took her home. then i went home." richard had replied, "you should have got it, she likes you. i got her drunk and got it once but she never would let me get no mo. but she likes you. you should get it." The old man had said nothing further, merely looked away, certain that richard would not understand that what the old man felt for mildred, although initiated by the sharpness of their sexual encounter, was, nonetheless, a feeling deeper than a good fuck.

many years later, when the old man was watching the house of representatives vote to impeach bill clinton for lying to the american people about the monica lewinsky affair, something terrible took hold of him. although he continued to see mildred for over twenty years and even had a kid with her, the old man had never told his wife. and he felt intensely guilty. intensely.

he felt horrible. felt like he had felt at richard's funeral. sitting in the catholic church before a closed casket. the body had been too brutalized to have a public viewing. the police had shot his good friend richard, shot him in the head.

———

while he sat between his wife and two daughters on one side and his young son on the other side, the old man was thinking about his dead friend when he looked up and saw mildred looking over at him with those large, limpid, brown eyes. nearly every time he stole a glance her way, she seemed to be looking directly at him. he could not read her eyes.

but his friend richard was dead. and his wife and legitimate children were at his side and his woman was across the aisle staring at him, and the old man felt really guilty about how he was living his life, and he put his head in his hands and just wanted to ball up and die. and he didn't realize he was crying until his wife daubed his face with her handkerchief.

10

a murder is a crime against society. we look at pictures of murderers and wonder about them. wonder what led them to do it. wonder do they have feelings like the rest of us.

what motivates one human to lynch another?

in the case of a suicide, everyone who survives wonders not only what led to the murder but also, particularly for those who were close to the victim, we wonder what could we have done, what "should" we have done to prevent the murder.

murder is a crime condemning society and suicide is particularly damning of those who were close to the murderer (who is also the murderee). if you think about someone close to you committing suicide, you have to ask yourself, what did i fail to do that would have prevented that person from committing self-murder? while sometimes we ask that question of a mass murderer—what could have been done to prevent them from acting the way they did—we always ask that question of a suicide. and why? if we cannot stop people from committing large and impersonal murders, how can we hope to stop small murders, the most personal of murders: the suicide? the question is perplexing.

after a while though, you come to an awful realization: maybe it is impossible to stop people from killing each other and themselves. indeed, is it not a certainty that it is impossible to stop suicide?

11
if you are shot in the head with a large handgun it can be messy.

12
if you shoot yourself in the head with a large handgun it can be messy.

13
the old man's casket was sealed before the funeral mass just like richard's had been. a closed casket is a terrible death for it is a death which suggests that this death is much more worse than ordinary death. this is a death you cannot look in the face. and what can be more horrible than imagining how horrible death looks when the corpse is too horrible to look at?

14
mildred was at the old man's funeral. so was their son, who favored his mother but had his father's skin color. mildred had not talked with the old man in over two months, and then it was only briefly over the phone. he had said something about being sorry he had never been brave enough to marry her. and hung up. mildred had waited in vain for him to call back. as anxious as she had been, she had never once broken their agreement. she knew where he lived, knew his phone number, but she never called. never. and now he was

dead, gone. life is so cruel, especially when much of your life is lived cloistered in a box of arrangements shut off from what passes for normal life. to everyone mildred looked like the statistic of single mother with one child: a son, father unknown. but what she felt like was a widow, a widow who had never been married but a true widow nevertheless, her de facto husband's corpse sequestered in a closed box, not unlike her whole life, lived unrecognized outside of sight. isaac (mildred and the old man's son) used to ask who his father was, but he stopped asking after weathering junior high school taunts. and once he was married and had children of his own, he understood that what was important was not who his father had been but what kind of father he would be for his children. when his mother called and asked him to accompany her to the old man's funeral, isaac at last knew the answer without ever having to rephrase the question. mildred and isaac both remained dry-eyed throughout the service even though inside both of them were crying like crazy.

you cannot gauge the depths simply by looking at the surface. printed on the program was a smiling snapshot of the old man. next to the closed casket there was an enlargement of this same posed photograph. but what picture of the old man was in various people's minds?

moreover, what does a self-murderer look like whose death has left the corpse too gruesome to witness? certainly not like the smiling headshot on the easel surrounded by flowers.

was the look in the old man's eye as he pulled the trigger anything like that wild look in the eyes of white people staring at a lynched negro—of course not? But what did he look like looking at his own death?

15

have you ever seen a picture of the man who was convicted of bombing the baptist church in birmingham, alabama, and killing those four little girls? he looks like a white man. and once you get beyond the racial aspect of the murderer, he looks like a man. and once you get beyond the gender aspect of the murderer—a grown man killing four little girls—well, then, he looks like a human being. murderers are human beings. they look like what they are. it is a conceit to think that murderers look different from "ordinary" human beings. what does a killer look like? look at the nearest human being.

16

while i admit i have not seen a lot of pictures of white people—and then again i have undoubtedly seen more pictures of white people than of black people when you consider how the image of whiteness surrounds us and bombards us in school, in commerce, in television, in entertainment, in advertisements, everywhere—but anyway, i don't remember seeing many white people in the classic negro pose of yore nor in the contemporary iconic hand-to-the-crown-of-the-head pose.

in examining the photos of lynchings i see none of the concern for the future that the hand to the head would indicate. that hand to the head indicates that a person has a heart. that a person is feeling life, and though the life that is felt may not be pleasant, at least we are still feeling.

but when you watch and listen to and smell a person dying, and when you cut off your feelings for the fate of another human being, well . . . and you know it is not biological. have you read about the civil wars in africa typified by the hutu-versus-tutsi conflict? how literally thousands of people are hacked to death. it is one thing to fire a gun or drop a bomb, it is another thing to whack, whack, whack with a machete slaughtering a human being as though assailing a dangerous beast or a tree that was in the way of progress. when any of us, be we white, black, or whatever, when we sever our feelings to the point that not only do we methodically and unfeelingly commit acts of mass murder or acts of ritual murder, when we can watch murder and not feel revulsion, then obviously we have moved to the point that death gives us pleasure.

when i first raised the issue about death and pleasure you may have thought, "oh, how absurd." but the next time you are chomping your popcorn and sipping your artificially flavored sugar water while watching thrilling scenes of mayhem, murder and mass destruction on the silver screen (perhaps i should add that you have paid for the privilege of this pleasure), but the next time the bodies fly through the air, the bullets rip apart a young man in slow mo, the very next time you watch an image of death and get pleasure from it, see if you can remember to say "oh, how absurd."

i think you won't be able to, any more than at the moment of orgasm you would holler "oh, how absurd." for you see pleasure in and of itself is never absurd, perverse perhaps, but never absurd. and taking pleasure in someone else's death: oh, how . . . what? how do we describe that pleasure? what is human about enjoying death? or perhaps, since deriving pleasure from someone else's demise seems to be a norm today, maybe i should ask, what is inhuman about enjoying death?

there is much that is wrong.

F. BRETT COX

Madeline's Version

F. Brett Cox has published fiction in Century, Black
Gate, Indigenous Fiction, The North Carolina Literary Review, Carriage House Review, Say . . . , Lady
Churchill's Rosebud Wristlet, *and elsewhere. His essays,
reviews, and interviews have appeared in numerous publi-
cations, including* The New England Quarterly, The
New York Review of Science Fiction, Paradoxa, Sci-
ence Fiction Studies, Locus Online, The Robert Frost
Encyclopedia, and Science Fiction Weekly. *Brett has
served as a juror for the Theodore Sturgeon Award and as a
member of the advisory board for the current edition of*
Contemporary Novelists *and is currently editing* Twenti-
eth-Century American Science Fiction and Fantasy
Writers, *a multivolume component of the* Dictionary of
Literary Biography *reference series. He holds an M.A. in
English with emphasis in creative writing from the University of South Carolina, where he studied with William
Price Fox and James Dickey, and a Ph.D. in English with
emphasis in American literature from Duke University. A
native of North Carolina, Brett is assistant professor of*

English at Norwich University in Northfield, Vermont. He lives in Northfield with his wife, the playwright Jeanne Beckwith. This marks the first publication of "Madeline's Version."

I

She had been sick a long time, and when the physician finally declared recovery impossible, no one was surprised. Not even her brother, prostrate by her bedside, his lamentations shrill and echoing upward to be lost in the arched ceiling. His flesh and blood and very self. What would he do, what, what? The dim lamp by her bedside lit without illuminating; the torches on the wall flickered and cast random shadows. She could see the physician standing in the corner of the room, muttering to the nurse. "No, good God, they can't come in here. Tell them I'll be out presently." Her hearing was unusually acute. The nurse went out; her brother pressed her pale hand to his paler face. She tried to smile at him but failed, contented herself with what she hoped was a loving glance into his gleaming mad eyes. She was cold despite the covers. Everything seemed so far away.

She said nothing. For even longer than she had been sick, she had said nothing. There was no longer any need to speak.

2

They had been taught, when they still had tutors, that while brother-and-sister twins were not uncommon, it was impossible that they be identical; the laws of biological science would not have it so. Nonetheless, there they were, she and her brother. The broad brow; the large, liquid eyes. The thin lips; the finely molded chin, wanting prominence. The soft, weblike hair; the death-pale skin. She fancied that all of these features were more pronounced in her brother than in her, that perhaps her chin was a touch stronger, her hair a bit thicker, her skin a shade less pale. But everyone who had ever seen them together—fewer and fewer as they grew older—remarked the same: they were identical. Not mirror images, as a mirror is a reflection and reversal; not a duplication, with one the original and the other a copy. Identical.

A servant, attached to the household since before Madeline's birth, had grown talkative in her dotage. Before her death, she had told Madeline that their parents had dressed them alike during their infancy and well into their childhood, sometimes in dresses, sometimes in breeches and coats. Madeline did not remember this. She barely remembered their parents at all: dim figures treading slowly, arm in arm, through the great house, or around the grounds, surrounded by the dull, gray mist that perpetually enveloped their home, that seemed to ooze from the trees and rise from the ground itself. Their faces had been the image of their children's. One day the physician had appeared and told her and her brother that their parents had died. She never saw the bodies, was not told of a funeral. Since then it had been only her brother, and her, and the vast, crumbling house.

3

She awoke, unaware of how long she had been asleep. The nurse, seeing her awake, came to her bedside, helped her with the chamber pot, and proceeded to bathe her. She could tell that the cloth was soft and the water warm, but she could barely register either sensation. She heard voices down the hall, in the upstairs drawing room: her brother's, and that of an unknown man. She looked at the nurse inquiringly. "His lordship has a visitor, m'lady," she said, turning Madeline to reach the small of her back. "An old school friend, I'm told. His lordship seems pleased for the company, though it's hard to tell, he's still so dreadful nervous. He worries about you so, m'lady. I hope his friend can revive his spirits."

She tried to take this in. Someone else in the house? She remembered the one period of her life when she and her brother had not been together, when he had been away at school. His visits home had included references to his schoolmates, and one in particular with whom he had established a relationship of some sympathy. She remembered her discomfort at this, and how he had had to hold her close and kiss her eyes and assure her that he would not leave. And he did not. Adam? Andrew? She could barely tolerate the presence of the servants, but something within in her needed to know. What was the man's name? With some effort, she pushed herself upright and pointed toward her wardrobe.

The nurse helped her as far as the drawing-room door; Madeline pushed her away, leaned on the doorsill, and listened.

"It is the curse of this family," her brother was saying. "The stem of our race, time-honored as it is, has put forth, at no period, any enduring branch. The entire family lies in the direct line of descent, and has always, with tri-fling variation, so lain. Small wonder that I am stricken so. There is nothing to alleviate our condition, which is passed on undiluted from generation to generation."

"But Rod, dear fellow," the stranger said, his accent marking his South-ern origins. "Is there truly nothing to be done? Perhaps a sojourn from this—this too-familiar environment. Let me take you—"

"No!" he cried, his voice strangled with agitation. "No, Allan, I cannot leave this place! The most insipid food is alone endurable; my eyes are tor-tured by even a faint light—how, then, might I survive out in the ungovernable world? You are right; the physique of these gray walls and turrets has surely poisoned the morale of my existence. Yet, I cannot—I dare not—leave."

"But would it not also be beneficial to Madeline? A change of scenery, at least, if not in fact different treatment from a different doctor—"

"Madeline! She is gone!" His voice broke. "It is more than I can take. We have been together always; she is of me, and I of her. Her decease will leave me—me, the hopeless and the frail—the last of the ancient race of—"

Their conversation ceased upon her entrance. The room, as always, oppressed her. Dark draperies obscured the walls; armorial trophies rattled as she strode upon the black floor. The scattering of books and musical instruments left an impression not of activity but of disuse. She was too weak to traverse the great length of the room, but passed through it at an angle, away from her brother and his visitor. They were obscured in the dim light; curious as she was, she could not bring herself to look directly at them. But out of the corner of her eye she apprehended the stranger: well-dressed, of an age with her brother, and—she paused, imperceptibly, at this—although not of an absolute likeness, bearing a passing resemblance to the two of them! The same high forehead, the same nose; the thin line of the lips obscured beneath an elegant moustache. He stared at her as she crossed to the side door, a look of astonishment on his face.

Once out the door, she stopped and leaned against the wall, panting for breath. "Good God," she heard the stranger say. "Her figure, her hair, her features—"

"I dread the events of the future," her brother said. "Not in themselves, but in their results. I feel that I must inevitably abandon life and reason together in my struggles with some fatal demon of fear."

The nurse found her where she had fallen and helped her back to her room. As they passed the staircase, her gaze fell downward. The physician stood in the foyer addressing two men. Their thick, ugly faces were smeared with dirt, as were their tattered clothes. One wore an eyepatch; the other's teeth were rotting out of his head. "It won't be long now, boys," she heard the physician say. "When I give the word, be ready."

4

There had been moments of comfort, of relative contentment and peace. When Roderick had finally returned from school to stay, she had felt an overpowering sense of relief. There had been many pleasant hours. He had played his guitar; she had accompanied him on her flute. There had been many books and many conversations. The absence of others seemed no absence at all.

But as they moved through their twenties, he changed. He had always talked, in moments of depression, about "the family curse," "the flaw in their house." She had paid him no heed when he was in those moods. Did they not have the house, and servants, and money? Did they not have each other? They needed nothing else, no one else. She would inevitably wean him from his sadness, and everything would be as it was.

As the years passed, though, her strategies gradually failed. He grew into himself and away from her. His nature, always sensitive, grew more and more intolerant of the sensations of life. Her flute, he said, pierced his ears like nails; she abandoned it. The light hurt his eyes, so the house went dark. Their conversations became monologues, she listening patiently to his increasingly eccentric pronouncements:

"Do not question the acuteness of my senses! You call them morbid? Observe!" he would cry, holding his index finger aloft. "If I venture to displace the microscopial speck of dust which lies now upon the point of my finger, what is the character of that act upon which I have adventured? I have done a deed which shakes the Moon in her path, which causes the Sun to no longer be the Sun, and which alters forever the destiny of the myriads of stars!"

The sounds of his guitar became muted and erratic; his paintings, which she had formerly enjoyed, became abstract, unfathomable. His looks grew wild; sometimes he seemed to regard her with nothing less than pure loathing. Then he would break down, grab her in his arms and sob that she was all he had, was everything; he could not lose her; they could not lose each other.

Over time, she ceased to feel. Her senses, with the lone exception of her hearing, attenuated. Avoiding Roderick's chambers, she wandered through the creaking hallways, peering into unused rooms whose dim light only worsened the darkness. Down sometimes even beneath the house into the vault where they had played as children, not realizing then the fierce use to which the room, as a dungeon, had been put in remote feudal times, nor its more recent incarnation as a repository for powder and other combustibles. She walked about the grounds, circling the tarn in which their house lay reflected. She would stop and gaze at the house, its vacant, eyelike windows seeming to pierce her where she stood. There was a scarcely noticeable crack in the stonework, beginning underneath the roof and zigzagging down to the ground. She breathed deeply of the unceasing fog which seemed to rise from the stagnant water and the moldering walls. She wished she could disappear into it.

Eventually she no longer left the house. Her strength ebbed; her body grew gaunt; her sleep was increasingly prolonged. The physician could do nothing. Her brother wept. She fell silent.

5

She felt her eyes open but could see nothing. Had she finally gone blind as well? Then her vision cleared, and she found herself staring at a thick white cloth. She thought someone had pulled a blanket over her head, but the whiteness held several inches from her face. She tried to reach up and touch it, but her arms would not respond.

Then she felt a sudden shock beneath her, a bump and a scraping sound.

She was inside something and was being moved. Her eyes fell shut again. She had no perception of her own breathing.

Down, and then down again; she was being carried beneath the house—if, indeed, she were still in the house. For the first time in months, she felt the urge to speak, to cry out, but her voice was frozen along with her limbs.

She came to a halt, was set down with a thud. There was a soft creaking sound and a sudden gush of air; someone had opened the lid. She was dimly aware of two male voices from somewhere above her, fading in and out:

"—faint blush upon her bosom and face. Almost—"

"—oh my sister, my love! You cannot understand—"

Allan. Roderick.

"—sympathies of a scarcely intelligible nature have always existed between us. It is the end of the line, our line—"

She was in her coffin. They thought her dead and were preparing to bury her.

"But are you certain this is what you wish, Rod? Would it not be perhaps more fitting to give her a proper burial, with proper rites?"

"We had the priest in last night. And as I conveyed to you earlier, I have no choice. You yourself remarked on the commingling of perplexity and low cunning on the physician's face. A rare malady such as Madeline's calls to the betrayer of Hippocrates as surely as the dead and rotting animal calls to the vulture. I dare not entrust her to the remote and exposed situation of our family burial ground."

She tried with every fiber of her being to move, to speak, but remained motionless and silent. Allan muttered something in Latin; Roderick moaned, "Farewell, dear sister!" There was a gentle thump followed by the tightening of screws. Footsteps, a tortured screech of metal, a final, hopeless thud. Mercifully, the lassitude overcame her once more, and she slept.

6

One day when they were fifteen, lounging in his bedchamber, she told him what the old servant had said of them being dressed alike as children. "I remember," he replied. "That would be passing strange now, would it not?" She had laughed at the thought and, for a joke, left the room and returned wearing one of his outfits, shirt and breeches and a slightly oversized vest. "We are truly identical now," she had declared. He looked at her with eyes shining even brighter than usual. He walked over to her, caressed her cheek with his hand. "On the outside, yes. But what about underneath?" He unbuttoned his shirt and stripped it off. She looked at his chest, as naked and smooth as his face. He reached to the top button of her shirt; she finished for him and let it fall to the floor. She had removed her corset but kept her other undergarments on. He dropped to his knees, pulled off her trousers, buried his face in her belly. She could feel his breath through the thin white linen. She stroked his hair, stared up at the ceiling. He rose and removed the rest of his clothes. She stared at the wisp of hair, the rope and sac of flesh beneath. She had seen his body before, when they were children, but not like this. She felt her own private parts clutch, moisten. She let the linen fall as she followed him to his bed. It was quickly done. Over time, they learned more. It was the easiest and most natural of things; years later, when he finally drew away from her and she fell silent, she missed it dreadfully until feelings left altogether and she no longer missed anything.

7

She awoke again to voices, but this time unknown, muffled by the closed lid:

"Hurry up, damn you!"

"Why? She ain't goin' nowhere." Laughter and the creak of wood pried from wood.

"I don't care. God knows you made enough noise getting us in here to have the whole house down on us. I don't like this place, and I don't like this job, and I don't like you much either, so get that damned lid off and let's be done with it."

"Whining like a woman, Christ Almighty. I suppose you'd rather be back on that worthless farm squeezing cow tits."

"I'd rather be in bed squeezing your wife's tits."

A harsh, mirthless laugh. "Goddamn you, I'll give you something to squeeze when I get this lid open." A final sharp, wrenching sound. "Ah! There we go." She heard the lid open, felt—felt!—a gush of cool, damp air, followed by heat. A light burned through her closed eyelids. "Take a look, eh? She got right peaked there at the end, but she's still a woman. Shame for the doc to want to cut all that up." A hand rested on her right breast, grasped roughly, callouses scraping against her skin. Foul breath washed over her face.

"For God's sake, Jeremy, are you mad? It's bad enough what we're doing—"

She opened her eyes and sat up. The man with the rotting teeth jumped back from her coffin screaming and dropped his torch on the floor. The one with the eyepatch, standing at the foot of the coffin, shouted "Christ save us!" and fled through the open door.

She blinked her eyes wildly; even the dim light seeping in from the open door seemed bright, and the glow of the torch cut painfully into her vision. She was in the vault beneath the house. Her coffin rested on two pillars; there was nothing else in the room. She raised her arms, clutched the side of the coffin, winced from the agony of unused muscles.

The man who had been molesting her stopped screaming. "Devil!" he cried, pulling out a knife. "Back to hell with you!" He ran to her, swinging the knife wildly. It cut her shoulder and her face. The wounds burned like fire. She tried to cry out, but the only sound that emerged was more like the hiss of a snake. Her arm shot up reflexively, and her untrimmed nails scraped the man's face. He screamed again and fell unconscious to the floor.

She pulled herself out of the coffin and stumbled bleeding to the door. The entire room was lined with copper, walls and floor alike the same reddish brown hue. A gritty substance crunched under her feet. As she staggered into the corridor, she heard the crackle and buzz of something igniting behind her. Her wounds were superficial but bleeding profusely. She wiped her face and went to find her brother.

8

Once she had awakened in the middle of the night to find him standing over her with a knife. The light from the doorway gleamed off the blade and illuminated his eyes. Much of madness and more of sin. He was unaware of, or ignored, her uncomprehending gaze. Then he lowered the knife, turned, and walked away.

9

The doors to the drawing room were shut, but she heard voices within. Her hearing, so acute for so long, failed her; she recognized Roderick's voice, and thought the other belonged to Allan, but she could not make out what they said. Roderick's voice grew louder. As she reached the door, his words came clear in a scream that frightened her more than the men in the vault: "Madman! *I tell you that she now stands without the door!*"

She pushed the doors open. Allan sat in a chair in the middle of the room holding a large, leather-bound book, which he let fall to the floor as she entered. The windows were thrown open; a tremendous storm raged outside, and the curtains were soaked. Lightning dazzled the room. She stood motionless, trembling with a sudden chill, weak from her paralysis and loss of blood. Roderick stared at her, all expression gone from his face. She tried to call out his name but could only manage a wordless moan. She moved to him, lost her balance, threw out her arms. They fell to the floor together, and Roderick did not move again.

She heard Allan run out of the room as she lay motionless atop Roderick. She raised her head and looked down at her brother. She tried to weep, knew she should weep, but there were no tears. She closed his eyes and mouth, smoothed his hair, kissed him gently on the forehead. With great effort, she arose and made her way out of the room, down the corridor and staircase, and out of the house through the nearer back entrance.

She got only a few steps before she collapsed. She lay sprawled on the grass and looked up at the house. The sky churned with the final spasms of

the storm. There was a rumbling sound from within and beneath the house;
the windowpanes began to shatter, and one by one the rooms went dark, like
eyes closing.

There was a great cracking sound from the other side of the house, and
the fissure that ran along the front suddenly appeared under the back eaves
and ran like a fuse down to the ground. There was more rumbling, and
more, and an explosion, and another, and the house crashed down before her
under the light of the blood red moon. Beyond the rubble of her home she
could see the tarn churning as if it boiled, and beyond that, the figure of a
man running away.

She lay on the ground for a very long time. Then she got up, brushed
herself off as best she could, and began to walk toward the road that ran
some distance away from the house. As she neared it, she could see the light
of torches and the shadows of wagons come to investigate the catastrophe.
When the wagon arrived, she regarded its startled occupants, took a deep
breath, and cleared her throat. "My name is Madeline," she said. "Please
help me."

LYNN PITTS

Tchoupitoulas Bus Stop

Lynn Pitts was born and raised in the south Louisiana town of Houma. She has spent most of her adult life in New Orleans, where she was a public relations specialist, newspaper columnist, and associate director of NOMMO Literary Society, an African-American writer's workshop. She now lives in Harlem, where she makes something resembling a living as a freelance writer and creative writing teacher. She received her M.F.A. in creative writing from Sarah Lawrence College in May of 2003 and is at work on her first novel. Her fiction has been published in Lumina, Big City Lit. New York Edition, and Drum Voices Review. *This marks the first publication of "Tchoupitoulas Bus Stop," her first professional fiction sale.*

Her profile reminded him of the Nefertiti medallions people sold at tables in the French Market, coils of night black braids sweeping back from her forehead and piled on top her head like a crown. He didn't know what the rest of Nefertiti looked like, but this woman was tall. WNBA tall. He was six-four and she looked him square in the eye. She could have been a model or something except she wasn't skinny. Nothing skinny about her. She had breasts and hips and big legs, big fine legs that he got a peek at every time she took one of those long, long strides, making the dress ride up. The dress was bright white beneath the streetlights. In the shadows it was ghostly against the dark. Thin and gauzy, it lay like skin, revealing sinew and muscle.

The woman hadn't given him the brush off when he'd stepped to her at the corner of Tchoupitoulas and Louisiana. She hadn't offered her name or asked him to walk with her either, but all that mattered was that she hadn't given him the look—the pursing of the lips, the swift cut of the eyes, the slight downward tilt of the head. Usually, trying to step to a sister at an uptown bus stop got him the look. But this woman had actually stopped when he'd called out: "Hey—where you going so fast, baby?" (Because she had been striding past him at a noticeably hurried pace, hips, breasts, flesh, moving unrestrained beneath the skin-thin white dress.) "Especially out here by yo' fine self."

"I'm going get my baby," she said, turning to him and pointing up Tchoupitoulas Street.

"Oh, all right," he murmured, nodding, noticing for the first time that the dress wasn't just thin, it was wet. Rather, it had been wet and was now just damp. A few beads of moisture still clung to the plump, muscular flesh of her upper arms and glistened like pearls in her hair.

Floyd felt a shudder run through him as he imagined her emerging from the shower, dripping, slipping on the flimsy dress without even bothering to dry off. She must be in a hurry to get to the kid to come in the street like that, by herself, fore'day in the morning. But then, she was a fierce-looking sister—face like it was carved from stone—even a fool would think twice before stepping to her with some bullshit.

He wondered how much farther she had to go, but before he could ask, a faraway look singed her face and she turned away from him, murmuring: "He go'n be looking for me. I promised I was coming for him." And she was off again, the long legs carrying her away from Floyd and the bus stop.

Because she hadn't given him the cutting look, Floyd broke into a little trot and caught up with her, wondering why he was putting himself out like this. Just because she was fine? It was four in the morning and he had to be at the construction site downtown by five-thirty. Why was he headed uptown behind some woman who seemed like she could be a little off? He looked back over his shoulder at the bus stop, deserted and submerged in the light of the streetlamp. His legs kept moving forward.

Floyd was thinking that the dress looked an awful lot like a nightgown or a slip, but didn't say so. A lot of women's dresses these days looked like underwear.

"So, what's your name?"

"They call me Nay," she said absently.

After that, the next few blocks were filled with Floyd's compliments—how fine she was, how long her legs were, how much she looked like an African queen—and her silence. So the blocks after that were occupied with Floyd's regrouping. Unwilling to give up, he reconsidered his approach and they were accompanied by only the sounds from the wharves along the river to their left—the ships' horns and the screech and clang of the train. Every so often she would turn a nervous gaze toward the river side of the street and Floyd would watch her eyes—black and glittery like the button eyes of a stuffed animal—thinking they looked watery, as though she could cry at any moment.

"You a'ight?" he inquired carefully, his mind flickering over the situation. He just wanted to get her number—her real number—and find out if she was married or had a man or what and if she liked to listen to music and if he could call her later this week maybe for a few drinks. A little something to eat. All that before the bus passed. They were definitely go'n walk up on the bus headed toward downtown and he'd have to get on it because he couldn't be late again. He couldn't lose this job. He was just getting regular with the child support and the people were off his back and Keela wasn't bitching. So he didn't have much time, but first he needed to find out if something was wrong with "Nefertiti"—if it was just some something that had her upset right now or if it was some shit he couldn't afford to get involved in.

"I'm just worried about my baby," she said.

"That's why you out here by yourself in the dark and shit?" Floyd watched her profile carefully. "I mean, your old man or somebody couldn't come with you?"

"No," she answered without hesitation. "It's just me."

"Oh, all right," Floyd nodded, looking up to see if approaching head-lights and gasping engine belonged to his bus. A fire engine rumbled by without warning lights or siren.

The woman picked up her pace, and Floyd matched it, unable to shake the sense of foreboding that had tried to get him to stay at his bus stop. They were approaching Napoleon Avenue and he was thinking that common sense would have him hold down a spot at this corner and wait for the bus.

That's what he would do. Just get her name and number. He'd come far enough.

"Say, so, uh, I can get that number?"

"What?" She had been staring toward the river again as they crossed the intersection at Napoleon, where there were fewer buildings blocking the view of the wharf buildings and the space above the river beyond them.

"Uh, I wanted to know if I could call you sometime. Maybe have a drink or something. What you like to do?"

She did not answer, instead, turning her attention from the riverfront and fixing her gaze on some distant point farther up Tchoupitoulas, she increased her already speedy pace.

Floyd matched her once again, his mind worked feverishly. He had gone too far out of his way not to get the number. "Look . . . um . . . I'm go'n have to stop right here and catch my bus. Got to get downtown." He reached into his back pocket and pulled out a small, battered address book and a stub of a pencil. "You can give me your number and stuff."

She stopped abruptly and when he looked up her eyes flickered with panic. "Oh, no, please, come with me. It's not much further." The woman reached out to clutch his arm.

At first he was just surprised at her sudden attentiveness. "Well . . . damn, baby, you know I'd like to help you out . . . you out here by yourself and everything, but the bus coming."

And the bus was indeed approaching. It lumbered no more than four or five blocks in front of them, headed in their direction, squealing brakes heralding its arrival.

Then she was pulling on his arm, her grip disturbingly powerful, and moving forward again. "Come with me," she said, and the water that welled up in her eyes was not his imagination.

Floyd decided that it was not going to work. Definitely not. He was definitely getting on the bus. "Look, baby . . . I can't come with you." He tried to free his arm and was alarmed at her strength. She tugged at him urgently, the tears slipping down the carved mahogany of her face.

"Please," she said, in a voice that sounded like it burned in her throat. And that's when she released his arm, covered with the sleeve of the blue work shirt, and took his bare hand in hers.

The contact with her skin made his legs weak and blistered his hand with the fire of her despair.

"Please," she pleaded again.

Floyd just wanted to be on the bus, under the familiar glare of the harsh neon lights. But it didn't seem as though his legs would have the strength to climb the bus's steps. He couldn't do anything but stare at his hand, encased in her strong, soft ones, the flames hissing and scorching, traveling through his fingers and up his arm. He felt tears pooling in his throat.

"What you doing to me?" he demanded, angry and afraid. "Let goa' me!"

But she only clutched him tighter and Floyd looked frantically around the deserted intersection for help, and then toward the approaching bus, which was still a good two blocks away.

"Do you have babies?" she asked, leaning into him, pressing his hand in hers to the soft space between her breasts. She smelled like baby powder and perfume and peppermint—and something else, he couldn't say really, like smoke, like water.

"Yeah, uh . . . I got a little girl . . . live with her momma," he said, distracted, slightly, by the smell of her but more by the feel of his callused palm on the tender flesh of her chest. "Just let me—"

"Then you understand. . . ." the woman cut him off, pulling him again, gently, pleading.

He stumbled forward, the pool of tears mixing with the flames that had reached his chest, all of it coming out in ragged, steamy breaths.

"You have to help me." And her own tears slipped out and she sobbed, a sound like everything crumbling. And it crumbled in Floyd too. He could feel it all. And she was pulling him again and begging, tugging him farther away from the bus stop. His hand was still near her breasts and he wondered why he couldn't stop thinking of his daughter—the soft sweetness of her—and the smoky, watery smell of the woman. And the sadness that was overwhelming to him.

The bus was pulling up to the corner and he pulled away from her with all his strength, even though he didn't want to let go of her softness. His stomach hurt and the tears still came and the burning steam in his chest still scorched him even after his hand was free and he was stumbling up the steps of the bus and the woman's white dress was running away up Tchoupitoulas followed by her sobs.

The bus driver and the handful of others on the bus stared at him and hugged themselves as he walked down the aisle to the seats at the back.

He swallowed hard and slumped in his seat, resting his cheek against the cool smooth of the bus window.

By the time he got off the bus he'd decided he was going to forget everything that happened. It was just some crazy, whack shit and he wasn't going to think about it or how his hands still felt hot or how he kept smelling smoke and baby powder.

He did okay until lunch.

For lunch, Floyd met Nathan—whom all the young men on the site called Big Poppa or Poppa—at The Commerce where they got a hot plate every day. They sat eating meatballs and spaghetti and reading the paper. Actually, Poppa read the paper and when he came across an interesting story he summarized it for Floyd. Sometimes they had something to say about the story before Poppa moved on to the next, sometimes they didn't.

"Check this out, Floyd," Poppa said from behind the paper, an it's-a-shame grunt in his throat. "House caught fire up on Valmont yesterday— five-hundred block, that's right at Tchoupitoulas. Chick was living there with her little boy, wasn't but two. They had just got home from church and she was fixing dinner and the little boy was upstairs asleep when the fire started—electrical, they say. Man, people got to stop messing round with these amateurs doing that wiring . . ."

"Yep," Floyd mumbled, a mouth full of meatball. "Can't be playing with electricity."

"I know that's real," Poppa intoned from behind the paper. "Anyway, they say the momma—woman named Naomi Francis—couldn't get to the baby before he burned up . . . they could hear him crying and shit from out-side . . . woman kept trying to get the neighbors to help her go back in there but wouldn't nobody do it."

Poppa looked up from the paper at the sound of Floyd gasping for breath. "You a'ight?"

"Yeah," Floyd sputtered, gulping his soda. "Meatball went the wrong way."

Poppa went back to the paper. "Girl family said she just couldn't believe wouldn't nobody help her . . . people live right next door. Guess they was scared. Still a shame, though." Behind the paper, Poppa shook his head slowly.

Floyd was silent.

"And get this. That's not all. They sent the chick home with one of her relatives, live over in Algiers. Girl got out the house and went jumped in the river—killed herself. They still ain't found the body. That's fucked up."

Poppa put the paper down to take a mouthful of spaghetti and red sauce and glanced at Floyd. "My man." Poppa gestured in Floyd's direction. "Got something on your chin . . . yeah. . . ."

Floyd fumbled with the napkin dispenser and wiped at his chin and then his entire face with a wad of napkins.

Poppa stared, brow furrowed. "You a'ight?"

"Yeah. Uh, look, um . . ." Floyd stammered. "You live uptown, right?"

Poppa nodded.

"I could get a ride with you in the morning?"

BRAD WATSON

Water Dog God: A Ghost Story

Brad Watson was born in Alabama. His acclaimed first collection, Last Days of the Dog Men, *was published by W. W. Norton in 1996 and received both the Sue Kaufman Prize for First Collection from the American Academy of Arts and Letters and the Great Lakes Colleges Association New Writers Award. His 2002 novel* The Heaven of Mercury *was a finalist for the Southeastern Booksellers Association Award, the Southern Book Critics Circle Award, and the National Book Award. He holds an M.F.A. in fiction writing from the University of Alabama, has taught writing at the University of Alabama and Harvard University, and recently served as visiting writer-in-residence at the University of West Florida and the University of Alabama at Birmingham. He lives on the Alabama Gulf Coast. "Water Dog God" was previously published in* The Oxford American. *This marks its first book publication.*

Back in late May a tornado dropped screaming into the canyon, snapped limbs and whole treetops off, flung squirrels and birds into the black sky. And in the wet and quiet shambles after, several new stray dogs crept into the yard, and upon their heels little Maeve. You've seen pictures of those children starving on TV, living in filthy huts and wearing rags and their legs and arms just knobby sticks, huge brown eyes looking up at you. That's what she looked like.

These strays, I sometimes think there is something their bones are tuned to that draws them here, like the whistle only they can hear, or words of some language ordinary humans have never known—the language that came from Moses' burning bush, which only Moses could hear. I think sometimes I've heard it at dawn, something in the green, smoky air. Who knows what Maeve heard, maybe nothing but a big riproaring on the roof: the black sky opens up, she walks out. She follows an old coon dog along the path of forest wreckage through the hollow and into my yard, her belly huge beneath a sleeveless bit of cloth you might call a nightslip.

I knew her as my uncle Sebastian's youngest child, who wouldn't ever go out of her room, and here she was wandering in the woods. They lived up beyond the first dam, some three miles up the creek. She says to me, standing there holding a little stick she's picked up along the way, "I don't know where I'm at." She gives it an absent whack at the hound. He's a bluetick with teats so saggy I thought him a bitch till I saw his old jalapeno.

I said, "Lift up that skirt and let me see you." I looked at her white stomach, big as a camel's hump and bald as my head, stretched veins like a map of the pale blue rivers of the world, rivers to nowhere. I saw her little patch of frazzly hair and sex like a busted lip wanting nothing but to drop the one she carried. Probably no one could bear to see it but God, after what all must have climbed onto her, old Uncle Sebastian and those younger boys of his, the ones still willing to haul pulpwood so he hadn't kicked them out on their own, akin to these stray dogs lying about the yard, no speech, no intelligent look in their eyes.

This creature in Maeve would be something vile and subhuman.

I said, "The likes of those which have made your child, Maeve, should not be making babies, at least not with you. It was an evil thing that led to it."

She said, "Well, when the roof lifted off the house and blew away I climbed on out. They was all gone, out hiding or gone to town."

She took to wearing the little blue earphones radio I got in the mail with my Amoco card. I had no idea what she was listening to. She wandered around looking at nothing, one hand pressing a speaker to an ear, the other aimless, signing. She scarcely ever took them off, not even when she slept. She was quiet before, but now with her head shot through with radio waves she was hardly more than a ghost.

She would never even change out of her nightslip, though when I'd washed it for her it nearly fell apart. She was pale as a grub, hair a wet black rag all pressed to her head. Not even seventeen and small, but she looked old somehow. She'd seen so very little of the world and what she'd seen was scarcely human. She would forget, or just not bother to use, the toilet paper. Climb into the dry bathtub and fall into naps where she twitched like a dreaming dog. She heaved herself somehow up the ladder and through the little hole in the hallway ceiling to sit in the attic listening to her headset until she came down bathed in her own sweat and wheezing from the insulation dust. Maybe the little fibers got into her brain and improved her reception.

I made her put on a raincoat over the nightslip and took her to the grocery store, since I didn't want to leave her alone. I thought if I took her there she wouldn't think herself so strange compared with some of the women who lurk those aisles. Town is only three miles away but you would not think it to stand here and look at the steep green walls of the canyon. And what does it matter? The whole world, and maybe others, is in the satellite dish at the edge of the yard, and I have sat with Maeve until three in the morning watching movies, industrial videos, German game shows, Mexican soap operas. It's what Greta would do sometimes while she was dying, her body sifting little by little into the air. When I started to get the disability and was home all the time I could see this happening, so I wasn't surprised when one morning I woke and she didn't. I grieved but I wasn't surprised. She was all hollowed out. We'd never had a child as she was unable, and near the end I think she believed her life had been for nothing.

I felt the same way about myself after some twenty-odd years at Chem-Glo. Sometimes it seems I wasn't even there in that job, I'd only dreamed up a vision of hell, a world of rusty green and leaky pipes and tanks and noxious fumes. But as I was not there anymore and was not dead, I began to believe or hope my life might have some purpose, though nothing had happened to confirm that until Maeve appeared.

At the grocery store I couldn't get her away from the produce section. She wouldn't put on any shoes, and she was standing there in her grimy, flat, skinny bare feet, the gray raincoat buttoned up to her chin, running her dirty little fingers all over the cabbages and carrot bunches, and when the nozzles shot a fine spray over the lettuce she stuck her head in there and turned her face up into the mist. I got her down to the meat and seafood area, where she stood and looked at the lobsters in their tank until I had everything else loaded into the cart, and I lured her to the cashier with a Snickers bar. She stood behind me in the line eating it while I loaded the groceries onto the conveyor belt, chocolate all over her mouth and her fingers, and she sucked on her fingers when she was done. And then she reached over to the candy shelf in the cashier chute and got herself another one, opened it up and bit into it, as if this was a place you came to when you wanted to eat, just walked around in there seeing what you wanted and eating it.

I looked at her a second, then just picked up the whole box of Snickers and put it on the conveyor belt.

"For the little girl," I said.

The cashier, a dumpy little blond woman with a cute face who'd been looking at Maeve, and then at me, broke into a big smile that was more awkward than fake.

"Well," she said to Maeve, "I wish my daddy was as sweet as yours."

Maeve stopped chewing the Snickers and stared at me as if she'd never seen me before in her life.

Understand, we are in a wooded ravine, a green, jungly gash in the earth, surrounded by natural walls. This land between the old mines and town, it's wooded canyons cut by creeks that wind around and feed a chain of quiet little lakes on down to ours, where the water deepens, darkens, and pours over the spillway onto the slated shoals. From there it rounds a bend down toward the swamps, seeps back into the underground river. The cicadas spool up so loud you think there's a torn seam in the air through which their shrieking slipped from another world.

One evening I was out on the porch in the late light after supper and saw Maeve sneak off into the woods. The coon dog got up and followed her, and then a couple of other strays followed him. When she didn't come right back I stood up and listened. The light was leaking fast into dusk. Crickets and tree frogs sang their high-pitched songs. Then from the woods in the direction she'd headed came a sudden jumble of high vicious mauling. It froze me to hear it. Then it all died down.

I went inside for the shotgun and the flashlight but when I came back out Maeve had made her way back through the thicket and into the ghostly yard, all color gone to shadowy gray, the nightslip wadded into a diaper she held to herself with both hands. I suppose it wasn't this child's first. She walked through the yard. What dogs hadn't gone with her stood around with heads held low, she something terrible and holy, lumpy stomach smeared with blood. She went to the lake's edge to wash herself and the slip, soaking and wringing it till she fell out and I had to go save her and take her into the house and bathe her myself and put her to bed. Her swollen little-girl's bosoms were smooth and white as the moon; the leaky nipples big as berries. I fed her some antibiotics left over from when I'd had the flu, and in a short time she recovered. She was young. Her old coonhound never came back, nor the others that went out with him, and I had a vision of them all devouring one another like snakes, until they disappeared.

I couldn't sleep and went out into the yard, slipped out of my jeans and into the lake. I thought a swim might calm me. I was floating on my back in the shallows looking up at the moon so big and clear you could imagine how the dust would feel between your fingers. My blood was up. I thought I heard something through the water, and stood. It was coming from across the lake, in the thick bramble up on the steep ridge, where a strange woman had moved into an empty cabin some months back. I heard a man one night up there, howling and saying her name, I couldn't tell what it was.

I'd seen her in town. She carried herself like a man, with strong wiry arms, a sun-scored neck, and a face hard and strange as the wood knots the carvers call tree spirits. I heard she's an installer for the phone company.

When I stood up in the water I could hear a steady rattling of branches and a skidding racket, something coming down the steep ridge wall. I waded back toward the bank, stopped and looked, and she crashed out of the bushes overhanging the water, dangling naked from a moonlit branch. She dropped into the lake with a quiet little splash, and when she entered the water it was like she'd taken hold of me. I didn't do that to myself anymore, though maybe I should've because I was sometimes all over Maeve in my sleep until she began to shout and scratch, for she was too afraid to sleep alone but must not be touched even by accident. But now here I was spilling myself into the shallows where the water tickled my ankles.

I saw her arms rise from the water and wheel slowly over her round, wet head and dip again beneath. She made no noise. She swam around the curve up into the shallows, stood up and walked toward me and never took her eyes off my own.

She took my hand, and looked into the palm. She had a lean rangy skinned-cat body, and a deep little muttering voice.

"Small slim hands," she said, "a sad and lonely man. You see the big picture, but you have no real life." She grumbled a minute. "Short thin fingers, tapered ends. A stiff and waisted thumb, hmmm. Better off alone, I suppose." She pressed into the flesh below my thumb. "Umm-hmm," she said, tracing all the little cracks and stars and broken lines in the middle of the palm with a light fingernail. She looked at it close for a second, then dropped it. She turned and sighed and looked back across the lake. I turned my eyes from her saggy little fanny and skinny legs.

"My name's Callie. I'm your neighbor," she said.

"I know it," I said.

She said, "Who's that little girl you taking care of?"

"My niece," I said. She was my younger cousin, but I had told her to call me uncle because it sounded more natural. I said, "She's had a hard life."

"Mmm," she said, and we were quiet for a while. "Well, the world ain't no place for an innocent soul, now is it?"

"It is not," I agreed.

"Must be hard on a man," she said.

"I don't know what you mean."

"I mean being alone out here with a pretty little girl."

"She's my niece, I'm not that way."

She turned and looked at me and then at the house for a minute.

"Why don't you come on up to the ridge sometime and pay me a visit?" Her thin lips crooked up and parted in a grin. She raised a hand and walked back into the water and swam around the curve into the cove and out of sight. I sat down on the bank. There was a sound and I turned my head to see Maeve up from bed and standing unsteady on the porch, fiddling with the little blue headphones radio, which she didn't at the moment seem to understand how to use. Then in a minute she had them on again, and just stood there.

Now that she wasn't carrying, she roamed the canyon with the strays. She ate raw peanuts from a sack I had on the kitchen counter, and drank her water from the lake down on her hands and muddy knees. She smelled like a dog that's been wallowing in the lake mud, that sour dank stink of rotten roots and scum. I finally held her in the bathtub one day, took the headphones off her head, and plunged her in, her scratching and screaming. I scrubbed her down and lathered up her head and dunked her till she was squeaky, and plucked a fat tick out of her scalp. But when I tried to dress her in some of Greta's old clothes, shut up in plastic and mothballs all these years, she slashed my cheek with her raggedy nails and ran through the house naked and making a high, thin, and breathless sound until she sniffed out the old rag she wore and flew out through the yard and into the woods buck naked with that rag in her hand and didn't come back till that evening, wearing it; smelling of the lake water again, and curled up asleep on the bare porch boards.

When I went to the screen door she didn't look up but said from where she lay hugging herself, "Don't you handle me that way no more."

"I had to clean you, child."

"I can't be touched," she said.

"All right."

"That woman at the big store said you was my daddy."

"But you know I'm not, I'm your uncle."

"I don't want no daddy," she said. "I just come out of the woods that day I come here, and I didn't come from nowhere before that."

"All right," I said, though my heart sank when she said it, for I wanted her to care about me in some way, but I don't think that was something she knew how to do. I fixed her a makeshift bed on the sofa in the den where I finally convinced her to sleep. As long as I kept my distance and made no sudden moves toward her and did not ever raise my voice above the gentle words you would use with a baby, we were all right. But it was not a way any man could live for long and I wondered what I could do—send her back to Sebastian's place, where she was but chattel? I feared one day she would wander into the woods and go wild. I might have called the county, said, Look, this child, who has wandered here from uncle's house, is in need of attention and there is nothing more I can do.

Who would take in such a child but the mental hospital up in Tuscaloosa?

I figured Sebastian thought she'd been sucked up into the twister and scattered into blood and dust, until the afternoon I heard his pickup muttering and coughing along the dam and then his springs sighing as he idled down the steep drive to the house, and then the creaking door and I was out on the porch waiting on him. He stopped at the steps and nodded and looked off across the lake as if we were lost together in thought. Uncle Sebastian was old and small and thin and hard as iron and he had the impish and shrewd face of all his siblings. His face was narrow and his eyes slanted down and in and his chin jutted up so that if you viewed him in profile his head was the blade of a scythe and his body the handle. He blinked in the sun, and said, "We been most of the summer fixing up the house after that tornado back in the spring."

I said, "Anybody hurt?"

"Well, we thought we'd lost little Maeve." And he turns to me. "Then I hear tell she's showed up over here, staying with you."

"Where would you hear that?" I said, and he said nothing but I saw his eyes shift just a fraction up toward the ridge where the crazy woman's house is perched.

The strays had shown little interest in Sebastian's arrival and kept mainly to their little scooped-out cool spots under the bushes, a flea-drowsing shade. Hardly moved all August, through the long hot days all you'd hear was the occasional creaking yawn, wet gnashing of grooming teeth, isolated flappity racket of a wet dog shaking out his coat. Hardly any barking at all. We heard a rustling and Maeve stood at the edge of the yard in her headphones, a scruffy little longhaired stray at her heels.

"She was with child," Sebastian said.

"She lost it."

"That late?" he said, and looked at me a long moment, then back at Maeve. "You keeping her outdoors and living with dogs?"

"If it was true, it would not be so different from what she came from," I said.

"Go to hell," Sebastian said. "Living out here by yourself, you going to tell me you ain't been trying some of that?"

"That's right."

"Them boys of mine done all wandered off now she's gone. I ain't got no help."

He walked slowly toward Maeve, who was standing there with two fingers of one hand pressed to the speaker over her right ear, head cocked, eyes cut left looking out at the lake. The little stray slinked back into the brush. Only when Sebastian laid his hand on Maeve's arm did she lean away, her bare feet planted the way an animal that does not want to be moved will do. He began to drag her and she struggled, making not a sound, still just listening.

I walked up behind Sebastian and said his name, and when he turned I hit him between the eyes with the point of my knuckle. Small and old as he was, he crumpled. Maeve did not run then but walked over to the porch, up the steps, and into the house.

I dragged the old man by his armpits to the water, and waded out with him trailing. Maeve came out again and followed in her nightslip to the bank, and stood there eating a cherry Popsicle. She took the Popsicle out of her mouth and held it like a little beacon beside her head. Her lips were red and swollen looking. She took the blue headphones off her ears and let them rest around her neck. I could hear the tinny sound of something in there, now it wasn't inside of her head.

"What you doing with that man?" she said.

"Nothing," I said.

"Are you drownden him?"

I said the first thing that came to mind.

"I am baptizing," I said. "I am cleansing his heart."

It was late afternoon then. I looked back over my shoulder at Maeve. She was half lit by sunlight sifting through the leaves, half in shadow. A mostly naked child in a rotten garment.

Underwater, Uncle Sebastian jerked and his eyes came open. I held him harder and waded out to where it was up to my shoulders and the current strong toward the spillway, my heart heavy in the water, the pressure there pressing on it. Behind me, Maeve waded into the shallows.

"I want it too, Uncle," she called.

Sebastian's arms ceased thrashing, and after a minute I let him go. I saw him turning away in the water. Palms of his hands, a glimpse of an eye, the ragged toe of a boot dimpling the surface, all in a slow drifting toward the spillway, and then gone in the murk. Maeve lifted the gauzy nightslip up over her head as she waded in, her pale middle soft and mapped with squiggly brown stretch marks. I pushed against the current trying to reach her before she got in too deep. There was such unspeakable love in me. I was as vile as my uncle, as vile as he claimed.

"Hold still, wait there," I said at the very moment her head went under as if she'd been yanked from below.

The bottom is slippery, there are uncounted little sinkholes. Out of her surprised little hand, the nightslip floated a ways and sank. I dove down but the water slowed me and I could not reach her. My eyes were open but the water was so muddy I could barely even see my own hands. I kept gasping up and diving down, the sun was sinking into the trees.

She would not show again until dusk, when from the bank I saw her ghost rise from the water and walk into the woods.

The strays tuned up. There was a ringing from the telephone inside the house. It would ring and stop a while. Ring and then stop. The sheriff's car rolled its silent flickering way through the trees. Its lights put a flame in all the whispering leaves. There was a hollow taunting shout from up on the ridge but I paid it no mind.

I once heard at dawn the strangest bird, unnatural, like sweet notes sung through an outdoor PA system, some bullhorn perched in a tree in the woods, and I went outside.

It was coming from east of the house, where the tornado would come through. I walked down a trail, looking up. It got louder. I got to where it had to be, it was all around me in the air, but there was nothing in the trees. A pocket of air had picked up a signal, the way a tooth filling will pick up a radio station.

It rang in my blood, it and me the only living things in that patch of woods, all the creatures fled or dug in deep, and I remember that I felt a strange happiness.

FRED CHAPPELL

Mankind Journeys Through
Forests of Symbols

Fred Chappell has published many books of poetry and fic-
tion, including First and Last Words, Midquest, More
Shapes Than One, Dagon, Brighten the Corner Where
You Are, *and* I Am One of You Forever. *He has received*
the T. S. Eliot Prize, the Bollingen Prize in Poetry, two
World Fantasy Awards, and the Prix de Meilleur des Livres
Étrangers of the Académie Française. In 1997, he was
named poet laureate of his home state of North Carolina. He
is Burlington Industries Professor of English at the Univer-
sity of North Carolina at Greensboro. "Mankind Journeys
Through Forests of Symbols" was first published in the
author's collection More Shapes Than One.

I

There was a dream, and a gaudy big thing it was, too, and for six hours it had been blocking Highway 51 between Turkey Knob and Ember Forks. The deputies came out to have a look-see, tall tobacco-chewing mountain boys, and they stood and scratched their armpits and made highly unscientific observations like, "Well, I be dog, Hank," and "Ain't that something, Bill," and so on, you can just imagine. Finally Sheriff Balsam arrived with his twenty years of law-enforcement experience, but he, too, seemed at a loss.

The dream would measure about two stories tall and five hundred yards wide and it lay lengthwise on the highway for a distance of at least two miles. It was thick and goofy, in consistency something like cotton candy. Its predominant color was chartreuse, but this color was interlaced with coiling threads of bright scarlet and yellow and suffused in some areas with cloudy masses of mauve and ocher. It had first been reported about seven o'clock in the morning, but it had probably appeared earlier. Traffic was light on that stretch.

Sheriff Balsam observed that it would be a problem. No dream of such scale and density had been reported before in North Carolina, and this one looked to be difficult. Balsam had never dealt much with dreams, and there was a lot to this one. It was opaque and complex; you could see it working within itself like corn-whiskey mash in a copper cooker.

Balsam and the boys set up the blinking barricades down the highway, detouring the traffic onto a circuitous gravel road, and then there was nothing to do but wait. The theory was that when the dreamer woke, the dream would go away, disappear like a five-dollar bill in a poker game. And who could afford to lie in bed all day dreaming? Balsam and Hank and Bill returned to the sheriff's office in the Osgood County courthouse to busy themselves with lost dogs and traffic citations.

But by lunchtime the telephone began ringing and didn't let up. Folks were irate. Whose dream was it out there on the highway and what, by God, was Balsam going to do about it? "I voted for you last time, Elmo Balsam," said the vexed farm wife.

"I was the only one running, Ora Mae," Balsam said.

Finally he left the receiver off the hook and looked over at Hank and Bill, who were sharing a newspaper and a spittoon. "Boys," he said, "looks like we got bigger troubles than we thought."

"Yup," says Hank, and Bill says, "Looks like."

Balsam said, "What if whoever is dreaming that damn thing is drugged?"

Now there was a thought. Crazed drug freaks everywhere these days. Just think of the high school over there. Hank and Bill thought of the high school and shook their heads mournfully. *These days anymore, boy, you just don't know.*

"Might be quite a while before he comes out of it. And it could be even worse."

Worse brightened their interest considerably. They looked at Balsam in mute wonder.

"He might could be in a coma. Might be weeks and months. Might be years."

They looked at one another.

"I think we ought to get an expert up here from the State Office," Balsam said. He looked the number up and paused with his finger in the dial. "What do you boys think?"

Whew, Lordy, the State Office. Bill thought it over and said, "Yup," but you could tell he considered it an extraordinary step to take. Bill was the slow and earnest thinker. Hank, the ebullient enthusiast, was intoxicated by every whim that sailed down the pike.

They watched astonished as Balsam spoke into the telephone. They fully realized it was the State Office on the other end of the line.

Balsam hung up and told them that the State Office had already dispatched an expert; he ought to have been here by now. Seemed that a farmer flying over in his Cessna had spotted the dream and radioed the highway patrol and they'd gotten in touch with the State Office. The State Office had

said a lot of other things to Balsam that they would of course regret saying
later on, so he wouldn't repeat all that. But they were to keep an eye out for
this expert, Dr. Litmouse his name was, who ought to have been here by now.

Just at that precise moment a state-patrol car pulled up in front of the
sheriff's office, blue light twirling, siren whining. Two men entered. One
was only a patrolman, but it was easy to see the other was an expert, the genuine article. His pinstripe gray suit was too large for him, as if he'd wandered into someone else's clothing by accident. He had but a paucity of hair
and what there was was white and frazzly. The thick lenses of his spectacles
so magnified his eyes, they looked like they were pasted on the glass. He was
carrying a quart mason jar of brownish liquid.

"I'm Dr. Litmouse," he said. "I hope I'm not late."

Balsam rose with unaccustomed alacrity and shook his hand. Introduc-
tions all around.

"I guess you're anxious to get out on Fifty-one and see about that
dream," the sheriff said. "We'll drive you out."

"Kind of you," Dr. Litmouse said. "I wonder if you have a safe place
where I might store this." He held up his quart jar.

"Sure thing, Doc. What is it?"

"I suppose you might call it a kind of secret formula," the expert said.

Balsam gave the muddy liquid an uneasy look. "We'll put it in the
safe . . . No, better put it in the filing cabinet," he said, remembering that
he'd forgotten the combination to the safe. It wasn't needed; Balsam and Bill
and Hank were not often entrusted with secret formulae.

"Fine."

Balsam and Dr. Litmouse got into one car, Hank and Bill into another,
and the patrolman followed them. Dr. Litmouse seemed preoccupied, saying not a word the whole trip. This guy wouldn't look like much if you saw
him just anywhere, Balsam thought, but once you knew he was an
expert . . . That was what Science would do for you. Balsam began to regret
that he wasted his evenings watching championship wrestling on TV
instead of reading chemistry books.

When they arrived at the famous dream, they found a little girl, a tow-
head about eight years old, standing just this side of it. She wore jeans and a
blouse and was popping bubble gum.

Balsam hollered at her. "Hey, little girl. You get back away from that thing."

She snapped a bubble. "There's already three cars drove in there."

"Good Lord," he said. "Didn't they see the detour sign?"

"Sure they did," she said. "Drove right around it."

"They must be crazy."

"They didn't look crazy."

"Well, you stand back now."

Dr. Litmouse had already begun to examine the dream. He paced back about fifteen feet and surveyed it from there, then walked over and stared closely, like a man peeking through a keyhole. He pulled his earlobe, pushed his glasses up on the bridge of his nose. "Bring me my case out of the car, please," he said.

Hank fetched it.

"What do you think, Doc?" the sheriff asked.

"I'm not quite sure," he said. He set the case on the ground and squatted to open it. It was a large square box of black leather, lined with blue plush. Inside were flasks and bottles and test tubes, forceps, big hypodermics, clamps, and other unrecognizable stainless-steel instruments. He took out a two-liter beaker and a pair of shiny clamps and went back. He inserted the clamps gently into the surface of the dream and gave them a slight twist and slowly withdrew. A hand-sized blob of it came away like greenish cobweb, trailing filmy rags. The expert stuffed this blob into the beaker and held it up against the sunlight to judge whatever he was judging. He shook his head.

From his vest pocket he took a book of papers like cigarette papers except that they were blue and pink. He blew on them and tore out one of each color. He lowered the blue paper down into the dream blob and took it out and looked. Obviously dissatisfied, he threw it to the ground. Then he tried the pink paper.

Bill nudged Hank. *Damn, boy, look at him go.*

The stooped gray expert held the beaker to his face and sniffed—carefully. Then, very gingerly, he put his finger into it. When he brought his finger out, it was tinted pale green and dream threads clung to it. They watched, muscles tensed, as he put his finger into his mouth.

Almost immediately a fearful transformation came over the scientist.

He trembled head to toe in his too-large suit like a butterfly trying to shed its cocoon. His eyes rolled crazily and blinked back, showing the wild whites. His voice was high and thin and visionary when he cried out:

"La Nature est un temple ou de vivants piliers
Laissent parfois sortir de confuses paroles:
L'homme y passe à travers des forêts de symbols
Qui l'observent avec des regards familiers."

Then he keeled over flat on the ground, unconscious.

Balsam sprang into action. "Hank, Bill! Pick that man up and bring him over here. Hurry up. And stay away from that stuff, whatever it is."

Hank and Bill deposited Dr. Litmouse at the sheriff's feet, and he knelt to examine him. The doctor's eyelids quivered and he began to breathe more regularly, regaining his senses. He sat up and rubbed his face with both hands.

"You okay, Doc?" Balsam asked.

"I'll be all right in a moment," he said. He put his head between his knees and breathed deeply.

"You took a bad turn there. Had us all worried," Balsam said. "What is that stuff, anyhow?"

Dr. Litmouse rose and brushed ineffectually at his baggy suit. "It's a more serious problem than we thought. The mass we have to deal with here is not a dream but something rather more permanent. Unless we can think of a solution."

"What is it then?"

"I hate to tell you," Dr. Litmouse said, "but I believe it's a symbolist poem. I'd stake my professional reputation that it's a symbolist poem."

"You don't say," Balsam said.

Hank nudged Bill with his shoulder. *Damn-a-mighty, boy, symbolist poem. You ever see the beast?*

The little girl came over to stare at Dr. Litmouse and to pop a bubble at him. "What's the matter with you?" she asked. "You act like you're falling-down drunk."

2

Dusk had come to the mountains like a sewing machine crawling over an operating table, and Dr. Litmouse and Hank and Bill and Balsam were back in the sheriff's office. Balsam sat at his desk, the telephone receiver still off the hook. Bill and Hank had resumed their corner chairs. The three lawmen were listening to the scientist's explanation.

"Basically it's the same problem as a dream, so it's mostly out of our hands. Somebody within a fifty-mile radius is ripe to write a symbolist poem but hasn't gotten around to it yet. As soon as she or he does, then it will go away, just as the usual dream obstructions vanish when the dreamers wake." He took off his glasses and polished them with his handkerchief. His eyes looked as little and bare as shirt buttons and made the others feel queasy. They were glad when he replaced his spectacles.

"It's worse than a dream, though, because we may be dealing with a subconscious poet. It may be that this person never writes poems in the normal course of his life. If this poem originated in the mind of someone who never thinks of writing, then I'm afraid your highway detour will have to be more or less permanent."

"Damn," Balsam said. He leaned back in his swivel chair. "What do you mean, more or less?"

"Death," replied the expert.

"Say what, Doc?"

"If it doesn't belong to a practicing poet, you may be stuck with it until the originator dies."

"Damn," Balsam said. "And there ain't nothing we can do? Nothing at all?"

"In Europe they've been heavily afflicted, but in America we've been lucky," Dr. Litmouse said. "The largest American symbolist obstruction is in California, and is, I would estimate, about twice the size of this one. Fortunately, it's at the bottom of a canyon in Whittier National Park and no real inconvenience. But it's been there, Sheriff Balsam, for fifteen years."

Hank and Bill exchanged glances. *Fifteen years, boy.*

Balsam said, "Doc, we can't leave that thing there fifteen years. That's an important road."

"I sympathize, but I don't know what can be done."

The sheriff picked up a ballpoint pen and began clicking it. "Well, let's see. . . . There it is, and it'll go away if somebody writes it down on paper."

"Correct."

"What we got to do then is get folks around here started writing poems. Maybe we'll hit on the right person."

"How will you do that?"

He bit the pen. "I don't know. . . . Bill, Hank—you boys got any bright ideas?"

They shook their heads sorrowfully. Bill spat; Hank spat.

"Say, Doc," Balsam said, "you tested this here, uh, poem. Did you get any notion what it was about?"

"Very difficult to say. It affects the nervous system powerfully, sending the victim into a sort of trance. Coming out of it, I remember no details. I have only impressions. I would say that the poem is informed by tenuous allusion, strong synesthesia, and a wide array of hermetic symbols. But it was quite confusing, and I could gather no details, no specifics."

"That's too bad," the sheriff said. "I was hoping we could track it down. Because if it was about Natural Bridge, say, and we could find someone who had been visiting up to Virginia. . . ."

"It's a symbolist poem, Sheriff," Dr. Litmouse said. "Doesn't have to be autobiographical in the least. In this case, we're probably dealing with archetypes."

Hank winked at Bill. *We better watch out, boy. Them ole archetypes.*

"Well, what we got to do then is just get as many people as we can out there writing poems. Community effort. Maybe we'll luck out."

"How?" asked Dr. Litmouse.

He clicked his ballpoint furiously. He got a sheet of department stationery and began printing tall uncertain letters. The other three watched in suspense, breathing unevenly. When he finished, Balsam picked up the paper and held it at arm's length to read. His lips moved slightly. Then he showed them his work. "What do you think?" he asked.

The SHERIFF'S DEPARTMENT

of OSGOOD COUNTY

in cooperation with the

NORTH CAROLINA STATE HIGHWAY DEPARTMENT

announces

A POETRY CONTEST

$50 FIRST PRIZE

Send entries to SHERIFF ELMO BALSAM

OSGOOD COUNTY COURTHOUSE

EMBER FORKS, N. C. 26816

SYMBOLISM PREFERRED!!!

"I suppose it's worth a try," Dr. Litmouse said, but he sounded dubious.

3

Then opened the beneficent heavens and verses rained upon the embattled keepers of the law.

Sheriff Balsam kept his equanimity. He had posted Collins, Dr. Litmouse's escort patrolman, out at the site to keep an eye on the dream and report to the office. Collins radioed in every hour that there was no change.

The other four sat in the office, reading sheaf after sheaf of manuscript. Dr. Litmouse held each page by a corner, regarding every poem as if it were some new species of maggot. Balsam turned pages mechanically; his eyes looked tired. Hank and Bill read ponderously, chewing their plugs as if they were digging graves.

Balsam glanced up. "Anything look promising?"

"These are just all Spring and Mother," Hank said. He sounded aggrieved.

"How about you, Bill?" the sheriff asked.

"Kinda boring," he said. "Spring and Mother and all. But there was one—"

"What about it?"

"I thought it had something, but it didn't work out."

"Let's see it." Balsam squinted and read aloud. "'The bluebird in our firethorn tree, Fills the merry day with glee. . . . 'Aw, come on, Bill. This ain't the kind of thing we're looking for."

"Yeah, I know." He chewed. "But I was thinking if maybe it went different—"

"Different how?"

"Like if it wasn't no bluebird and glee and stuff. Like if it started off, 'The squalid eagle in the thornfire,' maybe we'd be on the right track."

Balsam gave him a steady gaze. "How you say that?"

"Say what?"

" 'Squiggly eagle in the bush'?"

"I was trying to think how it might go. The squalid eagle in the thornfire . . . I guess I've got the whole wrong idea."

They looked at him with fierce interest.

Balsam turned to the expert. "What do you think, Doc?"

Dr. Litmouse nodded slowly. "It's worth a try. Why not?"

A sputter of static from the radio on the sheriff's desk and then the tinny voice of the patrolman. "Collins here, out at the site. You there, Sheriff Balsam?"

Balsam leaned and flipped a switch. "Right here," he said. "Anything happening out your way?"

"I think maybe I saw some movement. Top of it got a little ragged like maybe the wind took hold of it."

"When was this?"

"Just a minute ago. Nothing happening now, though."

"Stay right there and keep watch," the sheriff ordered. "I'll send some help." He cut the switch and stood up and took his keys out of his pocket. "Doc," he said, "you drive my car and radio back when you get there. When we hear from you, we'll start working with Bill here."

"Work with me how?" Bill's brow furrowed plaintively.

The sheriff led Bill to the desk and seated him. He crowded papers out of the way and got a fresh sheet and two pencils and laid them before the deputy. "You ever wrote any poems, Bill?"

He looked down at his big wrists. "Not much," he said.

"Have you?"

His face and neck were scarlet. "Used to try one ever once in a while."

"I never knowed that!" Hank exclaimed. "Boss, I swear he never told me nothing about it."

"You're going to write one now, Bill," Balsam said.

"What do you want me to write?" He picked up a pencil as if it were loaded and cocked.

"Write it down about that squirrely eagle."

Bill wrote, sticking the tip of his tongue out of the corner of his mouth. "Now what?" he asked.

"Just go on from there," the sheriff ordered.

"I don't know nothing that comes next."

"You just settle down and see if it doesn't come to you."

"Come on, old hoss, you can do it!" Hank shouted.

Bill closed his eyes. His lips twitched. He opened his eyes and shook his head.

"Anything we can get to help you out?" the sheriff asked.

He thought. "Well, maybe, uh, maybe I could use a glass of wine?"

"Wine!" Hank was thunderstruck, but at a glance from Balsam recovered himself. "Damn right, good buddy. What you want? T-Bird? Irish Rose? Mad Dog?"

"Like maybe a pretty good burgundy," Bill said firmly.

"Hank, you zip down to the supermarket and see if they got any burgundy wine," the sheriff said. Hank started for the door, but Balsam halted him. "No. Hell. Wait. Get this boy the best Champagne they got. Don't spare the horses."

"Damn right," Hank said, and went out.

Again the radio rattled and spoke. "Sheriff Balsam, this is Dr. Litmouse. I'm in place out here at the site. We're ready to begin when you are."

Balsam switched on and said, "We're ready to go. We'll keep each other posted. . . . No, wait. Bill's going to be concentrating pretty heavy in here. Maybe we ought to stay off the radio for a while."

"Quite sensible," Dr. Litmouse said. "We'll wait for your call."

"Fine." The sheriff switched off and turned to Bill. "Don't worry about a thing," he said. "You just go on and write down your poem. Won't nobody disturb you."

"I don't know if I can," Bill said.

"Look here, Bill," Balsam said, "you're a deputy sheriff of Osgood County. I don't have to tell you what kind of responsibility that is. Sometimes the job is dirty and dangerous, but you knew that when you put on the badge. I never expect to see you back off from the job, boy. Never."

Bill swallowed hard. "Do the best I can," he said.

"Okay then. I'll be right over here in the corner. Anything you need, just holler. Don't forget we're all behind you one hundred percent." Balsam sat in a corner chair and pretended to read a sheaf of poems.

Bill lifted a pencil and laid it down again. He closed his eyes. His neck and shoulder muscles bunched and veins stood out in his temples. He breathed slow and harsh and a film of sweat covered his forehead.

He picked up the pencil and began to write, poking the tip of his tongue out of the corner of his mouth.

Hank came in with a bottle of Champagne. He started to speak, but Balsam silenced him with a gesture. Hank looked at Bill with an expression of tender commiseration. He gave the bottle to the sheriff, who took it into the washroom and worked the cork out and poured a water tumbler full of the wine and took it to Bill, setting it gently on the desk.

Bill didn't notice. He scratched out old words and wrote in new ones. In a while he drained the glass without appearing to realize he'd done it. The expression on his face was startling to look at.

Balsam and Hank sat watching Bill and glancing at one another. Time seemed to stop.

Bill wrote and rewrote, grunting. At last, with a savage anguished cry, he flung down the pencil and buried his face in his hands. When he turned to Hank and Balsam, his face was ashen and his brown hair had turned gray. "That's all," he said. "I can't do no more. I can't."

They took his arms and half dragged him to his usual chair in the corner. "See how he is, Hank. We can have an ambulance here in five minutes."

"I'll be all right," Bill said.

Balsam went to the radio. "Hey, Doc, are you there? How's it look?"

The excitement of the scientist was unmistakable. "It's all gone, Sheriff Balsam. Disappeared. You've done a fine job back there."

"All cleared up?"

"Well, there are a few scattered patches, but the highway is clear. No trouble. We can probably get rid of the leftovers if Bill wants to correct his meter and line breaks."

"Hell with that," Balsam said. "Bill has done enough for one day. You boys come on in." He clicked off and turned to his deputies.

Hank was punching Bill's shoulder and wrestling him about. "You hear that? You done it, old hoss! By damn, you done it!"

Bill smiled weakly and tried to look modest.

"We ought to celebrate," the sheriff said. "What say we finish off this here Champagne?"

When Dr. Litmouse and Patrolman Collins came in, they all switched to the corn whiskey Balsam kept in his bottom drawer. They poured a couple of farewell drinks and talked happily. Dr. Litmouse promised to turn in a glowing report about the sheriff and his deputies to the State Office. They shook hands and the other two departed. Patrolman Collins cut in the siren for a couple of blocks.

They listened, and then Balsam was struck by a memory. "Oh hell," he said.

"What's the matter?" Hank asked.

"The Secret Formula," he said. "The doc forgot his Secret Formula." He took it out of the filing cabinet and set it on his desk. They regarded it with apprehension.

"What do you reckon that stuff does?" Hank asked.

"I don't know," Balsam said.

"Well, hell," Bill said, "let's find out." He unscrewed the lid and stuck his finger into the liquid and tasted it.

Hank and the sheriff eyed one another. It was clear now that Bill had the courage of tigers; he was afraid of nothing.

"What is it?" the sheriff asked.

Bill licked his lips. "Barbecue sauce," he said. He thought for a moment, tasting. "With about a cup and a half of Chateau Beychevelle '78."

MARIAN MOORE

The Mikado's Favorite Song

Marian Moore lives in the New Orleans suburb of Harvey. She studied fiction writing with the late George Alec Effinger and is a member of NOMMO literary society of New Orleans. This marks the first publication of "The Mikado's Favorite Song," her first professional fiction sale.

My first thought was that I knew the voice—thin and fragile as wedding crystal but then it fractured into a thousand slivers of bitterness. Mr. Harriman must have seen the look on my face because he scooped the phone receiver out of my hand, momentarily listened, and then set it firmly back into the cradle. I glanced at the glamour photo of his wife on his desk and looked away quickly. None of my business, after all. But he had seen my fleeting look.

"Not my wife—"

Even worse, I thought, and tried to keep my expression impassive. I wasn't sure what the voice had been saying. Only that it had been female and blistering. With the window blinds tight against the view, and the lights dimmed for the video display, my mind insisted on wandering and wondering. One of the fluorescent lights overhead had been crackling electronic comments throughout Harriman's drone. I caught sight of a custom label in his jacket and idly fantasized about ten-year-old Chinese girls struggling with the thin gray strands of silk that made up its lining.

"Well, do you have any questions?"

Pinching my nose and trying to focus, I could see that Elliott Harriman's eyes were on me. *Repercussions*, I thought. *He hasn't mentioned repercussions*.

"I thought that employees could take as much sick time as they needed?"

"You always have a few who abuse that policy. For example, have you reviewed Morgan's absentee record?"

"I've never paid much attention," I said warily. Morgan was fond of disappearing after lunch, but he always got his work done.

"You're thinking like an employee again, Leah." He perched his butt on the edge of his desk, his emotionless eyes searching mine. "I can see it in your eyes. 'Yes, he skips out, but he's a good guy.' You're in management now."

I saw, rather than heard, the phone begin to ring again. Elliott Harriman suddenly clutched the blue, whiteboard pen that he had been wielding and leaned back, looking at the caller display. A muttered "damn" escaped his lips and he stabbed the release button with his finger.

Desperate to escape, I interjected—"If you need to take that . . ."

"No, I don't. My point is that Morgan has been here longer than you have. He's not likely to be particularly happy that you were promoted after one year and he wasn't."

"He says that he didn't want the job."

"So he says. It doesn't mean that he wanted you to have it." He stole a glance at the phone warily. "Have they finished your office yet? It will help to have you out of their immediate area. Maybe the distance will do all of you some good. In the meantime . . ."

The phone rang again, and I sprang up ready to leave. "Your phone doesn't forward to the secretary?" I had seen Andrea at her desk on my way in, typing on her keyboard.

"These calls don't forward," he said curtly, staring at the telephone as if expecting the handset to rise up on its coils like a cobra.

And then I was out the door, safe and in the relative quiet of the office floor watching the morning sunlight silently combating the artificial simulation of noon by proper corporation lightbulbs.

It was the wrong thing to say, and I knew it immediately. Morgan stared up at me from his low chair, his arm stretching to hang up his phone. He kept missing the switch hook until he finally gathered himself, glanced left and pulled the handset over the hook forcefully.

I used that moment to tug at my skirt and flick a lint speck off my blouse. By the time Morgan looked back, I had composed my face into a faintly severe frown.

"I thought that you were going to have that document for me today, Morgan."

He stiffened, so I decided to be more disarming despite Harriman's advice. Kicking off my heels, I sat down in the extra plastic chair in his office—the so-called visitor chair.

"You know, if you have to, you can sign up for one of the project rooms. With no phones to bother you, you'd be finished in no time."

"My son, Raymond, is sick today," he said dully. "I was just checking up on him."

"Yes, of course." I shot a quick look outside his cubicle opening. The three other team members were either hunched over their desks or typing at their terminals. They didn't fool me one minute. The moment that I left, they would be over here commiserating with Morgan about their slave-driver boss.

"But I need that document for tomorrow's meeting. Why don't you take Project Room B?" Slipping my heels back on, I rose and paused in the doorway. "Look. I'll have everyone transfer any calls from home to you. I'll check on your progress after lunch."

I was congratulating myself on a successful encounter with an employee when I saw Shavti Patel poke her head out of her cubicle and wave me over holding a note.

"Are you able to break for coffee?" she sang, obviously for other ears.

The two other team members were studiously avoiding our conversation and I peered at the scrawl on the scrap of copy paper. *We should talk*, she had written.

"It's only nine A.M."

She danced the note in front of my eyes until I relented.

As soon as we cleared the elevator and any possible listening ears, I turned to her. "What's the problem?"

"Your reprimand of Morgan." Keeping my eyes on the hallway between the coffee bar and us, I adjusted my ears mentally to her Indian/British lilt. "It was all according to policy and all perfectly wrong."

I had to restrain my annoyance. Shavti had been up for this job also and had turned it down. When we arrived at the coffee kiosk, I waved away her movement towards her coin purse. After all, rank has its obligations as well as privileges.

"This is Harriman's first hurdle for me, Shavti. That's all. He practically laid it out. Make sure Morgan is at his desk every day. He's late or out altogether too often."

As she always did, Shavti sniffed at the amount of cream and sugar I dumped into my coffee. Swirling her own unadulterated tea reflectively, she stared into its depths.

"Now is not the time, however. His son is very ill. I heard him say that his fever is over a hundred and two degrees." She nodded to acquaintances from another department and we drifted towards the redbud trees, greenery, and benches that went toward making an informal lounging area. It was early yet and few had ventured out to take an attitude-adjustment break.

I was surprised to see a couple of kids loitering around the edge of the green area. Driving through school zones this morning made me certain that school was still in session.

"You're making me feel like Ebenezer Scrooge, Shavti. Isn't Morgan married? This son didn't come from nowhere, did he?"

"His wife is at the hospital. He was talking to her when you came up."

"You hear a lot over there," I commented wryly.

"Ah, but I'm only one cubicle away." Sighing, she added, "And Morgan can be quite dramatic. I am sure that he wanted us to hear everything."

The jagged beginning of a tension headache made my eyes throb. They kept wandering back to the young girl and boy circling the edge of the artificial mall park. The girl could not have been more than twelve and an undernourished twelve at that. Her arms, the color that Hanes pantyhose had christened gentlebrown, looked no thicker than the stick shift on my car.

"Can you let Morgan go today?" Shavti continued, jerking me back to our conversation. "He isn't going to get much work done this afternoon."

"And who's going to do his work?" Then quickly before she could respond, "No, I'm not going to get started on that path. If he needs to relieve his wife tomorrow, fine. But not today. He's the one who designed the process that I have to present tomorrow. He's the only one who knows it. And we both know why he's the only one who knows it. He's always bragged about his idea of job security." I took a breath before closing my case. "I have to make the presentation tomorrow. He can have his day off then."

"Are you going to tell him that?"

"I'll talk to him."

Shavti almost looked relieved. Had she been afraid of being drafted, I wondered, and added aloud, "Don't you want this job? We always had all of these plans of what we would do when women were in charge."

A guilty laugh jerked out of her. "Too much pressure." She crumbled the Styrofoam cup and tossed it into the wire trashcan at the perimeter. "I decided that my family was more important. Jay is six now and school has more meaning." My eyes had followed the path of her cup to meet the faces of the staring youngsters. And I was certain that they were staring—even though their dark eyes seem to slide away every time I determinedly looked in their direction. I was surprised that Shavti didn't say anything about the two. Usually, she was quick to equate indulgence with neglect when it came to American parents and their children.

"But you backed out after only one week," I pressed as we started back up the narrow corridor to the elevator lobby.

"Too much e-mail, too many calls," she said enigmatically.

Morgan's desk was quiet when I passed. Panicking me until I remembered that I had offered him the project room to work in. Ready to struggle with my first project plan and budget, I sat at my desk. I was driving the mouse up and down its pad aimlessly when the phone rang. I longed for a display console like Harriman's but that wouldn't come until the long-awaited office. Should I let it roll to phone mail? After the fourth loud electronic buzz—the volume button had just decided to break—I pulled the receiver from its base.

"Hello, this is—" I began.

"Mommy, Jafar won't stay at school!" a voice cried, a girl's voice, so of course, I thought of the child in the park.

Cradling the receiver between my head and shoulder, I pushed more imaginary numbers into the spreadsheet that I was working on, watching the totals climb. "I'm sorry. You have a wrong number." I looked up to find Harriman watching me. Hurriedly, I began to transfer the handset back to its cradle.

"No, Mommy. Please don't hang up." I wondered at a child who expected her mother to hang up on her, but pressed the receiver down firmly.

"How is it going?"

"Well enough." Hiding my slow progress, I minimized the project diagram.

"Are you still free for lunch? We can go over some of your projections."

"Yes, yes." Nervously, I pulled my jacket sleeve back down my wrist, remembered my training, and forced myself to look straight into Elliott's eyes. I doubted my plan would be finished by lunchtime, but confidence was more important than truth.

"I noticed that Morgan wasn't at his desk?"

"I sent him to the project room so that he wouldn't be disturbed."

"Very good—I'll stop by at noon, then."

He strode away, poking his head into Shavti's cubicle to make a comment. It was nearly 10:30 and I should check on Morgan—especially if Harriman wanted figures by noon. But I could hardly go now. One ear on the muted conversation down the aisle, I opened the project plan again and tried to work.

After the voices faded, I eased out of my own cubicle and headed to the project room at the end of the hall. Opening the door, I found the room dark, one computer terminal softly humming to itself. Damn, this was the only group room on the floor—where had Morgan gone? A nudge of the mouse deactivated the screen saver revealing a sketchy document on the screen. He had been here long enough to get started, at least. While I stood there, the phone began to ring.

He's forwarded it, I thought. *So he has to be around here somewhere*. I zigzagged back towards his desk, hesitating beside each row of cubicles. Perhaps he had stopped to borrow a manual from someone's desk? Andrea and I almost collided at the end of the fourth row.

"Andrea, have you seen Morgan?" I said after apologizing. "I needed to get some figures from him."

"No. Morgan's gone."

"What?" My voice started to rise before I thought better and tried to pull my voice back from a soprano shriek. Andrea's eyes edged past me as if plotting a get-away path. "When did he leave? Do you know where he went?"

"Almost an hour ago . . ."

Of course, I thought. *Right after I left the office with Shavti*.

"He got a call and left, but he left a note. I saw him write one."

"I didn't get one."

"I saw him write it." Striding to my desk, she led the way. When I reached the desk, she was waving a pink while-you-were-out note triumphantly. "You see—I knew that he'd written one."

"I've been sitting here since ten. It should have been here when I came back from break." I stared at the brief note. It was in Morgan's handwriting. He'd left no contact number. There was no option—I would simply have to make up any estimates that I didn't have. As I stood there, the phone began ringing again and I noticed that the message light was blinking angrily. Waving Andrea away, I scooped up the receiver.

At first, all I heard was music. Something vaguely classical. Was this an automated sales call? I was returning the receiver to its base when a voice cried out. I brought the headset back to my ear.

"Mother?"

My hand tightened automatically, but the voice sounded older than the child who'd called before. "You have the wrong number. Who are you calling?"

"Mother, Jafar says that he's hungry. What should I give him?"

Offering no pleasantries, I hung up. After a moment's thought, I headed to the secretary's desk.

"Andrea—I'm getting prank calls on my phone. Is there a way I can find out where they're originating?"

"What kind of prank calls?"

And what difference does that make? The thought must have been transmitted to my face because she went on.

"It costs us to trace calls."

"I thought that your phone displayed the telephone number of the caller. I could transfer my calls here."

"And all the display would say is 'transferred from Leah Ford.' "

"Then if I could get one of those display phones . . ."

She sighed and punched a key on her keyboard. "I'll make a note. Aren't you scheduled to have lunch with Mr. Harriman? I'll see if we can borrow one while you're out."

I thanked her and headed back to my desk. I only had thirty minutes to finagle some numbers into a reasonable estimate for Harriman.

Elliott Harriman spread my summary papers over the white tablecloth. He had insisted on spending lunch away from the usual places within walking distance and within my usual budget.

"This looks fine, Leah," he said slowly. "The numbers are more conservative than the estimate Morgan gave me earlier, however."

"You talked to Morgan."

"Briefly, yesterday. We left around the same time." He looked up from the pages of text and numbers.

"Well . . ."

The waiter chose that moment to come over and take our food order. So I had another two minutes for my stomach to churn over my response. The cheapest thing on the menu was soup and salad and that was twelve dollars.

"You don't have to worry—I plan on getting this."

Reviewing his trim figure and the tailored clothes again, I demurred. "No, this is what I want. With so many hours at my desk, I have to watch what I eat."

He passed the order on and turned back to me with an expectant gaze.

"Actually, I didn't get a chance to talk to Morgan to get his numbers. According to Andrea, he got a call and left in a hurry this morning."

"I understand that his son is in the hospital."

"Yes." Forcing my hands to unclench, I folded them in my lap and waited.

All Harriman did was swirl the ice around in his iced tea; his face had a sour look. Seeing his eyes flicker over my shoulder, I turned to see the waiter approach us with a small portable phone.

"Mr. Elliott Harriman?" Harriman only nodded. "I have a call for you."

"Leave it there."

The young man laid the disembodied receiver on the table and retreated. Taking the waiter's lead, I nodded toward the phone and asked if he needed me to leave. I would have welcomed a chance to catch a breath, even in the bathroom that I had noted at the end of the smoke-filled bar.

"No." He picked the phone up, listened briefly and set it back down, flipping the switch back to ready mode. It began to ring again almost immediately. He ignored it, only turning the ringer down when it was obvious that other tables were watching us.

Chiding myself, I began to silently repeat my morning mantra—*This is none of my business. . . . This is none of my business. . . .*

"I'm surprised that you haven't received some of these phone calls yourself, Leah." Harriman said casually. His salad and my soup arrived and we busied ourselves with flatware and napkins.

"What type of phone calls?" I said cautiously.

"Prank calls. At least that is what they would seem like at first. Andrea told me about your discussion with Morgan. He was quite upset from what I understand."

Ignoring Andrea's eagerness to pass on my employee relationships, I jumped at the chance to lay out my suspicions. "Is Morgan arranging these calls?"

"Then you have gotten some strange calls?"

"Yes."

He speared a leaf of romaine, turning it over as if in inspection. "You said arrange . . . then it doesn't sound like Morgan?"

"No. Like two children—well, actually one child who is taking care of another. Would Morgan arrange to have them call me? I would swear that I saw two kids in the park this morning."

Harriman shook his head and pointed to my soup. "That's going to get cold if you don't eat it. It would be a shame to toss Wollensky's turtle soup. It's excellent."

Sighing, I picked up the soupspoon and sampled a taste of the dark broth. The only irritant was the phone that still buzzed away on the small table.

"Go ahead." Harriman said, seeing my aggravated glare.

Picking it up, I flipped the switch to answer mode. A jumble of noises greeted me. All I was certain of was the sound of a child crying. The tinny sound of music from a television was in the background. "There's no one there. . . ."

Then a tired voice rang over the tiny receiver.

"Mother."

The voice took a heavy breath and I imagined her pushing away her shrieking brother. "Jafar has a temperature. The school won't let him stay if he has a fever. I have a science test today. What should I do?"

"This isn't funny." I retorted, as much to Harriman as to the girl. I started to lay the phone back on the table, then jerked it back up again. "What is your name, anyway? Why are you doing this?"

"It's Moena, Mother. Don't you recognize my voice?"

Pressing the switch to off, I set the phone back on the tablecloth. Glaring at Harriman, I watched him nonchalantly finish his salad. My bowl was still more than half full when the waiter returned.

"You're not finished . . . do you want more time?"

I waved the bowl away, gripping the edges of the table. The phone was ringing again.

"Hand me that, will you?"

I pushed the small receiver over to his area with one finger, watched him pick it up, listen for a minute and then pass it quietly to me.

The sharp, slightly familiar voice that I'd head that morning issued from the receiver in jagged tones. Some woman was demanding more money and more time. Complaints and protests fell into my ears like burning lead. He waved the phone back, hanging it up and began to attack his recently arrived steak. Looking down, I saw that my salad had arrived in the interim.

"Did you recognize the voice?"

"No," I said hesitantly.

"I'm not surprised. Few people recognize their own voice, even in recordings." He raised his hand, restraining my objections. "Oh, I know that it wasn't you. At times, it sounds like my wife. At times, like Shavti. Although I have to admit that the occurrences of Shavti have gone down since she backed out of this job." He attacked the steak with his knife. "Your salad."

As if prompted by a watching parent, I picked up my fork and selected a piece of tomato. He nodded and continued to eat.

"You haven't explained who they are."

"I don't know really. The Furies, Karma?" He laughed loudly and I glanced at the neighboring tables to see if we had attracted attention. "I've had Andrea trace some calls to no avail. If it sounds like my wife, then it is from my home number. If it sounds like you or Shavti, then the phone displays one of your numbers. And walking over to your desk only proves that it is not one of you making the call.

"The question is, Leah, how much do you want this job? The phone calls are just an annoyance."

"And the children I saw?"

He sipped his glass of wine, his eyes pensive. "Does it matter?" His eyes fastened on mine, he lowered the glass to the table. "As I said, the question is, do you want the job?"

"Why is it so important to you?"

"It's no secret that increasing minority representation in management is a company goal." He rotated his glass between his fingers precisely. "One of my measures during my annual review. And you're a good worker. You have drive. If you make it, that's all the better for me."

"And you'd be my mentor."

"As much as I can. But don't expect me to be around forever. I have my own ambitions as well." Crossing his knife and fork on his plate, he leaned back in his chair. "I still haven't heard your decision."

If I looked past him, out the windows onto the busy downtown street, I already knew what I would see. Jafar and Moena peering into the darkened restaurant like hungry waifs. If I left a take-out order on my doorstep tonight, would they be able to eat it?

"I want the job," I said. The phone began to ring.

SENA JETER NASLUND

The Perfecting of the Chopin Valse No. 14 in E Minor

Sena Jeter Naslund is the author of the acclaimed best-selling novel Ahab's Wife: or, The Star-Gazer, *listed by* Time *magazine as one of the top five fiction books of 1999. She also wrote the novel* Sherlock in Love; *her short fiction has been collected in* Ice Skating at the North Pole, The Animal Way to Love, *and* The Disobedience of Water. *Her latest novel is* Four Spirits. *She is the Distinguished Teaching Professor at the University of Louisville and program director for the brief-residency M.F.A. in writing at Spalding University in Louisville. A native of Birmingham, Alabama, Naslund received the 2001 Harper Lee Award for Distinguished Alabama Writer of the Year and the 2001 Alabama Literary Association Award. She is a former grant recipient from the National Endowment for the Arts, the Kentucky Arts Council, and the Kentucky Foundation for Women. Naslund lives with her husband in Louisville, Kentucky. "The Perfection of the Chopin Valse No. 14 in E Minor" was first published in* The Georgia Review.

One day last summer when I was taking a shower, I heard my mother playing the Chopin Valse no. 14 in E Minor better than she ever had played it before. Thirty years ago in Birmingham, I had listened to her while I sat on dusty terra-cotta tiles on the front porch. I was trying to pluck a thorn from my heel as I listened, and I remember looking up from my dirty foot to see the needle of a hummingbird entering one midget blossom after another, the blossoms hanging like froth on our butterfly bush. Probably she had first practiced the Valse thirty years or so before that, in Missouri, in a living room close enough to a dirt road to hear wagons passing, close enough for dust to sift over the piano keys. How was it that after knowing the piece for sixty years, my mother suddenly was playing it better than she ever had in her life?

I turned off the shower to make sure. It was true. There was a bounce and yet a delicacy in the repeated notes at the beginning of the phrase that she had never achieved before. And then the flight of the right hand up the keyboard was like the gesture of a dancer lifting her arm, unified and lilting. I waited for the double forte, which she never played loudly enough, and heard it roar out of the piano and up the furnace pipe to the bathroom. Perhaps that was it: the furnace pipe was acting like a natural amplifier, like a speaking tube. Dripping wet, I stepped over the tub and walked through the bathroom door to the landing at the top of the stairs. She was at the section with the Alberti-like bass. Usually her left hand hung back, couldn't keep the established tempo here (and it had been getting worse in the last seven or so years), but the left hand cut loose with the most perfectly rolled over arpeggio I had ever heard. Rubinstein didn't do it any better.

I hurried down the steps; she was doing the repeated notes again as one of the recapitulations of the opening phrase came up. I tried to see if she had finally decided to use Joseffy's suggested fingering—2, 4, 3, 1—instead of her own 4, 3, 2, 1 on which she had always insisted. But I was just too late to see. She finished with a flourish.

"Bravo!" I shouted and clapped. The water flew out of my hands like a wet dog shaking his fur. She leaned over the piano protectively.

"You're getting the keys wet," she said, smiling.

"You played that so well!"

"Suppose the mailman comes while you're naked?"

"Didn't you think you played it well?"

"I'm improving. You always do, from time to time."

"This was *super*."

"Thank you," she said and got up to make her second cup of coffee.

"Did you remember to take Hydropres?" I yelled. She is quite deaf, but refuses to wear her hearing aid while she practices. You know how music sounds over the telephone, she said to me once; that was what a hearing aid did to sounds.

"Did you take H?" I shouted a little louder.

She threw one of her white sweaters over the Walter Jackson Bate biography of Keats. "Don't read the last two chapters late at night," she said. "It makes you too sad."

I had taken to reading about romantic poets and their poetry, too, to relieve the glassy precision of my work at the pharmaceutical lab. I left the books around, and as she had done since I was a child, she read what I read—usually two hundred pages ahead of me. I put on her sweater, its wool sticking to my damp skin.

"I took H early this morning," she continued. "Did you take A?"

Aldomet is my high-blood-pressure drug. She takes it, too, but not till afternoon. I take it three times a day.

"No," I said. "I've forgotten again."

And I forgot about the Valse in E Minor. Maybe that performance was a fluke. Maybe I was mistaken.

It was not long after this that a rock in the garden began to move. It was thigh-high and pockmarked, and the pocks were rimmed with mica. The arcs of mica had the same curve as a fingernail clipping or the curve of a glittering eyelash.

Our garden was on a small scale by Louisville standards—about fifty by forty feet. We had landscaped it, though—rather expensively for us. A stucco wall hung between four brick columns across the back. Herringbone brick walks were flanked by clumps of iris, daylilies and chrysanthemums so that we had spots of spring, summer and fall bloom. There was a small statue of a girl looking up at the sky and spreading her stone apron to catch the rain. The apron was a birdbath. It was that sort of yard. Pretty, costly per square foot, designed to console us for our lack of scope. I had some dwarf fruit trees across the back, in front of the stucco wall.

The previous owner had had the mica boulder placed over a large chipmunk hole so no one would accidentally step in. The placement was imperfect aesthetically, and my mother said it ought to be moved, but I didn't want to go to the bother to hire somebody to do it. Sometimes I'd see her lean against the rock, her basket full of the spent heads of iris or daylilies, or windfall apples, or other garden debris. We were neat.

One bright night when the mica was arcing in the moonlight, I saw her going out there in her pajamas. She carried one of the rose satin sofa cushions, and its sides gleamed in the light. She put the cushion on top of the rock, climbed up, and sat on it. She looked like a bird sitting on a giant egg, a maharani riding an elephant, a child on a Galápagos tortoise.

I felt unreal, frightened, standing beside the bedroom curtain peering out. And stunned. I sat down on the bed, touched another satin cushion, smoothed it, soothed it. I held the cool satin against my cheeks. My tears made dark blotches on the fabric. I wanted to lie down, to deny her madness in the garden. And I did. I turned the cushion to the dry side, lay down on it and went to sleep.

In the morning the teakettle shrieked, she poured the water for her instant coffee, called "Good morning" to me, and all was ordinary.

When I walked in the garden, I noticed the rock had shifted. Around the base was a crescent of damp stone where crumbs of still-moist earth clung. The boulder had rotated a little, as though Antarctica on a giant globe had slipped northward a hundred miles into the South Pacific. Perhaps the rock had been more precariously balanced than I had thought. Perhaps her weight had caused it to shift—a slow-motion version of a child sitting on a big beach ball.

But from that morning I began to see a change in her health. She was tired. She was less ready to smile, and her eyes took on a hurt quality. Each day she seemed to get up later. She asked to eat out, and she ate ravenously, at Italian restaurants. She ate like a runner—huge quantities of pasta.

But the food did no good. Each day she was weaker.

And each day the ugly earthy area on the rock rose higher and higher out of the ground. What had been a slight crescent of dirt became a huge black island covering several thousand miles in the Hawaii area.

She changed her diet from high carbohydrate to high protein. I wanted to speak to her about her eating, but it was as though there was a bandage across my mouth.

I tried once, in the kitchen, to say "Mama, why are you eating in this crazy way?" But all I could say was "Mmmm, Mmmm . . ."

She glanced at me in that quick, hurt way, and I hushed.

Then the gag seemed to change its location. Instead of being across my mouth, it seemed to be tied on top of my head and to pass under my chin. It was the kind of bandage you see on the dead in nineteenth-century etchings—something to hold the jaw closed, something Jacob Marley might have been wearing when he first appeared to Scrooge. Again, I felt it in the kitchen. I tried to say "Mama, Mama, what are you doing to yourself? Why are you so tired?" But I couldn't even drop my jaw, couldn't get my mouth open for a murmur.

That night I stayed awake to watch the rock. At midnight, I knelt on my bed and peered out the window. There was no human form perched on the rock. Nevertheless I watched and watched. About 1:00, when I was quite drowsy, the rock suddenly glittered. It was as though the mica were catching light at a new angle. Sometimes this happens if a lamp is turned on in the house, or one is turned off. But there was no change in the lighting and yet this sudden sparkling, flashing out of light. My mouth tried to open in a silent and spontaneous *Oh!* but it was as though the binding cloth were in place. I was not permitted this small gesture of surprise.

Then I saw her rise up from behind the rock. She moved very slowly. Her movement was the kind I make in dreams when I feel panic, panic and also a heaviness, an inertia that scarcely permits forward motion. Her shoulders stooping, her hands and arms hanging like weights, she slowly began to walk down the bricks toward the house. I wanted to leap to meet her, to tell her, to tell her *Never mind. Never mind you don't have to do it, I'll hire a crane, I'll hire the neighborhood boys, I'll hire a doctor day and night, Don't try this, here, here let me help*. But I was immobilized.

The cloths that had bound shut my jaw now bound my entire body. I could not flex my knees. I tried to heave myself off the bed; I would roll to her help. But my body was as rigid as a statue.

I was forced to remain kneeling on the coverlet, looking out the window, watching her toiling past the ruddy daylilies. At a certain point, she passed beyond my sight line. There were three small steps there; and my ears strained to tell me that she had negotiated them all right, that now she was opening the storm door, now she was coming in from the night, that she had not fallen at the last moment, that she was not lying hurt right at her own safe door, that she had not struck her head on the steps—but my hearing failed, too. All of my senses were suddenly gone, as though I had received a blow to the head.

I awoke in the early hours to a loud thunderclap. The weather was changing early. It was late summer, and the fall rains were coming. Our air seemed like the ice water you stand strips of carrots and celery in to crisp. Daylilies were drooping and the chrysanthemums straining upright, ready to grow and take over the garden. I checked the statue of the girl. Serrated yellow leaves from a neighboring elm had blown into her apron.

The boulder had rotated 180 degrees from its original position. The black cap rode at the north pole. Below it the rock was clean and traces of mica sparkled in the sunlight. But I fancied the darkness was spreading, an earthen glaciation coming down to nullify the brightness of human accomplishment.

I knew it was hopeless to attempt to ask her any questions. Even as I tried mentally to formulate an inquiry, my body stiffened. I resisted that stillness. I would not be frozen into stone in my own garden in late summer. I would not take on that terrible rigidity. I would not allow my body to imagine death.

Her health began to improve, but it gave me no joy. I knew that this improvement was temporary. That August, gesturing toward the garden, a friend who raised berries told me that death was part of life; she pointed at the seasonal changes. We stood on the patio talking while the Chopin Valse no. 14 rolled out the windows.

I explained that each time my mother played it now, it was better. Sometimes it was improved only by the way a single note was played, but suddenly that note, once dead, leaped into life. And then the next time, the notes around it would be more vital, would be like flowers straining toward the light, inspired by one of their number who had risen above them. The whole surface of the music was becoming luminous.

I told my friend that the gulf between the seasonal lives of flowers and the lives of human beings was unbridgeable. The forte drowned out my voice, a forte big enough now to fill the garden.

Our garden was the perfect place for a garden party, but I had never had one there. I preferred to have one friend over at a time, or two. But two weeks after the weather change, I discovered that invitations had been issued to almost every person of my acquaintance to join me and the chrysanthemums for a gourmet dinner. *Gourmet!* To join *me and the chrysanthemums!* They weren't ready!

As usual, I had worked late at the laboratory. When I came out to the car, the pink glow of the sunset was reflected in the windshield. Amidst the wash of pink, a folded card had been placed under the wiper: an invitation for six o'clock. It was already half past six. There wasn't a potato chip in the house, and we'd eaten our last TV entree; I was supposed to get more on the way home. While I stood there fingering the stiff paper, I realized how many people had smiled at me that day, had said *See you later* or *Looking forward to it* or *Thanks for asking*—all mysterious, muttered fragments scattered over the day, everybody being especially gracious to me, or worse, *encouraging*.

Could I run home, maybe cook flowers? I was a very poor cook; my mother was no cook. We had long benefited from eating out and from TV dinners. They were the expensive TV dinners—pretty and tasty, even if always too salty.

As I sped home, I thought that at least my mother would be there to greet them. Like an illuminated billboard, the invitation flashed at me again. I recognized the handwriting. It was her writing. Large letters, angular, the capital A half-printed, looking like a star.

There were so many cars that I had to drive past the house looking for parking. Other latecomers—there was my supervisor—were sauntering down the sidewalks toward home. I parked almost two blocks away.

As I walked home as fast as I could; half a block away, I smelled the party. I gasped. Yes, my jaw *was* allowed to drop in amazement: Oh! Heavenly aromas.

There was roast beef! No, not just roast beef—something richer, more savory. Beef Wellington. I could envision the pastry head of a steer decorating its flank. But the odor of bacon, too, why bacon? It couldn't be, but there was a choice of entrees, just like when we had two separate frozen Stouffers. Trout was broiling under strips of bacon. There! There was a waft of garlic butter, for escargot.

And desserts had been freshly baked. That was angel food cake in the air, and there was the sweet cinnamon of apple brown Betty, and there, the orange liqueur that goes flambé with crêpes suzette. She had prepared three desserts. But you can't just have main courses and desserts! Where were the vegetables? She had forgotten the vegetables. Memory was becoming uncertain: I *had* heard her hesitate to enter the second theme of the *Valse*.

My supervisor was poised at the head of our walk, sniffing. I shouldered past him.

"Vegetables?" I exclaimed.

"Who cares?" He inhaled deeply.

I managed to make myself enter the house quietly. There was that civilized murmur in the room. The sound you hear in the finest restaurants, the bliss of conversation elevated by the artistry of food, of the tongue bending this way and that in ecstasy.

There she stood chatting, her hearing aid in place. She who had been reclusive, a devotee of music alone, for years. I noticed there was a dusting of flour on her hands and arms, up to her elbows. She seemed unaware of the flour, stood relaxed and comfortable as though she were wearing a pair of evening gloves.

"Mother," I said, "are you all right?"

She reached out and squeezed my elbow. Her grip was steadying. "Of course," she said. "I was just telling your friend we should have parties more often. I'm enjoying myself so much."

"All this food?" I said lamely.

"I can read a book, as you know. I got down James Beard, Irma Rombauer. I hadn't looked in Fanny for years."

"Are there any vegetables?"

"Sauteed celery, new peas in sherry sauce." She pointed at some covered dishes. "Here comes the mailman."

Other people began to arrive. People I had lost track of years before. How did she find them? I started to ask, but the hinge of my jaw began to resist; the familiar paralysis gently threatened. Questions had become out of order.

My salivary glands prompted me. Eat, *eat*. She had my plate ready for me—flamboyant and multicolored. It held something of everything. When I inhaled, I seemed to levitate six or seven inches—or float, that feeling you get walking neck-deep in a swimming pool on your big toes. Glancing down, I saw my food had been arranged on a new plate, the tobacco-leaf pattern that I had admired in the Metropolitan Museum catalogue. Seventy-nine dollars *per*. And each guest had one. I was rich.

One guest held no tobacco-leaf plate. Indeed, he wasn't eating. I didn't know him, had never known him, I was quite sure. He was standing beside the piano talking with mother. He was grossly fat, with reddish hair, what was left of it; he was mostly bald. Only his nose seemed familiar. It was a large and romantic proboscis, lean and humped—no, arched. They were discussing fingering. Mother was drumming the air—4, 3, 2, 1—and he was responding 4, 2, 3, 1. But then on 1, he gave the rug a quick jab with his foot. Ah, he was suggesting the last of the repeated notes be quickly pedalled. What an idea! Joseffy certainly never hints at such an effect.

Mother looked delighted. She too jabbed the rug with her foot. No, he shook his head, *not quite fast enough*. He actually reached over and grasped her right leg above the knee, grasped the quadricep muscle and forced a quick tap of the imaginary sostenuto pedal. Now he was savoring the unheard sound. With his face tilted up in the lamplight, I suddenly recognized him. At least I recognized a part of him. It was the nose of Frederick Chopin.

My mouth fell open. It was to gasp, I thought. But instead these words fell out, double forte, "Let's all go into the garden now." And I rotated—gracefully I could tell—to lead the way through the French doors. But why, when the chrysanthemums weren't ready?

The garden was ablaze in torchlight. Real torches, like the Statue of Liberty holds up, but with long handles planted in the ground, or jutting out from the back wall, torches like you see in some paintings of the garden of Gethsemane with that rich Dutch light flickering everywhere. And the chrysanthemums had been multiplied.

No longer just my neat mounds of red cushion mums. There was rank on rank of mums of all colors and forms. Spider mums in oranges and yellows. Giant football mums in purples, lavenders and whites, star-burst mums, fireballs and a thousand tiny button mums massed against the stucco wall. All the guests were gasping with delight. They hurried to stand among them, cupped individual blossoms like the chins of favored children; long index fingers pointed through the flickering light at flowers just beyond. When the guests knelt to study whole clumps, their bodies disappeared among the rows of flowers and their heads floated among them, heads themselves like large flowers or cabbages. Above us smiled the crescent moon.

I wanted to turn, to say *Mother, come look, come join us, they are so beautiful, thank you, thank you, they have never been so beautiful,* and of course I could not turn back. My body gasped with grief. The dreadful rigor seized me. Then all that was replaced with the turbulence and then the gaiety of the Chopin Valse no.14 in E Minor.

Could I hold my breath throughout? Could I thus make the moment permanent? Could I make the air hold that music forever, vivid as a painting, more permanent than stone, sound becoming statuary of the air? And would the performance be perfect at last? Who played? Was it *he* or *she*?

I held my breath on and on as each passage of loveliness, the lightest, most gay of sounds, swept past. But where was the pedal touch on the fourth of the repeated notes? Of course it was withheld, withheld till the phrase was introduced for the last time, and then the pedal, a suggestion of poignant prolonging, a soupçon of romantic rubato, a wobble in rhythm, the human touch in the final offering of art. Then it ended.

Then, only then, the air rushed from my lungs. *"Bravo!"* I shouted. Unbound, my jaw seemed to be permitted to open all the way to my heart. *"Hooray! Hooray!"* I shouted, raising my fist and punching the air over my head. All the guests shouted *"Bravo!"* their fists aloft. And dozens of Roman candles, skyrockets, pinwheels shot up into the air, burst gloriously high above our heads, bloomed like flowers forced by a movie camera. I felt her standing behind me, her hand a warm squeeze on my elbow.

The next morning I found her note saying that she wanted to vacation in England. She had taken a morning flight. England because they spoke her language there. I walked into the bright garden. Of course, she had hired a clean-up crew to take away the spent torches and the mess. The gauzy crescent moon, the ghost of a thorn, hung in the blue.

I visited the rock. It had been rolled six feet west, to the artistically correct place. The dark continent had returned to the bottom of the world, no longer visible at the juncture of rock and grass. The rock was right side up and mica glittered over its dome. Where it had stood gaped the chipmunk hole, wide enough for a human thigh. A dark, pleasant hole.

Ah, there was the chipmunk already, poising at the rim of damp earth, blinking in the sunlight.

IAN MCDOWELL

Making Faces

Ian McDowell has published two novels, Mordred's Curse *and* Merlin's Gift. *His short fiction has appeared in numerous magazines and anthologies, including* The Magazine of Fantasy and Science Fiction, Asimov's Science Fiction, Weird Tales, Cemetery Dance, Deathrealm, Borderlands, Love in Vein, *and* The Year's Best Horror Stories. *He received an M.F.A. in creative writing from the University of North Carolina at Greensboro, where he still lives in bohemian squalor with an amiable uromastyx and a morose iguana. In his spare time he studies Pai Lum kung fu and Chinese lion dancing. "Making Faces" was first published in* Cemetery Dance *magazine. This is its first book publication.*

"If you steal one more french fry," I mumbled at Rob through my mouthful of deliciously salty country ham, "I'll stab you with my fork." Considering what a sloppy job Waffle House did cleaning their silverware, that was a pretty serious threat.

"Sorry, Lucy," he said, doing the big-eyed waif-boy thing that I guess he thought made him look fuckable, "Maybe the redneck ambiance didn't kill my appetite after all. Say, you want to come with me to the free vegetarian dinner the Hare Krishnas are having tonight?"

I washed the salty ham down with satisfyingly sweet iced tea. "Hell, no." Looking like a regular alterna-girl does *not* mean I'm some kind of vegan. Mom used to call me her little green-eyed carnivore, laughing when I tore into a nicely bloody steak. Mom laughed at a lot of stuff; sometimes I even imagined her laughing right until the car went off the road. That was four years ago, and since then it's just been me and Dad and my little brother, who was still in the bathroom. If he didn't come out soon, I was going to eat his icebox lemon pie.

I nodded in the direction of the men's room. "Would you mind seeing what Jeremy is doing in there?" I didn't want him out of sight too long, as some pretty scary characters hung out at Waffle House, even during daylight hours. Of course, that's probably what our big-haired waitress thought about Rob with his tattoos and piercings, or even me with my dyed hair and nose ring.

"Masturbating, probably," said Rob, still looking covetously at my food. "I'd started when I was his age."

I lobbed a french fry at his exceedingly large head. "Thanks for the info, perv-boy." He plucked it from his spiky hair as casually as a grooming chimp and popped it in his mouth, then reached for another. "No," I sighed, moving the plate out of his reach. "Jeremy's probably drawing monster faces on the wall. That's all he ever does anymore, draw pissed-off-looking monsters. He does them in his notebooks and in the margins of his school-

books and everywhere else. Dad had a fit when he found them in his Bible—
you should have heard the Help-me-Jesuses!" I laughed, but it wasn't funny.
Oh, it didn't bug me that my brother liked to draw monsters and skulls and
stuff—what kid doesn't? But he was getting more and more withdrawn and
obsessive about it, and Dad was getting more and more into the religious
thing, and that just wasn't a good combination.

"I don't know how you can stand to live there," said Rob, trying to balance three packets of nondairy creamer on top of the Heinz bottle. "You're
over eighteen now—you can move out anytime."

Finished with the ham, I started on the fries (I've always eaten my food
in stages). "I know that. So does Dad. That's why he doesn't get on my case
much. But if I move out, it will be just him and Jeremy, and, well, I'm worried about Jeremy, that's all." I was also getting a bit pissed at Rob, for ducking my request to go make sure my brother was okay. And the boy
wondered why he couldn't get into my pants. Whatever filled up that huge
head of his must not be brains.

Fortunately, Jeremy emerged at that moment. The uncapped Flare pen
he'd stuck back into his shirt pocket was leaking a great spidery splotch, so
I'd been right about what he'd been up to. At least it was Dad's turn to do
the laundry.

"Everything squirt out okay, squirt?" said Rob. Jeremy gave him the
finger and attacked his pie. We looked so much alike, with the same big
eyes and odd squashed little nose and Jack Nicholson eyebrows, although
his hair was its natural brown and so far he'd shown no signs of getting
my height. I'd often wondered about that, since Mom wasn't tall and Dad
isn't. Sometimes it seemed like the only thing I got from my father was my
temper.

"I really like that Tori Amos CD you gave me," I said to Jeremy.
Indeed, I liked it so much that I'd bought it two years ago, but the fact that
my little brother had noticed enough of what was going on outside his head
to buy me a birthday present was worth remarking on.

Jeremy actually looked up at me. Was that a grin? "She sure pisses Dad
off, doesn't she? He doesn't like the way she talks about God."

"I'm sorry I wasn't here for your birthday," said Rob, who'd spent the
weekend in Atlanta doing God knows what and almost certainly wasn't a bit

sorry. "I got you a present, though. I was going to wrap it, but I should probably just give it to you now, so I don't forget later."

I was bemused to think that he'd actually spent *money* on me. Somebody in Atlanta must have had lots of free drugs.

He reached deep into his much-patched and safety-pinned coat and pulled out a little carved stone thing a bit smaller than the palm of his hand. The chiseled folded-up legs made me think of a crude scarab beetle, but when I turned it over there was a face on the other side, with glaring eyes and protruding tongue and stubby horns. I'd seen carvings like it in books on Medieval and Renaissance art.

"Wow," said Jeremy, eyes even bigger than usual. "That's really cool."

"Yeah," said Rob. "It reminds me of an evil version of those little faces R. Crumb draws on corks and stuff. It's from Italy. My grandfather found it there during World War Two, in what was left of some old monastery that had been hit by a bomb. Apparently the monks had been carving stuff like this for hundreds of years. Granddad said it symbolized the evil thoughts they were trying to get rid of, that they'd carve demon faces on little pieces of slate and throw the rocks down the dry well they used as a crap hole, showing they were purging themselves of sin. The well was where the bomb hit, and these little carved stones were all over the place."

So he hadn't spent money on me after all. "Along with centuries-old monk shit. How lovely."

Rob shrugged. "Any crap left would have been fossilized. The monastery had been abandoned long before the war, and I'm sure Granddad cleaned the stone off good when he found it."

I turned it over and over. "Why the legs?" The thought of a disembodied face scuttling around on bug legs was pretty neat, in a creepy kind of way.

Rob frowned, which always made him look cross-eyed. "I asked Granddad about that. He'd studied for the ministry, before the war made him realize he didn't believe in God, and knew a lot about this kind of stuff. He said it wasn't unusual for get-away-from-the-world religious types to imagine that demons were crawling all over them like ticks and fleas, biting the hell out of them—or into them, I guess. They probably had plenty of real ticks and fleas, so imagination-wise it wasn't a stretch to think that demons were like that, only bigger."

Jeremy reached out an ink-stained hand. "Can I see it?"

"Sure, hon." I handed it to him. "Thanks, Rob, that's really sweet, to give me something your grandfather gave you."

He looked momentarily furtive, and I wondered if his granddad had really *given* it to him. "Well, yeah, I just wanted it to be something special, that's all."

Jeremy took out his pen and began copying the face on the laminated menu. I was impressed by the way he captured it with a few deft strokes. I thought of Rob's reference to R. Crumb. I'd seen that movie about him over at Rob's house one night, or at least some of it, as I kept getting distracted by *somebody's* groping hand (at least until I bent a couple of fingers so far back that the somebody in question yelped like a dog). With my family's luck, poor Jeremy would turn out more like one of Robert Crumb's crazy brothers. As soon as I'd had that thought, I wished I could throw it away from me, just like one of those old monks with their demon stones.

It was my turn to do the dishes that evening. Unfortunately, I wasn't alone in the kitchen. Dad had bought an old mimeograph machine, of all the stupid outdated things, at some yard sale, and the kitchen table was the only place where he had enough room to set it up. So I washed while he cranked out his little newsletter, part of his current campaign to get the grade schools to stop celebrating Halloween.

"People would take you more seriously if you shelled out to have those done at Kinko's," I said as I scraped macaroni and cheese into the trash can. Not that I wanted people to take him seriously, but at least it would get him out of the house more.

He brushed thinning hair from his protruding ruddy forehead. "I'd have too much trouble keeping my temper if I went there. All those Marilyn Manson kids in their black T-shirts and trench coats, what's the world coming to? I don't even want to know what kind of Satanic filth they're making copies of."

"If you're talking about the so-called goth kids who hang out on Tate Street, they mainly go in Kinko's to use the bathroom." It was the slightly older punks and waspafarians that actually made copies of their 'zines and band flyers. "Lately, there's been some church types down there every night preaching to them. Maybe you ought to check it out, help with the missionary work."

He shambled over to the sink and proceeded to wash blue gunk off his big broad hands. The smell of his aftershave was very strong. Was it covering up something else? No, don't think that; he'd given up booze for God.

"Don't make fun of me, Lucy. I know you think me a fool, but please don't make fun of me. I'm trying to find my way, to do what's right, to make sense of the world and live in it the best way I know how." The cops had said the accident wasn't his fault, but it couldn't be easy, living with the possibility that he might have been able to dodge that station wagon if he'd been a little more sober.

Jeremy came into the kitchen. He opened the fridge and got a Chilly-Willy.

"Your homework done yet?" asked Dad.

"No," mumbled Jeremy, biting the plastic off one end and spitting it into the sink. "In the trash can, twitboy," I said, popping him gently on the head with the dishtowel.

"Just what have you been doing up there?" said Dad. "You've been in your room for hours."

He sucked his Chilly-Willy, his face unreadable. "Yeah, that's why I'm going out." Saying that, he headed for the door.

Dad made after him. "Come back here," he shouted, "you aren't going anywhere at this hour." I don't know what he meant by the "at this hour"—it was still daylight outside, although not for long. My brother must have been too fast for him, for I heard the front door open and slam shut, and then the sound of Dad pacing in the living room, before coming back to the kitchen.

His face was nearly as red as the dye in my hair. Sitting at the table, he shoved his elbows up against the bulky mimeograph machine and clasped his hands against his blazing forehead. I didn't pay attention to the words, but there were a lot of Jesuses. Walking over to him, I put my hand on his shoulder, which tensed under my palm. He didn't look up at me.

"He's a kid, Dad," I said, "just a kid. Like I used to be. I gave you lots of shit, too." I hadn't meant to bait him by using the word "shit," but I was tired and grumpy and my period was coming on.

He looked up at me and for a moment his eyes were fierce. "Don't use that kind of language, Lucy. Not in my house."

Fuck that, I thought but didn't say. What I did say wasn't much better. "I think Mom would rather have heard me cuss than you pray." It was a low blow, even though she'd been agnostic to the point of atheism, but the "my house" bit really pissed me off. Dad had been out of work for four months now, and the money I made waiting tables at Valencia's five nights a week had been going towards the bills. Putting off college for a year so that drunken UNCG professors could grab my ass while I poured their sangria put me in no mood to hear his crap.

"I'll finish the dishes," he finally said in a low cold voice, his eyes as distant and unreadable as Jeremy's. "Leave your poor mother out of this, and leave me alone to talk to the God you sneer at, but who loves you just the same." His grip convulsed on the crank of the mimeograph machine, which came off in his hand. "Blast it!" he hissed, putting more vehemence into the word than I normally used for "fuck," then threw the handle. He hadn't been aiming for anything in particular, but it shattered a pane of the dusty kitchen window.

We stared at each other in silence. Through the broken window came the metallic sound of cicadas buzzing in the trees outside. A neighbor's dog began to bark.

"Look what you just made me do," he said softly, looking down at his scuffed loafers.

"Not me, Dad," I said, drying my shaking hands. "Must have been the devil."

He nodded as if I'd been serious. "He's so strong in me. I renounce him, but can't shake him off. Yesterday, on my way home from the Employment Security office, I stopped at the ABC store and bought a bottle. I couldn't pull into our driveway with it in the car, though; I threw it in the garbage can."

"That's good," I said, keeping my voice calm. "That you threw it away, I mean." I'm sure the garbage men thanked him for it. "I'm not sure the prayers are any better for you than the booze, though." Fuck, that's not what I meant, at least not exactly—I have nothing against faith, even though I don't share it, just Dad's particular brand.

His face flushed again. "Watch your tongue. I lie awake every night, wishing there was some way I could keep you out of hell. Your mother died without finding salvation."

I wanted something heavier than a dishtowel to throw, but threw it anyway. It missed him and slapped against the refrigerator. There was shocked shame in his eyes and probably the beginning of an apology on his lips, but I was no mood to hear it. "Go fuck yourself until you bleed."

As I stomped out of the room and up the stairs, his renewed prayers began droning behind me.

I paced in my room a bit, then decided I wanted a cigarette. The cool lighter engraved with the poster for *Horror of Dracula* that I'd bought at Hypnotica was still there, but my Marlboros weren't. The little carved devil face, which had been sitting beside them on my dresser, was gone too. Anyone who's ever had a sibling knows who the chief suspect was. At least he hadn't taken the lighter.

I checked his room, in case he'd left the stone or the rest of the cigarettes behind. Nope. His spiral notebook was open on his desk, page after page covered in sketches. There were varied monsters and demons, Darth Maul from *The Phantom Menace*, Malebogia from *Spawn*, and, it appeared most recently, the face from the stone carving. He'd drawn several of these on the solid old rolltop desk that had once belonged to my late grandfather, using a ballpoint pen, so they were scratched into the finish. Jesus, Dad would have a cow.

I decided to go for a walk.

I found Jeremy sitting with two other kids, skatepunks from the look of them, on the steps of the little Primitive Baptist Church on the corner of Tate and Carr Streets, a block and a half away. The church was some sort of landmark here in the College Hill Historical District that bordered UNCG—a plaque on the wall gave its dates as 1907–1964. It wasn't abandoned; there was no pastor or congregation, but the grounds were kept mowed and maintained and the small brick structure didn't look the least bit dilapidated, its modest stained glass windows, decorated with abstract swirls of what looked like fingerpaint, clean and unbroken, its air-conditioning unit humming away on the other side of the porch. The church that Dad attended on Florida Street was much larger but didn't look half so nice. I knew the College Hill Historical Society, those anal retentives who were always trying to "preserve" the neighborhood by driving away undesirable elements like college students (the Hysterical Society, Mom used to call them) sometimes had meetings here, and their newsletter, which showed up on our doorstep each month, ran frequent stories saying they were debating what to do with the small building, which was no bigger than many of the surrounding houses.

I sat beside Jeremy on the stone step. One of his friends gave me the eye. "My sister," said Jeremy, puffing a Marlboro. The skatepunk continued to stare appraisingly. "Hot stuff."

"Shut up," said Jeremy.

How sweet; he was being protective. I put my arm around him affectionately. "Give me my damn cigarettes, ratboy."

He handed them over. "And the carving Rob gave me."

"Ah, come on," protested Jeremy. "You don't really want that. You don't even like Bighead all that much."

"Don't call him Bighead," I said, biting back my smile.

"Why not? You do! Anyway, what's the big deal about the stone? You're a girl; you can't be that much into weird stuff."

Well, that sure showed how much attention my little brother paid to what I said or did. "The hell I'm not, but that's beside the point. You took it off my dresser."

He looked down, and I wondered what it cost him to give in in front of his friends. "I'm sorry. Can't I just hang on to it a little longer? I think it's really neat."

I rubbed his buzzed head, making him grimace like a monkey. "Sure, Jere, but if you lose it, it's your ass, okay?"

The kid who'd called me hot reached down and held out a bottle in a crumbled brown bag. "Swig?"

I took it and looked inside. Aristocrat vodka. Not the kind of thing you want to drink straight, but I swigged anyway. If it had been Jack or good scotch, I might have been tempted to have more.

"Where'd you guys get this?"

"Found it yesterday in a trash can."

Ah, so the garbagemen hadn't enjoyed Dad's change of heart after all. "Well, then you're not out any money." I upended the bottle and poured the rest out. Good thing no cops were cruising by.

"Hey!" yelled the kid.

"You guys are too young," I said, shaking out the last few drops onto the brick steps.

"So are you, bitch, and you drank some."

Standing up, I grabbed the kid's ear and twisted till he yelped. "You call me or any other woman a bitch again, I'll shove your skateboard up your ass."

"Yes ma'am," he whimpered.

I let go of his ear. "Make sure they know I'm not kidding," I said to Jeremy. "And if you come home drunk or otherwise fucked up, I'll kick your butt. Dad's in a really foul mood tonight, and I'd like to have as much peace in the house as possible."

He nodded. I stopped scowling and gave him a thumbs-up, then headed down the street. Maybe these kids weren't the best of companions, but hell, at least he was hanging out with *somebody* and not just being an antisocial troll-boy. Behind me, I heard the kid who'd never spoken say "Your sister's really rad."

"I know," said Jeremy.

Despite my anger, I smiled at that. Wish it were true, Jere.

I went to the coffeeshop and tried to read the tattered paperback copy of Leonard Cohen's *Stranger Music* I'd found on a table there last week and been browsing ever since. Unfortunately, the usual quartet of college libertarians at the next table were braying about some Ayn Rand movie their organization was showing on campus, and they wouldn't crank the volume even when I did my best to glare like Brigitte Lin in *The Bride with White*

Hair, my newest favorite movie ever since the guy at College Hill Video practically begged me to watch it. At least they were too preoccupied by their argument to stare at my tits, the way they usually did when any woman sat near them. In my experience, Libertarians are just as horny and frustrated as comic-book geeks and sci-fi nerds, but much more loud and in your face about it.

I decided to get an iced Clockwork Orange to go and sit on the hill in front of the music building, even though it was now too dark to read. At least the goth kids weren't on the hill. Oh, I didn't really mind them, and think folks who are afraid to come down to Tate Street because of them are idiots (it's the rednecks at Spoon's Pool Hall who are dangerous), but I wanted to be left alone, and several of the babybats kept making clumsy attempts at picking me up. Um, sure I'd like to go to College Hill Video and rent some Tim Burton movie or that bootleg of *Neverwhere* with you, but let's wait until you're at least a high school senior, okay?

The cool grass felt good on my calves and the palms of my hands, and if they weren't such a bitch to unlace, I would have taken off my boots. My mom once told me that this had been called Hippie Hill back when she was an undergraduate here, just after UNCG first went co-ed (and changed its name from the Women's Normal College—hah!—to the University of North Carolina at Greensboro). When I was a kid, there were thorny shrubs here, which the university had planted back in the '70s to get rid of the hippies, but about five years ago they tore them all up and now folks can sit on the hill again.

Skateboard wheels echoed on pavement and two forms appeared in the streetlight. "Hey, you're Jeremy's sister, aren't you?"

"Yeah." It was the kids whose booze I'd taken away. They had good eyes, to recognize me up here on the dark slope. *Don't you dare come up here and sit with me*, I thought.

"Man, Jeremy said you were cool. Why the hell did you have to go tell your dad where we were?"

Oh shit. "I've not seen Dad since before I talked to you, and I sure haven't told him anything."

"Well, your old man just came busting in, smacking your brother up alongside the head and yelling something awful. We got the hell out, but Jeremy's probably still there, getting his ass chewed out."

I slid down the hill, not caring about grass stains on my butt, and hopped off the low brick wall at its base. "What? Inside—inside the church? What were you doing inside? Isn't it locked?"

The kid spat on the sidewalk. "Duh. Josh was bitching about how the Historical Society is always giving his dad grief for not painting his house and for putting garbage cans out on the curb too early, and we figured we'd fuck some shit up. We had a crowbar and got inside pretty easy. Your dad must have been out looking for Jeremy and seen the light through the window, I dunno, or maybe heard our voices. He busted in on us. They yelled at each other and he hit your brother pretty damn hard. Me and Josh got out of there."

Fuck fuck fuck fuck fuck fuck. The kid said something else, but I was already running down Tate Street, dodging a jeep full of shouting fratguys when I crossed Walker, tearing past the window of New York Pizza, where people looked up with strings of mozzarella hanging from their mouths, past Spanish Disco Night at Valencia's and then the darkened residential block, the sounds of the college strip fading to the hum of streetlights and cicadas, dry leaves crunching underfoot, a poodle yapping when I nearly bowled over its old lady owner, my heart pounding, smoker's lungs wheezing, goddamn it why did I ever start the stupid habit?

There was the church, its front steps illuminated by one of the faux-vintage streetlights that the Hysterical Society installed on this block last year. The door was open a couple of inches, black scuff marks on the painted wood, and light shone inside. I pushed on in, stubbing my toe on the crowbar that was lying on the floor. Past the bare vestibule, the space opened up into the sanctuary. There was a simple lectern and pulpit on either side of the small plain altar and maybe five or six rows of unpadded wooden pews. A familiar demon face had been spray painted onto the partially unfurled movie screen that hung above the abstract cross, and similar faces decorated the white plaster walls and the swirly glass windows.

My father and Jeremy were kneeling together over the central drain of what looked like a round recessed bathtub, about the size of a backyard wading pool and made of cracked porcelain. This must have been what they used to baptize people. Dad was kneeling by choice, but Jeremy was all big-eyed protest, his lips quivering and his face flushed, and then I saw that his small right hand was gripped tightly in Dad's much larger one.

"Let go of that thing," growled my father. "Give it to me now!"

"No," said Jeremy through gritted teeth. "It belongs to Lucy. If I give it to you, you'll only throw it away."

"Don't you dare defy me!" roared my father. "Not after what you've done here!" He savagely twisted and I heard a noise like dry twigs breaking and the thud of stone hitting porcelain after being dropped from broken fingers. Jeremy yipped like the little dog I'd almost run into earlier and slumped limply, his head on his patched knees. Dad stared at him, his own eyes wide, his brow glistening with sweat. His lip quivered as he looked down at the hand he still gripped in his own.

"Motherfucker!" I yelled. Backpedaling, I fumbled for the crowbar, picked it up, and strode towards the baptismal pool. "Get the hell away from him *now*!"

Dad looked at me, tears streaming down his red and white face, then back at Jeremy, who raised his head, gasping, his own wet stare meeting my father's.

"I'm sorry," said Dad hoarsely. "I'm so very sorry."

"Please let go of my hand, Daddy," said Jeremy. "Please. It hurts."

My father let go. Jeremy came scrambling up out of the tub, careening into me, the impact shoving me back and forcing me to sit on the first row of pews. I wrapped my arms around him without letting go of the crowbar. He shook in my embrace, his body wracked by heaving sobs.

"It's all right, baby," I said, "it's all right. I'll get you out of here."

"Damn you, Satan!" howled my father, the word "damn" sounding so odd on his lips. "Get out of me. Get out of me now!" Doubling over, he smashed his own head hard against the bottom of the porcelain pool, once, twice. When he lifted it again, there was a dull red scrape on his protruding brow. Putting a hand to it, he brushed lank hair out of the gash, then looked blankly at the stain on his fingers. "Help me, Jesus," he mumbled, crossing himself in blood across the front of his sweat-stained T-shirt. Clasping his hands, he began to pray, the words coming out so fast and low and garbled I couldn't understand them.

He's lost it, I thought, *he's completely lost it*. With luck a neighbor had already called the cops. Dammit, where were the sirens? Surely we'd hear them soon. There'd be police, to take my father away, and an ambulance, to patch up Jeremy's hand. And what? Social workers? Shit, that was a scary thought. If I'd moved out, the way Rob kept suggesting I should, I could petition to be Jeremy's guardian, but my living with dad would make that difficult. Well, I wouldn't be living with him long.

Jeremy turned his head out of my neck, twisting so that he sat on my lap the way he'd done when he was much smaller, his good hand clutching the arm that clutched him. "Look," he said, pointing gingerly with his injured hand.

A few inches from dad's knees, the small carved piece of stone that Rob's grandfather had found in the bombed-out monastery was . . . glowing.

It wasn't a bright glow, not like some movie special effect. Instead, it was like a lump of ash in a fire that's almost burned out, a lightning bug in thick grass. Somehow, without looking any bigger, it seemed closer than everything else in the room, as close and sharp as if it was right in front of me. My fillings ached and the cicadas outside seemed to be buzzing in my head, their drone taking on the crackly sound of high-pitched laughter on a distant radio. And then there was the *cold*, waves of it coming off the glowing stone, cold that I felt through my leather jacket, that turned the sweat on the back of my neck to ice drops.

Not noticing, Dad continued to pray. He could have been speaking in tongues for all I could make out his words.

The faces leered at us from the walls, the windows, the small movie screen above the altar. Jeremy had been very busy with his friends' spray paint. "Why'd you do that, honey?" I said, not sounding accusatory, just asking a mundane question as a way of ignoring the bigger one of why the stone was glowing. And not just the stone. Those faces were glowing too, as though Jeremy had used fluorescent paint and somebody had turned on a black light.

"I dunno," said Jeremy dully, looking at it all but maybe not seeing any of it. "I was mad at Dad. Mad at this place because it's a church and he's so into that. Josh and Ronnie started to get bored, just watching me paint that face on stuff. They wanted me to draw other stuff, but it was like I couldn't.

They said they were going to smash up things, but they were scared to. They started yelling for me to leave with them. I guess that's when Dad was going by outside, and heard them shouting my name."

The faces leering at us began to change.

I blinked, and would have rubbed my eyes if I'd dared let go of either Jeremy or the crowbar. No longer defined by blurry lines of paint, they swelled into shape and color, emerging from the surfaces on which they'd been painted like blisters swelling on flesh. They were the color of bruises, with wet red eyes winking above purple-black tongues that poked out of grinning toothless cunt-mouths framed by blue-black lips, the bumps sticking out of their foreheads looking more like tumors than horns.

Jeremy whimpered and I knew he was seeing them, too. So much for the theory that some prankster at the coffeeshop had put acid in my Clockwork Orange.

The faces writhed with indescribable expressions, winking, leering, nostrils flaring, tongues flapping in and out. They made wet, whistling, hooting noises; then started echoing Dad's prayer in a quavering falsetto. He didn't stop, didn't even seem to notice his impossible chorus.

That wasn't the worst of it. The worst was when they began to peel away from the walls and windows and screen, sloughing off like scabs and flopping onto the hardwood floor, where they lay quivering before rising on spindly legs and scuttling forward like spiders or beetles carrying soft fleshy masks on their backs.

Jeremy seemed incapable of surprise. "This is because of me," he said in the soft dead tone of someone in shock.

With horrible selfishness, I was actually grateful for his presence, as it shook me out of my own shock and gave me something else to concentrate on. "No, it isn't," I said, shifting him off and standing up, holding the crowbar tightly and finding comfort in its solid cold realness. If it was real, so was everything else. There was no time to think of why or how; the faces simply were. Like Dad's craziness, like Mom's death, they were a fact and could be dealt with. There was no point in screaming that this couldn't be happening.

Even though that was exactly what I wanted to do.

Two faces scuttled towards us, hooting. That spurred Jeremy out of his stupor, and he scrambled up onto the pew. I smashed the first to reach me with the crowbar, making one of its eyes burst like a huge pimple and crushing several of its legs. It dragged itself away, cackling. The other retreated, scuttling to join its fellows, which were converging on my father.

They swarmed up him, giggling. He noticed them then and started shrieking, thrashing about in the dry baptismal tub, tearing at them and himself, especially where the two were joined. There seemed to be more of them than had been painted on various surfaces in the church, but I wasn't counting. They flopped against him like fleshy purple pancakes, emitting fluting cries of triumph. In thrashing and tearing, he pulled off his T-shirt and half-squirmed out of his pants, but that only made it easier for them to dig their multijointed telescoping legs into his flesh, embedding themselves in him like giant chiggers, so that my father had many faces, all screaming in unison.

But only briefly. He heaved one last time and then the screaming stopped and his motions became less violent. He lay there, quivering, his body first blinking and gasping all over, then draped in drooling smiles.

At his feet, the carved slate face pulsed in cold bright waves. That's what was doing this. If this was real, that old stone carving had caused it.

Jeremy started forward, pulling against the arm with which I held him back. "We've got to get those things off him!"

"Go stand in the doorway," I said. He didn't react. "Do it! I can't handle this if I'm worrying about you!"

He went and stood, holding his bad hand in his good one, his forgotten broken finger as purple and swollen as the faces on our father.

I stepped gingerly into the dry tub, crowbar raised.

My father looked at me, but his rolling-eyed gaze was not his own, instead mirroring that of the grinning things rooted in his sweaty red flesh. He rose stiffly, jerkily, a puppet pulled by strings. Leering faces swelled from his sagging mantits and hanging belly like 3-D tattoos. His crotch seemed swollen, distended, and when he shifted his weight, a mottled face winked at me through the vent in his checkered boxer shorts. More faces hung in a folded quivering shroud from his shoulders, from the sides and back of head and from his thick neck, so that he was cowled in drooling grins.

"My pretty little girl," all the mouths, his own and those attached to his body, chimed in unison. "You look so much like your mother." *No, I don't,* thought some distant crazy part of me; *she was much prettier than me, small and dainty rather than tall and gangly*. Thinking irrelevant trivial stuff like that kept me from screaming and running away, or throwing up, or fainting. I had to get those faces off him, for Jeremy, hell, for him; no matter what kind of bastard, no matter how much he'd hurt my brother, he was still my dad.

I stepped closer. Bending low, keeping my eyes locked on all the rolling pink eyes watching me, I picked up the glowing piece of slate, my whole left side going numb from the cold. Handling dry ice might feel like that, except that the skin of my fingers didn't stick to it. Keeping the crowbar raised, I backed up to the edge of the tub.

I turned around to scramble out, and that's when Dad rushed me.

The faces gave a chorus of giggling battle cries and he slammed into me, his weight pinning me to the side of the pool. Twitchy hands groped my chest, his mouth wetly inhaled my hair, other mouths nuzzled toothlessly at my back. I bit my lip till I tasted something hot and salty and ignored them, even when the face in his crotch probed my denim-protected ass with its tongue, which then snaked upwards to lick the exposed base of my spine where my jeans rode low beneath my jacket.

The carved slate glowed icily in my numb left hand, the crowbar was still in my right. Somehow knowing this was more important than fighting off the thing that pressed itself against me, I brought the crowbar down on the carving, not bothering to move my left hand out of the way until the second or third blow, breaking the stone into pieces. The giggles behind me turned to keening shrieks as its glow went out.

My father slumped off me, gasping, and I kicked him in the chest as I scrambled out of the sacramental pool, scuttling crabwise beyond his reach, heaving in gulps of suddenly warm air, wanting to puke but not daring to be vulnerable. The room smelled like a blown circuit. My blood pounded in my head, my lungs ached. I was dimly aware of my father's muffled breathing. No more hooting, snickering chorus, though.

It seemed like a long time before I could stand up.

I walked gingerly to the edge of the pool. Dad lay on his side, his boxer shorts exposing his pale butt crack, his stained khakis crumbled at his ankles. His chest and gut were mottled with big blotchy welts where the faces had been. His eyes were half-closed, but his breathing was more regular, in time with his fluttering eyelids. He wasn't in control, I told myself, it was the faces in his flesh had made him press that flesh against me, not him. Maybe I didn't quite believe that, and even if I did maybe I'd always hate him for hurting Jeremy, but I couldn't leave him lying there with his ass exposed. Stepping down into the sacramental pool, I knelt cautiously beside him, trying not to see hints of grimacing faces in the glistening patterns of sweat on his torso, in the purple bruises. It wasn't easy getting his pants back up around his waist, and at the first touch of my skin on his I bit my already raw lip so hard the pain drowned out everything else, but I managed. Taking off my scuffed leather jacket, I wadded it up and stuck it under his head, then climbed stiffly out of the pool.

I don't know when Jeremy had stopped standing by the door, but he was at my side, steadying me now. "Will he be all right?"

"I don't know." It took lots of effort to even whisper those simple words. What kind of magic had been performed here, compounded of guilt and shame and all the old poisonous Christian fears and doubts, that called demons from the air? Whatever it was, let that be all of it, let it be over. Please.

A siren sounded on the street outside. There was nothing I could do for Dad; he would have to lie there, waiting for the paramedics we'd tell the cops to summon.

Squeezing Jeremy's shoulder, I let him lead me outside to meet them.

JOHN KESSEL

Every Angel Is Terrifying

*John Kessel won the Nebula Award for his 1982 novella
"Another Orphan," the Theodore Sturgeon Memorial and
Locus Awards for his 1992 short story "Buffalo," the 1994
Paul Green Playwright's Prize for his play* Faustfeathers,
*and is a multiple finalist for the Hugo and World Fantasy
Awards. His 1989 novel* Good News from Outer Space *is
one of the most highly praised works of modern science fiction satire and was reportedly sitting on Fox Mulder's
bookshelf on the set of* The X-Files. *His other books
include the novels* Freedom Beach *(with James Patrick
Kelly) and* Corrupting Dr. Nice, *and the collections*
Meeting in Infinity *and* The Pure Product. *He is co-
editor, with Richard Butner and Mark L. Van Name, of*
Intersections: The Sycamore Hill Anthology *and cofounder of the Sycamore Hill Writers Workshop. He also
edited* Memory's Tailor, *a posthumous novel by Lawrence
Rudner, published by the University Press of Mississippi in
1998. He is professor of English and director of the Creative
Writing Program at North Carolina State University and*

lives in Raleigh, North Carolina, with his wife, the graphic designer Sue Hall, and their daughter, Emma. "Every Angel Is Terrifying" was first published in The Magazine of Fantasy & Science Fiction.

Railroad watched as Bobby Lee grabbed the grandmother's body under the armpits and dragged her up the other side of the ditch. "Whyn't you help him, Hiram," Railroad said.

Hiram took off his coat, skidded down into the ditch after Bobby Lee, and got hold of the old lady's legs. Together he and Bobby Lee lugged her across the field towards the woods. Her broken blue hat was still pinned to her head, which lolled against Bobby Lee's shoulder. The woman's face grinned lopsidedly all the way into the shadow of the trees.

Railroad carried the cat over to the Studebaker. It occurred to him that he didn't know the cat's name, and now that the entire family was dead he never would. It was a calico, gray striped with a broad white face and an orange nose. "What's your name, puss-puss?" he whispered, scratching it behind the ears. The cat purred. One by one Railroad went round and rolled up the windows of the car. A fracture zigzagged across the windshield, and the front passenger's vent window was shattered. He stuffed Hiram's coat into the vent window hole. Then he put the cat inside the car and shut the door. The cat put its front paws up on the dashboard and, watching him, gave a pantomime meow.

Railroad pushed up his glasses and stared off toward the woodline where Bobby Lee and Hiram had taken the bodies. The place was hot and still, silence broken only by birdsong from somewhere up the embankment behind him. He squinted up into the cloudless sky. Only a couple of hours of sun left. He rubbed the spot on his shoulder where the grandmother had touched him. Somehow he had wrenched it when he jerked away from her before he shot her.

The last thing the grandmother had said picked at him: "You're one of my own children." The old lady didn't look anything like his mother. But maybe his father had sown some wild oats in the old days—Railroad knew he had—could the old lady have been his mother, for real? It would explain why the woman who had raised him, the sweetest of women, could have been saddled with a son as bad as he was.

The idea caught in his head. He wished he'd had the sense to ask the grandmother a few questions. The old woman might have been sent to tell him a truth.

When Hiram and Bobby Lee came back, they found Railroad leaning under the hood of the car.

"What we do now, boss?" Bobby Lee asked.

"Police could be here any minute," Hiram said. Blood was smeared on the leg of his khaki pants. "I'm worried somebody might of heard the shots."

Railroad pulled himself out from under the hood. "Onliest thing we got to worry about now, Hiram, is how we get this radiator to stop leaking. You find a tire iron and straighten out this here fan. Bobby Lee, you get the belt off'n t'other car."

It took longer than the half hour Hiram had estimated to get the people's Studebaker back on the road. By the time they did it was twilight, and the red-dirt road was cast in the shadows of the pine woods. They pushed the stolen Hudson they'd been driving off into the trees and got into the Studebaker.

Railroad gripped the wheel of the car and they bounced down the dirt road toward the main highway. Hat pushed back on his head, Hiram went through the dead man's wallet, while in the backseat Bobby Lee had the cat on his lap and was scratching it under the chin. "Kitty-kitty-kitty-kitty-kitty," he murmured.

"Sixty-eight dollars," Hiram said. "With the twenty-two from the wife's purse, that makes ninety bucks." He turned around and handed a wad of bills to Bobby Lee. "Get rid of that damn cat," he said. "Want me to hold yours for you?" he asked Railroad.

Railroad reached over, took the bills, and stuffed them into the pocket of the yellow shirt with bright blue parrots he was wearing, that had belonged to the husband who'd been driving the car. Bailey Boy, the grandmother had called him. Railroad's shoulder twinged.

The car shuddered; the wheels had been knocked out of kilter when it rolled. If he tried pushing past fifty, it would shake itself right off the road.

Railroad felt the warm weight of his pistol inside his belt, against his belly. Bobby Lee hummed tunelessly in the backseat. Hiram was quiet, fidgeting, looking out at the dark trees. He tugged his battered coat out of the vent window, tried to shake some of the wrinkles out of it. "You oughtn't to use a man's coat without saying to him," he grumbled.

Bobby Lee spoke up. "He didn't want the cat to get away."

Hiram sneezed. "Will you throw that damn animal out the damn window?"

"She never hurt you none," Bobby Lee said.

Railroad said nothing. He had always imagined that the world was slightly unreal, that he was meant to be the citizen of some other place. His mind was a box. Outside the box was that world of distraction, amusement, annoyance. Inside the box his real life went on, the struggle between what he knew and what he didn't know. He had a way of acting—polite, detached—because that way he wouldn't be bothered. When he was bothered, he got mad. When he got mad, bad things happened.

He had always been prey to remorse, and now it hit him full on. He hadn't paid enough attention. He'd pegged the old lady as a hypocrite and had gone back into his box, thinking her just another fool from that puppet world. But that moment of her touching him—she'd wanted to comfort him. And he shot her.

What was it the old woman had said? "You could be honest if you'd only try. . . . Think how wonderful it would be to settle down and live a comfortable life and not have to think about somebody chasing you all the time."

He knew she was only saying that to save her life. But that didn't mean it couldn't also be a message.

Outside the box, Hiram asked, "What was all that yammer yammer with the grandmother about Jesus? We doing all the killing while you yammer yammer."

"He did shoot the old lady," Bobby Lee said.

"And made us carry her off to the woods, when if he'd of waited she could of walked there like the others. We're the ones get blood on our clothes."

Railroad said quietly, "You don't like the way things are going, son?"

Hiram twitched against the seat like he was itchy between the shoulder blades. "I ain't sayin' that. I just want out of this state."

"We going to Atlanta. In Atlanta we can get lost."

"Gonna get me a girl!" Bobby Lee said.

"They got more cops in Atlanta than the rest of the state put together," Hiram said. "In Florida—"

Without taking his eyes off the road, Railroad snapped his right hand across the bridge of Hiram's nose. Hiram jerked, more startled than hurt, and his hat tumbled off into the backseat.

Bobby Lee laughed, and handed Hiram his hat.

It was after 11:00 when they hit the outskirts of Atlanta. Railroad pulled into a diner, the Sweet Spot, red brick and an asbestos-shingled roof, the air smelling of cigarettes and pork barbecue. Hiram rubbed some dirt from the lot into the stain on his pants leg. Railroad unlocked the trunk and found the dead man's suitcase, full of clothes. He carried it in with them.

On the radio sitting on the shelf behind the counter, Kitty Wells sang "It Wasn't God Who Made Honky-Tonk Angels." Railroad studied the menu, front and back, and ordered biscuits and gravy. While they ate Bobby Lee ran on about girls, and Hiram sat sullenly smoking. Railroad could tell Hiram was getting ready to do something stupid. He didn't need either of them anymore. So after they finished eating, Railroad left the car keys on the table and took the suitcase into the men's room. He locked the door. He pulled his .38 out of the waistband, put it on the sink, and changed out of the too-tight dungarees into some of the dead husband's baggy trousers. He washed his face and hands. He cleaned his glasses on the tail of the parrot shirt, then tucked in the shirt. He stuck the .38 into the suitcase and came out again. Bobby Lee and Hiram were gone, and the car was no longer in the parking lot. The bill on the table, next to Hiram's still-smoldering cigarette, was for six dollars and eighty cents.

Railroad sat in the booth drinking his coffee. In the window of the diner, near the door, a piece of cardboard had been taped up, saying, Wanted: Fry Cook. When he was done with the coffee, he untaped the sign and headed to the register. After he paid the bill he handed the cashier the sign. "I'm your man," he said.

The cashier called the manager. "Mr. Cauthron, this man says he's a cook."

Mr. Cauthron was maybe thirty-five years old. His carrot red hair stood up in a pompadour like a rooster's comb, and a little belly swelled out over his belt. "What's your name?"

"Lloyd Bailey."

"Lloyd, what experience do you have?"

"I can cook anything on this here menu," Railroad said.

The manager took him back to the kitchen. "Stand aside, Shorty," the manager said to the tall black man at the griddle. "Fix me a Denver omelet," he said to Railroad.

Railroad washed his hands, put on an apron, broke two eggs into a bowl. He threw handfuls of chopped onion, green pepper, and diced ham into a skillet. When the onions were soft, he poured the beaten eggs over the ham and vegetables, added salt and cayenne pepper. When he slid the finished omelet onto a plate, the manager bent down over it as if he were inspecting the paint job on a used car. He straightened up. "Pay's thirty dollars a week. Be here at six in the morning."

Out in the lot Railroad set down his bag and looked around. Cicadas buzzed in the hot city night. Around the corner from the diner he'd noticed a big Victorian house with a sign on the porch, Rooms for Rent. He was about to start walking when, out of the corner of his eye, he caught a movement by the trash barrel next to the chain link fence. He peered into the gloom and saw the cat trying to leap up to the top to get at the garbage. He went over, held out his hand. The cat didn't run; it sniffed him, butted its head against his hand.

He picked it up, cradled it under his arm, and carried it and the bag to the rooming house. Under dense oaks, it was a big tan clapboard mansion with green shutters and hanging baskets of begonias on the porch, and a green porch swing. The thick oval leaded glass of the oak door was beveled around the edge, the brass of the handle dark with age.

The door was unlocked. His heart jumped a bit at the opportunity it presented; at the same time he wanted to warn the proprietor against such foolishness. Off to one side of the entrance was a little table with a doily, vase and dried flowers; on the other a sign beside a door said Manager.

Railroad knocked. After a moment the door opened and a woman with the face of an angel opened it. She was not young, perhaps forty, with very white skin and blond hair. She looked at him, smiled, saw the cat under his arm. "What a sweet animal," she said.

"I'd like a room," he said.

"I'm sorry. We don't cater to pets," the woman said, not unkindly.

"This here's no pet, ma'am," Railroad said. "This here's my only friend in the world."

The landlady's name was Mrs. Graves. The room she rented him was twelve feet by twelve feet, with a single bed, a cherry veneer dresser, a wooden table and chair, a narrow closet, lace curtains on the window, and an old pineapple quilt on the bed. The air smelled sweet. On the wall opposite the bed was a picture in a dime-store frame, of an empty rowboat floating in an angry gray ocean, the sky overcast, only a single shaft of sunlight in the distance from a sunset that was not in the picture.

The room cost ten dollars a week. Despite Mrs. Graves' rule against pets, like magic she took a shine to Railroad's cat. It was almost as if she'd rented the room to the cat, with Railroad along for the ride. After some consideration, he named the cat Pleasure. She was the most affectionate animal he had ever seen. She wanted to be with him, even when he ignored her. She made him feel wanted; she made him nervous. Railroad fashioned a cat door in the window of his room so that Pleasure could go out and in whenever she wanted, and not be confined to the room when Railroad was at work.

The only other residents of the boardinghouse were Louise Parker, a schoolteacher, and Charles Foster, a lingerie salesman. Mrs. Graves cleaned Railroad's room once a week, swept the floors, alternated the quilt every other week with a second one done in a rose pattern that he remembered from his childhood. He worked at the diner from six in the morning, when Maisie, the cashier, unlocked, until Shorty took over at three in the afternoon. The counter girl was Betsy, and Service, a Negro boy, bussed tables and washed dishes. Railroad told them to call him Bailey, and didn't talk much.

When he wasn't working, Railroad spent most of his time at the boardinghouse, or evenings in a small nearby park. Railroad would take the Bible from the drawer in the boardinghouse table, buy an afternoon newspaper, and carry them with him. Pleasure often followed him to the park. She would lunge after squirrels and shy away from dogs, hissing sideways. Cats liked to kill squirrels, dogs liked to kill cats, but there was no sin in it. Pleasure would not go to hell, or heaven. Cats had no souls.

Life was a prison. Turn to the right, it was a wall. Turn to the left, it was a wall. Look up it was a ceiling, look down it was a floor. And he had taken out his imprisonment on others; he was not deceived in his own behavior. The world was full of stupid people like Bobby Lee and Hiram, who lied to themselves and killed without knowing why.

Railroad did not believe in sin, but somehow he felt it. Still, he was not a dog or a cat, he was a man. *You're one of my own children.* There was no reason why he had to kill people. He only wished he'd never have to deal with any Hirams and Bobby Lees anymore. He gazed across the park at the Ipana toothpaste sign painted on the wall of the Piggly Wiggly. *Whiter than white.* Pleasure crouched at the end of the bench, her haunches twitching as she watched a finch hop across the sidewalk.

Railroad picked her up, rubbed his cheek against her whiskers. "Pleasure, I'll tell you what," he whispered. "Let's make us a deal. You save me from Bobby Lee and Hiram, and I'll never kill anybody again."

The cat looked at him with its clear yellow eyes.

Railroad sighed. He put the cat down. He leaned back on the bench and opened the newspaper. Beneath the fold on the front page he read,

Escaped Convicts Killed in Wreck

Valdosta—Two escaped convicts and an unidentified female passenger were killed Tuesday when the late-model stolen automobile they were driving struck a bridge abutment while being pursued by State Police.

The deceased convicts, Hiram Leroy Burgett, 31, and Bobby Lee Ross, 21, escaped June 23 while being transported to the State Hospital for the Criminally Insane for psychological evaluation. A third escapee, Ronald Reuel Pickens, 47, is still at large.

The lunch rush was petering out. There were two people at the counter and four booths were occupied, and Railroad had set a BLT and an order of fried chicken with collards up on the shelf when Maisie came back into the kitchen and called the manager. "Police wants to talk to you, Mr. C."

Railroad peeked out from behind the row of hanging order slips. A man in a suit sat at the counter, sipping sweet tea. Cauthron went out to talk to him.

"Two castaways on a raft," Betsy called to Railroad.

The man spoke with Cauthron for a few minutes, showed him a photograph. Cauthron shook his head, nodded, shook his head again. They laughed. Railroad eyed the back door of the diner, but turned back to the grille. By the time he had the toast up and the eggs fried, the man was gone. Cauthron stepped back to his office without saying anything.

At the end of the shift he pulled Railroad aside. "Lloyd," he said. "I need to speak with you."

Railroad followed him into the cubbyhole he called his office. Cauthron sat behind the cluttered metal desk and picked up a letter from the top layer of trash. "I just got this here note from Social Security saying that number you gave is not valid." He looked up at Railroad, his china blue eyes unreadable.

Railroad took off his glasses and rubbed the bridge of his nose with his thumb and forefinger. He didn't say anything.

"I suppose it's just some mixup," Cauthron said. "Same as that business with the detective this afternoon. Don't you worry about it."

"Thank you, Mr. Cauthron."

"One other thing, before you go, Lloyd. Did I say your salary was thirty a week? I meant twenty-five. That okay with you?"

"Whatever you say, Mr. Cauthron."

"And I think, in order to encourage trade, we'll start opening at five. I'd like you to pick up the extra hour. Starting Monday."

Railroad nodded. "Is that all?"

"That's it, Lloyd." Cauthron seemed suddenly to enjoy calling Railroad "Lloyd," rolling the name over his tongue and watching for his reaction. "Thanks for being such a Christian employee."

Railroad went back to his room in the rooming house. Pleasure mewed for him, and when he sat on the bed, hopped into his lap. But Railroad just stared at the picture of the rowboat on the opposite wall. After a while the cat hopped onto the windowsill and out through her door onto the roof.

Only a crazy person would use the knowledge that a man was a murderer in order to cheat that man out of his pay. How could he know that Railroad wouldn't kill him, or run away, or do both?

Lucky for Cauthron that Railroad had made that deal with Pleasure. But now he didn't know what to do. If the old lady's message was from God, then maybe this was his first test. Nobody said being good was supposed to be easy. Nobody said, just because Railroad was turning to good, everybody he met forever after would be good. Railroad had asked Pleasure to save him from Bobby Lee and Hiram, not Mr. Cauthron.

He needed guidance. He slid open the drawer of the table. Beside the Bible was his .38. He flipped open the cylinder, checked to see that all the chambers were loaded, then put it back into the drawer. He took out the Bible and opened it at random.

The first verse his eyes fell on was from Deuteronomy: "These you may eat of all that are in the waters: you may eat all that have fins and scales. And whatever does not have fins and scales you shall not eat."

There was a knock at the door. Railroad looked up. "Yes?"

"Mr. Bailey?" It was Mrs. Graves. "I thought you might like some tea."

Keeping his finger in the Bible to mark his page, Railroad got up and opened the door. Mrs. Graves stood there with a couple of tall glasses, beaded with sweat, on a tray.

"That's mighty kind of you, Miz Graves. Would you like to come in?"

"Thank you, Mr. Bailey." She set the tray down on the table, gave him a glass. It was like nectar. "Is it sweet enough?"

"It's perfect, ma'm."

She wore a yellow print dress with little flowers on it. Her every movement showed a calm he had not seen in a woman before, and her gray eyes exuded compassion, as if to say, I know who you are but that doesn't matter.

They sat down, he on the bed, she on the chair. She saw the Bible in his hand. "I find many words of comfort in the Bible."

"I can't say as I find much comfort in it, ma'am. Too many bloody deeds."

"But many acts of goodness."

"You said a true word."

"Sometimes I wish I could live in the world of goodness." She smiled. "But this world is good enough."

Did she really think that? "Since Eve ate the apple, ma'am, it's a world of good and evil. How can goodness make up for the bad? That's a mystery to me."

She sipped her tea. "Of course it's a mystery. That's the point."

"The point is, something's always after you, deserve it or not."

"What a sad thought, Mr. Bailey."

"Yes'm. From minute to minute, we fade away. Only way to get to heaven is to die."

After Mrs. Graves left he sat thinking about her beautiful face. Like an angel. Nice titties, too. And yet he didn't even want to rape her.

He would marry her. He would settle down, like the grandmother said. But he would have to get an engagement ring. If he'd been thinking, he could have taken the grandmother's ring—but how was he supposed to know when he'd killed her that he was going to fall in love so soon?

He opened the dresser, felt among the dead man's clothes until he found the sock, pulled out his savings. It was only forty-three dollars.

The only help for it was to ask Pleasure. Railroad paced the room. It was a long time, and Railroad began to worry, before the cat came back. The cat slipped silently through her door, lay down on the table, simple as you please, in the wedge of sunlight coming in the window. Railroad got down on his knees, his face level with the tabletop. The cat went "Mrrph?" and raised its head. Railroad gazed into her steady eyes.

"Pleasure," he said. "I need to get an engagement ring, and I don't have enough money. Get one for me."

The cat watched him.

He waited for some sign. Nothing happened.

Then, like a dam bursting, a flood of confidence flowed into him. He knew what he would do.

The next morning he walked down to the Sweet Spot whistling. He spent much of his shift imagining when and how he would ask Mrs. Graves for her hand. Maybe on the porch swing, on Saturday night? Or at breakfast some morning? He could leave the ring next to his plate and she would find it, with his note, when clearing the table. Or he could come down to her room in the middle of the night, and he'd ram himself into her in the darkness, make her whimper, then lay the perfect diamond on her breast.

At the end of the shift he took a beefsteak from the diner's refrigerator as an offering to Pleasure. But when he entered his room the cat was not there. He left the meat wrapped in butcher paper in the kitchen downstairs, then went back up and changed into Bailey Boy's baggy suit. At the corner he took the bus downtown and walked into the first jewelry store he saw. He made the woman show him several diamond engagement rings. Then the phone rang, and when the woman went to answer it he pocketed a ring and walked out. No clerk in her right mind should be so careless, but it went exactly as he had imagined it. As easy as breathing.

That night he had a dream. He was alone with Mrs. Graves, and she was making love to him. But as he moved against her, he felt the skin of her full breast deflate and wrinkle beneath his hand, and he found he was making love to the dead grandmother, her face grinning the same vacant grin it had when Hiram and Bobby Lee hauled her into the woods.

Railroad woke in terror. Pleasure was sitting on his chest, her face an inch from his, purring loud as a diesel. He snatched the cat up in both hands and hurled her across the room. She hit the wall with a thump, then fell to the floor, claws skittering on the hardwood. She scuttled for the window, through the door onto the porch roof.

It took him ten minutes for his heart to slow down, and then he could not sleep.

Someone is always after you. That day in the diner, when Railroad was taking a break, sitting on a stool in front of the window fan sipping some ice water, Cauthron came out of the office and put his hand on his shoulder, the one that still hurt occasionally. "Hot work, ain't it, boy?"

"Yessir." Railroad was ten or twelve years older than Cauthron.

"What is this world coming to?" Maisie said to nobody in particular. She had the newspaper open on the counter and was scanning the headlines.

"You read what it says here about some man robbing a diamond ring right out from under the nose of the clerk at Merriam's Jewelry."

"I saw that already," Mr. Cauthron said. And after a moment, "White fellow, wasn't it?"

"It was," sighed Maisie. "Must be some trash from the backwoods. Some of those poor people have not experienced the benefit of a Christian upbringing."

"They'll catch him. Men like that always get caught." Cauthron leaned in the doorway of his office, arms crossed above his belly. "Maisie," Cauthron said. "Did I tell you Lloyd here is the best short-order cook we've had in here since 1947? The best *white* short order cook."

"I heard you say that."

"I mean, makes you wonder where he was before he came here. Was he short-order cooking all round Atlanta? Seems like we would of heard, don't it? Come to think, Lloyd never told me much about where he was before he showed up that day. He ever say much to you, Maisie?"

"Can't say as I recall."

"You can't recall because he hasn't. What you say, Lloyd? Why is that?"

"No time for conversation, Mr. Cauthron."

"No time for conversation? You carrying some resentment, Lloyd? We ain't paying you enough?"

"I didn't say that."

"Because, if you don't like it here, I'd be unhappy to lose the best white short-order cook I had since 1947."

Railroad put down his empty glass and slipped on his paper hat. "I can't afford to lose this job. And, you don't mind my saying, Mr. Cauthron, you'd come to regret it if I was forced to leave."

"Weren't you listening, Lloyd? Isn't that what I just said?"

"Yes, you did. Now maybe we ought to quit bothering Maisie with our talk and get back to work."

"I like a man that enjoys his job," Cauthron said, slapping Railroad on the shoulder again. "I'd have to be suicidal to make a good worker like you leave. Do I look suicidal, Lloyd?"

"No, you don't look suicidal, Mr. Cauthron."

"I see Pleasure all the time going down the block to pick at the trash by the Sweet Spot," Mrs. Graves told him as they sat on the front porch swing that evening. "That cat could get hurt if you let it out so much. That is a busy street."

Foster had gone to a ball game, and Louise Parker was visiting her sister in Chattanooga, so they were alone. It was the opportunity Railroad had been waiting for.

"I don't want to keep her a prisoner," he said. The chain of the swing creaked as they rocked slowly back and forth. He could smell her lilac perfume. The curve of her thigh beneath her print dress caught the light from the front room coming through the window.

"You're a man who has spent much time alone, aren't you," she said. "So mysterious."

He had his hand in his pocket, the ring in his fingers. He hesitated. A couple walking down the sidewalk nodded at them. He couldn't do it out here, where the world might see. "Mrs. Graves, would you come up to my room? I have something I need to show you."

She did not hesitate. "I hope there's nothing wrong."

"No, ma'am. Just something I'd like to rearrange."

He opened the door for her and followed her up the stairs. The clock in the hall ticked loudly. He opened the door to his room and ushered her in, closed the door behind them. When she turned to face him he fell to his knees.

He held up the ring in both hands, his offering. "Miz Graves, I want you to marry me."

She looked at him kindly, her expression calm. The silence stretched. She reached out; he thought she was going to take the ring, but instead she touched his wrist. "I can't marry you, Mr. Bailey."

"Why not?"

"I don't love you."

Railroad felt dizzy. "You could sometime."

"I'll never marry again, Mr. Bailey. It's not you."

Not him. It was never him, had never *been* him. His knees hurt from the hardwood floor. He looked at the ring, lowered his hands, clasped it in his fist. She moved her hand from his wrist to his shoulder, squeezed it. A knife of pain ran down his arm. Without standing, he punched Mrs. Graves in the stomach.

She gasped and fell back onto the bed. He was on her in a second, one hand over her mouth while he ripped her dress open from the neck. She struggled, and he pulled the pistol out from behind his back and held it to her head. She lay still.

"Don't you stop me, now," he muttered. He tugged his pants down and did what he wanted.

How ladylike it was of her to keep so silent.

Much later, lying on the bed, eyes dreamily focused on the light fixture in the center of the ceiling, it came to him what had bothered him about the grandmother. She had ignored the fact that she was going to die. "She would of been a good woman, if it had been somebody there to shoot her every minute of her life," he'd told Bobby Lee. And that was true. But then, for that last moment, she *became* a good woman. The reason was that, once Railroad convinced her she was going to die, she could forget about it. In the end, when she reached out to him, there was no thought in her mind about death, about the fact that he had killed her son and daughter-in-law and grandchildren and was soon going to kill her. All she wanted was to comfort him. She didn't even care if he couldn't be comforted. She was living in that exact instant, with no memory of the past or regard for the future, out of the instinct of her soul and nothing else.

Like the cat. Pleasure lived that way all the time. The cat didn't know about Jesus' sacrifice, about angels and devils. That cat looked at him and saw what was there.

He raised himself on his elbows. Mrs. Graves lay very still beside him, her blond hair spread across the pineapple quilt. He felt her neck for a pulse.

It was dark night now: the whine of insects in the oaks outside the window, the rush of traffic on the cross street, drifted in on the hot air. Quietly, Railroad slipped out into the hall and down to Foster's room. He put his ear to the door and heard no sound. He came back to his own room, wrapped Mrs. Graves in the quilt and, as silently as he could, dragged her into his closet. He closed the door.

Railroad heard purring, and saw Pleasure sitting on the table, watching. "God damn you. God damn you to hell," he said to the cat, but before he could grab her the calico had darted out the window.

He figured it out. The idea of marrying Mrs. Graves had been only a stage in the subtle revenge being taken on him by the dead grandmother, through the cat. The wishes Pleasure had granted were the bait, the nightmare had been a warning. But he hadn't listened.

He rubbed his sore shoulder. The old lady's gesture, like a mustard seed, had grown to be a great crow-filled tree in Railroad's heart.

A good trick the devil had played on him. Now, no matter how he reformed himself, he could not get rid of what he had done.

It was hot and still, not a breath of air, as if the world were being smothered in a fever blanket. A milk-white sky. The kitchen of the Sweet Spot was hot as the furnace of hell; beneath his shirt Railroad's sweat ran down to slick the warm pistol slid into his belt. Railroad was fixing a stack of buttermilk pancakes when the detective walked in.

The detective walked over to the counter and sat down on one of the stools. Maisie was not at the counter; she was probably in the ladies' room. The detective took a look around, then plucked a menu from behind the napkin holder in front of him and started reading. On the radio Hank Williams was singing "I'm So Lonesome I Could Cry."

Quietly, Railroad untied his apron and slipped out of the back door. In the alley near the trash barrels he looked out over the lot. He was about to hop the chain-link fence when he saw Cauthron's car stopped at the light on the corner.

Railroad pulled out his pistol, crouched behind a barrel and aimed at the space in the lot where Cauthron usually parked. He felt something bump against his leg.

It was Pleasure. "Don't you cross me now," Railroad whispered, pushing the animal away.

The cat came back, put its front paws up on his thigh, purring.

"Damn you! You owe me, you little demon!" he hissed. He let the barrel of the gun drop, looked down at the cat.

Pleasure looked up at him. "Miaow?"

"What do you want! You want me to stop, do you? Then make it go away. Make it so I never killed nobody."

Nothing happened. It was just a fucking animal. In a rage, he dropped the gun and seized the cat in both hands. It twisted in his grasp, hissing.

"You know what it's like to hurt in your heart?" Railroad tore open his shirt and pressed Pleasure against his chest. "Feel it! Feel it beating there!" Pleasure squirmed and clawed, hatching his chest with a web of scratches. "You owe me! You owe me!" Railroad was shouting now. "Make it go away!"

Pleasure finally twisted out of his grasp. She fell, rolled, and scurried away, running right under Cauthron's car as it pulled into the lot. With a little bump, the car's left front tire ran over her.

Cauthron jerked the car to a halt. Pleasure howled, still alive, writhing, trying to drag herself away on her front paws. Her back was broken. Railroad looked at the fence, looked back.

He ran over to Pleasure, knelt down. Cauthron got out of the car. Railroad tried to pick up the cat, but she hissed and bit him. Her sides fluttered with rapid breathing. Her eyes clouded. She rested her head on the bloody gravel.

Railroad had trouble breathing. He looked up from his crouch to see that Maisie and some customers had come out of the diner. Among them was the detective.

"I didn't mean to do that, Lloyd," Cauthron said. "It just ran out in front of me." He paused. "Jesus Christ, Lloyd, what happened to your chest?"

Railroad picked up the cat. "Nobody ever gets away with nothing," he said. "I'm ready to go now."

"Go where?"

"Back to prison."

"What are you talking about?"

"Me and Hiram and Bobby Lee killed all those folks in the woods and took their car. This was their cat."

"What people?"

"Bailey Boy and his mother and his wife and his kids and his baby."

The detective pushed back his hat and scratched his head. "Y'all best come in here and we'll talk this thing over."

They went into the diner. Railroad would not let them take Pleasure from him until they gave him a corrugated cardboard box to put the body in. Maisie brought him a towel to wipe his hands, and Railroad told the detective, whose name was Vernon Scott Shaw, all about the State Hospital for the Criminally Insane, and the hearselike Hudson, and the family they'd murdered in the backwoods. Mostly he talked about the grandmother and the cat. Shaw sat there and listened. At the end he folded up his notebook and said, "That's quite a story, Mr. Bailey. But we caught the people who did that killing, and it ain't you."

"I know what I done."

"Another thing, you don't think I'd know if there was some murderer loose from the penitentiary? There isn't anyone escaped."

"What were you doing in here last week, asking questions?"

"I was having myself some pancakes and coffee."

"I didn't make this up."

"So you say. But seems to me, Mr. Bailey, you been standing over a hot stove too long."

Railroad didn't say anything. He felt his heart about to break.

Mr. Cauthron told him he might just as well take the morning off and get some rest. He would man the griddle himself. Railroad got unsteadily to his feet, took the box containing Pleasure's body, and tucked it under his arm. He walked out of the diner.

He could not find his pistol in the lot. He went back to the boarding-house. He climbed the steps. Mr. Foster was in the front room reading the newspaper. "Morning, Bailey," he said. "What you got there?"

"My cat got killed."

"No! Sorry to hear that."

"You seen Miz Graves this morning?" he asked.

"Not yet."

Railroad climbed the stairs, walked slowly down the hall to his room. He entered. Dust motes danced in the sunlight coming through the window.

The ocean rowboat was no darker than it had been the day before. He set the dead cat down next to the Bible on the table. The pineapple quilt was no longer on the bed; now it was the rose. He reached into his pocket and felt the engagement ring.

The closet door was closed. He went to it, put his hand on the doorknob. He turned it and opened the door.

F. Brett Cox has been published in many major magazines. Originally from the South, he now lives and teaches in Vermont.

Andy Duncan is the winner of the World Fantasy Award, the Theodore Sturgeon Award, and other awards for his fantasy and SF stories. He's had stories published in major SF and fantasy magazines and anthologies. He's published a story collection, *Beluthahatchie and Other Stories*. He lives in Northport, Alabama.